THE FAIRFIELD
MURDERS

RICHARD J. TRACEY

 SterlingHouse Publisher, Inc.   Pittsburgh, PA

THE FAIRFIELD
MURDERS

PEMBERTON

ISBN-10: 1-56315-408-0
ISBN-13: 978-1-56-315408-9
Trade Paperback
© Copyright 2008 Richard J. Tracey
All Rights Reserved
Library of Congress #2008924339

Requests for information should be addressed to:
SterlingHouse Publisher, Inc.
7436 Washington Avenue
Pittsburgh, PA 15218
info@sterlinghousepublisher.com
www.sterlinghousepublisher.com

Pemberton Mysteries
is an imprint of SterlingHouse Publisher, Inc.

SterlingHouse Publisher, Inc. is a company
of the Cyntomedia Corporation

Cover Design: Brandon M. Bittner
Interior Design: Kathleen M. Gall

Printed in U.S.A.

DEDICATION

In memory of Margaret L. Tracey, my mother,
who gave me the inspiration to finally put the words on paper.

To Gloria J. Tracey, my wife,
who stood behind me and gave me the motivation
to see this through.

ACKNOWLEDGMENTS

Grateful acknowledgment is made to the
Barbara Bauer Literary Agency
for taking a chance on me.

CHAPTER ONE

Racer lay motionless in his bed. He never heard the phone ringing. It was his day off, which meant he spent last night at Barney's, the local hangout for the men and women in blue. It was a place to unwind and tell war stories.

Racer lived alone. He had been engaged once but a week before he was due to get married, his fiancée ran away with an old high school flame. Since then he had vowed not to get serious with any female. As a matter of fact, he tried to stay totally away from them. In his mind, they only meant trouble. Racer didn't get home from Barney's until four o'clock in the morning and he didn't intend to get up before noon. When he finally realized that the phone was ringing, the sound seemed to be coming from miles away. By the time he made it to the phone, it stopped. *The answering machine will catch it*, he thought. Peering through half-closed eyelids at the clock, he noticed that it was a quarter after ten. He threw his legs over the side of the bed, got up slowly and headed for the kitchen to make some fresh coffee. On the way he saw the red light of the answering machine. Pushing the button, he listened.

"Racer, this is Captain Peterson. I would like to see you in my office at two this afternoon."

That was it. A smile came over Racer's face; he knew. He had been following the murders in the papers since they started. He knew things weren't going real well for the homicide division, but what did this have to do with him? Peterson had him reassigned to traffic and he wasn't his boss anymore. His first instinct was to call Peterson and tell him that, but he stopped short. Coffee first, then a shower.

Racer headed for the shower. He settled in under the pulsating shower head and let himself drift away. He wanted to shower, dress and grab some lunch before he decided if he wanted to see captain Peterson or not. After Racer pulled himself away from the shower, he finished his coffee and got dressed. Glancing at his watch, he saw that it was eleven-thirty. He started to leave the apartment when the phone rang again. Ignoring it, he closed his door and headed for the elevator. Taking it down to the lobby, he headed out to his 300ZX. It was his only pleasure left in life.

Peterson sat at his desk, chewing on one of his favorite cigars. He had one more person to invite to his meeting. The only problem was to convince Lieutenant Rogers to give this person up for the duration of the case. He pulled the phone off the cradle and dialed Roger's number. The phone only rang once when he heard Roger's voice.

"Yeah, what is it?" asked Rogers.

"Walt, this is Ben; I have a favor to ask you," said Peterson. "I need one of your people reassigned to homicide for a couple of weeks to help with this damn murder case. We are really in a jam here and the press is all over us."

"Okay, who do you want and when? I'm always willing to help Homicide," said Rogers.

Peterson told Rogers that he needed one of his Vice detectives by the name of Cindy Darling, and he wanted her to report to his office at two o'clock for a briefing. Hanging up, he could still hear Rogers grumbling in the background. He leaned back in his chair and decided that he had everyone he needed for the meeting. Now he had to figure out how he was going to handle Racer.

Racer pulled into the parking lot on Washington. This was one of the older sections of the city but kept up real nice by its residents. The houses were mostly three stories with fenced-in yards. Barney's sat just off the corner of Washington and Second Streets. A large neon sign with a shamrock in the middle of it hung in front of the tavern. Racer parked the 300ZX in the far corner of the lot. He didn't want to risk someone scratching his car. Turning the corner of the building, he pushed the door open.

It was dark inside after coming in out of the noon sun, and it took his eyes several seconds to adjust. Once they did, he headed over to the bar where Barney was still washing glasses from last night. Barney O'Shay, the owner of the bar, was a tall, burly guy who always had a smile on his face. He was eight years old when his parents immigrated to the United States, and when he opened his mouth you sure could tell he was Irish.

"How you feeling this morning, or should I say afternoon?" asked Barney. "I didn't expect to see you in here this early, especially after last night."

"Thought I'd stop and get one of those half pound burgers and a cold glass of beer," said Racer.

"Are you going to shoot darts tonight?" asked Barney, putting a frosted mug in front of Racer.

"I'll be here," replied Racer, taking a sip of beer.

"That's great. Tonight is ladies night. Maybe you can hook yourself up with someone," said Barney.

"Just get me that burger," said Racer, laughing.

As two o'clock approached, Peterson was putting the final touches on his game plan. Everything was falling right into place, or so he hoped. The phone rang and his secretary announced that Detman and his two detectives were waiting. Just as he planned, they were five minutes early. He told her to send them right in. Detman, Harlin and Piakowski entered the office, and Peterson motioned them to three chairs that he had placed to one side of his office. So far so good.

Racer pulled into the station lot at exactly two o'clock. He parked his car with the same care as he always did and headed for the rear door. Once inside, he walked up to Lieutenant Detman's office but no one was around. He talked to several of the detectives but no one had seen him. After looking around, he finally gave up and headed upstairs. When Racer got to Peterson's office, he started to feel anger build up in him. Here he was going, to meet with the same guy that kicked him out of Homicide, then turned around and reassigned him to Traffic. Traffic of all places.

But he was determined to hear Peterson out and see what kind of scheme he was cooking up.

When Racer entered the outer office, Peterson's secretary looked up from her typewriter and gave him the once-over. "Can I help you?" she asked.

"My name's Charles Racer and I'm here for a meeting with the captain," said Racer.

"Just a minute," said the secretary, buzzing the captain. "You can go in now. They are waiting for you inside."

Who are they? he thought. He got to the door, tapped on it and pushed it open. Peterson was sitting behind his desk. Racer didn't even notice the other people in the room. Stepping into the office, the captain motioned for him to take a chair just off the corner of his desk. Closing the door, Racer noticed Detman and his two detectives, Harlin and Piakowski, sitting on the opposite side of the room. Piakowski he didn't know but Harlin was a different story. They had worked together on a couple of cases in the past and never saw eye to eye on the way Racer handled them. He knew from the newspaper articles and television reports that Harlin and Piakowski were the lead detectives on the serial killer case. Racer sat down before Peterson spoke. "I'm glad that you could make it. I didn't know if my message got through to you in time."

"Oh, it got through to me all right," replied Racer. "Right in the middle of my day off. You know that it's a strenuous job directing traffic. Oh yeah, that's right—you transferred me there."

"I'm sorry if I disturbed your beauty sleep, but this is an important meeting and I wanted you here," said Peterson. "I'm sure that you have been reading the papers and watching the news reports over the last few weeks. This department has been getting hit hard lately concerning these murders. The Chief is concerned that three women have been murdered at the hands of a serial killer. This is the first time anything like this has happened in Fairfield. So he wanted me to get your feelings about returning to Homicide to help us out of a hole."

Racer looked at Detman and then his two detectives. He could tell by the look on their faces that this was as much a surprise to them as it was to him. He then turned back to Peterson. "You already have people working on the case. I'm sure you don't need me," said Racer, looking right into Peterson's eyes.

"Look, I'm asking you to accept a reassignment back into the Homicide division. We need your help to catch this killer," said Peterson, trying to control his temper.

"I think I'd like to stay were I am," said Racer.

"Come on and stop breaking my chops. How can I convince you to come back to Homicide?" asked Peterson.

"Well, let me see," said Racer.

"While Racer is hashing this over, I want your two detectives to wait outside in the outer office," said Peterson.

Harlin gave Detman a disgusted look and Piakowski nodded toward the door. They left the office, closing the door behind them.

"All right, let's cut the crap," said Peterson. "What will it take?"

"I'll return to Homicide, but this case is mine with no interference from outside sources. When it's solved, I want a permanent assignment back to Homicide with a promotion. That will do for starters."

"Do you have any problems with any of that?" asked Peterson, looking at Detman.

"None. Actually, I'll be glad to get Racer back into homicide, but what do I do with Harlin and Piakowski?" said Detman.

Without hesitation, Peterson said, "Take them off this case and reassign them to something they can handle. I'm sure you have enough cases to keep them busy."

"Yes sir," replied Detman. "I'll figure something out."

Peterson then redirected his attention back to Racer. "You've got it. This case is all yours. The only thing that I want is an update once a week until these murders are solved, which I hope won't take you too long," said Peterson.

"That won't be a problem," replied Racer.

Detman looked at Peterson and asked, "Is that all, sir?"

"I have one more thing. Racer needs a partner, and I have the perfect person for the job."

"I could assign Harlin. He definitely is familiar with the case," replied Detman.

Peterson fired off a firm "No" without hesitation. As he said this, he pushed himself away from his desk, stood up, and headed for his office door. He opened it and stepped outside. This gave Racer a chance to talk to Detman alone.

"Harry, why didn't you give me a heads up on this?" asked Racer. "It would have been nice if I could have been a little prepared."

"I didn't know what he was up to," said Detman. "Peterson kept this whole thing to himself."

Just then the door opened and Peterson was standing there.

"Gentlemen, I would like to introduce you to Racer's new partner. Her name is Cindy Darling."

With that, policewoman Cindy Darling walked into the office. She was a five-foot six inch brunette with dark brown eyes and a pleasant smile.

"Miss Darling was assigned to Vice until I convinced Lieutenant Rogers to reassign her temporarily to this case," said Peterson, smiling broadly.

Racer didn't say a word. He realized why Cindy Darling was assigned to Vice. She was about twenty-six years old with an hour glass figure. Finally, Racer raised himself out of his chair and headed for the door.

"Racer, where are you going?" asked Peterson. "I want you to get acquainted with your new partner."

"No thanks, I changed my mind. Partners just get in the way, and I don't need that," said Racer. "I appreciate the offer, but I'd rather just do my time in Traffic. No one shoots at you there."

"This isn't an option. This is your assignment. You either take it or you'll be reassigned to foot patrol in some of our nicer neighborhoods. So, say hello to your new partner, and I'm sure she'll be an asset to this investigation. Won't you, Officer Darling?" asked Peterson.

"Yes, sir," said Darling. Her smile could melt an iceberg.

"Great, everything has fallen into place. Now all we have to do is solve this case," said Peterson, clasping his hands together. "Lieutenant, I guess you better go and break the news to your two detectives."

"Yes, sir," replied Detman as he got up and started for the door.

"Is that it?" asked Racer.

"You can go and get started and I hope that we'll be seeing some results shortly," said Peterson, smiling again.

Racer headed for the door with Detman. Seeing Racer leave, Cindy got up and followed him.

"Detective Racer, wait a minute. When do we get started?" she asked.

"Tomorrow morning at seven sharp," replied Racer as he continued to walk away.

"Tomorrow? I thought we would start right away," said Cindy.

"I don't know about you but I'm going to finish my day off. So I'll see you in the morning in the lieutenant's office," said Racer, heading for the stairs.

It was two minutes to seven when Racer and Detman arrived the next morning. Racer was talking about some dart game he was in last night as they crossed the squad room. When Cindy saw them, she stood up and waited. When Racer and Detman reached her, she greeted them. Detman returned her greeting but Racer just nodded. Detman opened his door and they filed in. He motioned for them to have a seat. Cindy took a seat in front of his desk but Racer leaned against a metal filing cabinet.

"One thing Peterson wasn't kidding about yesterday was how important this case is. We need something and we need it before the killer strikes again," said Detman.

"I've been following the case in the papers but I'll be playing catch up," said Racer as he moved to the window. "I'll have to go through all the files and visit the crime scenes and see what I can come up with, but it isn't going to be a cake walk."

"I know," said Detman. "I have a desk for you and Cindy over in the corner with separate phone lines. Let me know if there is anything else you'll need. This case is priority one. And by the way, do you need a car assigned to you?"

"No, we'll be using my car," said Racer.

"Well, that's it," said Detman.

Racer looked down at Cindy and said, "Let's go."

Cindy tried to start a conversation with Racer but he just continued out the door and headed directly for Harlin's desk. Harlin wasn't anywhere around but Piakowski was on the phone.

"I need your notes on the murders," said Racer.

"Wait a minute, I'm on the phone," replied Piakowski.

Racer started going through the paperwork on the desk until he found three manila folders with the names of the three dead women. Piakowski gave him a dirty look but Racer just ignored him and headed for the desk Detman had assigned to them. Cindy walked around the desk as Racer started going through one of the folders.

Looking over his shoulder, Cindy said, "Look, you might not like working with partners, especially a female, but you're stuck with me and I'm not going to go away. This case means just as much to me as it does to you. So how can I help?"

Racer glared at her before he said, "Go down to the storeroom and pick up a cork board and stand it against the wall. We'll use it for tacking up any evidence that we collect."

Cindy returned 15 minutes later with two patrolmen carrying a large cork board with push pins. They looked at Racer and backed away. Racer shook his head and opened the second folder. He realized that Peterson and Detman were right. There wasn't much to go on. He wondered if the killer was that smart or was the department that dumb.

Racer decided that the best thing to do was to take the folders and visit each of the crime scenes one at a time. He gathered them up and motioned for Cindy to follow him. Just as they were about to leave, someone grabbed Racer's arm from behind. Racer spun and came face to face with Harlin.

"What's wrong with you?" demanded Racer.

"Where are you going with those files?" asked Harlin. "They're not suppose to leave the station without the lieutenant's permission."

"Jim, don't worry. This isn't your case anymore," said Racer.

Before Harlin could object, Racer was out the door with Cindy in close pursuit.

"Racer, he's right," said Cindy. "They are suppose to be signed out. We're going to get in trouble for this."

Racer just kept going. He waited for Cindy to slip into the passenger seat of his 300 ZX.

"Buckle up," said Racer as they squeal out of the parking lot.

"Where are we going first?" asked Cindy.

"Mary Wagner's apartment," said Racer. "That was the last victim and it's the warmest trail. Maybe we can come up with something that everyone else overlooked."

They sat in silence the rest of the way. After a few turns, they pulled up outside of 845 Apple Way.

Stepping out of the car, Racer could feel the heat rising from the concrete sidewalk. He and Cindy headed directly for the air-conditioned lobby. Once inside they took the elevator right to the third floor. When they got to apartment 3D, the doorway was blocked with yellow crime scene tape. Racer tried the doorknob, the door was unlocked. He pushed it open. They both ducked under the tape and entered. Finding themselves standing in the living room, Racer stopped but Cindy kept right on going. The air in the apartment was heavy with the smell of death.

Racer directed Cindy to checkout the living room and kitchen and he continued through the living room and entered the hallway, leading to the main bedroom. There were two other doors off the hall. One was the bath and the other was a smaller bedroom. Entering the smaller bedroom, Racer couldn't help but see the large bloodstain that covered the bed in the main bedroom. *It was such a waste of human life*, he thought. He knew that he had to catch this animal before he struck again.

Racer started going through the drawers in the dresser. Taking each one completely out, he dumped the contents on the floor. The first was full of bulky sweaters. He then did the same with each drawer but found nothing. He tried the nightstand but it was completely empty. Racer then went to the bed and pulled the bedspread and sheets back. It looked like no one had ever slept there. He flipped the mattress and box spring over but again found nothing. Next was the closet. He pushed the sliding door back and gazed into the closet. There were a number of coats, at least one for each season. He went through each one carefully. All he came up with was a couple of movie ticket stubs, a stack of tissues and a phone bill receipt paid last March. Looking up, he noticed four shoeboxes stacked on a shelf. He reached up and took them down. Racer removed the lid off the first box and found nothing but old utility bills held together by rubber bands. Racer fanned through them but there wasn't anything. The next box had a birth certificate, an insurance policy and greeting cards from various times of the year. The third box contained pictures, most of which seemed to have been taken a long time ago. Racer spent time going through them to see if there was anything current. No such luck. The final box had nothing more than a pair of shoes. Before he left the room, he got down on the floor and examined the carpet. Mary must have been an excellent housekeeper. There wasn't even a piece of lint on the carpet. Racer sighed, crossed the hall and entered the bathroom.

Racer went through the medicine cabinet. There were the usual supplies: band-aids, aspirins, first-aid cream and some feminine hygiene items. He checked the tank behind the toilet and dumped the clothes hamper out. Nothing. When he hit the hall, Cindy was waiting for him, and they entered the main bedroom together. Racer directed Cindy to start going through the drawers. He reminded her to go through everything piece by piece and not to leave anything go without looking at it. Racer took the closet. It was full of dresses, blouses, skirts, shoes and anything else you could name that a woman would wear. The only thing he could do was take them one at a time.

Cindy called over to Racer and held up a pair of sexy panties.

"Sure seems to be a lot of sexy lingerie here," said Cindy.

Racer looked, nodded and returned to what he was doing. As they went through everything, again there was nothing out of the ordinary. Racer walked around the bed and checked the trash can hidden between the bed and nightstand. There he spotted a pink dress in the trash can. Racer opened the file on Mary Wagner and read the evidence section but there was no mention of the dress anywhere. He thought that was strange. Reaching down, he pulled the dress from the trash can. It seemed to be brand new. He stretched it out on the bottom of the bed. All the buttons were there and he couldn't find any tears or rips. *Why would a perfectly good dress have been thrown away?* He thought. He saw Cindy watching him. "Would you throw away a nice dress like this?" Racer asked as he pointed to the dress.

"Certainly not," said Cindy. "I don't throw away anything."

"Make sure we take this dress with us," said Racer.

Racer then did his carpet thing again. He got down on all fours and scanned the carpet. Under the bed he spotted something black; it looked like it was stuck under the leg of the bed. He went to the other side of the bed, lifted it up and removed the object from under the leg.

"Did you find something?" asked Cindy.

"It looks like a cloth label," replied Racer. "You know, the kind that they sew into the collar of shirts and blouses."

Racer paused for a split second and then went back to the dress on the bed and looked for a label. It was missing. Racer looked at the label and read out loud, "Designer Dress Shop."

"She had expensive tastes," said Cindy. "That's a specialty shop for the rich and famous."

"Well, she was single and had a fairly good job, so maybe she splurged on herself," said Racer, shrugging his shoulders.

Cindy just nodded.

Racer picked up the dress and tossed it to Cindy, who placed it into a brown evidence bag. Sealing it, she wrote the required information on the outside label. Racer then placed the label in a plastic bag and put it in his jacket pocket. Now he had one final thing to do. He started to go to each window and check to see if there were any signs of forced entry that the initial investigation might have missed. After the windows, they checked the front door to the apartment. It had a lock in the handle and a deadbolt above the doorknob. There was no sign of forced entry. Turning to leave, Racer flipped the file open to see who found the body. It was a Betty Arnold. She worked with Mary. Apparently she stopped to pick her up for work when she found the body.

"Let's go and have a talk with Ms. Arnold," said Racer. "But first, let's grab a quick lunch at Barney's."

Racer pulled the ZX into Barney's parking lot. When they entered, Racer picked out a table away from the noon crowd. After placing their orders, Racer tossed a manila folder on the table and started to spread out the individual reports. Studying the reports, he looked over at Cindy and said, "With the exception of the dress and label, we came up empty. So all we have so far is a corpse, a new dress and a torn out label. The medical examiner reported the case of death was due to her bleeding out. Her jugular was severed with a sharp object. There was also evidence of sexual activity prior to death. But no signs of bruises, scratches or cuts."

"So it's possible that she could have been raped prior to her murder, though there was no evidence of forced entry, and nothing in her apartment seemed to be disturbed. That brings up the possibility that she could have known her attacker," said Cindy.

"That's a good possibility," said Racer, rubbing his chin.

In the meantime, Barney brought their orders to the table and left them alone. Racer now started to dig in with both hands. While they ate, Racer never took his eyes off the reports. When they both finished, he motioned for Cindy to gather up the reports while he headed for the bar.

"What do I owe you?" replied Racer.

"This one's on me," said Barney. "It was worth it. I don't want to spoil your first date."

Racer shook his head. He spun around and headed for the door where Cindy was waiting.

CHAPTER TWO

Racer headed down Washington until he reached River Road. He made a right and pushed the accelerator to the floor. He didn't let up on the gas until the speedometer hit eighty. When they reached Route Five, Racer turned left and the industrial park was on their right. He pulled into the entrance road and stopped in front of a large sign. The sign laid out the names and locations of each business in the park. Resources Incorporated, where Betty worked, was located right in the front of the park. Racer spotted the building, a white marble square with a lot of dark glass and a small lake with a bridge. Racer parked his 300 ZX in one of the reserved spaces and he and Cindy got out. They crossed the bridge and entered the building. The lobby was large and spacious and done in white marble. The floors were so clean that you could see your reflections in them.

After identifying themselves to the receptionist, Racer noticed a gentleman approaching from behind. He was six-feet tall, slim in build and had a mustache and goatee.

"Hello," said the gentleman, "I'm Bernard Shaver the General Manager."

"I'm Detective Racer and this is my partner Detective Darling. We're here to speak with a Betty Arnold," said Racer.

"Betty's department is at lunch right now but they should be back in about five minutes," replied Mr. Shaver. "I'll take you up and introduce you to Ms. Arnold's supervisor."

Shaver escorted them down a hallway and toward the elevators. They took the elevator to the fifth floor.

When the elevator stopped, they stepped out into a large room with at least a dozen cubicles. They walked straight across the room headed for an office on the far side. Shaver knocked on the door and walked right in. The man looked up with a startled expression on his face.

"John, this is Detective Darling and Detective Racer with the Fairfield Police Department. They are here to ask you a few questions about Mary Wagner," said Shaver. Then he turned to Racer and Darling. "Detectives, this is John Conners, Mary's supervisor. Now I'll leave you alone so you can talk. I'll be in my office if there is anything else that I can do for you," said Shaver. He nodded and left the office.

"Please, sit down," said Conners. "Is there anything that I can get you? Coffee, Coke, anything?"

"No, thanks," said Racer. "We just want to ask you a few questions concerning Mary Wagner."

"Sure. I'll help you in any way that I can," said Conners.

"How well did you know Mary?" asked Racer.

"Mary worked for me for about three years and we got along fine," said Conners.

"Do you know if she had anyone here that she might have spent a lot of time with?" asked Racer.

"No, no one that I can think of," replied Conners.

"No one she might have dated, gone on vacation with, had dinner?" asked Racer.

"No," said Conners as he shook his head. "She seemed to keep pretty much to herself, especially lately."

"What do you mean lately?" asked Cindy.

"Oh, over the last two to three months she seemed to stay pretty much to herself," said Conners. "When everyone would get together for lunch, she'd stay behind, things like that. It seemed as though she had something on her mind."

"Did you ever ask her if there was something wrong?" asked Cindy.

"No, I guess I thought it wasn't any of my business," replied Conners.

"Well then, could we talk with Betty Arnold?" asked Cindy.

"Sure," replied Conners. "Let me see if she is back from lunch yet." Conners got up and left the office to check.

"What do you think?" asked Cindy.

Racer watched Conners through the glass as he listened to

Cindy. "Right now, not much of anything," said Racer. "I hope this Arnold woman can remember something though." Racer watched as Conners returned to the office with a woman in tow. After Connors introduced Betty to Racer and Cindy, he excused himself from the office.

"May I call you Betty?" asked Racer. We would like to ask you some questions about Mary Wagner." Instantly, Racer could see tears starting to well up in Betty's eyes.

"I'll try to help you the best I can, but I already told the other officers everything that I know," said Betty.

"How well did you know Mary?" asked Cindy.

"I only knew Mary at work," said Betty. "We never went out anywhere. We ate lunch together and started to take turns driving to work to save some money."

"When did you start riding to work together?" asked Cindy.

"We started about a year ago when we found out how close we lived to each other," replied Betty. "We agreed that one week she would drive and the next week I would drive. It was my week to drive when I found her. She was supposed to be waiting outside for me. She was always waiting outside, but she wasn't that day."

"Did Mary ever talk about her private life?" asked Cindy.

"No, usually just about work," said Betty. "Until the last month or so, she didn't even talk about that. It was as though something was bothering her."

"She never said anything to you about what that might be?" asked Racer.

"No," replied Betty as tears started to roll down her checks.

"Can I get you anything?" asked Racer.

"No," replied Betty. "I'll be okay."

"Can you tell us what happened when you entered the apartment?" asked Racer. "Anything that you can remember, no matter how unimportant you might think it is. Take your time."

"I knocked on the door and it started to open," said Betty as she dabbed at her eyes with a tissue. "I went in and called Mary's name, but there was no answer. I went into the kitchen and didn't see her so I called again."

Racer stopped her for a second. "Did you see anything lying

around in the kitchen, such as a coffee cup, dishes, utensils, anything?" asked Racer.

"I don't remember seeing anything," replied Betty.

"Go on then," said Cindy.

"I left the kitchen and went into the living room. As I got to the hallway I could see into Mary's bedroom. I saw Mary's arm hanging over the side of the bed. I thought that she must have overslept so I went down the hall. I called her name several more times but she never moved." Betty burst into tears.

Cindy comforted her until she regained her composure.

"It was awful," Betty continued. "There was blood all over the bed, and her eyes... I'll never forget her eyes. They were staring up at the cross that was hanging on the wall by her bed."

"Did you go into any of the other rooms?" asked Racer.

"No," replied Betty.

"What did you do then?" asked Cindy.

"I guess I screamed and ran out of the apartment. I pounded on apartment doors until someone answered and they called the police," said Betty.

"Did Mary ever mention seeing anyone in particular?" asked Cindy.

"She never really said," replied Betty. "Though she seemed to be tied up on certain nights over the last several weeks. But I never saw her with anybody."

"When Mary left work the night before you found her, what was she wearing?" asked Racer.

"She had on a pretty pink dress," said Betty.

"Is there anything else that you can tell us?" asked Cindy.

"No," said Betty as she shook her head.

After the interview, Racer and Cindy stopped on the way to the elevator and thanked Connors for his cooperation.

"So it looks like Mary Wagner was preoccupied over the last several weeks. Now if we can find out what that was, we might have something," said Racer, when they were alone.

"Maybe it had something to do with throwing that dress out," said Cindy.

Racer and Cindy got back to the station around four-thirty and headed right up to the squad room. When they entered Detman was waiting for them. "Well, did you come up with anything?" asked Detman.

"We have a couple of things to check out but we don't know how they will tie into the case," replied Racer.

"Oh, by the way, why did you two remove files from the station without clearing it with me?" asked Detman. "You know the rules. If you need anything from here, see me first."

"Aye, aye, lieutenant," said Racer, thinking about that jerk Harlin.

Racer crossed the room and left Detman standing there. He started to make some notes and handed them to Cindy to pin up on the corkboard. The notes referred to the dress they found, the label, the fact that Mary had sex before she died, and that there were no signs of forced entry. He also added a note stating that Mary had no known boyfriends but put a question mark on it.

"Why did you do that?" asked Cindy.

"Remember Betty telling us that it seemed like Mary was preoccupied lately? Maybe she had a secret lover," said Racer.

Next he handed Cindy the two pictures that were in her file. One picture showed Mary standing next to some statue in a park and the other was Mary lying in her bed in a pool of blood.

"Well it's a start," said Racer. "Not much, but a start. Tomorrow we'll head over to Elizabeth Farley's place, but right now it's time to call it a day. I'll see you tomorrow, seven sharp."

"Wait, can I get a ride home from you?" asked Cindy. "I had to take a cab this morning. My car is in the shop for a tune-up and oil change."

"Sure," said Racer.

While Racer was driving Cindy home, she asked, "What happened between you and Peterson to get you reassigned to Traffic?"

Racer looked straight ahead for several seconds before he answered.

"I'd really rather not talk about that. It's a personal matter and let's just leave it at that," said Racer.

Cindy didn't push the issue.

"The next block and make a left," said Cindy. "It's the second building on the left."

Racer reached the corner, made the turn and pulled up outside the building. It was a seven-story brick building that was neatly landscaped with small trees and colorful flowers. Cindy opened the door and slid out of the car.

"Can I ask you for one more favor?" asked Cindy. "I need a ride to work in the morning because my car won't be done until noon."

"No problem," said Racer. "Just be ready around six forty-five."

"I'll be here," said Cindy as she turned away.

Racer watched her as she walked toward the canopied front entrance. After she disappeared inside, he pulled back out into the street.

Racer pushed his key into the lock and slid the deadbolt back. Sliding the door open, Racer stepped into his apartment, tossing his keys onto a table and kicking the door closed with a bang. Moving toward the kitchen, he began sorting through the mail he had picked up in the lobby. There was nothing but bills and junk mail. Removing the two manila folders he had tucked under his arm, Racer deposited them on the kitchen table. He went to the refrigerator and took a cold beer from the shelf. He twisted the top off and tossed it into the trash can under the sink. Sitting down at the kitchen table, he took a healthy drink from the bottle as he spread the next victim's file out in front of him. He sorted through the pictures of Elizabeth. They were similar to the ones of Mary Wagner. There was a picture of Elizabeth standing with a man next to a car and the rest were from the murder scene. They showed Elizabeth lying in her bed, on her back, with a deep cut across her throat. If it were not for Elizabeth's face you would swear it was a photo of Mary Wagner. He checked the report and read that Elizabeth was sexually assaulted. *Maybe she just had sex before she died*, he thought. He made a note to talk to the medical examiner in the morning. He continued to read the report. Elizabeth's sister found her when she didn't answer her calls. She also lived alone. Looking at her pictures, Racer thought she was a good-looking woman. He pushed himself away from the table, moved through the living room and stopped at his patio doors. He slid the door open and stepped out onto his balcony.

Scanning the skyline of the city, he recalled the day before when Peterson gave him this case and assigned Cindy as his new partner. He had something up his sleeve, but what was it? He knew he didn't particularly like to have a partner, especially a female, but he went ahead and assigned him Cindy. Racer knew he was a little hard on Cindy at first but it wasn't her fault that she was a pawn in Peterson's game. But he had to admit that she wasn't hard to work with and damn sure not hard to look at. But he had to remember to keep her at arm's length. He didn't want to get burned a second time.

Carolyn was a beauty and the envy of everyone on the force. She worked in records and drew men to her like bees to honey. Racer met her at Barney's one night, and it was love at first sight. They went together for eight months. They were unseparable. Until that spring day. An old high school boyfriend came to visit and that was the beginning of the end. Slowly they drifted apart and, two weeks before they were to be married, Carolyn ran away with her old flame. Racer didn't even get a "Dear John." He didn't want something like that to happen again. He pulled himself back to reality. Who was killing these women? He didn't know yet but he sure was going to find out.

Racer pulled up outside of Cindy's apartment at exactly six forty-five in the morning. She was standing there waiting for him, dressed in a red blouse and black slacks.

Cindy opened the car door and slid inside saying, "Good morning."

Racer just mumbled something in her direction and squealed away from the curb. Heading directly for the station, Racer had a few things to do before heading for Elizabeth Farley's place. He parked in an isolated space in the police lot and jumped out. By the time Cindy got out, Racer was halfway across the lot. When she got upstairs Racer was sitting at his desk making notes.

"What's with you this morning?" asked Cindy.

"I came across a few things last night going over Farley's file," replied Racer.

"Farley's file?" said Cindy. "You weren't suppose to take that out of the station. Didn't you hear what Detman said?"

"What he doesn't know won't hurt him," said Racer, never looking up.

Cindy leaned over his shoulder to see what he was writing. He ripped a piece of paper from the pad and handed it to Cindy. She tacked it up along with the two pictures that Racer sorted out last night. The note read, *Who is the man in the photo with Elizabeth?* As Cindy was tacking the note on the board, Lieutenant Detman peeked around the corner.

"Where are the two of you heading this morning?" he asked. "Peterson wants an update tomorrow, and I would like to have something for him."

"We're going over to the Farley place and check it out. Then we'll probably see if we can catch up with her sister to ask a few questions," said Racer. "By then I'm sure we can give you a few tidbits that you can feed to the captain."

"I'm going to hold you to that," said Detman as he walked away.

"Do you really think we will have something by tomorrow?" asked Cindy.

"We already have the dress and label," answered Racer. "It's a start. Remind me to take them down to the lab as we leave. I want to see if they can come up with anything. I want to make sure that the label and dress go together."

Racer phoned the medical examiner's office to clarify the statement that Elizabeth Farley had been sexually assaulted. After talking with the medical examiner, Racer found out the report had been amended to state that Elizabeth Farley had sexual intercourse within two hours of her death. He found this very interesting. The scenario was similar to the Wagner case.

Racer strolled across the squad room and plunked down into

Harlin's chair. He wasn't around but Racer didn't give a damn. He started going through the drawers in Harlin's desk. There was a load of manila folders of cases Harlin and Piakowski were working on. He opened the next drawer and noticed an envelope that was labeled with the initials M.W., E.F. and B.M. He opened the flap and removed several sheets of paper that were inside. There was one sheet for each set of initials and a couple of photos attached to each sheet. Harlin made up three sheets, one for each victim, with points of similarity between each crime. Racer went to the sheet that had the heading E.F. and found the amendment that the medical examiner had mentioned. It stated exactly what the medical examiner had told him. Now it was time to head to Detman's office. He didn't bother to knock but instead burst right in, envelope in hand. Detman was reading something on his desk when the door exploded. Detman looked up. Racer gave the door a shove and it slammed closed. "What do I owe this honor to?" asked Detman.

"What is going on around here?" shouted Racer. "I just found this envelope in Harlin's desk with information that should be in the files. How am I suppose to solve this damn case if there is a conspiracy around here to screw me up?"

"Wait a minute," said Detman. "You know that a lot of detectives keep separate notes on their cases. That's nothing new; no one is trying to screw you. Remember, Harlin was taken off this case and he probably forgot to put those notes in the files. I'll talk to him to see if there is anything else that he might have that will help you solve this case. Everyone around here wants these murders solved. It's been a black mark against this department for months. So calm down."

"Fine," said Racer as he walked out of the office.

"What did you find in Harlin's desk?" asked Cindy when Racer returned to the desk. "I saw you talking with Detman, or should I say yelling at him."

"Nothing," replied Racer sharply.

"Nothing?" said Cindy. "I thought you were going to take Detman's head off."

"Just get the dress and let's get it down to the lab," barked Racer.

Cindy grabbed the dress and followed Racer to the stairs. The lab was located in the basement of the building. It was the only place big enough to house all the equipment. As they passed through the swinging doors, Racer could see that the only one there was Sidney Waldo. Sidney was the senior lab technician and probably the most dedicated one of them all. Racer strolled over to Sidney, who was looking through a microscope, and asked him if he could do him a favor.

"I have a dress and label that I need you to look at for me. These are pieces of evidence from one of the homicides I'm working on," said Racer. "I'm sure you're aware of the three women that have been killed around Fairfield."

Sidney's face lit up. The thought that he could be part of the investigation that cracked this case was exciting. He took the dress from Cindy and placed it on the table. Racer reached inside of his jacket and removed the plastic bag with the label in it. He handed it to Sidney.

"I'll try to have something for you before the end of the day," said Sidney. "I'll make it top priority."

"Thanks. I'll be waiting for your report," said Racer.

Leaving the lab, Racer turned to Cindy and said, "We have a friend now. Let's get over to the Farley place and see if we can dig up anything else for Sidney to work on."

CHAPTER THREE

Racer pulled the 300 ZX to the curb outside of 5750 Riverdale Drive, which was situated in a nice middle-class neighborhood with one-story homes with small garages. Elizabeth Farley's was a light green house with white shutters. The neighborhood was unusually quiet. It was as if the place had been evacuated. By the time Racer got out of the car, Cindy was already at the front door. There again was the yellow police tape blocking the entrance. Cindy tried the doorknob. It was locked.

They went around the side of the house and opened the gate to the back yard. The back door also had the yellow tape across it. Cindy tried the knob but it was also locked. Racer walked up to the door and gave it a firm push with his shoulder. The door gave a little but still remained closed. Racer gave it one more try and the door swung open. Racer had to catch it before it crashed against the wall.

Racer waved to Cindy to follow him into the house. Ducking under the tape, they entered the house. When they got inside they found themselves standing in the kitchen.

"Let's get started. You take the kitchen and I'll try the rest of the house," he said.

Cindy started with the kitchen cupboards, pulling everything out of them as Racer walked into the dining room. It was small and barely had enough room for the table, four chairs and a buffet server. Racer went through the drawers in the server. He didn't find anything but serving utensils. He checked the front sliding door and found a punch bowl with glasses, a matched set of china, a tablecloth and matching napkins. Nothing out of the usual. Before he moved on, Racer stuck his head into the kitchen and saw that Cindy had everything out of the cabinets and spread across the counter top and kitchen table.

"How are things going?" asked Racer.

"A woman's work is never done," said Cindy as she shook her head.

Racer tried the living room next. There was a sofa, swivel rocker, coffee table with two end tables, a magazine rack, television and videotape recorder. Along the full wall was a set of bookshelves. Racer sat down on the sofa and pulled the manila folder from his jacket. He spread it out on the coffee table. He looked at the reports and didn't find anything noted under evidence. He knew that didn't mean too much. He went through everything but came up empty. As he was finishing, Cindy entered the room and watched as Racer got down on his hands and knees and scanned the floor.

"I can't believe this," said Racer.

"I know what you mean. There was nothing in the kitchen either. But we still have three bedrooms and the bath to go," said Cindy.

They went through each room but didn't find much. Racer found a picture of a man in the middle size bedroom, along with men's clothing. He made a note of this. Finally, they entered the master bedroom and again took in the sight of a large bloodstain that had spread across the bed. Racer noticed that the stain also made its way to the floor. Maybe this was an indication of a struggle. Again, he made a note of this. They started going through the dresser, chest of drawers, nightstand and the closet.

"Guess where Elizabeth did some of her shopping?" asked Cindy.

"Don't' tell me, let me guess," said Racer. "The Designer Dress Shop."

"Bingo," said Cindy.

Racer pulled a dress out of the closet. It was a very low cut black cocktail dress. He held it up so Cindy could see it.

"Very nice but it's not your color," said Cindy.

"There's about a dozen of them in here from that same shop," said Racer.

Cindy was now holding up a black lace bra in her hands.

"This is from the same place," she said. "Coincidence?"

Racer shrugged his shoulders.

They were just about done when Cindy whistled.

"What do you have?" asked Racer.

Cindy was over by the nightstand. She had pulled the drawer completely out, and taped to the bottom of the drawer was a picture. Racer walked over to Cindy and peered over her shoulder. It was a photograph of Elizabeth Farley sitting on the edge of a hot tub with a guy whose face was turned away from the camera.

"Must have been someone special," said Cindy.

"If it was someone special, then why did she hide it by taping it to the bottom of a drawer?" asked Racer.

"Didn't want anyone else to see it," said Cindy.

Racer took the picture from Cindy and slipped it into a plastic evidence bag.

They finished looking around but found nothing else. Racer checked the windows and doors for forced entry but there were no marks or scratches. As they headed back into the living room, Racer stumbled over Elizabeth's handbag. Somehow they had missed it the first time. He dumped the contents out on the floor and sorted through it. It was the usual woman's junk except for a key ring. Racer noticed one of the keys seemed out of place. After looking at it closely, he realized it was from a safety deposit box. He slipped the key ring into his pocket.

Racer looked at his watch and asked, "Are you hungry?"

"Don't tell me, Barney's for lunch," said Cindy.

Racer just smiled.

When they returned to the station after lunch, Racer headed for his desk. There was a large brown envelope waiting for him. Picking the envelope up, Racer opened it. He reached inside and slid a sheet of paper out. It was Sidney's report on the findings.

Racer read the report to Cindy, "The label was definitely from the dress. It was probably cut out with a knife. The dress itself was in perfect shape. There were five hairs found on the dress. Three of them were Mary Wagners', and the other two where from a male with dark black hair. That's it."

"Well, we finally have something to go on," said Cindy.

"Yeah," said Racer, "two hairs from a male with dark black

hair. That should cut it down to twenty or thirty thousand suspects."

Cindy glared at him.

"Well, let's put what we got up on the board," said Racer.

He started to make some notes and handed them to Cindy. A ring of keys in Elizabeth's purse; a picture of Elizabeth with an unknown man in a hot tub; bloodstains outside of bed; clothes from the Designer Dress Shop, and the fact that Elizabeth apparently had a male visitor who was in the habit of staying over. He handed Cindy the next slip and told her to place it under Mary Wagners' column. The note carried the information that Sidney had just given him about the label and the five hairs.

"Well, let's look her sister up and see if she can tell us anything. I would also like to take a look at what this Designer Dress Shop looks like. It might be far fetched, but there could be a connection there. Maybe they ran across each other there, or maybe they met their killer there," said Racer.

"Do you really think the dress shop could fit into this?" asked Cindy, sitting on the corner of the desk.

"I don't know, but both women shopped there," said Racer, pushing his chair back and staring at the corkboard. "What more can you ask for in a case like this, murder, sex and who knows what else?" said Racer.

"You know, I was just thinking. Why would a person keep an empty can of Coke in her refrigerator? I mean, I always throw them out when I'm done, don't you?" said Cindy.

"I probably do," replied Racer. "Why are you asking?"

"Because Mary Wagner had an empty Coke can stuck way back in a corner of her refrigerator. Almost like she was hiding it," said Cindy. "It's probably nothing. The contents probably just evaporated."

Racer thought about it for a second, then said, "Some people hid money or jewelry in cans and hide them in the refrigerator, hoping that burglars won't find them. It usually never works. But we shouldn't overlook anything. Let's go and check it out."

CHAPTER FOUR

Racer flew up to the curb and slammed on his brakes.

"Hey, take it easy! You're going to give me whiplash, damn it," said Cindy.

But before she got it all out Racer was already out of the car. Cindy had to run to catch up to him. They crossed the lobby, stopped in front of the elevator and rode it to the third floor. The doors opened and out they raced. When they got to apartment 3D, Racer turned the knob and pushed the door. It was locked.

"What's going on?" he said. "It wasn't locked when we were here yesterday, and the police tape is gone. Damn, they must have released this apartment back to the manager."

"I'll run down to the manager's apartment and get the key," said Cindy.

Racer held up his hand. Looking around, he kicked the door. Nothing happened.

"You can't do that," said Cindy.

Again Racer just held up his hand. He looked around and kicked the door one more time. The door finally gave way with a crash. The frame was in splinters and the door had two large footprints on it.

"What are we going to tell the manager?" asked Cindy.

"Don't worry about that now. We need to get to the refrigerator," replied Racer.

The one thing that was speeding through his mind was that someone had already cleaned the apartment up. Cindy got to the refrigerator first. She grabbed the handle and yanked it open. They both stood there staring into an empty refrigerator.

Racer turned to Cindy and told her to check the garbage in the apartment; he was going to head downstairs and look in the dumpsters. Hopefully the garbage men hadn't picked up the garbage yet. Racer hit the button for the elevator and waited several seconds. Then he headed for the exit and the stairs. Racer took them three at a time until he reached the first floor.

A man was picking up his mail at the row of mailboxes and Racer asked him where the dumpsters where. The man looked at Racer and pointed down the back hall to a door at the rear. Racer headed for that door at a trot. Racer hit the door and stepped outside, allowing the door to close behind him. He was in the rear parking lot for the apartment building. He searched the lot and found the dumpsters in the far corner of the lot. There were three of them all painted brown with the white lettering "City of Fairfield" on their sides. When he got to them he flipped the lid on the first one and peered inside. There were three bags of garbage and scattered newspapers. As he stood there, Cindy came up behind him with a tall black man.

"Racer, I found someone who might be able to give us a hand finding the right bag," said Cindy. "This gentleman is Mr. Al Bailey and he's the maintenance super here. He helped the housekeeper bring the bags down."

"I placed two bags in here," he said, pointing to the middle dumpster.

Racer flipped the lid up and saw that the dumpster was chock full of plastic garbage bags. There had to be about twenty bags jammed in there.

"Do you remember which ones they were?" asked Racer.

"Not really," said Mr. Bailey. "When I came out, the dumpster had about five bags in there. So I would guess they are somewhere in the middle."

Mr. Bailey stood there watching Racer and Cindy arguing over who was going into the dumpster. "I'll go into the dumpster and throw the bags out," said Mr. Bailey. "Both of you can go through the garbage."

Racer and Cindy nodded.

Mr. Bailey climbed into the dumpster and started tossing out plastic garbage bags. He had four out before Racer could say anything. "Whoa, wait a minute, that's enough for now," said Racer.

Cindy removed the tie off the first bag and dumped it out on the asphalt. Racer followed suit. They continued to sort through empty bottles, cans, potato peels and assorted other items. All they kept looking for was empty Coke cans. And they both knew how many people drank Coke. When they had finished with the first four bags, Racer motioned to Mr. Bailey to toss a few more out. This continued until Cindy opened the ninth bag and yelled, "I found it!"

Cindy squinted as she looked into the can.

"Do you see anything?" asked Racer.

"No," replied Cindy. "There's too much glare."

Racer took the can from Cindy and then removed a jackknife from his pocket. He put the can down on the asphalt, stuck the blade through the thin aluminum and slowly moved the knife around the top of the can. It only took a couple of seconds and the top was off. Racer folded the knife up and placed it back into his pocket. As he looked into the can, he smiled. "Well, well, look here," said Racer, reaching into the can and pulling out a set of negatives.

Captain Peterson was looking forward to tomorrow's meeting with Detman and his detectives. After these first few days, he was starting to wonder what they had come up with. Between the Chief of Detectives and the press, they were driving him crazy about the three murders. Just then the phone rang. He picked it up and listened. "Send them in," he said into the phone.

In a second, the door swung open and Harlin and Piakowski entered. Peterson motioned them to a chair and asked what they wanted. Harlin told the captain that there were a couple of things about his friend Racer that he might be interested in. This piqued Peterson's curiosity. He told Harlin to continue.

Harlin went on to explain how Racer and his partner have been removing files from the station without anyone's permission. And the complaint that was received from the super at Mary Wagner's apartment building about someone breaking into her apartment. And the sighting of Racer and Darling leaving the building, by a meter maid, just before the complaint came in.

Peterson sat there staring at them, smiling wryly. Then he asked, "Did you report this to the lieutenant?"

"We told him about the files but we don't know if he is aware of the apartment being broken into," said Harlin.

"Okay, go on," said Peterson, with a wave of his hand.

"We checked again this morning, after the lieutenant had a talk with Racer, and two of the files are still missing," replied Harlin.

"We just thought that you should know," added Piakowski.

"I sure appreciate you coming to me with this information, but I really think that the lieutenant is capable of handling this," said Peterson. "Though, if anything else comes up out of the ordinary, feel free to come to me with it."

"Sure will captain," said Piakowski

Peterson thanked them as they stood up and left the office. He pushed himself back into the tall brown leather chair and puffed on his cigar. *So Racer is still screwing up,* he thought. *How interesting. Tomorrow's meeting might be more fun then I thought. And that damn Detman. He's getting too soft with Racer to do anything about it. He's always been on Racer's side. Always trying to protect him. Well, he better watch out or he's going to get burnt. Detman better remember that it was he who recommended Racer for this case. Or at least, that is what the Chief thinks. How can I lose? If Racer is good enough to solve the case, I'll get a pat on the back and probably a commendation, and if everything goes to hell, Racer and Detman will have to face the music.* As he swiveled around to look out the window, a light mist began to fall on the city. It had been a hot, dry summer and they needed the rain. But it was going to get even hotter.

As the rain began to fall, Cindy and Racer made a dash for the car. Looking over his shoulder, he could see Mr. Bailey picking up the mess they had just left and stuffing it back into brown garbage bags. Mr. Bailey had griped about cleaning up the mess, but Racer slipped him a twenty and that seemed to quiet him down.

They both started running around the building at the same

time. When they got to the car they jumped in out of the rain. By now the rain was starting to fall in large, heavy drops that hit the windshield with a thud.

Racer pulled the negatives out and studied them one at a time. "It looks like a woman in different poses," said Racer, passing them to Cindy one at a time. "We better get them to Sidney so we can see exactly what's on them.

When they got back to the station, the sky had grown darker and the rain was falling so heavily the wipers were having a hard time keeping up. Racer parked in his favorite space and turned the engine off. They both sat there for several minutes until they realized that it wasn't going to stop raining anytime soon. It was time to make a mad dash to the rear door of the police station. By the time they reached the door they were both drenched.

Cindy told Racer that she was going upstairs to get changed.

Cindy headed for the stairs as Racer told her he was going to take the negatives down to the lab and have Sidney look at them. Racer pushed through the swinging door and searched for Sidney. He was sitting at a desk in a small glass enclosed office. Racer walked over that way.

"Sidney, I have some negatives for you to develop for me," said Racer.

Sidney took the negatives from Racer and held them up to the office light.

"How soon will you need these?"

"As soon as possible," replied Racer.

"I'll have them for you in two hours tops."

"That will be great," said Racer. "Send them upstairs as soon as you're done."

They left the office together. Racer headed for the swinging door and Sidney headed into another room with the negatives in hand. Racer headed up the stairs, he realized that it was getting late but he still wanted to visit Elizabeth Farley's sister before calling it a day. When he entered the squad room, Detman was sitting on his desk.

"The captain wants to see us in his office at ten sharp tomorrow for an update. Do you have anything for him?" asked Det-

man. "The press is still hounding him about results. He's been trying to keep you and Darling out of the news, but he doesn't know
how much longer he can do that."

"We should have a couple of things that should keep him
happy for another week," said Racer.

"Well, I have to run," said Detman. "Remember, ten sharp
tomorrow."

Racer watched Detman as he walked away.

"Is that our update meeting with Peterson?" asked Cindy.

Racer nodded as he sat down at his desk.

"How long before Sidney has the negatives developed?" asked
Cindy.

"About two hours," replied Racer.

"What's next then?" asked Cindy.

"Why don't you call Farley's sister and see if we can set up an
appointment with her for tonight?" asked Racer.

Cindy flipped Farley's file open and looked up her sister's
number. Picking up the phone, she dialed. After letting it ring a
dozen times, Cindy hung up. She told Racer there was no answer.
Racer told her to see if there was an address and phone number
for where she worked. He really wanted to talk to her before their
meeting with Peterson. He didn't know how much ammunition
he'd need to keep Peterson off their butts.

Cindy started going through Elizabeth Farley's file and came
up with an address and phone number. She picked up the phone
and dialed the number. Racer was watching her and the clock at
the same time. Racer listened as Cindy identified herself to the person on the other end of the phone. After a brief conversation,
Cindy hung up. She turned to Racer and said, "We're all set for
seven-thirty at Mary's Steakhouse. That's were she goes for dinner
break."

Racer kept looking at the clock, wondering where Sidney and
those pictures were. It had been almost an hour. Finally, at five-
twenty, Sidney entered the squad room and headed directly for
Racer's desk with a brown envelope.

"I think you're going to be surprised by these," said Sidney,
handing the envelope to Racer.

Racer opened the brown envelope and slid the eight by ten proofs out. There were 6 photos showing Mary in various poses and states of dress. Two of them had Mary dressed in sheer teddies, posing by herself. In two others, she was topless and being fondled by another woman, and in the last two, she posed with a man standing behind her. He had his arms around her with his hands cupping her breasts. The man conveniently hid his face behind Mary, though Racer could see that he had extremely dark black hair.

"What is going on?" asked Cindy.

"If nothing else they're very interesting. You did a great job on these. Can you tell what type of camera they might have been taken with?" said Racer.

"The pictures were taken by someone who knew what they were doing," said Sidney. "Not necessarily a pro. It was probably a 35 millimeter camera of high quality. I tried to bring as many things out of the background as possible to try and help you."

"Keep this under your hat. I don't want this to leak out before I'm ready," said Racer.

"I didn't even see them," said Sidney, heading back to the lab.

"These are definitely photos of Mary Wagner, but why was she hiding them in a Coke can in her refrigerator?" asked Racer.

"It appears as though she was ashamed of them, but why keep them?" asked Cindy.

"I know what you mean, but girls who pose for these types of pictures aren't usually ashamed of them. They usually use them to make money, like having them in a magazine or even skin flicks," said Racer.

"Do you think maybe this is why she was killed?"

"I don't know yet," said Racer. "But think back to when we searched Elizabeth Farley's place. We found a photo of her in a hot tub with a man. She was naked from the waist up, or that is all we could see, and she had that photo hidden under a drawer."

Cindy threw the photos of Mary Wagner on top of the desk. Racer took the photos and shoved them back into the envelope.

"Let's go and see if Gloria Simons can tell us anything about these photos of her sister. Maybe she knows who this guy with the dark hair is. And tomorrow after we have our meeting with Peterson, we'll head over to Molino's place and see what we can find there."

Racer pulled his car up to the curb across the street from Mary's Steakhouse and glanced at his watch. It was seven-fifteen. They were a little early. Crossing the street, Racer and Cindy entered the restaurant and approached the maitre'de. Glancing around the dining area, Racer noticed about eight or nine couples scattered throughout the room, either sipping drinks or attacking their meals.

A waitress came up to them and asked if they wanted smoking or non-smoking. Racer hadn't thought about it till then but neither Cindy nor he smoked.

"We're here to meet someone," said Racer.

"Then maybe you would like to sit at the bar," suggested the waitress.

Racer peered through the doorway and could see the bar lining one side of the wall. He would have a perfect view of the front door.

"Thanks, I think we will," replied Racer.

Racer headed for the bar with Cindy right alongside of him. He took a seat at the far end which gave him a total view of the dining room. Cindy sat down next to him.

The bartender, a short blond woman, approached them and asked, "What can I get you?"

"Give me a draft and whatever the lady wants," said Racer as he winked at Cindy.

"I'll have a Tom Collins," said Cindy.

Sitting there sipping at their drinks, Racer heard the door starting to open and close on a steady basis. He kept an eye on the dining room. He didn't know what Gloria Simons looked like but he felt confident he could pick her out. Cindy was just about done with her drink when a woman approached Cindy and tapped her on the shoulder. The woman was about 35 years old with light brown hair.

"Are you detective Darling?" she asked.

"Yes, and this is my partner Detective Racer," said Cindy.

"I'm Gloria Simons," she said. "You wanted to talk to me?"

"Yes, we would like to ask you a few questions about your sister's death, if you don't mind," said Racer.

"Sure, but I would like to order dinner first. I only get 45 minutes," said Gloria.

"No problem," said Cindy. "You lead the way."

They followed Gloria to a table in the dining room and they all sat down. Everyone waited until Gloria had placed her order with the waitress before they started asking questions.

"We'll try to keep this short," said Racer. "How did you come about finding your sister?"

"Well, Beth was supposed to call me that morning. We were going to have lunch together and do some shopping. We both had the day off. It was unusual for us to have the same day off and when we did, we usually planned something together. The problem was I never got the call. This was unusual for Beth. She always followed through on what she promised. So I went over to her place and let myself in. That's when I found her," said Gloria, her eyes filling with tears.

"Where was she when you found her?" asked Cindy.

"She was lying in bed," said Gloria. "Kind of leaning over the side. There was so much blood I couldn't take it. That awful cut across her throat."

"Can you tell us what your sister was wearing?" asked Racer.

"She didn't have anything on," said Gloria. "I thought that was strange because Beth always wore a nightgown when she went to bed. Couldn't stand being naked."

"Did you notice anything that seemed out of place?" asked Racer.

"No. I don't think so," replied Gloria.

"Just think for a minute," asked Cindy.

They all sat there in silence. The waitress approached the table with Gloria's dinner and placed it in front of her and, after asking if there was anything else, she departed.

"No, nothing," replied Gloria. "Sorry."

"How did you get into Elizabeth's place?" asked Racer.

"Beth gave me a spare key. She wanted me to keep an eye on the place whenever she went out of town, like on vacation or something like that," said Gloria.

"So the door was locked when you got there?" asked Racer.

Gloria thought for a few seconds and then said, "Come to think of it, I put my key into the lock but the door was open. I never thought about that."

Racer made a note of that. He removed the pictures from his jacket pocket and placed them on the table in front of Gloria. "I'd like you to take a looked at these pictures for a minute. I want to warn you, they are quite graphic," said Racer.

Gloria gave Racer a strange look as she picked them up one at a time and placed them back down on the table.

"Can you tell us anything about them?" asked Racer.

"This one is easy," said Gloria pointing to the picture of the older gentleman. That's our dad. He is a traveling salesman, and whenever he is in town he stays with Beth, mainly because she has that extra room."

"How about the other one?" asked Racer.

"I never saw that one before," replied Gloria with a shocked expression. "I can't believe that Beth would allow anyone to take a picture of her like this. She was so shy. All her clothes were modest. Nothing sexy."

Cindy looked at Racer. He made a motion for her not to say anything.

"Do you know who the guy is in the hot tub with your sister?" asked Racer.

"No, I never saw him before," answered Gloria.

"Was your sister dating anyone?" asked Cindy.

"No one in particular. It seemed like she was having a hard time finding the right guy, so she spent a lot of nights at home alone. That is why, when we were off at the same time, we spent that time together," said Gloria.

"I don't want to take up anymore of your time," said Racer. "Thanks for you help. If you remember anything else, give me a call. You have my card," said Racer.

"I sure will," said Gloria.

Racer and Cindy got up and started walking toward the main entrance. Gloria Simons called to them. Racer and Cindy stopped and walked back to the table. Gloria mentioned that the tape for the answering machine was gone. Racer wanted to know how she knew that. Gloria explained that when she went to the phone to call the police, she noticed that the cover was open and there wasn't any tape inside. That it was gone.

"And your sister always had a tape in there?" asked Racer.

"Yes," replied Gloria. "When she was home alone at night she never answered the phone. She always let the machine pick up the call."

"That's a big help," said Racer. "Remember, give me a call if anything else comes up."

Gloria nodded.

Heading to Cindy's apartment, to drop her off, Racer asked if she needed a ride in the morning. Cindy explained that her car wouldn't be done until noon, so she would need a ride. Racer reminded her six forty-five sharp. Cindy smiled and headed up the walk to her apartment building. Racer watched until she was inside, then headed for Barney's.

CHAPTER FIVE

Racer picked Cindy up in the morning and drove to the station. When they got upstairs, Racer sat down and opened the files on Mary Wagner and Elizabeth Farley. He started comparing similarities between the two cases. He wanted to get all the facts together before they had to meet with Detman and Peterson. He didn't want to go up there and make a fool of himself. He glanced over at Cindy; she was staring at the corkboard.

"I want to compare these two cases and see what matches up," said Racer.

"Let's get started then. We only have a little over an hour to get our facts together."

"We know that Mary Wagner and Elizabeth Farley posed for some nude pictures. They had sexy garments in their places and they did their shopping at an expensive shop called the Designer Dress Shop. They both lived alone and didn't seem to have much of a social life. They both had sexual relations shortly before they were killed. Both were found in bed nude with their throats cut. And it appeared that the doors were left unlocked. Is there anything else that I might have missed?"

"No," said Cindy, "you're doing fine."

"On the other side of the coin, we have no suspects or leads. But we do have one more place to search," said Racer.

"What do you make of all this so far?" asked Cindy.

"At a quick glance, I would say that these two women were either party girls making some money on the side posing or they were very lonely women picking up strange men," said Racer. "The first option would explain how they could afford shopping at the Designer Dress Shop. Why they were killed, I don't know yet. As far as the killer goes, he could be any one of a thousand guys in this city. Now doesn't that sound reassuring?"

"I don't think the captain will buy that," said Cindy.

Racer acknowledged that and looked at his watch. They had 20 minutes before they were due in the captain's office.

"Make a copy of Molino's file but don't let anyone see you," said Racer. "When we go up to Peterson's office I want to make sure that all the files are back in their right place. When you're done, we'll head up there and present our case."

He looked toward the back of the squad room and through the window into Detman's office. It was empty.

"I wonder where the lieutenant is," said Racer. "He's cutting it pretty close."

"Maybe he's already upstairs with Peterson," said Cindy. "The two of them are probably planning how to screw us."

"Detman wouldn't do that," said Racer. "As long as I have known him, he has always been straight with me. Even when they reassigned me to traffic, he was the only one who stuck up for me. Everyone else jumped on the bandwagon and pounded the knife in deeper into my back. Those are the ones I will never forget."

"Is that where the grudge with Harlin comes in?" asked Cindy.

"Good old James Harlin," said Racer. "By the book Harlin. He would turn his own wife and kids in if it would help him make some points with the brass. We had a few run-ins, to say the least."

"Let me make those copies and then we can head upstairs," said Cindy. "It's almost showtime."

They entered the outer office and saw Detman waiting for them. Peterson's secretary looked up and told them to go right in. Racer nodded and continued through. Detman held them back for a minute, and explained that he was smoothing things over with a certain apartment manager, and assured him that the department would pay for the damages. Racer just shrugged. Detman then knocked on the door and pushed it open.

"Come in and have a seat," said Peterson, sitting behind his desk with a large cigar hanging over the edge of his ashtray.

"Well people, the press is still beating us into the ground over this case," said Peterson. "I would like something that I could give them that would shut them up for a while."

Racer knew that this was his cue, so he spoke first. "Captain, we found a few more pieces to the puzzle but we still can't make out what the whole picture is yet," said Racer. "We have a dress and label found at Mary Wagner's place, and we have a couple of photos of both women that we're checking out. We know both women had sexual relations before they were killed. We think the women knew the killer, due to the fact we can't find any forcible entry into either place. That's were we are."

"What kind of pictures are you talking about?" asked Peterson.

"There were a couple of pictures with other people in them and we're trying to track them down," said Racer. "In one case we have identified Elizabeth Farley's father. So we're still working on them."

"I see," said Peterson, moving to the window. "There really isn't much I can give to the press. We sure as hell don't want to mention anything about sex. I guess I'll try to hold them off for another couple of days, but I'm going to need something, and real soon, before the mayor gets into this. It would be nice if we could just give him the killer."

"Yes, sir," said Detman.

"Oh, by the way, Racer, I hope that you're not up to your old antics like kicking doors down or removing files without signing them out," said Peterson, watching the sky cloud up.

"That's already been taken care of," said Detman before Racer could answer.

"I sure hope so," stated Peterson.

"Anything else Captain?" asked Detman.

"That's it for now," replied Peterson. "But I expect something a lot more substantial by the end of next week."

"Yes, sir," said Detman as they all got up to leave.

"Hold on a second," said Peterson, turning from the window and looking directly at Racer. "I would like to see those photos when you get a chance. You never know, it might be something that we can give to the press."

"Yes, sir," said Racer. "I'll have a double set made, one for you and one for the lieutenant."

When they got back down to the squad room, the lieutenant

went right to his office and closed the door. Racer and Cindy headed for their desk.

"Why didn't you tell the lieutenant about the pictures?" asked Cindy. "I thought he was your friend?"

"Somebody has a big mouth around here and I don't know who it is. The captain knew about the files and the apartment door. So until we catch the killer, we don't tell anybody anything. Is that clear?" said Racer with emotion.

"Sure," said Cindy.

"Let's head over to Barbara Molino's place and we can pick up some lunch on the way," said Racer.

"Okay, but it's my turn to pick the place to eat," said Cindy. "And don't forget about my car."

Racer and Cindy decided to eat at Sergio's Italian Restaurant. After they were seated, a waitress came over and placed two glasses of water in front of them. Cindy immediately ordered a pepper steak sandwich with fries and a large Diet Coke and Racer ordered the same, only with a Coke. A couple of minutes later, the waitress brought there sandwiches out and placed them and their drinks in front of them.

During lunch, Cindy tried to pry information out of Racer concerning his transfer to the Traffic Division. Racer kept changing the subject until he finally gave in. He explained that there was a time when he was considered a cowboy, gun in hand, kicking doors down, pushing suspects around until he got the information that he wanted. That is what eventually got him in trouble with the brass. There were complaints from his partners that no one wanted to work with him. But there was one thing that he did get and that was results. The district attorney's office never had one of his cases thrown out of court. He had the highest arrest record on the force. The trouble was, as Peterson put it, the department was getting tired of defending him from the press and the Chief. All he knew was, he got the job done. And to him that was what counted. And that was exactly what he was going to do in this case, get the job done.

The waitress approached their booth and asked if she could get them anything else. When they both shook their heads, she slipped the check on the table. Cindy started to reach for it but Racer got it first.

"It's my treat," said Cindy.

"I'll get it," said Racer, "it's the least I could do to repay you for listening to my story."

They both got up. Racer placed a tip on the table and headed over to the cashier as Cindy walked outside.

Soon Racer joined her. "Let's head over to Barbara Molino's place and see what we can come up with. Maybe we can cap the day off with a little more excitement."

As Racer pulled into traffic, Cindy said, "Don't forget, I have to pick my car up."

"Just tell me were I have to go," said Racer.

"My car is at Clifton Chevy," said Cindy.

Racer parked in the lot at Chifton Chevy to drop Cindy off. Before she got out of the car, Racer had a suggestion to make. While she took care of her car, he would go over to Barbara Molino's place and see what he could come up with and then they'd get together later. Cindy agreed after she found out her car won't be ready for another hour.

Racer pulled up outside of 1212 Bluebird Place. It was a nice new building in one of the higher income neighborhoods. The building was ten stories high and stretched out over the whole block. It was located near the mall, and Racer was sure that it took quite a few bucks to stay there. Walking up to the building, Racer noticed that there was an underground parking garage. The driveway dipped down under the building and there was a booth at the bottom of the ramp. Racer made this his first stop. He approached the booth and saw a man in a navy blue uniform standing inside. When Racer got close, the man stuck his head out and asked if he could help him. Racer flashed his badge.

"Always willing to help the police," said the attendant.

"What exactly do you do here?" asked Racer.

"Well, this is a security building. We have guards at all the entrances to make sure we know who is going in and out of the building. All visitors have to sign a log book," said the attendant. "Vehicles that enter the garage receive a parking ticket. The ticket is stamped with the time the vehicle enters, the apartment visited, and the time they leave.

"Is there anyway someone can get in without you knowing?" asked Racer.

"None," said the attendant, confidently.

"How long do you keep your records?" asked Racer.

"We keep the tickets for six months on a rotating basis and the log books are kept for one year."

"And where are they kept?" asked Racer.

"In the captain's office," said the attendant, "on the first floor behind the main desk."

"Thanks, you've been a great help," replied Racer.

Racer crossed the lawn and walked under the green and white canopy covering the entrance to the building. There was gold lettering on the glass door identifying the building as the Fairfield Towers. He pushed himself through the doors and entered a large lobby with a front desk and two guards stationed there. He took notice of the lobby to see if there was anyway that someone could slip past the guards. Everyone entering the building had to pass them on one side of the desk or the other. The elevators were to the left and the stairway was to the right. Racer determined that it would be almost impossible to get past the guards unless they weren't there or sleeping on duty. He also noticed that the lobby was equipped with video cameras mounted high above the floor. He started walking across the marble floor but before he reached the desk, one of the guards was already asking him if she could help him. Racer propped his elbows on the desk and showed his shield. The guard looked at it with little emotion.

"What can I do for you, detective?" she asked.

"I would like to take a look at Barbara Molino's apartment," replied Racer.

She turned to the other guard on duty and said something in a low voice. She turned back to Racer and asked, "Do you have a warrant with you?"

"I'm investigating her murder and the apartment is a crime scene," said Racer as he glared at her. "So if you have any objections, you better go get your boss."

She turned to the other guard and whispered to him again. He picked up the phone and hit three buttons.

"If you will wait a minute, I'll have my supervisor talk to you," said the male guard.

"You have about 30 seconds before I arrest both of you for obstructing an officer in an investigation," said Racer angrily.

The female guard backed away from the desk and was about to say something when Racer heard a voice in the background.

"Racer, you old fart. Still bullying people around, are you?" said a short, stubby man walking toward him.

Racer looked past the guards and said, "Bobby, how the hell are you? I thought you retired."

"I did," said Bobby Redding. "This is my retirement job. It gives me a few extra bucks. They put me in charge of security and I'm doing a darn good job of it, if I might say so. Or at least it was going real good until that Molino woman got herself killed."

"I know," said Racer. "With all the apartment buildings around, she had to pick yours to be murdered in."

"I thought someone told me that you were working Traffic," said Bobby.

"Well, you know how it is. When there's a big case and need someone to solve it, who do they call?" asked Racer.

"Sure, sure," said Bobby. "Now what can I do for you?"

"I need to see the Molino woman's apartment and I'll need to talk with you afterwards."

"No problem," said Bobby. "I'll take you upstairs myself."

Bobby Redding went around the desk to a cabinet mounted under the desk. He stuck a key into the lock and turned it. There must have been a hundred keys inside. Bobby looked over the keys and removed one with a white tab attached to it. Then he motioned toward the elevators.

They headed for the row of elevators. Racer asked Bobby if there was any way out of there where the guards' vision was obstructed. Bobby assured him that the only way out was right past the front desk. Then Racer asked the same about the garage. Bobby chuckled and told Racer not unless they ran the guard over, and he hadn't lost a guard out there yet.

Just then the elevator doors opened and they rode the elevator to Barbara Molino's floor, listening to elevator music. When they reached the sixth floor, they stepped out of the elevator and stood at the junction of the two hallways. Racer followed Bobby as he took the hall to his left. The apartments were situated along the rear of the building, so all the entry doors were on the right side of the hallway. The floor, the same gray marble as the lobby, was polished to a glassy finish. Bobby stopped in front of apartment 608. Bobby inserted the key, with the white tag, into the lock. When the deadbolt slipped back, he pushed the door open.

"The management doesn't want to rent this unit out for at least another month," said Bobby. "They want to give it a good going over and make sure everything is just right."

Racer nodded in acknowledgment.

When they got inside, Racer whistled. The place was a far cry from his apartment. The carpet was so thick, it was like walking on air. It was a rich cream color. The furniture in the living room was all white leather and there was a marble fireplace in the center of the wall. On the far wall was a set of sliding glass doors leading onto a balcony.

"How many rooms does this place have?" asked Racer.

"There's the living room, formal dining room, kitchen, breakfast nook and two very large bedrooms with their own baths," replied Bobby.

"How much does a place like this go for?" asked Racer.

"It's sure more than you or I can afford," replied Bobby.

"Is there anything else that I can help you with?" asked Bobby.

"No, but I would appreciate it if you would let me go through this place alone."

"That's no problem," said Bobby, handing Racer the key. "Lock up when you're done and I'll see you downstairs."

Racer nodded as Redding backed out of the apartment.

From the report that Harlin and Piakowski had filed, they had found a button and some fibers. The lab report stated that the fibers where from a blond hair wig. Barbara Molino had been married once. He husband had been killed in an automobile accident. *That must have been where the money came from for the apart-*

ment, Racer thought. The boyfriend had found the body. Racer would talk to him later. As he was searching the apartment, Racer thought about the security system setup for the building. The killer would have had to sign in that night so there had to be a record. No one could have slipped past the guards unless they were invisible. So this told Racer that Barbara must have known the killer. According to the guard, she would have to give them the okay to allow the person up to her apartment.

He didn't find anything out of the ordinary in the living room, so he moved on to the kitchen. Racer searched the kitchen, paying extra attention to the knife drawer. He went through everything, even checking the empty garbage can, nothing. He moved his search to the dining room and the two bathrooms but again found nothing unusual. He looked through the smaller of the two bedrooms and found old clothes, shoes, some luggage but not much of anything else. It looked like Barbara used this as her storage room.

Next was Barbara's bedroom. The original blood-stained sheets had been removed, but Racer could see the large stains on the mattress, which was leaning against the wall. A new mattress had replaced it. The stain was identical to those at the other crime scenes. He started with the closet and found about half a dozen dresses from the Designer Dress Shop. Racer then went to the dresser drawers, searching through them one at a time. He found bras, panties and nightgowns all from the Designer Dress Shop. So far, it was the only link between the dead women. He got down on all fours and scanned the floor area. It was clean. He then went back to the closet and started removing the clothes, looking for the garment that was missing a button. All the dresses from the Designer Dress Shop were low cut and slinky. Not many buttons on them. Then he came across a more conservative dress. He looked at the button that he removed from the evidence envelope. It was white around the edges with small gray squares in the middle of it. He laid the dress on the bed and took a closer look at it. It had the same buttons on the sleeves as the one he was holding in his hand. There was a button missing off the left sleeve. The dress appeared to be new. He started going over it carefully and noticed that there was a seam ripped under the right arm. Why would Barbara have hung this dress back up if it was ripped and a button was missing? And why would Mary Wagner throw away a perfectly good dress? Racer was puzzled. He spread Barbara's file on the dresser and studied it. The fibers were from a blonde wig. Racer didn't find any wig. Barbara Molino also had sex within a short time of her death. Her boyfriend might be able to clear that one up. Racer thought, *The scene was just like the last two.* A lot of clothes from the Designer Dress Shop, but he hadn't found any pictures yet.

Before leaving, he scanned the apartment one more time, wondering how three gruesome murders could have been committed without hardly any evidence being left behind. Someone knew exactly what they were doing. Turning, he headed for the door. Racer pulled the door closed and set the deadbolt. Stepping into the elevator, he headed down to Redding's office.

"I've been waiting for you," said Bobby, blowing blue smoke rings from a cigar.

"I just have a couple of questions to ask," said Racer, moving to a large window looking out on a small playground.

"Shoot," answered Bobby.

"How do you think the killer got into her apartment?" asked Racer.

"As I have been telling everyone, the only way that a person could get in is for her to let them in," replied Bobby. "There is no other way."

"The guard in the garage said that visitors have a ticket made up showing the time they enter, the apartment they visited and the time they left," said Racer.

"That's right," said Bobby. "I have the ones for the Molino apartment right here. I thought that you might be interested in them."

"Thanks," said Racer. "Also do you have the names of all the officers that were on duty that night?"

"I already gave them to the other detectives," said Bobby.

"Well, can you give them to me?" asked Racer.

"No problem," replied Bobby.

Bobby went to a filing cabinet and in a minute he had a list of six names. He handed them to Racer, who looked the list over. Bobby had written down the guards' name and the location they were working that night. "That's great," said Racer. "I'll have these tickets back to you before the end of the week."

"Hey, take as long as you like," said Bobby.

Racer folded the list and stuck it in his jacket pocket. He picked up the tickets that were in a small cardboard box and headed for the office door.

"Thanks again," said Racer as he left the office.

When Racer got to the station Cindy was patiently waiting. It was already after five and most of the day shift had left.

"What's taken you so long?" asked Cindy.

"The Chief of Security at Molino's apartment complex was an old friend of mine. Use to be a cop here," said Racer as he placed the box with the tickets down on the desk.

"Are you ready to call it a day?" asked Cindy glancing at the box.

"No, not yet," replied Racer. "I want to make a couple of notes for tomorrow. You can take off if you want."

Cindy said goodnight, grabbed her bag and headed for the door. Before she disappeared down the steps, she stopped and looked back at Racer.

"Don't stay too long. I don't want you to get burned out on me," said Cindy.

"I won't," said Racer.

She then disappeared through the door and down the steps to the parking lot.

Racer pulled a pad of paper out of the top drawer and started making notes. He ripped the sheet from the pad and folded it up. He tucked it into his shirt pocket, picked up the box of tickets and headed for the stairs. Raindrops were hitting hard against the windowpane like bullets.

Racer had to tuck the tickets under his coat so they wouldn't get wet as he made a mad dash into Barney's. He glanced at his watch: It was six-thirty. It was Thursday and that meant ladies' night. There wasn't much of a crowd yet, so Racer grabbed a table in the back corner and put the tickets on the table. Walking toward the bar, he noticed that Barney had a new bartender on duty. He was a young guy with blond hair and a dark tan. Barney must be pulling out all the stops for the ladies. A good-looking bartender never hurt. Racer took a stool at the bar and ordered a cold draft.

"The beer's always cold," said a voice from somewhere on the other side of the bar. Racer stood up on the stool and peered over the bar. It was Barney. He was kneeling down behind the bar checking his inventory. "What's up, Racer?" asked Barney.

"Nothing," replied Racer. "Just thought I'd stop by and have a cold one before going home."

"Remember, it's ladies' night," replied Barney, "I'm sure a nice tall lady could give you a hand with your homework," said Barney with a chuckle.

"No thanks," said Racer, holding up his hands.

Racer grabbed his beer and headed back to his table. He took his jacket off and rested it over the back of the chair. Sitting down, Racer took a drink from the frosted mug and started going through the tickets. The tickets were placed in order by the date stamped on them. He started two days before the murder and finished two days after the murder. Pulling tickets out of the box, sorting by date, he placed the ones that fit his time frame next to his beer. When he got done, there were five tickets lying there. He picked up the rest of the tickets and put them back in the box. He took another drink from his glass and fanned the five tickets out in front of him. Reaching behind him, he removed his notebook and pen from his jacket pocket. Finishing his beer, Racer motioned for the bartender to bring him another one. Now he lined the tickets up by date and time. The bartender brought him another frosty mug and a bowl of popcorn, placed them on the table and removed the empty glass. Racer never looked up.

The first ticket that Racer picked up showed that Barbara had a visitor two nights before she was killed. As a matter of fact, there were three tickets for that time. The fourth ticket showed she had a visitor the night before she died and the last ticket was the day the body was discovered. He sat there staring at them and tried to reason them out. The last ticket most likely was the boyfriend, so he pushed that one aside for the moment. Now he had four left, and he was sure that one of them was the killer. His next step was to talk to the guards that were on duty and hope that they could remember who belonged to each ticket. He would start with them tomorrow. It had been a little over a month now, and with the number of people that entered and exited that building every day, it might be hard for the guards to remember. Racer made some notes on his pad and returned it to his pocket along with the five tickets.

Racer downed half the contents of the mug as he noticed that Barney's was starting to fillup. The women outnumbered the men by about three to one, and he knew it would get worse as the night went on. He usually tried to avoid Barney's on ladies' night, but he didn't want to go back to his empty apartment quite yet. He got up and walked back to the bar. There were two bar stools left. He took one that was next to a tall redhead with green eyes. Racer put the box on the bar in front of him and gave her the once over. She gave him a smile and then turned back to her drink and the guy next to her. Barney approached him with another mug of beer.

"Well, did you find what you were looking for?" asked Barney.

"I think I might have, but I won't know until tomorrow when I get a chance to talk to a couple of people," said Racer.

"You going to stick around for a while?" asked Barney.

"Not too long," replied Racer.

Barney placed the mug on the bar in front of Racer and moved to the other end of the bar. Racer spun around on his barstool and surveyed the crowd. As he was taking a drink, he heard a familiar voice. The place was getting packed so he couldn't see without standing up on the bottom rung of the stool. He looked in the general direction the voice was coming from. Then his eyes settled on the person. It was Cindy. She was sitting at the same table that Racer left a few minutes ago. There were a couple of guys hanging around her. Racer recognized them as two detectives from robbery. Racer sat back down and turned to the bar and his beer. He wrestled with the idea of whether he should go over or stay right were he was. Finally he decided to finish his beer and just head home.

When he got half way across the room, Racer heard his name being called. Racer turned and saw Jim Harlin with his arm around Cindy's waist.

"The party is just getting started. I hear that Barney is going to have a wet T-shirt contest around eleven tonight and I think I already know who it going to win," said Harlin, looking at Cindy.

Racer looked at Harlin and then at Cindy. She had a pleasant smile on her face. He could tell that she had a few drinks too many.

"You really should stay," said Cindy looking directly into Racer's eyes.

"No, I really have to go," said Racer.

Racer pushed through the door and stepped outside into the rain. He knew that Harlin would take advantage of Cindy the first chance he got. It would be another trophy to add to his collection. It would start with the wet T-shirt contest. He looked at his watch and it was a little after nine. He decided to head home, get changed and return before the contest started. As he walked toward his car, the rain was starting to letting up.

While Racer was changing, all he could think about was that damn Harlin. Rumors had it that he scored every week with a different woman. How could a guy with a beautiful wife and two young sons openly cheat like this? Now he was trying to hit on Racer's partner. All he wanted to do was smash Harlin's face in.

In another part of the city, a young woman was sitting at her kitchen table in a small apartment, writing her husband a letter. She had tears in her eyes as she wrote. She told him how sorry she was that they had had a fight about moving back onto the military base before he left. She wanted him to understand that the apartment gave her more freedom and that her job and friends were all off base. Then she had something else to tell him. She said how sorry she was for what happened over the last couple of days. She didn't know how something like this could happen. She wanted him to understand that she had no choice.

There was a knock at the door. She put down her pen and slid the letter into a drawer under the table. A knock sounded again. She got up and slowly headed for the door. Crossing the living room, she approached the front door and asked who it was. She wanted to be careful, thinking about the recent string of unsolved murders. The voice on the other side of the door said they were from the Designer Dress Shop. A strange look crossed her face as she slid the deadbolt back. She turned the knob and opened the door as far as the chain would allow.

"What do you want?" she asked. "I thought that I was all done with you people."

"Not quite yet," said the figure standing there.

CHAPTER SIX

Racer was just getting ready to leave his apartment when the phone rang. He picked it up and listened.

"Racer, this is Detman. I have something for you. A patrol car was called to 1355 Roscoe Street for a disturbance call. When they got there to investigate, they found a young woman with her throat slashed. It couldn't have happened more than an hour ago. I want you to round up your partner and get your butts over there now," said Detman.

"I'm on my way," replied Racer.

This gave him a good reason to haul Cindy out of Barney's and away from Harlin. When Racer arrived, he hollered to Barney, "Where's Cindy?"

"I think she went back to the ladies room to change into her white T-shirt," yelled Barney.

"Thanks," said Racer.

When he got to the restrooms, Harlin was leaning against the wall. Racer could see that his eyes were getting glassed over. Racer pushed past him. When he did, Harlin grabbed Racer's arm. Racer spun around and faced Harlin. "Jim, take you hand off my arm before I shove it up your butt," said Racer.

Just then, Cindy came out of the ladies room. Racer and Harlin were standing there glaring at each other.

"What is going on out here?" asked Cindy.

"Nothing," said Harlin. "You look quite beautiful in that T-shirt."

Racer turned to Cindy and said, "Get your blouse back on, you're coming with me."

"She isn't going anywhere," said Harlin. "You're not her father."

Racer spun Cindy around and headed her back toward the

ladies room. He told her to get changed, now. Cindy gave him a dirty look but followed his directions. When she came out, Racer took Cindy's arm and started leading her through the crowd. After being in Barney's all night, she wasn't too stable on her feet. Harlin caught up to them and grabbed Racer's shoulder. Racer spun around with a driving leg kick, lifting Harlin two feet off the floor. By the time he landed, Racer was out the door with Cindy in tow. When he got her to the car, she pulled her arm free.

"I'm not going anywhere with you," said Cindy in a slurred voice.

"Look, this is business. They just found a body of another young woman and Detman wants us there," said Racer. "So pull yourself together and get in the car."

He opened the car door for her and helped her into the front seat. Her head fell back against the headrest. Racer stared at her as he brought the car to life. He squealed away from the curb and headed for Roscoe Street.

Sliding around the next corner onto Roscoe, Racer could see blue and white flashers up ahead. Racer parked between a couple of the patrol cars. He looked over at Cindy and she was resting her head against the car window. He tapped her on the arm and she slowly turned in his direction.

"I don't feel so good," she said.

"That's okay, you stay in the car. I think that I can handle it by myself," he replied.

Racer didn't really need her but he was glad that he had rescued her from the clutches of Harlin. It also felt good that he had a chance to lay Harlin out.

"No, I'm coming with you," replied Cindy.

"If you want," said Racer.

After Racer got out of the car, he removed his badge and tucked it into his breast pocket so it was exposed. He went around to the passenger side and helped Cindy out.

"I'm all right," said Cindy.

"Okay," said Racer, "just trying to help."

When they got to the front door of the building, a young patrolman was standing there. He looked at Racer's badge and told him it was the apartment at the rear of the second floor. Racer nodded.

When Racer and Cindy reached the second floor there were cops all over the place. He asked Cindy if she could find out who was the first one on the scene and see what they could tell her. She nodded and went off. Entering the apartment, Racer went directly to the bedroom. The medical examiner was still there going over the body. Two things struck Racer right away. First, there appeared to be signs of a struggle and secondly, the dead woman wasn't in bed. Racer turned to the medical examiner.

"What do you have for me?"

The medical examiner said, "We have a young white female, in her early twenties, with her throat cut. Cause of death most likely is exsanguination. She bled out."

"Has she been sexually assaulted?" asked Racer.

"Won't be able to tell until I get the body back and examine it. I'll have everything in my report tomorrow," replied the medical examiner. "One thing I can tell you is that she put up a struggle. There are a number of bruises on the body. It isn't like the rest."

"I can see that," said Racer. "Thanks, doc, I'll be waiting for your report."

Racer looked around, saw Cindy talking with a patrolman over in the corner of the living room, and headed that way. "Have anything?" asked Racer.

"Here's the story," started Cindy. "At around nine tonight, a Mrs. Caldwell was walking her dog in the back alley. Apparently she does this every night. As she passed behind the building she thought she heard someone scream. When she looked up, she saw what looked like two figures struggling with each other. The shade was pulled, so all she could see was their shadows, but she said it looked like a man and a woman. She wasn't going to call the police because she thought it probably was a family quarrel, but then she decided she better report it."

"Is the woman still here?" asked Racer.

"No, they sent her home but I have her address. She only lives three houses from here," said Cindy.

A patrolman walked over to Racer and asked if he was done with the body. The ME wanted to take it back to the morgue. Racer turned and headed back to the bedroom. Cindy was right behind him. Going directly to the body, Racer lifted the blood-stained white sheet. He noticed there was more than one cut on her throat. She was naked from the waist up, wearing only a pair of panties. Her eyes were fixed in horror and she had bruises on her upper arms, indicating that the killer was having a difficult time holding onto her. That probably explained why she was on the floor and not in bed. He knew this pretty woman was too young to die. He pulled the sheet back over her and motioned for the coroner to remove the body. Now it was time to check with the lab techs to see if they came up with anything.

Racer went over to a short, heavyset man that was dusting the front door for prints and asked if he had come up with anything. The tech shook his head.

Racer returned to the patrolman that was the first on the scene and wanted to know how he found the front door. He told Racer that it was closed but unlocked.

In the next hour, Racer watched as everyone slowly left. Now he motioned for Cindy to join him in the bedroom. He wanted to get started going over the apartment and maybe they could get out of there before midnight. This time they worked together.

As they went from room to room, Racer noticed the lack of furniture. It probably wasn't that unusual. Most people who lived in this part of town were in the lower income bracket. There was a group of small houses mixed in with some old apartment build-ings. A lot of elderly couples and young people just getting started lived here. He figured that the woman was married because he saw a wedding ring on her finger when he examined the body. But he thought it was strange that there weren't any pictures in the bed-room. He also knew that the victim was named Cheryl Ports-mouth. Racer also realized that if the same person was doing the murders, his M.O. has changed. Cheryl was the first married per-son he had picked.

Racer started going through the dresser drawers, taking them out one at a time, emptying the contents on the floor. The top three drawers had woman's undergarments, sweaters and night-gowns, and in the bottom three he found underwear, T-shirts, pajamas and socks for a man.

While Cindy continued through the drawers, Racer went to the nightstand. There were some old letters, some stationery, a phone book but not much else. He moved to the closet, pulled the door open, and found a bare lightbulb with a pull string hanging down. He pulled the string and the bulb lit instantly. There were clothes lined up on each side of the closet. One side was for Cheryl and the other side was for her husband's clothes. As he went through each piece of clothing, he found nothing more then an overdue electric bill, a couple of movie ticket stubs and some tissues.

Racer stuck his head out of the closet and asked Cindy if she was having any luck.

"Nothing," said Cindy still searching.

"Have you noticed the one thing that we didn't find?" asked Racer.

"Yeah, something from the Designer Dress Shop," replied Cindy. "Maybe this murder is unrelated, a copycat."

"Let's go to the kitchen," said Racer.

They walked through to the kitchen and stopped in the doorway. It was small, with the stove and refrigerator crammed into the corner. A small wooden table with two chairs was positioned in the middle of the floor. There was no microwave or dishwasher. They had checked just about everything when Cindy called for Racer's attention. Cindy had found the drawer under the kitchen table. Opening it, Cindy found the letter that Cheryl Portsmouth was writing. She carefully removed it from the drawer by the bottom corner and laid it out on the table. Racer removed a plastic evidence bag from his inside pocket and carefully slid the letter into the bag. After sealing it, Racer took it into the living room. They sat down on the couch. Racer held up the letter so they both could read it. It looked like she was writing a letter to her husband when she was interrupted.

"It looks like he is on a tour of duty right now," said Racer.

"We'll have to find out where he is and break the news to him," said Cindy.

"That's always a pleasant job," replied Racer as he continued to read the letter.

"What do you think she is talking about when she said she didn't think anything like this could happen to her and that she had no choice in the matter?" asked Cindy.

"I don't know," replied Racer. "You didn't find any other letters around, did you?"

"No," said Cindy.

"Something just doesn't fit here. The body was next to the bed, there appears to have been a struggle, there is no clothing from the Designer Dress Shop, and she's married. Nothing fits," said Racer rubbing his hand across his stubbled chin. "I'm going to take another quick look around to make sure we didn't miss anything."

Racer backtracked through the kitchen, living room and bath. He got down on his hands and knees and could see something under the cabinet that housed the television and video recorder. He crawled over and reached under but couldn't reach it. He went into the kitchen, found a broom and used it to remove a plastic container. He picked it up with his pen and looked closely at it. It looked like a plastic container for a roll of 35 millimeter film.

Racer pulled another evidence bag from his coat pocket and placed the container inside. Before stuffing it into his jacket pocket, he shook it. "It sounds like there might be a roll of film inside. We'll get this to Sidney as soon as we get back."

He went back into Cheryl's bedroom and got down on the floor again. There was something lying under the bed. He half crawled under the bed until he could reach the object. He scooped it up with his notebook and brought it out. It looked like a piece of balloon. As he was looking at it, he heard Cindy call him.

"What is this up here?" she asked.

Racer went over to the closet and saw a door way up in the ceiling. It looked like it had been nailed shut. Racer went to the kitchen and returned with one of the chairs. He placed it in the closet and climbed up. He removed his pocket knife and slipped the blade under the wooden frame. He worked it around until the door came free. It was easy to tell that it had been opened a few times before. The nail holes were starting to widen out. He couldn't see into the hole but carefully reached in with his right hand. Feeling around, he felt a package that seemed to have a string around it. Gripping the packet, he slid it to the opening. It appeared to be a cardboard box wrapped with brown paper and tied with a string. He handed it down to Cindy. She took it into the kitchen and placed it on the table. Racer jumped down and joined her. He untied the string and removed it from the package carefully. Next, he unfolded the brown paper and slowly opened the box. Cindy watched him closely. Then a big smile broke out across his face. Racer started pulling clothing from the box. There were bras, panties, and nighties, and they were all very sexy.

"And guess were they're from?" asked Racer.

"It wouldn't be the Designer Dress Shop, would it?" replied Cindy.

As he pulled items from the box and slowly worked his way to the bottom, he found two pictures. They were Polaroids. The first one had Cheryl sitting on the couch in the living room in nothing but a pair of sheer panties with her legs crossed. There was a guy sitting next to her with his arm around her shoulder. Since he was turned toward her, you could only see his profile. The second picture had Cheryl lying on the living room floor on her stomach, with her back arched, looking up at the camera. She wore a sheer pink nightie that was very revealing. The panties and pink nightie were part of the pile of garments that Racer had removed from the box.

"She must have been hiding these so she could get rid of them after her husband got shipped out," said Cindy.

"I wouldn't doubt that," replied Racer. "By the way, did you notice any pictures of her husband while we were going through the apartment?"

"Come to think of it, no," said Cindy.

"Take a look around all the rooms and see what you can find while I stuff these things back into the box," said Racer.

Cindy starting going around the apartment and found four pictures of the same man. All of them had been turned face down and stuck under something. She pointed them out to Racer and made the comment that Cheryl was either mad at her husband or she didn't want him to see what she was doing while he was away.

Racer looked at his watch: It was a quarter to twelve. He was starting to feel the fatigue settle in and he knew Cindy was about dead on her feet. He suggested they call it a night, and Cindy agreed without an argument.

As they left the apartment, they realized there was still a patrolman standing outside the door. Racer told him to make sure the apartment was secure before he left. The patrolman nodded, locked the door, pulled out a roll of yellow tape and started taping the door to the apartment.

When they got down to the ZX, Racer paused. "Tomorrow I want to go back to Molino's place and take one more look around. Something is missing. Every victim had clothes from the Designer Dress Shop and pictures of her in various forms of undress. I found the clothes in Molino's place but no pictures. Besides, I have to return the tickets the security people loaned me."

"What do you want me to do?" asked Cindy.

Racer reached into his jacket pocket and pulled out the list of security guards that were on duty when Barbara Molino was killed. Along with that, he had the five tickets that he removed from the box that Bobby Redding had given him. He handed everything to Cindy and told her that he wanted her to question the security guards about the five tickets and anything that they could remember about the visitors on those dates.

"Sure, I'll get on it first thing tomorrow," said Cindy.

"How about if we meet at around one at Barney's for lunch?" asked Racer.

"You got a date," replied Cindy.

"I'll drop you off at Barney's so you can pick up your car," said Racer. "Do you feel all right to drive?"

"I feel fine now," said Cindy.

After Racer dropped her off, he pulled around the corner and stopped. He watched Cindy get into her car and head home. He followed her all the way to make sure she made it safely. After she entered her apartment building, he waited five more minutes and then took off for home. The bed sure would feel good tonight.

CHAPTER SEVEN

All Racer could hear was a loud buzzing in his ear. He finally realized that his alarm had gone off. As he swung his arm around to shut it off, he knocked it clean off the nightstand. The worst part was it never stopped buzzing. Climbing out of bed, Racer shut off the alarm and headed for the kitchen. Trying to get his eyes focused on the wall clock, he finally realized it was nine-thirty.

After measuring some coffee into the maker, he shuffled off to the shower. He started the water for the shower but never waited for it to warm up. Racer always said the best way to wake up in the morning was to jump into a cold shower. By the time the water finally started warming up, he was ready to get out. He dried off a little and then wrapped the towel around his waist. The smell of fresh coffee was filling the air as he made his way back to the kitchen. Pouring himself a cup, he sat down at the table. Sipping the dark liquid, he started to lay his day out in his head.

First, he was going to go over to Barbara Molino's place and return the box of tickets that Bobby Redding had loaned him. Next, he was going to give her apartment one more going-over to see if he could locate any pictures that would tie her murder to the rest.

Then, he was going to talk with Mrs. Caldwell about what she had seen last night. Maybe she could add a little something to what they already knew. Then there was the film container, the piece of balloon, the box of sexy garments and the pictures that Cheryl Portsmouth had hidden in her closet. All he had to do was tie them into the recent murders. He went back into the bedroom and got dressed. Maybe by the end of the day he would have some answers to these questions. He sure as hell hoped so.

When he was done dressing, Racer clipped his .357 on his belt and finished his coffee. Checking his watch, he saw that it was time to head out.

When Racer got outside, he saw a woman sitting on a bench by the front entrance. He couldn't see her face until he got right up to her. That's when she turned to face him.

"Hi, I'm Marge Smyth, a reporter for the Fairfield Press. Can you give me a statement concerning last night's death of Cheryl Portsmouth?" she asked.

Racer kept on walking.

"Come on, detective, you'll have to talk to me sooner or later, so why not sooner?" asked Marge, chasing after him.

Racer paused. "What gives you the idea that I might want to talk to you at all?"

"Well, since you are in charge of the case and the body count has reached four, I thought you might have something to say to the women of Fairfield. You know, like how to stay safe," said Marge.

"No comment," replied Racer, ready to continue walking.

"Look, I'll make a deal with you. If you trust me with the story, I won't print anything until you give me the okay. How's that?" asked Marge.

"I really enjoyed our little chat but I have an appointment to keep," said Racer as he headed for his car.

"Well, at least think about my offer," said Marge. "You can catch me at the paper. Just leave a message if I'm not there."

Racer got into the ZX and quickly headed for Barbara Molino's condo. As he twisted and turned his way through the mid-morning traffic, he kept looking in his rearview mirror to make sure Marge wasn't following him. He wouldn't put anything past one of those damn reporters. Finally, he made a right; Barbara's condo was in the next block.

Racer pulled his car to the curb and grabbed the box of tickets off the passenger seat. He walked up to the entrance and pushed through the glass doors. There was only one guard at the front desk this time. Approaching the guard, he removed his badge from his pocket. Before the guard could say anything, Racer asked for Bobby Redding, showing his shield at the same time. The guard informed Racer that Mr. Redding wasn't there yet but should be arriving any minute. Racer mentioned that he had a box of tickets to return to Bobby, plus he wanted to get back upstairs to Barbara

Molino's apartment. The guard looked at him and then the badge and picked up the phone. It only took a minute for another guard to appear. One would watch the desk while the other escorted Racer up to Barbara Molino's apartment. Racer left the box of tickets on the counter and asked the guard to keep an eye on it.

When they got to the apartment, the guard let Racer in and asked if he could be of any help. Racer waved him off. The guard backed out of the apartment and told Racer that he would be right outside. When the door closed, Racer was all alone. He walked to the middle of the room and started to scan everything in sight. There had to be pictures. All the others had pictures. They had to be somewhere, but what if she destroyed them? That's what it seemed Cheryl Portsmouth was getting ready to do. He had gone through everything, even looking in the refrigerator for empty cans. He went back through every room, looking behind and under everything that he possibly could. He even pulled the carpet back in areas where he could. He was just about to give up when the guard poked his head in the door and asked if he was done.

"Yes," said Racer, "I guess I'm not going to find what I'm looking for."

"Is it something of value?" asked the guard.

"Could be," replied Racer.

"Well, we provide all our residents with safety deposit boxes for their convenience," said the guard.

"And where might they be?" asked Racer, smiling.

"They're kept in a room behind the guard's desk," he said.

Out the door they went and back down to the lobby. When they reached the lobby, the guard took Racer to a room next to Bobby Redding's office. Using one of the keys on his ring, the guard unlocked the steel door and pushed it open. Racer stepped inside and looked at rows of safety deposit boxes. There was one box for each condo, and each box was marked with an apartment number.

"I need to look in the one for Barbara Molino's apartment," said Racer.

"Can't do that," said the guard. "If the resident isn't present, the box can't be opened without the next of kin or a search warrant."

"I don't think Barbara Molino would mind," said Racer.

"I agree," said the guard, "but her survivors might."

"When does Redding get here?" asked Racer.

"Captain Redding? He should be here any minute," answered the guard.

The guard offered Racer a cup of coffee and led him to a break room. He poured Racer a cup of coffee from the glass container and then one for himself. Sitting there at a small table, the guard tried to make small talk but Racer was only interested in getting into Molino's safety deposit box.

Racer finally got up and started to head for the hall when the guard appeared with Bobby Redding behind him. Redding stepped around the guard and held out his hand. Racer took it and thanked Bobby for the use of the tickets. He informed Redding that they possibly could help them pinpoint who had seen Barbara Molino before she died. Racer wanted to grease Bobby a little before asking him for another favor. He wanted to get into Barbara's safety deposit box and he wanted to do it today.

"The guard tells me you want access to Barbara Molino's safety deposit box," said Bobby.

"That's right; there might be something important in there that could help this case," said Racer.

"That could be a problem," said Bobby.

"Yeah, I know. I just want to look," said Racer. "I won't touch anything."

Bobby thought for a second then said, "I don't see anything wrong with that. Come on."

They all turned back toward the safety deposit room. Redding told the guard to go ahead and open Molino's box. The guard removed the key ring from his belt and inserted two silver keys into the locks. Turning both keys at the same time, he pulled the small metal door open. Moving back from the open door, the guard nodded to Bobby and left the room. Racer moved over, removed the metal box from the wall and placed it on the small table provided. Bobby was right behind him.

"Would you mind standing by the door so no one walks in on us?" asked Racer.

"Sure thing," replied Bobby, slowly backing up.

Racer turned the box around so when he opened the lid it blocked Bobby from seeing what was in it. Racer could see several brown envelopes. There were insurance policies for the condo and her car. There were several stock certificates and savings bonds in another envelope. Racer figured there was about fifty thousand dollars worth. There were also some personal letters but nothing of importance. Then he came to a sealed envelope. There was no writing on the outside to identify what the contents were. Racer knew that he wasn't suppose to touch anything but he stuck his finger under the corner of the flap and worked it across the envelope quietly. Inside the envelope were six negatives and six black and white pictures of Cheryl and some guy in different positions. It appeared to be the same guy with the dark black hair. He always seemed to have his face hidden from the camera. He was of average build with no distinguishing marks visible. This was the thread that linked the four murders together.

"Did you find anything interesting?" asked Bobby.

"Not really. There only appears to be a bunch of personal papers" said Racer.

He peered over at Bobby and, when he wasn't looking, Racer slipped the brown envelope under his jacket. Closing the lid, he put it back into the opening in the wall. Bobby called the guard back into the room so he could lock it back up.

"I really appreciate this," said Racer. "It saved me a lot of time. We'll keep this between us."

"Hey, anything I can do to help," replied Bobby.

Cindy pulled up in front of a small frame house in one of the older sections of the city. She parked her car and headed up a brick walk. The neighborhood was starting to come alive with groups of small kids playing in front of the houses. School would be back in session in a couple of weeks and the streets would be quiet again. Cindy rang the doorbell and waited a few seconds before pushing it again. She could hear footsteps coming from inside. A lock slid back and the front door opened. A middle-aged woman peered out at her, with curlers in her hair, wearing a housecoat. Cindy identified herself and flashed the woman her badge and identification. The woman looked at it for a second and then looked back at Cindy. Cindy asked if a George Brown lived there, and explained that she needed to speak with him about a case she was investigating. When the woman offered some resistance, Cindy mentioned that she could either talk with him here or down at the station. Without another word, the woman closed the door in Cindy's face and left her standing there. She waited a couple of minutes and was about to start pounding on the door when it finally opened to reveal a man about five feet six inches tall, a little pudgy around the middle, with light brown hair. Cindy guessed that he was probably around forty-five to fifty years old.

"Hi, I'm detective Darling with the Fairfield Police and I would like to ask you a few questions concerning the death of Barbara Molino."

The guy gave Cindy the once over and then asked her to come in. Once inside, he offered Cindy a seat and sat down in a brown lounge chair covered with fake leather.

"How can I help you, detective?" asked Mr. Brown.

"You work for the American Security Systems and your duty station is 1212 Bluebird?" asked Cindy.

"Yeah, that's right," replied Mr. Brown.

"Were you on the night shift the week that Barbara Molino was killed?" asked Cindy.

"Right again," replied Mr. Brown.

"I have a couple of tickets from three separate nights that I want you to look at," said Cindy.

George Brown took the tickets from Cindy and studied each one for several seconds. "I was working the side door that week and visitors don't usually use the side door. Mostly everyone either goes through the main entrance or the garage, especially at night. It's a lot safer. I don't remember any visitors coming past my post at all that week," answered Mr. Brown.

"Do you remember any of the other guards talking about anything unusual happening during that week?" asked Cindy.

"Nope," replied Mr. Brown, his eyes straying to Cindy's blouse.

"Well, thanks for your help, Mr. Brown. I won't take up any

more of your time. But if you do remember anything, here is my card," said Cindy handing, him one of her cards.

George Brown watched her closely as she got up off the couch. "You can take up my time whenever you like," he said.

As Cindy moved to the door, she could see Mrs. Brown standing in the doorway that led to the kitchen. She had a coffee cup in her hand. Cindy thought that this guy must be a real dirtball.

Heading for the car, Cindy crossed George Brown's name off the list. Sliding in behind the steering wheel, she checked the list to see who was next. There was a name and address only ten blocks away. Pulling away from the curb, Cindy hoped she would have better luck with the next person.

Racer pulled up in front of the Roscoe Street address. He sat there for a minute, trying to figure out exactly what house Mrs. Caldwell lived in. It was the third house over but he couldn't remember if it was to the right or left. Just about then, he noticed a woman hollering and waving at him, and thought it must be Mrs. Caldwell. He got out of the car and walked down to meet her. After introducing themselves, he told Mrs. Caldwell that he had a few questions to ask her about Cheryl Portsmouth. Mrs. Caldwell invited him into her house where they could chat and have a nice cup of tea.

Racer followed her into the house. She was a cheery woman of about sixty-five. Her hair was almost completely white and she walked with a slight limp. Racer followed her right into the kitchen and took a seat at the kitchen table. Looking around, he could see that everything was kept spotless and in its place. All of a sudden his heart skipped a beat. An extremely large black dog was headed straight for him. Mrs. Caldwell called the dog's name and told it to behave in a calming voice. The dog came to an abrupt stop and sat down, staring at Racer.

"Oh, don't worry about King, he's such a pussycat," said Mrs. Caldwell. "He's a black Labrador, you know."

"No, I didn't know, but I'm glad you yelled at him to stop. Otherwise I might have had to shoot," said Racer laughingly.

"Oh, detective," said Mrs. Caldwell with a light laugh. "Now what would you like to ask me about last night? I think I told that nice lady every thing there was, but fire away."

"First, Mrs. Caldwell, please call me Racer. Now about last night, tell me in your own words exactly what you saw," he asked.

"Sure, Mr. Racer," said Mrs. Caldwell. "I always take King for a walk around the block around eight-thirty every night, no matter what the weather is. Well, last night was no exception. Just as we were passing the apartment building where that poor Mrs. Portsmouth lived, I could hear loud noises coming from inside. King barked a couple of times until I told him to quiet down. I heard this arguing, or at least it seemed to be. First, I thought that her husband was still home, but then I remembered her telling me that he had to leave for some place in California. He's in the service, you know."

"Yes, ma'am," said Racer. "Go on."

"I could see two figures go back and forth in front of the window but I couldn't see who the guy was because of the window shade. But he was taller than Cheryl was. Probably around six feet or so. Bigger than you, Mr. Racer," said Mrs. Caldwell.

"Now, you were in the alley right behind the apartment building?" asked Racer.

"Yes, "said Mrs. Caldwell, "When we return home from our walks, I always take King down the back alley and in the back door."

"Go on, Mrs. Caldwell," said Racer.

"I stayed there for about five minutes, trying to hear what they were saying," said Mrs. Caldwell.

"Did you hear anything?" asked Racer.

"I thought about that all last night," said Mrs. Caldwell. "He told her something about being with the same people that were there the other day and she said that he wasn't. He would grab her and she would break away from him. Finally, he grabbed her from behind and pulled her out of my view."

"Could you tell if they were wearing anything?" asked Racer.

"I couldn't tell because of the shade," said Mrs. Caldwell with raised eyebrows. "You don't think something was going on between them, do you?"

"I don't know anything right now," replied Racer. "I'm just

trying to determine if she might have been sexually assaulted."

"Oh, I see," said Mrs. Caldwell. "It appeared, now that you mentioned it, that they both could have been bare chested, but I couldn't be sure.

"After they disappeared from my sight I decided to head home, and that's when I heard her scream. It was short and not real loud but it was a scream. King barked toward the window. I listened closely for a moment but that was all I heard. I half ran home and called the police," said Mrs. Caldwell.

"Did you see anything after that?" asked Racer.

"No, I kept an eye on the street looking for a car or something, but he could have left while I was calling the police," said Mrs. Caldwell.

"Had you talked with Mrs. Portsmouth lately?" asked Racer.

"The morning before her death," replied Mrs. Caldwell.

"What did you talk about?" asked Racer.

"She was telling me about her husband having to leave for about three months. Then she told me that she was a little upset about a fight they had about her moving back to the base while he was gone. She told me that she wished they hadn't fought before he left," said Mrs. Caldwell. "She did mention that she had something very important to tell him but she never got the chance before he left. I guess if you think about it, if she had moved back to the base, she would still be alive. What a shame."

"She didn't mention what the important thing was, did she?" asked Racer.

"No. I took it to be something very personal," replied Mrs. Caldwell.

"Is there anything else that you can remember about that night?" asked Racer.

"No, but I will be sure to call you personally if I remember anything else."

Racer thanked her and she escorted him to the front door. As he walked out to the curb he turned and waved goodbye to Mrs. Caldwell, and she returned his wave.

*   *   *   *   *

Cindy found the house of guard Jim Paulson after the second time around the block. The house didn't have any street number on it that Cindy could see, and the numbers on the mailbox was so small you needed a magnifying glass to read them. She parked her car in front of the house. She slide out of the car and approached the house. Ringing the doorbell, Cindy waited a few seconds and then knocked. She was ready to knock again when she heard a voice come from the side of the house.

"Can I help you?" asked the voice.

This startled Cindy. She almost stepped back off the top step. Catching herself, she walked toward the voice.

"I'm detective Cindy Darling with the Fairfield Police. If you're Jim Paulson, I would like to ask you a few questions concerning the death of Barbara Molino," said Cindy.

"Sure," said Mr. Paulson. "Why don't you come around into the back yard? I'm doing some work on my flowerbeds. I always like to work on them in the morning before it gets too hot."

As Cindy walked through the gate, she was amazed at how beautiful the yard looked. There were all types of flowers in a variety of colors. Mr. Paulson explained that ever since his wife died it was the only thing that kept him busy.

"Oh, I'm sorry about your wife," said Cindy.

"Thank you. Now what can I do for you?" asked Jim.

"I'm investigating the death of Barbara Molino, and I understand that you were on duty that week," said Cindy.

"Yes, that's right. I was on the four to twelve shift all week and my post was the garage."

"I have a couple of tickets here for the nights that center around Barbara's death," said Cindy. "Can you tell me anything about them?"

Cindy handed him the tickets and waited. Jim took the tickets and studied them one at a time for several minutes. Then all of a sudden he looked up at Cindy.

"Pardon my manners, but can I offer you something?" he asked. "Coffee, tea, a soda?"

"No thanks, I'm fine," said Cindy.

"Let's go over to the patio and sit down while I look at these tickets one more time."

Jim led Cindy over to the patio, offered her one of the lounge chairs and collapsed in the other. "I remember this one, said Jim as he handed one of the tickets to Cindy." A car pulled up to my booth and there were three people in it. There was a man driving with dark hair, and I think the other two passengers were women. It was hard to see in the car because the windows were tinted, but I'm pretty sure they were women. I asked the driver who they were there to see and he told me Barbara Molino. I made the call to her apartment like I'm supposed to, and she gave me the okay to send them up. So I did."

"Do you know what kind of car he was driving?" asked Cindy.

"It was a '99 or 2000 Buick but I don't remember what model," replied Jim.

"No, that's great," said Cindy.

He looked at one of the other tickets. It was stamped with the front entrance on it, so Jim handed it back to Cindy and looked at another. "Yeah, I remember this one too," said Jim. "It was kind of funny because when I called Mrs. Molino to get the okay to let him in, she hesitated. Let me think. Yeah, she asked me what the guy wanted. I asked him and he told me that they had forgotten something the night before and they sent him back to pick it up. Then she gave me the okay to send him up and that was that."

"Do you remember what the guy looked like?" asked Cindy.

"No, he kind of stayed back in the shadows of the car," replied Jim.

"Did you see him come out?" asked Cindy.

"No. It was right at shift change, and I don't remember seeing him leave," said Jim. "And that last ticket you have there is the boyfriend finding the body," said Jim, "because I remember the guards talking about it the next night when I got to work."

"Didn't any of the other detectives ask you about who went in or out of the garage that night?" asked Cindy.

"Sure, and I told them all of the people that I could remember," replied Jim. "But they didn't asked me about a certain ticket or time."

"Well, thanks a lot for your help, Mr. Paulson," said Cindy as she got up to leave.

"It was a pleasure to help," said Jim. "And I do appreciate the company. I don't get visitors too often."

"If you think of anything else, please give me a call," said Cindy as she gave him one of her cards. Cindy crossed the street and looked at her watch. It was five minutes after twelve. She had one more person to talk to before she could keep her date with Racer.

As Cindy pulled up outside of Pat Bryant's house, she noticed a person getting mail out of the mailbox. Cindy hurried out of the car and approached the woman that was now heading back to the house. While asking the woman if she was Pat Bryant, Cindy pulled her shield and identification from her purse. The woman nodded, and waited for Cindy to catch up with her. When they were side-by-side, Cindy informed her that she had a few questions to ask about Barbara Molino's murder. Pulling the three tickets from her purse, Cindy handed them to Pat Bryant and explained they were from around the day that Barbara Molino was killed. Cindy pointed to the middle ticket that Pat Bryant was holding and asked if she remembered it. Pat nodded and told Cindy it was for Barbara Molino's boyfriend the day he found the body. Cindy asked if she remembered anything else about the other tickets and Pat shook her head.

"How long would you say the boyfriend was upstairs before he called the police?" asked Cindy.

"He was probably up there for about two or three minutes when he called downstairs for the guard to call an ambulance and the police," said Pat.

"Can you remember if anyone else went into the building that morning or even the night before?" asked Cindy.

"No," said Pat handing the tickets back to Cindy.

"Thanks for your help," said Cindy.

Cindy gave Pat Bryant her card and told her to call if she remembered anything else. Cindy crossed the street and climbed into her car to join Racer at Barney's.

CHAPTER EIGHT

By the time Cindy arrived at Barney's, the lunch crowd was starting to thin out. She checked the bar area first and noticed Racer sitting at the far end. Cindy started in that direction, but before she reached Racer, Barney intercepted her.

"Hi, Miss Darling, what can I get you?"

"'I'll have whatever Racer's having," she said sitting down next to Racer.

Barney headed for the grill and threw on two half-pound burgers and then went to the tap and drew a couple of drafts. He placed them in front of Cindy and Racer.

"Let's go over to one of those tables away from prying eyes," said Racer as he grabbed his beer.

"Sounds good to me," replied Cindy as she followed Racer to a table near the rear exit.

"Well, did you have any luck this morning with those guards?" asked Racer.

"I think I struck pay dirt," replied Cindy with a smile. "Jim Paulson, the guard stationed in the garage, told me that a car entered the garage with three passengers the night before Molino died. The driver was a young guy with dark hair. The other two passengers he thinks were women. When he called Barbara's apartment, he said it sounded like Barbara was expecting them. The next night another car entered the garage. It had a single male in it. The guard didn't get a good look at him. When he called Ms. Molino about this guy, she sounded a little apprehensive about letting him in but finally gave the okay. So Paulson let him in. Apparently, that was the last time that anyone had either heard from her or saw her alive. The next day the boyfriend arrived through the main entrance and called down two or three minutes later asking for help. That's when he discovered her body. This was verified by

Pat Bryant, the guard at the front entrance."

Racer then told her about the safety deposit box and the trouble he had getting into it without a warrant but Bobby Redding bailed him out. That's when he found the pictures of Barbara Molino. Racer removed the brown envelope, from his jacket pocket, and tossed it on the table. Then he said, "The one thing that ties all the murders together."

Before Cindy could look inside, Barney placed the burgers and two more beers down on the table. Once he headed back to the bar, Cindy looked inside. The pictures were just like the rest they found at the other crime scenes.

Racer went on to describe his interview with Mrs. Caldwell. He told Cindy about the two silhouettes she saw on the shade and how they appeared to be struggling.

"So she didn't get a description of the guy?" asked Cindy.

"Not unless she had x-ray vision," said Racer. "All she could tell me was she thought he was a big man. So after lunch we'll give the medical examiner a call to see what he came up with."

It was two-thirty when they finally returned to the station. Racer headed down to the lab and found Sidney in his office sitting behind a stack of paperwork. Racer stepped in and told Sidney that he had something for him. Pulling the film container from his jacket pocket, Racer said, "I know it doesn't look like much, but I thought I'd have you give it the once-over anyway."

"You never know what modern science might be able to come up with," replied Sidney, taking the container from Racer.

When Racer got upstairs, he walked across the squad room and sat down behind his desk. Picking up the phone, he dialed the medical examiner's office. When someone finally answered, he asked for Jack Campbell. He was immediately put on hold. Sitting there waiting for Campbell, Racer watched Cindy making some notes at her desk. Just then a voice came on the line.

"Campbell speaking," said the voice, a little out of breath.

"Jack, it's Racer. Have anything for me?"

"Hold on a second and let me get the file," said Campbell.

Racer was waiting again. A couple of seconds later Campbell was back on the line and reading the report on Cheryl Portsmouth. He went through the usual stuff like her height, weight, color of hair, color of eyes and so on. Racer listened impatiently. Then Campbell came to some interesting things. Cheryl's death was caused by a large slash across her jugular. She bled to death. She also had a number of small cuts on her hands that probably came from her defending herself against the killer. She had bruises on both her upper arms. She wasn't sexually assaulted but there was evidence that she did have intercourse within two to four hours before her death. Also, some skin was removed from under her fingernails. It was from a white male with a blood type of "A" positive. When Jack Campbell was done, Racer asked his first question.

"Did she die right away?"

"My guess is no. It probably took 10 to 15 minutes for her to bleed out," said Campbell.

"One other question; do you believe this is tied with the other murders?" asked Racer.

"In my professional opinion, yes," said Campbell. "The marks left by the murder weapon appear to match all the victims."

"Thanks, I'll be waiting for your report," said Racer as he hung up.

Racer filled Cindy in on what the medical examiner had just told him. What bothered him the most was that Cheryl lay there alive until she bled to death. Cindy could hear the emotion in his voice.

"Damn, we have to catch this maniac before he kills again," said Cindy.

On cue, Lieutenant Detman entered the squad room and headed right for Racer's desk. He informed Racer and Cindy that Channel Seven was going to run a special on Sunday about the four homicides. They called Peterson to ask if he wanted to send a police representative to answer any questions they might have. He decided to send Detective Darling.

"Why me?" asked Cindy.

"Because he felt you were a little more pleasing to the eye then either Racer or myself. Also, he needs someone who can intelligently answer some questions or avoid them if necessary without getting into a heated discussion," said Detman, looking at Racer.

"I don't know if I'm up to this. I've never been on television before," said Cindy.

"Don't worry, I'll be there to give you moral support," said Racer laughingly.

"No way! The captain made it perfectly clear that you are not to be within 10 miles of that studio on Sunday," said Detman. "Look, go over everything that you can think of with Cindy. Maybe we won't look so bad if we're prepared, but stay away from the studio," replied Detman.

Racer looked at Cindy and told her he would do everything that he could to prepare her for this witch-hunt. Detman started to head to his office when he stopped and turned to face Racer. "Do we have anything that we can give to the press that would help us?" asked Detman.

"I was really trying to keep all the evidence that we have out of the press, but I guess I'll give them a little tidbit. Maybe that will satisfy them for a while," said Racer.

Racer and Cindy watched Detman leave. "I really don't want to do this," said Cindy.

"Look, when I get done with you, you'll see: This little recital will be a piece of cake," said Racer. "As a matter of fact, it might work out to our advantage. We might be able to give them something that will allow the killer to think we might be on to him and that might keep him from striking again. It just might work. How about if we meet in front of the library on Grant at one o'clock?"

"That'll be fine," replied Cindy. "See you then."

Racer awoke at ten the next morning. Pulling himself out of bed, he stretched and shuffled off to the kitchen. Although he got in early the night before, he still felt like crap. He turned on the coffee maker and opened last nights' paper. Since this last killing, the papers were having a field day. They kept reminding the citizenry how lame the police department was. As if the press could do any better. Maybe he should get to know that reporter from the *Fairfield Press*. He tried to think of her name. Marge Smyth, that was it. He could leak small bits of information to her, information that could put the killer on the defensive and might cause him to make mistakes.

An article concerning the death of Cheryl Portsmouth, comments from her husband and the usual response from the police. He got up and poured himself a cup of coffee. Somehow this guy was getting into these women's apartments without any trouble, he thought. There was no forced entry, and it looked more and more like the killer was the one having sex with the victims. The odd thing about that was they seemed to be consenting to it. There was no evidence of a struggle until Cheryl's murder. If the sex was consensual, why murder them? But what changed with Cheryl? She was murdered the same why but with no sex. Could it be blackmail of some kind? There were no ties between the women other than their taste in clothes. But what did these dresses and night things from the Designer Dress Shop have to do with it, or was it just a coincidence? They didn't know each other, yet the killer apparently knew them all.

Before moving back to the table, Racer grabbed a pad of paper and a pen from a drawer alongside the sink. Sipping his coffee, he sat down at the kitchen table and started to make a list of items he was going to cover with Cindy. Since this was going to be her television debut, preparing her would be critical. He was glad it wasn't him going in front of the cameras. His relationship with the press wasn't always good. So it was important for Cindy to be strong but understanding of the situation. She had to make contact with the audience. Racer did know that the department needed some good press. They had been taking a beating lately. If only he would have been on this case from the beginning. *If,* was a big word. He felt confident that he would catch the killer, but he didn't know how many more women would be murdered before he did. Then the phone rang, breaking his chain of thought.

Racer went to the phone hanging on the wall and answered it.

"Detective Racer, this is Marge Smyth. Do you remember me?"

"Yes, I remember who you are," replied Racer.

"I understand that your partner, Detective Darling, will be on a talk show tomorrow, discussing the homicides that have recently struck our city," said Marge Smyth.

"That's correct," said Racer. "Now, what can I do for you?"

"I thought that you might consider giving me a scoop on this story," said Miss Smyth.

"There is no story to give you," replied Racer. "My partner is going to be interviewed to give the police department's comments on whatever issues are raised. That's it, no story."

"So you still have no comments on these murders?" asked Miss Smyth.

"That's right," replied Racer, holding his ground.

"Well, if you change your mind you know where you can get in touch with me," said Miss Smyth, as she hung up.

CHAPTER NINE

Cindy was early. The day had been cloudy but now the sun was starting to break through. The park across the street was starting to fill with people. People didn't want to waste their day indoors, especially when it was nice outside. She was the same way. Cindy always made sure she took advantage of the nice days, playing tennis, going to the lake with friends or just lying around outside, getting a nice tan. She wondered what Racer did on his days off. Feeling a hand on her shoulder, Cindy turned to see Racer standing beside her.

"You're early," he said.

"I was up early thinking about what we need to go over and what to expect from the television reporters tomorrow."

"Right, but first things first. There's a little sub shop on the other side of the park. I thought maybe we could get a sandwich and sit in the park and eat," said Racer.

"Sounds like a great idea to me," replied Cindy.

While they were strolling through the park, Racer pulled a folded piece of paper from his back pocket and handed it to Cindy, who unfolded it.

"While having my coffee this morning, I jotted down several questions that I'm sure you'll be asked. I also wrote some replies that you might consider," said Racer.

"I wish it was you instead of me. You have a lot more experience dealing with the press then I do," replied Cindy.

"Hey, you'll be fine. Just don't let them put words in your mouth. Make sure that you get your point across and don't let them cut you off. Keep your composure and don't get nervous," said Racer.

"That's easy for you to say," said Cindy.

They got through the park, crossed the street and entered the sub shop, where they placed their orders. After they received their sandwiches and drinks, they returned to the park. Finding a park bench under a nice full maple tree, they sat down in the shade. By then the sun was out in full force.

As they ate, Cindy wanted to know if Racer would be there tomorrow. He assured her that nothing would keep him away. They were partners and he would be there to support her. Not even Peterson's warning would keep him away.

Finishing their lunch, Racer collected the wrappers and threw them into the round garbage can. Standing there, he told Cindy they would meet in front of the television studio about an hour before the show. She nodded her head in acknowledgment.

"I have to get going," said Cindy, looking at her watch. "I have some shopping to do, and then I'm going to have dinner with my mother and father. They're retired and travel a lot, so I don't get a chance to see them very often."

"There's one more thing," said Racer.

"What?" asked Cindy.

"Try to wear something conservative to the studio tomorrow," said Racer. "A nice dress or suit."

"Don't worry, I'll make sure everything is covered," replied Cindy.

They said their good-byes and Racer watched as Cindy headed back toward the library and her car. He was starting to soften where Cindy was concerned and that wasn't good.

Racer knew exactly where he was going. After looking up the address for the Designer Dress Shop in the yellow pages, he headed for the Manchester Mall. He wanted to see what this place looked like without Cindy tagging along.

Racer pulled into the mall parking lot and started circling the shops. The place was like a madhouse. Several times cars cut him off, trying to beat him to a parking space. When he located the shop, he found a space and pulled in. Sitting there, Racer glanced over at the shop and saw the outline of a curvy woman with a bra, panties and garter belt on. Racer got out of the car and crossed over to the sidewalk. He stopped by the window and looked at the assortment of dresses, nighties, bras, and panties and some things that he couldn't identify. Peering into the shop, he noticed only a handful of people.

Entering the shop, Racer heard a low-sounding bell rang. It was bad enough that he was the only man in a woman's shop, but they had to announce it to everyone. That's when he noticed a guy behind the checkout counter with dark black hair. As he tried to get a better look, a salesclerk stepped in front of him. Looking past her, Racer saw that the guy was gone.

"Can I help you find something?" asked the clerk cheerfully.

"I'm looking for something for my wife. It's our anniversary tomorrow," said Racer.

"What does your wife look like?" asked the salesclerk.

"Oh, she's about five-foot-six with long brown hair, slim and probably a thirty-six. She has a nice tan and likes to show her figure off," said Racer.

Racer thought to himself that he was describing Cindy, but that was the only woman he really knew. The salesclerk led him to the middle of the shop. He tried to see her nametag but it was covered with a flower.

"The dresses are on racks along that wall, and the lingerie is on the counter right over there," said the clerk. "I'll let you browse for a few minutes and I'll check back with you in a couple of minutes."

"Take your time," said Racer. "I'm in no hurry."

The woman nodded and headed toward another customer. All the women in the shop were between 25 and 35. All were nice-looking with good figures. And all of them could fit the description of the murder victims.

Racer was making it look as though he really was trying to find something nice. He felt as if everyone in the shop were watching him. Five minutes later, the salesclerk returned. "Having any luck?" she asked.

"You have such a large selection it's hard for me to make up my mind," replied Racer.

"Take your time but I must remind you, we will be closing in half an hour," said the salesclerk.

Racer nodded and turned back to the lingerie. He slowly moved down the lingerie counter as he tried to look around. He couldn't believe that women paid so much to wear so little. He noticed only two salesclerks in the shop. The sales clerk returned one more time to see how he was doing.

"Any luck yet?" she asked.

"Yes," said Racer without thinking.

He handed her the garment that he had in his left hand. She took it from him before he realized what it was. It was a white teddy with a lot of lace across the breasts. To say the least, it was sheer. It also came with a garter belt and a pair of white mesh stockings. He followed the salesclerk to the checkout, wondering what in the world he was going to do with it.

Waiting for his sales transaction to go through, Racer looked around the shop and spotted a tall brunette watching him real close. When he met her eyes, she gave him a big smile.

"That will be 35 dollars and 97 cents," said the salesclerk.

Racer paid for it with his charge card and then headed out to his car. He popped the trunk, threw the bag in and stood there staring at it. Shaking his head, he slammed the trunk shut. He would return that thing in a couple of days and get his money back.

Racer was pacing across the street from Channel Seven's television studios. He kept looking at his watch. It seemed as if he had been waiting there for hours but it had only been 20 minutes. He knew he was early, but where was Cindy? He told her that he would meet her in front of the studio an hour before the show. Turning back toward the parking lot, he saw Cindy's car pull in. Racer met her car before she could get out.

"You're late," he said firmly.

"I'm right on time," said Cindy pointing at her watch.

She slid out of the car and they walked together to the studio entrance. Racer paused by the door and gave Cindy the once over. She was wearing a pretty pale blue dress with white flowers on it. The dress would be perfect.

Racer opened the door and held it for her. When they got inside they walked right over to the receptionist's desk and Cindy identified herself. The receptionist gave Racer a strange look. "We were only expecting a Detective Cindy Darling," she said.

"I'm her agent," replied Racer, leaning on her desk.

"Well, they're waiting for you in makeup," said the receptionist.

"You mean I spent two hours in front of a mirror this morning and now they're going to redo me?" said Cindy.

"Please follow me," said the receptionist, dryly.

Racer watched as the two of them disappeared behind two large glass doors. A minute later, the girl returned and asked Racer to follow her. She led Racer into the studio where the show would take place. He was seated in a section for VIPs. It was a small studio and the audience was starting to trickle in. The stage crew was busy getting the furniture on the set in the right places and then setting the camera angles. Sitting there, Racer tried to think of the interviewer's name. It was a woman that hosted the show but he couldn't remember her name. Just then, he saw the door open and to his surprise it was Detman.

"What are you doing here?" asked Detman as he spotted Racer.

"I'm here to give my partner moral support," said Racer.

"You know Peterson ordered you to stay away," said Detman.

"Peterson set this whole thing up, didn't he? Well, that's enough to make me suspicious," said Racer.

"Come on, Racer, Peterson is on the level about this," said Detman. "He thinks this will be good publicity for the department."

"Then why are you here?" asked Racer.

"Peterson wanted me here to make sure that you weren't," said Detman, smiling.

About 10 minutes before the hour, the host entered the studio with Cindy and a tall, good-looking guy, right behind her. The host took her place behind her desk and Cindy sat down to her left.

The guy took his place on the right.

"Who's this guy?" asked Racer.

"He's a reporter with the *Fairfield Press*. He'll have an opportunity to ask Cindy some questions," said Detman.

"So that's Peterson's angle," said Racer. "That's probably the guy that has been bugging Peterson for information about the murders. This is a way to get the reporter off his back. Offer Cindy up as a sacrifice."

Detman didn't say a word, but Racer sensed that Detman agreed with him. The stage manager gave the countdown and then pointed to the host of the show.

"Good afternoon, ladies and gentlemen," said the host, looking directly into the camera. "I would like to welcome you to Questions and Answers. This is the show that gives you the opportunity to ask our city officials about major issues that are happening in our town.

"Today, I would like to welcome Ms. Cindy Darling, a homicide detective with the Fairfield Police Department, and on my right Mr. Bryan Alexander, a reporter with the Fairfield Press. The issue that we are going to look into this afternoon is, how safe is our city? Everyone knows there have been four brutal murders of young woman committed over the last three months and the killer is still at large. The police department has been silent about these crimes. I'm sure that everyone here is anxious to hear from Detective Darling as to what type of action the police department is taking. But first, I would like to give the floor to Mr. Alexander."

Bryan Alexander was a short man, about 32, dressed in a blue pin-stripe suit. He told the audience, both in the studio and at home, how brutal these crimes were. As if the audience didn't know already. He then went on to explain how he had tried to contact the police to find out what was being done about them, but he was constantly being put off. He mentioned that the people had a right to know, and that this was a disgrace. The host turned to Cindy and asked if she would like to make a statement before they entered the question and answer segment of the show.

"Yes, I would," said Cindy.

Racer sat back in his seat and held his breath.

"Good afternoon," said Cindy staring into the camera. "My name is Cindy Darling and I'm a detective with the Fairfield Police Department. Every police officer that has worked on these homicides has worked extremely hard. The police department is not at fault here. If the public wants to blame someone, then let them blame the killer for carrying out these brutal and heinous crimes against our citizens. That is the person we should be taking out our anger on, not the police department. They are doing everything humanly possible to catch this maniac, and they will. Thank you."

The studio went dead silent. A smile crossed both Racer's and Detman's faces.

"Mr. Alexander, would you like to ask the first question?" asked the host.

"Why yes, thank you," said Alexander, turning to Cindy. "Miss Darling, why hasn't the police been more cooperative toward the press concerning this case?"

"Mr. Alexander, there are some things that the police cannot release to the press, like things that are essential to the success of finding the killer and convicting that person. If we divulged this information, we would jeopardize the case and the killer would go free. I'm sure that there is no one person out there that wants that."

"Does that mean that you have evidence that could lead to an arrest soon?" asked Mr. Alexander.

"No, not exactly," replied Cindy. "It means that when we catch the killer, we can match the evidence to that person and prove guilt in a court of law."

"Could you at least tell us if the killer is a man or a woman?" asked Mr. Alexander.

"Mr. Alexander, the police department has given out details of the four homicides, so you can make your own conclusions," answered Cindy, with a smile on her face.

The verbal sparring went on for another 20 minutes, with the only break being a one-minute commercial. Racer thought that Cindy did an excellent job. He didn't think that he could have done any better. At the end of the show, Cindy asked both Alexander and the host why they didn't back their local police department instead of hounding them for information that would only further their careers. With that question, the audience burst into applause. She had won them over. But Racer and Detman both knew that the goodwill wouldn't last if another murder occurred. As Cindy left the stage, Racer could see that she was totally drained.

"You were great," said Racer.

"And I second that," said Detman.

"Thanks, now I feel like a beer," said Cindy.

"Barney's," they all said at the same time and laughed.

As they were leaving the studio, Mr. Alexander stopped Racer by the front door and commended him on the excellent job he did coaching Cindy. Racer stressed the point that Cindy blew him away all on her own. Alexander pointed out that he couldn't believe a bubblehead from Vice could be that sharp. That was a big mistake. Racer grabbed Alexander by his fancy lapels and pinned him against the wall. Staring into Alexander eyes, Racer told him that he better never hear anything like that again, about his partner. "If I do, I'll rip the lapels off your jacket and shove them down your throat.

Alexander was visibly shaken. "Remove your hands from my suit or I'll have your badge for this," he said.

"You can have it anytime you think you're man enough to take it," said Racer, letting go of Alexander's suit.

"I won't forget this," said Alexander as he glared at Racer.

"That's funny, neither will I," replied Racer with a smirk.

Cindy grabbed Racer's arm and led him out to the parking lot saying, "Making some more friends with the press, I see."

CHAPTER TEN

Driving home from Barney's, Racer was wondering how Cindy felt. She kept up with them last night, drink for drink. He hoped her hangover wouldn't be too bad. One thing he couldn't take was someone tossing their cookies all day. But Cindy could be a different story. He'd find out before too long. Now, all he wanted to do was get home.

A short while later, in the shower, Racer thought about what they needed to do that day. First, they would have to sit down and sort through all the information they'd gathered so far. This would tell them what their first step would be. He also wanted to give Marge Smyth a call and set up a meeting for that afternoon. He hoped that it wasn't too early to leak information to the press, especially after Cindy's interview.

After getting dressed, Racer headed to the kitchen for a cup of coffee. The shower had felt great. He was wide awake now. He decided to give Cindy and Detman a call and see if they wanted to meet him for breakfast. After making a date to meet them at the Cup and Saucer, Racer finished his coffee.

When Racer walked into the restaurant, Detman was already sitting at one of the booths with a large picture window. He had a steaming cup of coffee in front of him. Seeing Racer, he waved in his direction. Racer stopped one of the waitresses, ordered a cup of coffee and pointed in Detman's direction.

"Well, how do you feel this morning?" asked Detman.

"Great," replied Racer.

The waitress came to their table with the coffee for Racer and a refill for Detman. She asked if they were ready to order.

"Sure am, I'm starved," replied Detman.

"Could you give us just a few more minutes?" asked Racer. "Someone else will be joining us."

The waitress nodded and headed to a different table.

As they were waiting, Detman asked, "What happened between you and that guy Alexander?"

"I have no idea what you're talking about," said Racer.

"Well, when I got home last night, the wife said I had a strange message on the answering machine. It was from Bryan Alexander and he said to keep you away from him or he'll file charges against the department for harassment. Then he hung up," said Detman.

"Oh, it was just a little misunderstanding, that's all," said Racer.

"Yeah, I know about your misunderstandings," said Detman. "That's how I got my ulcers."

Racer was ready to say something when he noticed a large smile spread across Detman's face and his gaze went past Racer.

"Well, good morning, Detective Darling. "How are you doing this fine morning?" asked Detman.

"Tired," replied Cindy, "just plain tired. I probably could have stayed in bed for another couple of hours. But someone had to wake me up with this strange proposition about buying me breakfast."

"Whoa, wait a minute," said Detman. "You never promised to buy me breakfast."

"Okay, okay, I'll buy both of you breakfast," said Racer, putting his hands up in front of him.

Cindy slid in next to Detman. The waitress was back to take their orders, and Racer waited until the waitress was gone before he started the conversation back up.

"I wanted to get the two of you to breakfast this morning to discuss this case. I thought it would be better to do it away from the station and prying eyes. I don't want anything to get out yet, but here is what I think has been happening," he said.

Racer went on to explain his theory as Cindy and Detman listened carefully. He felt that somehow these women were being coerced into posing for these pictures. The pictures were probably being used for illicit purposes in magazines, videos or even on the Internet. When the women served their purpose, or when they threatened to go to the police, they were killed. When Racer was finished, he waited for comments. But before anyone could speak, their breakfast was placed in front of them. The waitress refilled their coffee cups and left.

"I think that is the best scenario we've had yet," said Detman. "I definitely think you should pursue it."

Racer nodded as everyone started eating their breakfast.

When they arrived at the station, Racer sent Cindy to the property room to gather up the dress and label they had found at Mary Wagner's place. He removed one of the pictures, which showed the man with the black hair, off the corkboard and slipped it into his pocket.

"Do these items have something to do with us going shopping?" asked Cindy.

"That's right," replied Racer.

When Racer got to his desk, there was a message for him. A Mrs. Caldwell had called and wanted to speak with him and only him. Racer tucked the message into his shirt pocket. Unlocking one of his desk drawers, he removed one of the pictures that were in safekeeping there. He slipped it into a small envelope and tucked it into his inside jacket pocket.

Five minutes later Cindy returned with a plastic bag. She told Racer that the dress was in the bag and the label was in her pocket. "If we leave now, we should be at the mall just about the time they are opening up," he said.

They arrived at the Manchester Mall a little after nine. Racer parked in the back row of the parking lot but directly in front of the Designer Dress Shop. He didn't want anyone to see that he and Cindy were together. He told Cindy to wait there while he got out of the car. She watched as he went to the trunk and removed a package. A second later, he was back behind the wheel. Beside him was a white plastic bag with the Designer Dress Shop logo printed on the front. He explained to Cindy that he wanted her to go in first and exchange the item. While she was in the shop, she was to look around and keep an eye out for a guy with dark black hair. When she was done, she would not go directly to the car. That would signal him to enter the shop and question the clerk.

She took the plastic bag from him and peered inside.

"Very nice. You have good taste," said Cindy.

"That's exactly what the salesclerk told me," replied Racer.

Cindy got out of the car and made her way across the parking lot. Racer watched her slip between the parked cars and finally made it to the sidewalk. Racer thought that Cindy was perfect for this shop. She fit the exact mold of their type of shopper. After Cindy disappeared into the dress shop, Racer looked at his watch.

After five minutes had passed, Racer slipped out from behind the steering wheel and made his way to the shop. He carefully moved to the display window, looked inside and saw Cindy over by the lingerie counter. She was talking with one of the salesclerks, a young brunette around 30, definitely not the same girl he had talked to the day before. Scanning the store as well as he could, Racer realized that she was the only salesclerk on duty. Racer watched as Cindy handed the bag to the clerk. She removed the contents and said something to Cindy. Cindy picked up another garment from the counter, headed for the far wall and disappeared into one of the dressing rooms. A few minutes later, Cindy reappeared and headed back to the counter, where the sales clerk joined her. They conversed for a couple of minutes and then the sales clerk placed the garment in the plastic bag and handed it to Cindy. Racer watched as Cindy walked to the front door. When Cindy got outside, she turned in the opposite direction, away from Racer. Now it was his turn.

Racer entered the shop and didn't make it half way across the store before he was intercepted by the same salesclerk who had just helped Cindy. "Can I help you, sir?" she asked.

Racer reached into his jacket pocket and removed his badge and identification. Showing it to the clerk, the woman immediately seemed nervous. "What can I do for you, detective?" she asked.

"Can we move over to the counter?" said Racer, taking the woman by the arm.

When they got to the counter Racer removed the dress from the brown bag and handed it to the woman. "Do you recognize this?" he asked.

The salesclerk took the dress from him and looked it over

carefully. Racer watched as she checked the dress for a label. After a few minutes she placed the dress down on the counter. "It looks like a dress from a shipment we received a couple of months ago. I'm sure we sold all those dresses," she said.

That's when Racer reached into his pocket, removed the label and showed it to the salesclerk.

"Is this the standard label that you sew into all your clothes?" asked Racer.

"Yes, the ones that we sell under our own name," replied the clerk.

"Do you keep sales records for purchases made from your store?" asked Racer.

"Yes we do," replied the salesclerk. "This is to protect ourselves. Some people want to return garments that they didn't purchase here. These records help us."

Racer asked to see the receipts but the clerk informed him that she had specific instructions not to give out any information without the manager or store owner's permission. Racer wanted to know how to get in touch with either only to find out the store's owner was out of town and the manager was off on Mondays. He wanted to know who was in charge then. The clerk informed him she was until noon. "Then Miss Thompson comes in. She is the assistant store manager."

Racer wanted to know if any men worked there. He was informed by the salesclerk that they had a stockman who helped to unload merchandise from the trucks and also filled in as a cashier when they got real busy. Racer wanted to know if he was there. The salesclerk told him that the stockman didn't come in until later. The salesclerk was getting nervous answering all these questions and asked Racer if he could come back when Miss Thompson came in. She was afraid of getting into trouble for saying something she shouldn't.

"I understand," said Racer. "Oh, by the way, could you tell me the name of the owner?"

"I guess I can tell you that," said the sales clerk. "Her name is Madeline Stein. She owns this store and a couple more both here and in Springdale."

"Thanks for your help. I'll be back later," said Racer.

He gathered up the label and dress, tucked them into the bag and headed for the door. While walking toward the car, he saw that Cindy had made it back.

"Well, what did you find out?" asked Cindy.

"I found out that the dress is definitely from their shop, but other than that, nothing. The salesclerk is by herself. No dark haired guy. We'll have to wait until this afternoon before we can talk to the assistant manager. I want to look at their records," said Racer.

He turned the key and the engine came to life. Racer pulled the ZX out of the lot and turned left onto Cleveland Avenue. He told Cindy that Mrs. Caldwell left a message at the station that she wanted to talk with him. So that's where they were headed.

Racer parked the car, and he and Cindy got out and started up the sidewalk. Before they reached the house, Mrs. Caldwell was already standing on the front porch, waiting for them.

"Good morning, Charles," she said.

"Good morning, ma'am," said Racer, a little embarrassed.

Mrs. Caldwell invited them into her house and led them right into her kitchen. Racer could smell the coffee. Mrs. Caldwell offered them a seat and placed coffee cups in front of them.

"I got your message, Mrs. Caldwell," asked Racer, positioning the cup just so.

"Well, Charles, after you left the other day, I started thinking if there was anything else that I needed to tell you about the night poor Mrs. Portsmouth was killed. I kept running this thing over and over in my mind. And then something dawned on me," said Mrs. Caldwell. "When I started down the alley with my dog that night, I remember walking past a dark car sitting at the end of the alley. There wasn't anybody in it, though."

"Is it unusual for a car to be parked there?" asked Racer, lifting the cup to his mouth.

"Definitely. Parking in the alley is prohibited. There are signs posted on both ends."

"Do you know what kind of car it was?" asked Cindy, blowing into her cup.

Mrs. Caldwell's gaze never turned away from Racer. "I'm not

good about cars, but I did start to watch the television commercials a lot closer to see if I could recognize it. I believe it was a Buick."

"Do you know what color the car was?" asked Cindy.

Mrs Caldwell ignored Cindy as she gave her answer. Racer was starting to get a kick out of this. Cindy asked the question; Racer got the answer. She never looked at Cindy.

"It was either a black or a dark blue car," said Mrs. Caldwell.

"You didn't happen to notice the license plate number, did you?" asked Racer.

"No, I'm sorry, Charles," said Mrs. Caldwell.

She offered them another cup of coffee, before she continued. Mrs. Caldwell told Racer that after she called the police, she noticed that the car was gone. Racer wanted to know if she had ever seen this car in the neighborhood before but she couldn't remember. Thanking her for the coffee, Racer mentioned what a help she has been and to call him if anything else comes to mind.

"I sure will, Charles," said Mrs. Caldwell.

Mrs. Caldwell stood on the porch and watched them as they drove away. When Racer looked in his rear view mirror, she was still waving.

"That sounds like the same car that the guard described, entering the apartment building before Barbara Molino was killed," said Cindy, with a wry smile.

"It sure seems like it," said Racer.

"It's a shame that Mrs. Caldwell didn't take her dog for a walk sooner. Maybe she could have scared him off and Cheryl Portsmouth would still be alive," said Cindy.

"I don't think that was the problem. I think that she stood there too long watching what was happening instead of calling the police right away," said Racer, looking at his watch. "Ready for lunch yet?"

"Don't tell me, Barney's again," said Cindy.

"No, we're going to the Watering Hole today," replied Racer. "I have a lunch date with Marge Smyth from the Press and I got conned into buying."

"Why are we meeting a newspaper reporter?" asked Cindy, with concern in her voice.

"Well, I was thinking that maybe we can use her to our advantage," said Racer. "Especially after the television interview, it might be the right time."

Racer had been to The Watering Hole just once before. It was a hole in the wall, in a line of old stores on Jefferson Boulevard. At one time, it was one of the busiest places in the city until they started building malls all over the place. Now, the only people that frequented this area were lower-income folks and reporters. One thing that Racer could say about the place was, it had great sandwiches. Racer parked across the street from the bar. As he and Cindy got out of the car, Racer noticed that the street was almost deserted, with just a sprinkling of people and almost no traffic. Racer held the door open as they entered the bar. Much to his surprise, the place was nearly packed. There wasn't any room at the bar and most of the tables were taken. He finally spied an empty table by the pool table. Not a good location for holding a conversation, but it would have to do.

Cindy headed for the table and Racer to the bar. He returned with a Diet Coke for her and a draft for himself. After sitting down, he told Cindy what the game plan was for this afternoon when they returned to the dress shop, keeping a close eye on the door while they talked. He explained that he would go in first to talk with the assistant manager. He'd wanted to get a look at those receipts. "After that, we'll hang around until the salesclerk from this morning leaves and then you can return whatever you have in that plastic bag." Cindy sounded disappointed when Racer told her this. All of a sudden, he was out of his seat, headed for the door. Soon he returned to the table with a petite woman in tow. When they got to the table, Racer introduced Marge Smyth to Cindy.

"Does anyone want to order, or shall we just have drinks first?" asked Racer.

"I'll have a Tom Collins for now," said Marge.

Racer headed back to the bar and soon came back with her drink.

"Now, what are we all here for? I would think that, after Miss

Darling's performance on television yesterday, you sure wouldn't need the newspaper to help you out," said Marge, sipping at her drink.

"That show was a con job. I want to handle this case my way. So I decided to make you an offer," replied Racer.

"I'm listening," said Marge.

Racer then told Marge that he would feed her information that might or might not pertain to the case, and all he wanted her to do was print it. Marge wanted to know what exactly Racer meant by *might or might not pertain to the case*. Racer explained that he might want her to print an article or two that might help him flush out the killer, but it might not be exactly the truth. Marge laughed out loud. She wanted to know if Racer thought she was a total idiot. Racer took a sip of beer and then set the glass on the table. He explained that if she agreed to do this, he would give her the exclusive story and credit for helping the police crack the case, but only if she helped him. Then he dropped the hammer. "If you don't, I'll make sure you are the last person to know." He did this without batting an eye.

"I'll have to think about this. You're going to be putting me in a difficult position."

"I'll tell you what, you think about it and call me tomorrow," said Racer. "If I don't hear from you by four o'clock, I'll take it as a no and look elsewhere for help."

"Agreed," said Marge. "Now how about lunch? I'm starved."

Racer took their orders back up to the bar and placed them with the bartender. After they finished eating, Racer reconfirmed his deal and Marge nodded in agreement. After she left, Cindy looked at Racer, puzzled. "Are you nuts? You of all people asking the press for their help," she said.

"That's right," replied Racer. "We can use her to feed the killer the information that we want him to have. Plus, I don't see anything wrong with us trying to improve our image with the media. Peterson will love us for that."

"I hope you know what you're doing," said Cindy, shaking her head.

CHAPTER ELEVEN

Thirty minutes later Racer and Cindy were sitting in the parking lot outside of the Designer Dress Shop. After going over their plan one more time, Racer walked toward the shop. He swore that he saw a black Buick pulling away from in front of the shop, but he couldn't be sure. When he got to the sidewalk, he walked right into the shop.

"Can I help you?" asked a voice from behind him.

Racer turned and said that he was looking for a Miss Thompson.

"I'm Susan Thompson," said the woman.

He showed Miss Thompson his badge and identification but she never looked at it. As a matter of fact, her eyes never left his. He explained that he was in there this morning and spoke with one of her salesclerks and she pointed him in her direction.

"I was expecting you," said Miss Thompson.

"Can we go somewhere private?" asked Racer.

"Sure, we can go into my office in the back," she said.

With that, she turned to a salesclerk, who was doing some pricing, and told her to keep an eye on the floor. She then turned back to Racer and told him to follow her. Susan Thompson was in her late thirties or early forties. It was hard to tell with all the make-up until you looked closely at her face. She was definitely wearing one of the dresses that the shop sold, pale pink with buttons down the front. It hugged her body tightly.

Racer followed her into the office. It was barely large enough to hold two people. It was jammed with a desk, chair, and three filing cabinets. Susan Thompson grabbed a folding chair that was leaning against the wall and opened it for him.

"Thanks," said Racer, taking a seat.

"Now, what can I do for you?" asked Susan Thompson.

Racer removed the dress and label from the bag he had been carrying. He placed it on her Desk, explaining that the salesclerk had identified it as one the shop carried. He asked Miss Thompson if this was correct. Miss Thompson stared at it for several seconds and then agreed it was from her shop. This gave Racer the opening to ask for copies of the store receipts for the last three or four months. Though Miss Thompson acknowledged that the shop kept the receipts for a period of six months, she stressed that the confidentiality of those receipts had to be maintain do to the class of their clientele.

"Well, Susan, I'm investigating a homicide and I really need your cooperation," said Racer. "Of course, I could get a search warrant, but I'm sure you wouldn't want that."

Miss Thompson informed Racer that she would have to make a phone call. Racer nodded. Picking up the phone, Miss Thompson dialed a number that Racer couldn't see.

After talking for several minutes, Miss Thompson said, "Yes ma'am, thank you. I'm sorry to have bothered you. Goodbye."

Susan Thompson told Racer that he would have to get a warrant if he wanted to see the receipts. Mrs. Stein had told her that their customers put their trust in them and that she must uphold that trust the best she could. She was sorry, but no receipts without a warrant. That would show her customers that she didn't just hand them over.

"Thanks, anyway," said Racer. "I'm sure that you will be seeing me again real soon, and next time I won't be so polite."

As Racer was leaving the office, he spotted a guy working in the warehouse, moving boxes around. He didn't get a chance to see his face but he did notice his dark black hair. Walking back through the shop, Racer noticed that the salesclerk who was there that morning was gone. It was a good time for Cindy to return the item.

Racer left the shop and meandered through the parking lot while Cindy came from two stores down. Racer watched Cindy enter the shop. Once she was inside, he returned to the car, waited for almost half an hour and finally saw her leave the shop. Cindy walked along the line of shops, looking in the windows. Racer started the car up and circled the parking lot. When Cindy got to the last shop, Racer was waiting for her. He pulled out of the mall parking lot and into the lot for a fast food restaurant across the street. "Okay, what happened?"

Cindy went on to tell Racer how strange it was. One of the salesclerks came up to her and asked if she could help, but a Miss Thompson interceded. "I explained to her that I wanted to exchange a gift that my boyfriend bought for me. We moved to the counter, where she removed the nightie from the bag and looked it over. She made some small talk, asking me what college he went to and how long he was going to be gone.

"Did you give her all that information?" asked Racer.

"I told her that he was going to UCLA and that he wouldn't be home until Thanksgiving. She asked me if I wanted to exchange it since it was a present, or if I wanted my money back. I told her I wanted to exchange it. She told me that was no problem. She led me over to the lingerie counter and told me to take my time, then she excused herself. I watched her slip through a doorway in the shop. As I was looking over the garments on the counter, I noticed her standing there talking with a young guy. He was about six foot even with a muscular build. Appeared to be somewhere between 20 and 25 years old and with the darkest black hair," said Cindy.

"Sounds like the same guy I noticed," said Racer.

"Well, I pretended that I was picking out something when this Miss Thompson returned and asked if I had found anything. I told her that I had two teddies picked out and she suggested that I try them on. She showed me to one of the dressing rooms and waited outside. I had this funny feeling that someone was watching me. You know how you get that feeling," said Cindy.

"Yeah, I know what you mean," said Racer.

"After I was done, we walked over to the cash register and I made the exchange. She wanted me to fill out some type of form that asked for my name, address and phone number. She explained that it was so they could mail me their store fliers. I told her that I really didn't have the time. When I opened the door to leave, I saw that same guy standing in the doorway, watching me. He was trying his best to stay out of sight."

"Do you think it could be our guy in the pictures?" asked Racer.

"I'd say it's a good possibility," replied Cindy.

When Cindy and Racer returned to the station, it was a little after four. There was a message from Sidney that he had his report ready on the film container. Racer picked up the phone and dialed the lab. It must have rung 30 times before someone picked it up. Racer asked for Sidney and was told he just missed him. Racer thought for a second, then asked the lab tech if Sidney had left anything for him. When he was told that there was a sealed envelope on Sidney's desk with his name on it, he asked if someone could run it up to homicide. The lab tech said she'd have it there in five minutes.

Cindy looked over and asked if he wanted a cup of coffee. Racer yelled "Black!" as she headed for the break room.

Cindy returned at the same time that the lab tech showed up with the envelope. She put the coffee in front of Racer and plunked herself into one of the wooden chairs. Racer ripped the envelope open, removed a single sheet of paper and started reading the report.

"The container was used for thirty-five millimeter film, and there was a perfect print on the outside of the container. A right index finger. Sidney is trying to match it in COTIS, plus he sent a copy to the FBI."

"We'll have to keep our fingers crossed for a match," said Cindy.

Just then Detman appeared from his office. "Anything new on the case?" he asked.

"Something strange is going on at the dress shop. I'm going to need a warrant to get a look at their receipts. Also, Sidney found a print on that film canister," said Racer.

"I guess we'll have to wait and see if that print can be matched," said Detman. "We're about ready to catch a break. By the way, Cindy, I was up in Peterson's office this afternoon and he was in a good mood over the way you handled yourself in that interview yesterday," said Detman.

"Why thanks, lieutenant," said Cindy with a big smile.

"Well, while everything is quiet, I'm going to get the hell out of here," said Detman. "I'll see the two of you in the morning. And by the way, Peterson is going to be looking for an update by the end of the week. Remember, that was part of the deal."

"Yeah, I remember," replied Racer, staring down at the report that he just read.

Detman slipped into his office, grabbed his hat and made a bee-line for the stairs. After Detman disappeared down the stairs, Racer turned to Cindy. "The first thing tomorrow, I want you to check-out the owner of the Designer Dress Shop. See what type of background information we can dig up. While you do that, I'm going to call on one of my buddies at the Internal Revenue Service and see if I can find out exactly who is on their payroll," said Racer, leaning back in his chair. "How would you like a late dinner?"

"What's the catch?" asked Cindy.

"We'll have to eat it in the car. We're going to stake out the dress shop at closing and see who leaves and what they're driving. It might give us a lead to our killer."

Cindy reached down into a greasy paper bag and pulled out a large french fry. Racer was still chewing on his Quarter Pounder when the lights started to go out in the shop. They had been sitting there for about 30 minutes when the last customer left the shop at about eight fifty-five; someone followed them right to the door and locked it behind them. Racer didn't know for sure who was left in the shop, but he wanted to find out.

After about 10 more minutes, someone unlocked the door and a guy and girl left. Racer could see in the parking lot lights it was the same guy who was in the shop earlier. He didn't recognize the girl. The two walked together to the corner of the parking lot, where they got into their own cars. The girl got into an old, beat-up Mustang and the guy got into a red Camaro. Racer asked Cindy to see if she could get the license plate number for the Camaro. Then his attention was drawn back to the shop. The shop went entirely dark. A woman stepped out onto the sidewalk and locked the door. It was Susan Thompson. Racer's eyes followed her across the parking lot to a dark blue or black, late model Buick LeSabre the same type of car that Mrs. Caldwell had described. He watched as she unlocked the car door and got in. Then he motioned for Cindy to follow the Buick.

Cindy waited until the Buick was in motion before she started her car. When the Buick entered traffic on Melrose, she turned her headlights on and started to follow. They followed Susan Thompson through the city and out onto the highway. Just as they were leaving the city limits, she turned off the highway and onto Route Twenty-one. They followed her for about another mile before Cindy noticed her signal and watched as the Buick made a right turn into one of the expensive new subdivisions that were springing up around Fairfield.

Cindy turned her headlights off and followed the Buick through a maze of streets until they came to a two-story brick home. The Buick pulled into the driveway and stopped. Slipping up to the curb about a block away, Cindy killed the engine. They watched the Buick until the garage door opened and the car disappeared inside. Then the door closed, hiding the Buick. They continued to watch until the lights inside the house came on.

"Let's get the address and get out of here," said Racer.

Cindy started the car and drove by the mailbox slowly. Racer jotted down the address: 4790 Hunington Lane. They continued on until they found their way out of the subdivision. Racer waited until Cindy was back on the highway before he asked her if she got the plate number off the Camaro.

"Yep, it's BB8-63J," said Cindy.

"Good. Now you have something else to check on in the morning."

Cindy was quiet the rest of the way back to town. When she pulled into the station parking lot, she turned to Racer. "Do you think that Susan Thompson's Buick is the same car that was spotted at two of the murders?" asked Cindy.

"We can't jump to conclusions. There are a lot of dark-colored Buicks around the area. But it's possible," replied Racer.

"I wish that Mrs. Caldwell could have gotten a number off that car," said Cindy. "That would have been a big help." As Racer got out of her car, Cindy added, "If that is the car, then maybe our whole theory is wrong."

"What do you mean?" asked Racer, frowning.

"Well, if that is the Buick, then Miss Thompson could be the killer," said Cindy. "All along, we have been assuming the killer is a man, based on the assumption that the victims had intercourse with the killer before they died."

"Don't disregard the fact that she could be part of a killing team. She watches as this guy has sex with them and then slits their throats. A possibility but not probable," said Racer.

"Why not?" asked Cindy.

"Because Mrs. Caldwell told us that she saw Cheryl Portsmouth struggling with a fairly large man, not a woman. And secondly, Miss Thompson would have trouble controlling these women before she could kill them," stated Racer.

"That's true, but what if she was watching Cheryl struggle with this guy and waited until he left? While Mrs. Caldwell was calling the police, she could have slipped in and murdered Cheryl. That might account for why the car was gone when Mrs. Caldwell looked back outside. And remember, we found synthetic hairs from a wig at one of the crime scenes."

Racer slid back into the bucket seat of Cindy's car and thought for a moment.

"You know, you have a good point there. But you still haven't convinced me yet. I still believe the killer is a man," said Racer.

"Then I guess we're back to considering a killing team," said Cindy. "Susan Thompson and a male accomplice. Maybe the dark-haired guy at the store."

"Boy, your mind is really working overtime tonight. Let's go home and sleep on it. We can talk about it in the morning," replied Racer.

"That sounds like a good idea to me," answered Cindy.

CHAPTER TWELVE

Cindy beat Racer to the squad room the next morning. She had a hard time sleeping thinking about all the possibilities that they had. When Racer arrived, he reminded her of the phone calls they had to make as soon as everything opened up.

When the clock hit nine, Cindy was already calling the Department of Business Licenses to find out who owned the Designer Dress Shop. Looking over at Racer, she saw that he was also on the phone. She guessed that he was getting his list of employees for the Designer Dress Shop from his buddy. When someone picked up the phone on the other end, Cindy identified herself as a detective with the police department and told them what she wanted. She waited a few minutes and then started writing notes down on her note pad.

They hung their phones up at the same time. Cindy looked over at Racer and he looked up at her. They tried to talk at the same time. Cindy held up her hand and motioned for Racer to go first.

"I'll have the list of employee's names and addresses by the end of the day. How about you?" asked Racer.

"Madeline Stein lives up in the Mulberry Hills area."

"Good, check her out and see if there's anything on her. I'm going to run downstairs and see if Sidney got anything back on that print."

They both got up. Cindy walked off toward the computer room, and Racer headed for the lab. He found Sidney standing by one of the tables along the far side of the room. As he approached, Sidney said, "No luck."

"Great," said Racer a little dejected.

"One thing, though, it's a perfect print, so we won't have any trouble matching it to a suspect when we get one," said Sidney.

"Yeah, all we need is a suspect," replied Racer.

As Racer was talking with Sidney, Cindy stopped at the second floor and headed down the hallway until she came to a door that was lettered with a "No Admittance—Authorized Personnel Only" sign in big red letters. She paused for a second and looked around. No one was in the hall except her. She turned the knob and stepped out of the hallway. When she got inside, the room appeared to be empty except for the computers. Then she heard a woman's voice calling her name. Cindy looked around and saw a head of blond hair sticking over the top of a computer in the back of the room. Cindy walked toward the voice. There, sitting on a chair, was her old street pal from Vice, Penny Stewart. They had both started out in Vice together. Penny only lasted about a year when some crazy stabbed her with a switchblade. After she recovered, they reassigned her to IT and the computer room.

"What can I do for you?" asked Penny. "I know you're not here just to visit me."

"I need a favor. I have a name I would like you to run for me."

"Sure. I hear you're assigned to Homicide now," said Penny.

"Yeah, I'm temporarily assigned to these murder cases," said Cindy.

"Is that where this name is from?" asked Penny.

Cindy nodded. After a few seconds, Penny asked for the name, holding her hand out. Cindy handed her the name of Madeline Stein written on a piece of paper. She stood there and watched Penny punch the name into the computer. While waiting for the computer to bring up the information, Penny reminded Cindy that she could get reprimanded for this. Cindy told her how much she appreciated it. Then all of a sudden the information started coming up on the screen. Cindy asked for a printout. Penny pointed to a printer by the wall. Cindy moved over to it and waited for the machine to start. Penny hit the print button and reminded Cindy not to leave it lay around. A second later, the printer printed out a single sheet of paper. Cindy removed the page from the tray. She stood there reading the information.

"Good stuff?" asked Penny.

"Yeah, thanks a lot and don't worry, I'll keep this information under wraps. If you ever need a favor, don't be afraid to ask. I owe you one," said Cindy.

"You sure do. Remember, I want this dirt bag caught just as bad as you," replied Penny, seriously.

Cindy folded the sheet and placed it in the pocket of her slacks. She didn't want anyone to see her leaving the computer room with a printout in her hand. Opening the door, she waved goodbye to Penny and left. Turning to head back upstairs, Cindy ran square into Jim Harlin.

"My, what a pleasure it is bumping into you," said Harlin. "What are you doing in this neck of the woods?"

"Penny is an old friend. We started in Vice together. Thought I'd drop in and say hi while I had a minute," replied Cindy.

"How nice," said Harlin. "Oh, are you going to be at Barney's Thursday night? It's ladies night."

"I don't know, this case is eating up a lot of my time right now," answered Cindy.

"I'm sure," said Harlin. "By the way, how's the case going? Have any real substantial leads yet? I'm sure that your partner is breaking every rule trying to solve it."

"We're working on it," was all Cindy would say. She squeezed by.

Damn, I would have to run into him, she thought as she pushed the door open to the stairwell. When she got back to the squad room, Racer was on the phone again. She pulled a chair over to his desk and pulled the paper out of her pocket. After saying thanks, he hung up the phone. He turned his attention to Cindy and wanted to know what she had found out. Cindy handed him the printout on Madeline Stein.

"It says she's the owner of the Designer Dress Shop in Fairfield, which we already know, but she also owns a photography shop in Springdale. She's had a few traffic citations here in town but here is the thing that is interesting. She was arrested once in Denver for involvement in a pornography ring but the charges were dropped. Lack of evidence, it says."

"That's quite interesting, since we have been finding some very suggestive photos of our victims at each scene," said Racer.

"That's what I was thinking. Who were you talking to on the phone?" asked Cindy.

"That was the motor vehicle department. I wanted to make sure who owned the car that Susan Thompson was driving. And believe it or not, it belongs to none other than Susan Thompson."

"So, that makes her our prime suspect then," said Cindy.

"I don't know, but we're starting to get quite a few pieces to the puzzle. Now all we have to do is start fitting them together. I think we should go and have a talk with Madeline Stein. Or should I say me. I don't want them to know that you're a cop yet," said Racer. "You could be our ace in the hole."

"Then what do you want me to do?" asked Cindy.

"I want you to get a picture of Thompson's car and see if that guard at Molino's building can identify it."

"Okay, I'll give him a call and make sure he's home," replied Cindy.

"I'll met you at Barney's around noon," said Racer.

"Barney's again," said Cindy.

"I do my best work there," said Racer.

Cindy watched as Racer disappeared down the steps. What would Racer ever do if Barney's closed down, she wondered?

Heading out to his car, Racer took a look at the printout to see exactly where Madeline Stein lived. It was 10049 Honeysuckle Circle in Mulberry Hills. There probably wasn't a house in Mulberry Hills that didn't go for less than a cool million. The rich folk moved out there years ago, because of the favorable tax structure.

Racer got into his car and pulled out into traffic. As he was driving, Racer started going over the case in his head. The Designer Dress Shop was the connection to all four women, the thread that held them together. And that stock boy with the dark black hair.... He would bet a week's salary that it was the same person in those photos. But the one thing that he couldn't figure out was the Buick and Susan Thompson. He had to dig into that a little further.

Racer headed out of town on highway 21. It was a beautiful sunny day. The heat had finally broke, and even though the temperature was still in the upper eighties, the humidity was just about gone. He could drive like this for hours, the air conditioner off, the windows open and fresh air whistling through the car. *What a day for a picnic*, he thought. He didn't know why that popped into his head. He wasn't in the habit of going on picnics. As he was daydreaming, he almost missed the turnoff for Mulberry Hills.

Right in the middle of the four-lane road was a sign that welcomed visitors to Mulberry Hills. Right behind the sign was a guard shack. Even though the sign said *welcome*, you had to prove to the guard that you had business there or he would turn you away. Racer pulled the ZX up to the shack and stopped. A portly guy in a guard's uniform came out.

"Who are you here to see?" asked the guard, a clipboard in his hand.

Racer pulled his shield and identification from his jacket pocket and presented it to the guard. The guard looked at it closely, then asked him again whom he was there to see.

"I'm here to see a Madeline Stein," said Racer.

The guard gave Racer a sheet of paper with a layout of the Mulberry Hills subdivision. He pointed out the directions to the Stein residence on Honeysuckle Circle. It was the middle house on the circle. Thanking the guard, Racer put the car in gear and pulled away from the guard shack.

He drove down the street, looking from left to right as if he were watching a tennis match. There were houses with winding drives; some had high stone walls and some had automatic gates. There were no mailboxes. When he got to the stop sign, he made a right and noticed a fancy sign pointing the way to Mulberry Hills Country Club Members Only. He followed the curve until he came to the first right. He had no trouble finding which house Madeline Stein lived in. There were only three houses on the circle and Madeline Stein's was dead ahead. Just as the guard described.

The house put him in mind of the Deep South, with the wraparound porch and tall white pillars. It had a circular drive lined with small trees and sprawling bushes. The lawn was beautifully manicured. Pulling his car into the drive, Racer could see someone come out of the house and onto the porch. He pulled up in front of the house and before he could get out of his car, a large gentleman was standing by his car door.

"Sir, may I ask what you're doing here?"

"Sure, my name is Racer. I'm a detective with the Fairfield Police Department and I would like to speak with Madeline Stein."

"Do you have an appointment?" asked the Incredible Hulk.

"No, I didn't realize I needed one," said Racer

"Well, Miss Stein is a very busy woman and I doubt if she will be able to see you without an appointment," he said.

"I'm here on police business," said Racer as he pushed the car door open.

"Sorry, sir, this is private property," said the guy as he pushed the car door closed.

Racer knew that he was at a disadvantage while he was sitting in the car, so he had to equalize the situation.

"Look, pal," said Racer, "we can do this two ways. Either you tell Miss Stein that I'm here to see her or I'm going to get out of this car, get Miss Stein, and take her down to the station and talk with her there. It's your choice."

A smile crossed the hulk's face. Racer had a good idea what he was thinking.

"Well, it's your move, pal," said Racer.

"Sir, just call tomorrow and set up an appointment with Miss Stein. I really don't want any trouble here," said the hulk.

"Have it your way," said Racer.

Racer put the car in reverse and hit the gas pedal. The car lurched backward for about 20 feet before Racer slammed on the brakes. In a flash, he was out of the car and heading toward the hulk.

"Look, all you have to do is tell Miss Stein that I'm here to see her. So let's make it easy on both of us."

"And what if I don't?"

"Well, you are going to get hurt and I'm still going to talk to Miss Stein," said Racer.

"You're right about one thing; someone is going to get hurt."

When the hulk got right in front of Racer, the man grabbed his jacket in both hands. Racer looked him straight in the eyes and told him he was under arrest for interfering with a police investigation. The hulk laughed. That was his second mistake. Racer forced his arms up inside of the hulk's and broke his grip. He then grabbed one of the hulk's tree-like arms and tried to bend it behind him. As Racer reached for his handcuffs, the hulk broke Racer's grip. There was no doubt the hulk was stronger than Racer first thought. The hulk tried to throw a left at Racer's head, but Racer blocked it and countered with the heel of his right hand, catching the hulk right under the chin. Racer heard the man's teeth crunching together. As the hulk bent over holding his mouth, Racer caught him under the chin again with his right foot. Bone and blood came from the hulk's mouth. He straightened up and came running at Racer, swinging wildly. Racer side-stepped him and slammed a left into the hulk's kidney. The hulk went down on one knee. Racer spun around and caught the hulk on the side of his head with his right foot. That was all she wrote. The hulk went down for the count.

Racer rolled him over and cuffed his hands behind his back. They just about fit. He took a look at the hulk and decided that he would need some extensive dental work to repair his smile. He hoped that Madeline Stein provided a good dental plan. Then Racer headed for the porch. He took the steps one at a time and pushed the doorbell. He could hear the chimes ringing inside the house. In a minute, a woman answered the door.

"Yes, can I help you?" asked the woman, dressed in a maid's uniform.

"I would like to see Madeline Stein," said Racer as he showed the woman his badge.

The woman excused herself and said that she would be right back.

A minute or two later the door opened again and the woman said that Miss Stein would see him.

"Thanks," said Racer with a smile.

The woman led Racer down a long hallway that must have split the house in half. At the end of the hall was a big room with a pool table, jukebox, bar and big screen television. There was a double set of french doors that led out into the backyard. The woman opened the door for Racer and pointed the way. The backyard had an Olympic-size swimming pool, tennis courts, hot tub and a large putting green. Madeline Stein was lying on her back with the top of her bikini unhooked. The lounge chair was positioned so she would catch the full rays of the sun.

Moving around the pool, Racer could see another well-built guy sitting in the shade, reading a magazine. This goon looked even larger then the guy lying in the driveway. Miss Stein never looked up as Racer approached.

"Miss Stein," said Racer.

"Yes," she answered turning her head in his direction.

"I'm detective Racer with the Fairfield Police Department, and I'm investigating the recent string of homicides that have taken place in town. I would like to ask you a few questions, if I may."

"Of course, but what does this have to do with me?" asked Madeline Stein.

"You are the owner of the Designer Dress Shop?" asked Racer.

"Yes. You must be the same detective that was in the shop the other day asking to see my records," asked Madeline, looking over her sunglasses.

"You have me there. But you know, if you would have let me see those records, I probably wouldn't be here right now," replied Racer.

Racer sat down on the chair right next to her. He couldn't get a good look at her face but she had the body of a 20 year-old. Finally, she grabbed a towel and rolled over carefully. Racer could see that she was a very attractive woman. He guessed that she was more like 40, but she must have taken good care of herself. Miss Stein pulled herself up carefully and hooked the top of her bikini.

"Apparently you didn't have too much trouble with Frederick," said Miss Stein.

"Oh Frederick, nice guy. I had to show him some self-defense moves," said Racer.

"So do I dare ask where he is?" asked Miss Stein.

"He's lying in the driveway handcuffed. I sure hope that you provide your employees with a good dental plan because Frederick is going to need one," replied Racer.

"If you have hurt him, I'll have to speak to your superiors about it," said Miss Stein nonchalantly. "That's the trouble with you cops, you're all alike. You think all you have to do is bully people and you can go wherever you want."

"Look, all I want to do is my job. And right now my job is to ask you a few questions. If you would just allow me to do that, I'll be on my way."

"All right, detective, let's get this over with. Exactly what do you want to know?" asked Miss Stein.

"I would like the names of the people who work for you," said Racer.

"I suppose if I don't answer your question you'll beat it out of me," said Miss Stein.

"No, I'll just get a warrant and confiscate all your records," said Racer, but the thought of beating it out of her seemed appealing.

"I run a small business, so I only have seven employees working for me. I'll have to go in the house and get the list of names for you. Why are you so interested in my dress shop anyway?" asked Madeline Stein.

"It seems the women that have recently been murdered all frequented your shop. Besides that, they have quite a collection of your garments. So, it appears to be the thread that connects them together," said Racer.

"You would be surprised to see who shops in my store. And it's not always for the wife," said Miss Stein. "So that is why we keep our records confidential."

"How well do you know the people who work for you?" asked Racer.

"I make it my business to know everything there is about my people," said Miss Stein.

"By the way, what kind of car do you drive?" asked Racer.

"I have a 2006 Mercedes Benz convertible. Why do you ask?"

"Just curious. I understand that you also have a photography studio in Springdale?" asked Racer.

"Yes, I do. That studio was my husband's pride and joy. When he died, I didn't have the heart to sell it," said Miss Stein.

"Do you run it yourself?" asked Racer.

"As a matter of fact, I do," said Miss Stein. "I have two people that help me out."

"I'm curious; have you ever been arrested?" asked Racer.

"So that's what this is all about. Yes, I was arrested once in my life and the charges were dropped because they found that I was innocent," Miss Stein answered angrily.

"What charge did they arrest you on?" asked Racer.

"Detective Racer, I think that this meeting just ended," said Miss Stein sternly. "I don't have to sit here, in my own home, and have some cop insult me."

"I'm sorry if you took that as an insult. I only wanted to know what the charge was."

Madeline Stein took a deep breath before she answered. "It was for dealing in pornography. You see, my husband was the one that was involved in it, not me. It started out as a hobby of his. Taking pictures of nude models. Then he progressed to videos, and I'm sure you know what came next."

"How did your husband die?" asked Racer curiously.

"He had a heart attack. I guess he couldn't take all that excitement. Now, if you would excuse me, I'll get that list for you so you can be on your way."

"I appreciate it, ma'am. And by the way, can you send the mountain man sitting there out front to pick up his partner?" asked Racer, pointing behind him with his thumb.

Madeline Stein made a motion and the guy was gone.

After Miss Stein handed the list over to Racer, he said, "Before I leave, I have one more question. Is Stein your married name or maiden name?"

"Why do you ask?"

"Because you go by Miss Stein," said Racer.

"When you're attractive, have money and available, you want people to know. I hate to be alone," replied Madeline Stein.

Leaving the house, Racer could feel that someone was watching him. He slid into the front seat of his car and cranked the engine up. He thought to himself that Miss Stein didn't tell him anything more then he already knew. The part about her husband was interesting though. He would have to check into that a little further when he got back.

CHAPTER THIRTEEN

Cindy pulled up outside Jim Paulson's place. She had called him to set up an appointment. It was a few minutes before eleven and the late morning coolness was changing into a warm sunny day. Jim seemed real enthusiastic when Cindy mentioned about them meeting again. She felt a little more comfortable this time. She had on a pair of baggy slacks and a loose fitting cotton blouse. Nothing to break his concentration. She got out of her car and headed up the walk. Pausing at the steps, Cindy thought about the last time when Jim startled her and she almost fell off the top step. She went over to the fence and unhooked the gate. Jim was in the backyard on his knees, playing in the dirt. He looked like a little kid having fun.

"Anybody home?" Cindy said in a soft voice.

"Only me," replied Jim, turning toward Cindy. "Come on in. I just put on a fresh pot of coffee. Would you like a cup?"

"Sure, that sounds great."

"Have a seat and I'll be back in a jiffy," replied Jim, pulling off a pair of garden gloves.

Cindy watched as he disappeared into the house. She walked over to a lounge chair and sat down. She thought that Jim was the kind of neighbor everybody would like. He was a real likable guy, very cheery and pleasant.

"Here we go," said Jim as he came back with two coffee cups. He placed them on the table and sat down opposite Cindy. Before Cindy could say anything, Jim started the conversation. "I haven't come up with anything new since you were here the last time but it sure is nice to see you again."

Cindy was starting to get the feeling that Jim liked her.

"Well, maybe I can jog your memory, if you don't mind," said Cindy.

"Not at all," said Jim as he took a sip from his cup.

"Going back to the night before Barbara Molino was killed, you said that a car with three people came in through the garage," stated Cindy.

"Yes, that's correct. The driver was a guy and the other two appeared to be women. Even though I couldn't get a good look at them, I still believe they were women," answered Jim.

"Could you recognize the guy if you saw him?" asked Cindy.

"I think so," said Jim.

Cindy reached into her purse and pulled out one of the pictures they had collected from the murder scenes. It was the one with the guy and girl in the hot tub. The girl's face was covered. Cindy handed the picture to Jim and waited to see if he could identify the guy in the photo. Jim took the picture and studied it for quite some time. While he was looking at it, Cindy started sipping on her coffee.

"It's pretty hard to say. It doesn't really show the guy's face very good. But looking at his hair and his profile, I would say it's the same guy."

Cindy took the picture from Jim and placed it back into her purse.

"Do you think that this is the guy that killed Barbara Molino?" asked Jim.

"We really don't know. We're just trying to sort out all the details. Now, the next night another car came into the garage with a man driving. He also wanted to see Barbara, is that correct?"

"That's right," said Jim.

"Can you tell me again what kind of car he was driving?"

"That is the one thing I've been thinking about. I'm pretty sure now that is was a dark model Buick. I would say a '99 or 2000," replied Jim.

"Do you happen to know what model it was?" asked Cindy.

"It was either a LeSabre or Park Avenue," answered Jim.

"Did it look like this?" asked Cindy, showing him a picture of Susan Thompson's Buick.

"That's it," replied Jim, nodding.

"Is there anything else that you can think of about those two nights, anything unusual? A stranger hanging around or a fender bender?"

"No, I'm sorry, that's all I can think of," replied Jim.

"I really appreciate your help," said Cindy.

"Glad to be of help, and I'm sure glad to have the company," replied Jim with a broad smile.

When Racer arrived at Barney's, Cindy was already sitting at the bar, chatting with Barney and sipping a Diet Coke. The regular lunchtime crowd was there. With the exception of Cindy, there was no one else at the bar. Everyone was sitting at tables, having their lunch and talking business.

"How was your morning?" asked Cindy when Racer got close enough.

"Quite interesting. I got to see how the rich and famous live. Had a nice chat with Miss Stein and got a little workout in the process. How about you?'

"Jim Paulson just cleared up a couple of things. I showed him the pictures and he identified the car and was pretty sure that the guy in the hot tub was the driver. He couldn't remember anything else about the women in the car."

"Great, things are starting to fall into place," said Racer. "Now, let's order."

"How'd you make out with Madeline Stein," asked Cindy.

"Miss Stein tried to give me a hard time. She seems to have a thing about cops. Doesn't trust them. I did get the list of her employees though, but only after I threatened to take her down to the station. I found out an interesting thing. Her late husband died of a heart attack. He apparently was running a porno ring out of his photo studio."

"Must be where she got her money from," replied Cindy.

"Must be. He was also into pictures and videos, according to Miss Stein. Apparently he was using her as one of his models. She was arrested on porno charges but they were dropped. She wanted me to believe that it was her husband that the vice squad was after."

"What do you believe?" asked Cindy.

"I believe that Miss Stein was in it up to her pretty blue eyes. Who knows? She might have been her husband's leading actress. We'll have to dig into that a little further."

"Sure will, that's the line of work I'm use to," said Cindy.

"Also, here's the list of employees that she gave me," said Racer as he removed it from his pocket and spread it out on the bar.

Barney had placed their drinks in front of them and was gone.

"It sounds like she leaves the running of the dress shop to her assistant manager. She runs the photo studio in Springdale herself, which tends to make me believe that she might not be out of the porno business altogether. That would tie into all those pictures we've been finding at the murder scenes."

"You think that she has been using these women and then, when they finally call it quits, she has them killed?" asked Cindy.

"So far, that's the way the arrow is pointing," replied Racer.

With that Barney returned. Cindy ordered a salad, and Racer ordered a double bacon cheeseburger with fries and another draft. After Barney left, Racer told Cindy that he would match up the list that Miss Stein gave him with the one from the Internal Revenue Service, which his friend was providing that afternoon. Cindy stared at her drink.

"What's wrong?" asked Racer.

"Okay, let's say that Miss Stein is somehow getting these women involved in pornography. She uses them and then, when she's done, decide for one reason or another to get rid of them. But the person that is driving the Buick is a woman and the person seen in the car at the murder scene is a man. So how do we explain all of this?"

"Easy," said Racer. "Miss Stein is either using one of her employees to do the dirty work or she is hiring someone from the outside. Other choices could be the oversize bouncers she has or this elusive black-haired guy."

"That's possible, but why kill Mary, Elizabeth, Barbara and Cheryl? It's one thing to get them involved in porno, but to murder them? That's taking a big risk," said Cindy.

"That's what we can't be sure of. We have to ask ourselves if they were doing this of their own free will or were they being blackmailed," said Racer.

Their conversation was interrupted when Barney returned with Cindy's salad and Racer's burger.

Taking a bite of his burger, Racer looked over at Cindy. She was just picking at her salad. "Now what? All of a sudden you're not hungry?" asked Racer wiping his chin.

"Oh, it's not that. It's just that I'm thinking about four attractive women who got mixed up with the wrong people and wound up losing their lives for their trouble," said Cindy.

"It happens," said Racer as he took another bite of burger.

"Yeah, I know," said Cindy as she finally started eating.

When Racer was about half done he pointed to one of the names on the list. Cindy followed his finger.

"That's probably a good place to start," she said.

Racer was pointing to Danny Tonelli. He was the only male on the list.

Arriving back at the station, Racer found a message taped to his phone. Cindy watched as he read it.

"What's up? asked Cindy.

"It's from our fearless leader, Captain Peterson. He would like my presence in his office in 15 minutes," said Racer.

"Do you want me to go along?" asked Cindy.

"No, he made it clear he wanted just me," said Racer. "But while I'm with Peterson, you can check out Miss Stein."

"Will do," said Cindy.

Racer pushed himself away from his desk and started the long walk to the stairs. As he made his way upstairs to see Peterson, Racer was pretty sure that this meeting had something to do with dental insurance and who was responsible for paying it. Miss Stein didn't waste any time filing a complaint. Entering the Captain's office, Peterson's secretary motioned him to take a seat.

"The Captain will be with you in a minute," said the secretary.

"Trouble?" asked Racer as he sat down.

She nodded as she continued clicking the keys on her computer. A few seconds later the phone on her desk rang. Listening, she then motioned to Racer that he could go in.

When Racer entered Peterson's office, he was seated behind his desk with one of his large cigars in his mouth. There was no smile on his face. He pointed for Racer to sit in the chair directly in front of him. Peterson took his cigar out of his mouth slowly and placed it in the ashtray that was shaped like a badge.

"What in the hell were you doing out at the Stein place?" asked Peterson in a low calm voice. "I just got off the phone with the Chief and my butt is still sore from the chewing out I received. Miss Stein is a very prominent citizen and she called to lodge a complaint about a certain Fairfield detective for police brutality. A worker of hers may need some dental work and she wants to know where to send the bill. Do you have any idea what I am talking about?"

"I went out to the Stein place to question her about the homicides and this large mastodon wouldn't let me do my job so I had to protect myself," replied Racer.

Peterson picked the cigar back up and stuck it between his teeth.

"You could have come back here to get a warrant if you wanted to talk to her that bad," said Peterson, his voice getting a little louder.

"Yes, I could have, but I was already out in Mulberry Hills and I didn't want to waste time," replied Racer.

"Listen to me carefully. I almost had to kiss the Chief's butt to get you back into homicide and assigned to this damn case, so don't screw it up," said Peterson.

"Yes, sir. Is that all?" asked Racer pushing himself out of the chair.

"No, there is one more thing. Are you aware that the computer room is off limits and that you need permission from your superior officer if you need to use it?" asked Peterson.

"Yes sir, I'm aware of that," said Racer.

"Well, you better make sure that your partner is aware of this policy," said Peterson.

"Yes sir, I'll make sure," said Racer.

"Get out of here," said Peterson as he waved his large hand toward the door. When Racer got back to his desk, Cindy was gone. He sat down at his desk and stared at the list that Miss Stein had given him. He picked up a pencil and made a check mark next to Susan Thompson and then another next to Danny Tonelli. If a car entered the garage at Barbara Molino's the night before she died and it contained a man and two women, he would bet that the two women were Susan Thompson and Madeline Stein. That meant that Danny Tonelli was the driver. But who was driving the Buick the following night? If he knew that, he'd have his killer.

"Hey, what are you looking at so intently?" asked Cindy.

She had just come through the doorway and was crossing the room heading for his desk.

"What did you find out?" asked Racer.

"So far her story checks out. It was her husband that was doing all the dirty work. But they are still digging into it for me. Should know more by tomorrow," said Cindy.

When Cindy got to the desk, she peered over Racer's shoulder and saw the check marks next to the two names.

"What's up with the check marks?" asked Cindy.

"Oh, I was just trying to put two and two together, but I'm still coming up with five. Susan Thompson owns the dark Buick, Danny Tonelli has the black hair, and our gal Miss Stein has a background in porno and owns a photo studio in Springdale. All our murder victims had sexy garments from the Designer Dress Shop in their possession."

"First, we'll have to prove that Miss Stein had something to do with her husband's business," said Cindy.

"Come on now, she had to know what was going on. Besides, a woman with her looks could well have been a participant," replied Racer.

"So what are you telling me?" asked Cindy.

"My guess is that Stein, Thompson and Tonelli were in the car that visited Barbara Molino the night before she was killed. They were probably there to blackmail her."

"But how are we going to prove it?" asked Cindy.

"The first step is for me to ask Mr. Tonelli a few questions and see if I can make him nervous," said Racer.

"What do you have in mind for me?" asked Cindy.

"I want you to go sit outside of Madeline Stein's place and follow her every where she goes. Get some real good shots of her and everyone that she associates with. You can sign a camera out from the lab," said Racer.

"Why will we need a picture of Madeline Stein?" asked Cindy.

"You'll see," said Racer.

Racer pulled into a parking space about three stores down from the Designer Dress Shop. He made sure that he had a good view of the shop's entrance and turned his engine off. It was starting to get late and he hoped that he hadn't missed Danny. He wanted to follow him home and question him there. Sitting there, he noticed the number of good-looking women that did their shopping in the Manchester Mall. And a good portion of them spent time in the Designer Dress Shop. His mind started wandering. If there was some kind of porno ring going on, how many other women were involved and how many of them had their lives in danger? Racer figured that if he could start to put some heat on the principals, then maybe the killer would show his hand.

Racer noticed a young guy come out of the dress shop. He recognized him as Danny Tonelli. He headed across the lot to his car. Racer kept an eye on Danny as he slid the key into the door lock and opened it. Danny looked around nervously, as though he were expecting someone. Sliding into the driver's seat, Danny started the car and backed out of the space. Putting it into drive, he headed for the exit. Racer paused a moment and just before he was ready to put the ZX in gear, another car several rows over pulled out in front of him and headed in the same direction that Danny went. It was a light blue Pontiac Grand Am. Racer didn't know if it meant anything but he decided to hang back until he found out. As he pulled in behind the Grand Am, he copied down the plate number.

When Danny got to the exit, he stopped and then made a right, heading for the center of town. The Grand Am made the same turn. Racer knew that there was another exit up a little further so he hit the accelerator and the ZX took off. He got there just as the cars passed. Racer moved into traffic, cutting off an elderly woman in a Lincoln. Now he had to make sure that neither car spotted him. Danny came to the light at Pearson and made a turn onto Archer. The Grand Am was right behind him. Racer allowed a car to slip in between his ZX and the Grand Am. If they continued on Archer, it would lead them into the older section of the city. When Danny got to Archer and Ninth, he found a parking space and pulled over. The Grand Am passed him and made a right at the next corner. Racer maneuvered the ZX to the curb about fifty yards behind Danny. He watched as Danny got out of the car and ran across the street. He entered a building that once was a fancy hotel but now was a low rent place for drug dealers and hookers. Racer glanced down the street to the corner where the Grand Am disappeared and saw a well-dressed man standing against one of the run-down buildings, with his attention also focused on the hotel where Danny just disappeared.

Racer was too far away to see the guy's face but he looked to be a little over six feet and about 220 pounds. He had a mustache and what appeared to be light brown hair. He was wearing a gray suit. Racer looked down and checked his watch. It was five-thirty, and Danny had been inside for about 10 minutes. When Racer looked up, he saw Danny appear in the doorway and check the street in both directions before heading back to his car. Racer then checked the guy on the corner. He was already gone. When he looked back, Danny was pulling out into traffic. Racer decided to hesitate again. Sure as hell the Grand Am pulled right in behind Danny's car.

Racer slowly moved away from the curb and made sure that another car had slipped in between them. After about 15 minutes, Danny pulled up in front of an old two-story building on Herbert Street. The Grand Am again slid by. Racer drove past the house and made a left at the next corner. He stopped so he could still see the building. Danny got out of the car and headed to the rear of the building. Racer looked for the Grand Am but it was nowhere in sight. He parked the ZX again and checked the streets. Still no Grand Am. He got out of the car and started walking down the opposite side of the street. Passing the building, Racer noticed a flight of steps that went up to a door on the second floor. That must be Danny's apartment, thought Racer. He continued to walk to the end of the block. There still wasn't any sight of the Grand Am. Apparently, the person driving the Grand Am had found out what he wanted to know.

Racer crossed the street and headed right for the building. When he got there, he checked one more time for the Grand Am before heading around back. He climbed the steps, keeping an eye out for anybody watching the building. When Racer got to the top of the steps, he stood to the side of the door and knocked. When no one answered, he knocked louder.

"Who is it?" asked a voice from inside.

"It's the police," said Racer. "I would like to talk to a Danny Tonelli."

Racer put his ear to the door and he could hear movement inside. Then the door opened a crack.

"Can I see some kind of identification?" asked Danny.

Racer reached into his pocket and removed his badge and identification. Danny studied it for a second. "I guess it's okay. Come on in," said Danny.

Racer stepped into what was the living room. It was spotless. Danny closed the door and locked it. He moved around to face Racer.

"Aren't you the cop that was asking questions at the dress shop the other day?" asked Danny.

"That's right. You're very observant."

"What do you want with me?" asked Danny.

"Can we sit down?" asked Racer.

Danny motioned toward a couch. He sat down in a straight back chair, and Racer took a seat on the couch right across from Danny. Racer told Danny that he would like to ask him a few questions concerning a couple of customers that frequented the dress shop. Danny said, "I'm not a salesclerk and I don't wait on customers."

"I know, but you do serve as a part-time cashier, don't you?" asked Racer.

"Yeah, sometimes I help out," replied Danny.

"Okay then, I want you to take a look at a couple of photos that I have. See if you can tell me if you recognize anybody in them," said Racer, pulling a pile of photos from his inside pocket and handing them to Danny one at a time. Racer paid close attention to Danny's expression after he looked at each picture. Racer had brought the pictures from each of the murder scenes. He could see Danny wince after looking at each one.

"I never saw any of these women," said Danny. "What happened to them?"

"They have all been murdered and the strange thing is, they all were customers of the Designer Dress Shop," said Racer, never taking his eyes off Danny's face.

Danny kept shaking his head.

"Are you sure you don't recognize any of them? Take a closer look at them," said Racer, nudging him on.

"I don't want to see them anymore," said Danny.

Racer then handed Danny the photo of the hot tub scene, and asked if he recognized anyone. Danny sat there staring at the picture. Raising his voice, Racer asked the question again, if he recognized anyone in the photo. Danny again shook his head. Racer pointed out the guy with the black hair. Danny looked at Racer, and he could see the fright in Danny's eyes.

"No, I don't know who that guy is," said Danny.

"Gee, I was sure that you would be able to help me out here but I guess not," said Racer. Racer took the picture back and looked at it himself and then he looked at Danny. Danny avoided Racer's eyes. "You know, I would almost have to say that the guy in this picture resembles you. I have never seen a guy with hair this dark."

"It's not me and I don't know who it is," replied Danny defensively.

"Okay, calm down. If you think of anything that might help, here's my card. Call me anytime," said Racer.

Racer got up and headed for the door. When he got there, he paused for a moment.

"You know Danny, someone like you should stay away from

Archer and Ninth. It isn't a very nice neighborhood for a clean-cut guy like you," said Racer.

Danny's jaw dropped. Racer turned, unlocked the door and left.

Stepping out onto the landing, he heard the door slam shut behind him and the locks being applied. He knew that he had given Danny a little something to think about. Now, he had to wait and see what effect it would have on him.

Racer drove into the parking lot of a convenience store and pulled his cell phone out of his coat pocket. He dialed the squad and waited.

"Detective Darling speaking. What can I do for you?" asked Cindy.

"This is Racer. Did you get the picture I wanted?" asked Racer.

"No problem," said Cindy. "As a matter of fact, she almost posed for me."

"Great," said Racer. "I'm on my way back."

CHAPTER FOURTEEN

Upon returning to the station, Racer filled Cindy in on his visit with Danny Tonelli. Explaining how he showed the pictures of the crime scenes and how Danny's facial expression changed when he saw the hot tub photo. He was sure that Danny was involved in this whole mess. So he was going to pay Danny a visit again tomorrow to keep the heat.

"While you were visiting Danny, I called a friend of mine in Springdale and asked if he could remember anything about the Stein case. All he could remember was they were ready to prosecute Mr. Stein when he had his heart attack and died. But there was one important thing about the case. Madeline Stein was involved in his first couple of movies. Apparently, her show biz name was Misty Blue. He couldn't remember the title of the movies, but he was positive that was how Mr. Stein got started in the pornography business. They couldn't get enough evidence on her, so they had to let her go. So how's that?" asked Cindy with a smile of satisfaction.

"Nice work, but we have to be careful until we can prove that she was in those movies," said Racer. "And I know a guy that might be able to help us."

"How does this tie into the murders though?" asked Cindy.

"My feeling is that the Designer Dress Shop is a front for enticing young women into photo sessions. If we can crack the ring, I'm sure we can catch our killer," said Racer.

"Well, let's get at it," said Cindy.

"Okay, I'll tell you what: I'm going home to change and I'll pick you up at your place at eight. We'll have dinner and then we'll head to a place called The Jungle."

"See you at eight," said Cindy without batting an eye.

Racer was outside of Cindy's apartment at eight sharp. She came out in a pale green dress and slide into the front seat. She asked Racer where they were going for dinner. He said he had a nice placed picked out. Cindy thought, *Yeah, I can imagine.*

They made some small talk as Racer drove. Racer turned onto Lincoln Boulevard and then turned right into the parking lot for the Rendezvous Restaurant. Racer looked over at Cindy, "Does it meet with your approval?" he asked.

"Definitely," said Cindy, with a smile.

When they left the restaurant, darkness had fallen on the city. The summer was sailing by and fall wasn't far behind. Getting into his car, Racer looked at his watch and mentioned that The Jungle should be jumping by the time they got there.

Easing the ZX out of the parking lot, Racer headed for a four block square area of downtown that most people in the city weren't too proud of. But every time the city aldermen tried to get the place cleaned up, the owners would find some Philadelphia lawyer to file injunctions to keep them open. If there wasn't a bar on every corner it was a strip joint.

The Jungle was one of the classier places on the strip. An old buddy of Racer's owned it. They had been in Special Forces together. Steve Howard wanted Racer to join him in this venture, telling him that it would be a gold mine. It sure as hell had turned into one. Steve ran a very tight ship. No hookers, no drugs and only the best-looking girls. It was hard to run a place like this, but he fired any employee who allowed such vices.

It was ten-thirty when they got to the Jungle. A nice looking blond met them and asked if they had a preference on where they wanted to sit. Cindy spoke right up.

"Right up front if we can," she said.

The girl led them to a table, to the right side of the stage. Racer watched her all the way. She was wearing a skimpy bikini in a leopard skin pattern. His eyes were moving right along with her hips.

Most of the people were still crowded around the large horse-shoe bar. The show usually started at eleven but everyone knew that the first two acts where just to warm the crowd up. The good stuff came on around midnight. That's why the tables weren't all taken.

When they were seated, another blond approached their table asking if they would like to order drinks. After she took their orders Racer asked if Steve was around.

"He's here but I don't have any idea where," said the blond. "I'll see if I can find him."

"Tell him that Racer is here to see him," said Racer, slipping her a five.

The girl got back just as the curtain was going up. She placed their drinks on the table and mentioned that she hadn't seen Steve yet. Racer shook his head. Their attention now went to the stage. An older gentleman came out in a black tux. He started firing off jokes one after the other, none of which Racer thought were very funny, but apparently Cindy did. She was laughing at every one. The guy realized this and it seemed that he was directing every joke in Cindy's direction. When he finished, he told the audience to get ready for the best show in town. He then disappeared behind the black curtain.

A sheer curtain came down, the lights dimmed even further and the music started. This was the signal for everyone to make a mad dash to their tables. The announcer presented the first dancer, Shelia. Shelia came from behind the curtain and started her rhythmic dance. She had on a red sequined dress with long white gloves. As she moved around the stage, Shelia seductively removed pieces of her costume until all she had on was a G-string.

Racer looked around the room, and from what he could see there was about twenty men to each woman present. The blond returned and asked if they would like another drink before the next dancer came on. Racer nodded. She mentioned that she still hadn't seen Steve yet. After about five minutes, the lights went down again.

The announcer's voice came over a speaker announcing the next act as Tara the Tigress. As Tara went through her routine, the blond returned with their drinks. She told Racer that she had given the message to Steve and that he would be right with him. Racer thanked the girl and slipped her another five. When Tara was done, the lights went back up and the jukebox kicked in.

"Is that it?" asked Cindy.

"No, there will be more. Just be patient," said Racer with a smile.

Turning to scan the crowd one more time, Racer saw Steve Howard standing behind him. Steve was a burly guy standing even at six feet tall, with a light-colored mustache.

"Well, what did you think of the show so far?" asked Steve looking at Cindy.

"Not too bad," said Racer.

"Are you going to introduce me?" Steve asked.

"This is my partner, Detective Cindy Darling," replied Racer. "We're here to ask you for your help."

"Anything for an old buddy. Why don't we go back to my office, where we can talk?" said Steve, leading them away.

Cindy and Racer followed Steve behind the stage and down a narrow hallway, past the performer's dressing rooms. Going into Steve's office, they all sat down. The walls of his office were covered with photos of girls in various costumes.

"Okay Charlie, what can I do for you?" asked Steve.

"We're trying to find a movie with a girl that calls herself Misty Blue. It's probably a few years old," said Racer.

"Do you have a picture of this Misty Blue?" asked Steve.

Cindy pulled the picture from her purse and handed it to Steve. He studied the picture for several minutes. "It sure would help if you knew the name of the movie," said Steve.

"If I knew that I wouldn't need you," said Racer. "But I do know who made the movie: an amateur film producer from Springdale by the name of Stein."

Steve thought for a few seconds, then told Racer he remembered the name. It had something to do with a pornography ring in Springdale where the guy died before the cops could put him away. Racer nodded. Steve said that it would take him a couple of days to dig up the information. Racer told him it wouldn't be a problem.

"Well, if that's it, you can get back out and catch the rest of the show. The last act will be coming up and it's great. The girl has a large German shepherd that pulls her clothes off," said Steve.

"No thanks, we have an early day tomorrow," said Racer. "Maybe another time."

The next morning Racer was in early. He wanted to get that license number to the motor vehicle department as soon as it opened. So he could find out who owned that light blue Grand Am. He would also like to know what business they had with Danny Tonelli. Racer went over to the coffee maker and poured himself a cup of coffee. As soon as the clock hit eight, Racer picked up the phone and called Harry Able at the DMV.

"Harry, this is Racer. How the heck are you?" he asked.

"Racer you old son-of-a-gun, I haven't heard from you in ages. What's up?"

"I need you to run a number for me."

"Okay, give it to me. I'll see what I can do," said Harry.

Racer read off the plate number for a light blue Grand Am. Harry asked Racer to hold a minute. While Racer waited, he looked at his watch and wondered where Cindy was. Then Harry came back on the line.

"That number is registered to a vehicle owned by a Madeline Stein. It says that it's a 2002 blue Pontiac Grand Am. Do you need her address?" asked Harry.

"No, I have a pretty good idea where she lives. Thanks a lot, I owe you one."

"You bet you do, and I have a good memory," answered Harry, laughing.

Racer hung up and started to make some notes on his yellow pad. He wrote Miss Stein's name, then draw a line to the Grand Am. After that he wrote, used for trailing Danny Tonelli. It looked like Miss Stein was keeping a close eye on one of her employees. But for what reason? Maybe she was checking to make sure that he wasn't talking to somebody he shouldn't. Racer heard someone coming up the steps. It was Cindy, and she was swearing to herself. She was still talking as she approached his desk.

"What in the world is wrong with you?" asked Racer.

Without answering, Cindy pulled a brown envelope from her purse and tossed it to him. Racer took the envelope and opened it. He removed several pictures from inside. Racer looked through the photos, then suddenly his eyebrows went up and he whistled.

"They were in my mailbox when I got home last night. As you can see, they weren't sent through the mail. Someone hand delivered them. And do you know where I had those outfits on? In the fitting room of the Designer Dress Shop," said Cindy.

"Remember when you told me that it felt like someone was watching you? Well I guess you were right," replied Racer. "And they weren't only watching you, they were photographing you. These pictures look like they have been touched up, so it looks like you could be just about anywhere. Is that all that was in the envelope?" asked Racer.

"That's it," said Cindy.

"I'm sure the person who sent these will be getting in touch with you," said Racer.

"That's great, just what I needed, a damn pervert stalking me," said Cindy, throwing herself into one of the wooden chairs.

"Now wait a minute, let's think this through. Say our four victims had the same experience. They had photos taken of them in various stages of undress while trying on lingerie. Then a brown envelope arrives with the photos. A few days later, someone contacts them and sets up a meet. Somehow this person convinces them to pose for explicit photos, and all of a sudden they are hooked. Not long after that they turn up dead. We might have to play this out."

"What do you mean, play this out?" asked Cindy.

"We have to wait and see if this person contacts you to set up a meeting," said Racer. "Which means we'll have to be careful, since they may be watching you. Right now they don't know that you're a cop. This could be the break that leads us to the killer. And that Grand Am that was tailing Danny Tonelli, it belongs to Madeline Stein. I want you to tail Stein again and see where she goes. I'm going to have another talk with Danny Tonelli. I'm going to shake him up real good this time."

Cindy nodded her head.

"When you get out to the Stein place, keep an eye out for that light blue Grand Am. If you happen to come across it, try to see who the driver is," said Racer.

"Sure will," said Cindy as she grabbed her purse and started for the steps right behind Racer. "Catch you later."

Racer pulled his car into a parking space outside the Designer Dress Shop. A few minutes passed after he saw several customers enter the shop, he slid out and headed for the entrance. When Racer got inside, he saw Susan Thompson waiting on one of the customers, who had just entered the shop. Another salesclerk was hanging up some dresses on a rack, on the other side of the shop. No one had realized yet that he was there. He slowly moved behind the counter and stuck his head through the curtain leading to the back. He didn't see anybody. The office was empty and there was no movement. Racer looked back into the shop and saw Susan Thompson leading a young woman to one of the dressing rooms. The woman had a couple of garments draped over her arm. Someone came up behind him and asked if they could help him. Racer must have jumped a foot off the floor. Catching his composure, he said, "Yes, you can get my heart beating again."

"Oh, I'm sorry, I didn't mean to startle you," said the salesclerk.

Racer looked at her nametag. It read "Monica Klein—sales associate." Racer pulled out his shield and showed it to Monica.

Racer wanted to know if Danny Tonelli was around. Monica informed him that Danny didn't show up this morning and never called. Racer wanted to know if this was normal for him. Monica shook her head. Racer thanked Monica and noticed Miss Thompson heading in his direction.

"Well detective, is there anything that I can do for you?"

Racer said that he had a couple of questions for Danny Tonelli but Monica told him Danny never showed up this morning. After Miss Thompson confirmed this, Racer then asked how long she had known Madeline Stein.

"I've known her ever since the store opened," said Susan. "She was the one who interviewed me."

"So you didn't know her before you started working here?" asked Racer.

"No, why do you ask?"

"No particular reason. I'll come by tomorrow and see if I can catch Danny."

Heading for the door, Racer could feel Susan Thompson looking at him. He walked right to his car, backed out of the parking space, stopped short of the exit and circled the mall until he came back to a space that gave him a full view of the shop. After about 15 minutes, Racer watched as Susan Thompson came out of the shop and walked down the sidewalk. When she came to the corner, she turned left and out of sight. Racer got out of his car and followed her. When he got to the corner, he saw Susan about a hundred feet in front of him at a pay phone, dialing. Racer got as close as he could without taking a chance of being spotted. He watched Susan intently, trying to decipher anything that he could about her conversation. He would lay odds that Susan was calling good old Danny boy, to warn him that the cops were on his trail. Apparently no one answered. Susan hung up without saying a word and dialed again. This time, she started talking almost immediately. Racer was positive that he could make out the words "Miss Stein." It was a short conversation. Susan hung up and headed back to the dress shop. Racer ducked into a bookstore so he wouldn't be spotted. When Susan was out of sight, Racer went to the phone and called the operator. After identifying himself and giving his badge number, Racer found out where the last call was placed from that pay phone. After writing it down, he walked back to his car and started thinking that he must have hit a nerve. Danny was still his best bet. He would have to catch up with him later.

CHAPTER FIFTEEN

When Racer returned to the station, he headed right for Detman's office. Tapping on the door, he walked right in. Detman was reviewing some reports stacked on his desk.

"I think we're getting close," said Racer, before Detman could say anything. "I'm positive that Madeline Stein, Susan Thompson and a kid by the name of Danny Tonelli are running a porn ring out of Springdale."

"What does that have to do with this case?" asked Detman.

"I think they found a way to blackmail our victims into posing for them. When the victims threaten to go to the police, they turn up dead. The problem is, I'm not sure yet who is actually doing the killing," said Racer.

"Well, at least you're making progress. Have you mentioned any of this to Peterson yet?" asked Detman.

"You must be out of your mind. I don't want him blabbing this to the press quite yet. I still have some leads to follow up on. By the way, do you remember the Stein porno case that took place in Springdale years ago?"

Detman rubbed his chin and thought for a few seconds.

"Yeah, that's the guy that owned the photography shop and started dabbling in nude photos of young girls, which eventually led to videos."

"That's him," replied Racer. "Well, Madeline Stein was his wife at the time. I'm trying to tie her into his operation."

"If that's the route you're taking, then you should talk to Robert Shane," said Detman. "He's a detective in the Springdale police department."

"What did he have to do with the case?" asked Racer.

"He was the lead investigator on the case, and there were rumors that he was getting pretty friendly with Madeline Stein while he was working on it."

"That's interesting. Maybe I'll just do that. Is he still on the force?" asked Racer.

"I'm pretty sure he is. As a matter of fact, I think he is in charge of robbery."

"Thanks a lot, Harry," said Racer, as he left the office.

It was almost noon. Cindy had been sitting outside of Madeline Stein's house for over four hours now. She was getting tired of sitting and doing nothing. In four hours, no one had entered or left the house. It had been dead quiet. Cindy was starting to wonder if Madeline Stein was even home. She also was wondering if Racer had any luck with Danny Tonelli. Just then the front gate opened and a new Lincoln came down the drive. She couldn't tell if Madeline was in it or not. The windows were tinted so that it was virtually impossible to see in. Cindy waited until the Lincoln was halfway down the street before she started her engine.

Keeping her eyes on the Lincoln, Cindy made sure that she kept a safe distance behind it. She sure didn't want to be spotted. The Lincoln made its way out of the subdivision and headed for the highway. Instead of turning toward Fairfield, it went up the ramp marked Springdale. This was a good indication that Madeline Stein was in the car. She was probably on her way to the photo studio. It was about a 45 minute drive, so Cindy settled back and allowed the Lincoln to open up a bigger gap. Once they approached Springdale, Cindy positioned herself two cars behind the Lincoln. The Lincoln made its way into the business district and eventually eased to the curb right in front of Stein Photography Studio. Cindy passed the Lincoln and stopped at the corner. She could see Miss Stein step out of the car and head into the studio. The Lincoln drove off.

Once Madeline Stein was out of sight, Cindy made a U-turn and pulled to the curb on the other side of the street. She now had a clear view of the studio. After about an hour, a car pulled up in front of the place and two men got out. Five minutes later the closed sign was put in the window. Getting out of her car, Cindy walked up close to the studio and took a good look at the men's car. It was a light blue Grand Am with license plate number CSX-749, the same car that Racer had spotted tailing Danny Tonelli. Apparently, these men worked for Madeline Stein, but Cindy couldn't understand why the *closed* sign had been placed in the window.

Cindy continued down the sidewalk, stopped in the doorway of a drugstore, and kept an eye on the photo studio. Several minutes later the door opened and the two men stepped out onto the sidewalk. They were carrying two boxes about the size of a small television. They slipped the boxes into the trunk of their car and drove away. A few minutes later the Lincoln pulled back up in front of the studio. Madeline Stein came out and climbed into the back seat. Cindy watched as the car headed back to the highway. She hurried across the street, jumped into her car and took up tail. She followed the Lincoln right back to the Stein residence. Taking up her position again, Cindy decided that she would stick it out until four-thirty, then call it a day.

Racer arrived at Danny's just after one o'clock and parked across the street from the apartment. He crossed the street and headed up the back stairs. When he got to Danny's door he knocked, but no one answered. Racer tried to peer in one of the windows but all the curtains were drawn tight. He decided to head back to his car and wait.

About five minutes later, Racer heard tires squealing and saw Danny's car fly into the driveway. Danny jumped out and ran for the steps to his apartment, a brown envelope tucked under his arm. It was the same type of envelope that Cindy had received. Racer wanted to see what was in that envelope. Seeing that the street was deserted, he hurried to the rear steps. When Racer got to Danny's door, he pounded on it.

"Who's there?" shouted Danny.

"It's Detective Racer. I need to talk to you."

Racer saw the curtain move back and Danny peer out. The lock slipped back and Danny opened the door a crack. There was a night chain on the door.

"What do you want?" asked Danny. "I told you all I know."

"I don't think so. I need to clear up a few things," said Racer, trying to peer inside.

"Why don't you leave me alone? You are going to get me fired," replied Danny nervously.

"Look, you can either talk to me here or we can take a ride down to the station. I'm sure that wouldn't look too good, you talking to the cops," said Racer.

Danny hesitated for a second, then slipped the chain and opened the door just enough to let Racer ease inside. Then Danny closed the door and locked it behind Racer. Racer knew he was spooked about something. They both sat down.

"Danny, I have an eyewitness that told me they saw you entering the garage, at Barbara Molino's apartment building, the night before she was killed. What do you have to say about that?" Racer watched Danny's face closely.

"I don't know what you're talking about," replied Danny, rubbing his hands on his pants.

"Danny, that gives me enough to arrest you. So why don't you tell me who was in that car with you and what you were doing there," said Racer.

"I was nowhere near that building and I don't know anybody by the name of Barbara Molino," said Danny.

Racer reminded Danny that he had the picture of him in the hot tub with one of the victims. So he told Danny that if he would help him, he would talk to the DA in his behalf. Danny told Racer again that he had no idea what he was talking about.

Racer looked around the room, trying to spot the brown envelope that he saw Danny carry in. "When I saw you get out of your car, you were carrying a brown envelope. It was the same type of envelope that a couple of women have been receiving, with some very interesting photos. You wouldn't want to show that envelope to me, would you?"

"Detective Racer, I would like you to leave now," demanded Danny. "And please, don't come back unless you have that warrant with you."

"Have it your way, Danny. You'll be seeing me real soon, with or without a warrant."

Racer got up and slowly strolled to the door. He still couldn't locate the envelope.

"Think about what I said and, if you feel a change of heart, you can reach me at this number." He handed Danny his card.

Racer made his way back to his car. Looking up at Danny's window, Racer could see him looking out from behind his curtains. Racer watched until Danny disappeared back into his apartment, and then he slid in behind the wheel and drove off. He circled the block and stopped at the corner, where he had a good view of Danny's apartment.

Racer had been sitting there for about 15 minutes when Danny came out, got into his car and drove off. Racer slumped down in his seat as Danny sped past and then pulled out behind Danny. Racer followed him all the way to the post office.

Racer watched as Danny got out of his car, the brown envelope under his arm. He disappeared inside the large double doors. Three minutes later, Danny came out and got back into his car without the envelope. When Danny's car was out of sight, Racer entered the post office, walked up to the counter and asked for the postmaster.

A gentleman came out from behind the counter and introduced himself as Edgar Wholling, the postmaster. Racer pulled his badge from his pocket and explained to Mr. Wholling what he needed. Mr. Wholling explained that it was against federal law to allow him to have the envelope. Racer shook his head, telling Wholling that it wasn't the envelope he wanted but the mailing address. The postmaster pulled Racer to the side and asked what this was all about. Racer explained that the brown envelope could be a key piece of evidence in a murder case. The postmaster thought for a second and then told Racer that he still couldn't give him the envelope, but if the envelope was sitting out he couldn't prevent Racer from seeing it.

Racer watched the postmaster walk behind the counter and grab the brown envelope from a mail bin. He placed it on the end of the counter and walked away.

Racer made sure that no one was watching and moved to the end of the counter. Leaning over, he could see the address. Taking out his notepad he wrote down the name Amanda English and her address. Racer nodded to Mr. Wholling and headed for his car.

Racer drove to one of the newer subdivisions outside the city and parked near a small new ranch home at 9027 Cumberland Circle. Getting out of the car, Racer saw a tall, slim woman in the garage. He approached her and introduced himself. He asked if she was Amanda English. Amanda nodded. Racer asked if they could go inside so he could explain why he was there. She led Racer through the garage and into the house.

After they were seated in the living room, Racer explained to her that she was going to receive a brown envelope, in the next day or two and he would like to be present when she opened it. Amanda English looked puzzled and wanted to know how he knew this.

"Let's say that the person who mailed this is under investigation," said Racer.

"Under investigation for what?" asked Amanda English, still not understanding.

Avoiding the question, Racer asked, "Are you married?"

"Yes," replied Miss English. "My husband is a salesman and travels a lot."

"Do you shop at the Designer Dress Shop?" asked Racer.

"Not usually, but I decided to buy a couple of things to surprise my husband with. What does all this have to do with me?" she asked.

"I believe that the contents of that envelope are important to a case that I'm working. So I really need your help." said Racer.

"If it's that important to you, yes, I will help you," said Mrs. English.

"I really appreciate your help," said Racer as he pulled his card from his pocket and handed it to her. "You can call me anytime day or night."

Leaving the English's house, Racer hoped that Amanda English would follow through and call him when that envelope arrived.

There were a couple of notes on Racer's desk when he got back to the station. One was from Cindy who said she couldn't wait any longer. She was headed for a Mexican restaurant around the corner. The other note, taped to his phone, told him to call Detman when he had a chance. When he dialed Detman's number, Detman picked it up on the second ring.

Racer filled Detman in on Danny Tonelli, the brown envelope and his meeting with Amanda English. Detman wanted to make sure that Mrs. English wasn't in any danger. He told Detman, not to worry, he had everything covered, and that Amanda English would call him as soon as she's contacted. Before Detman hung up, Racer said that he would keep him posted.

After hanging up, Racer checked his desk one more time. He was really hoping to hear from Steve to see if he had found anything out about Madeline Stein, but there were no more notes. He got up from his desk and decided that it was time for a taco.

Racer walked around the corner to the Mexican restaurant and found Cindy sitting at one of the tables, sipping on a Diet Coke. Racer could tell that she was just about done from all the empty dishes in front of her. He waved to her as he stepped up to the counter to order. After he got his meal, Racer sat down at Cindy's table.

"Hey, busy day?" asked Cindy.

"I think it has been a very productive day," replied Racer. "Before we start comparing notes, give me a chance to finish my meal."

After they were finished, Racer explained his interview with Danny Tonelli and told Cindy about the brown envelope. Racer also told her that he believe Amanda English was going to be the killers' next target. Cindy sat there listening. When he finished, it was her turn. She started telling him about the trip to Springdale and the two guys loading boxes into a blue Grand Am. She suspected that the boxes were filled with pornographic material heading for distribution. After this was done, she followed Stein back to the mansion, where she settled in. Racer thought for a minute, then asked Cindy if she knew anyone in the Springdale police department that could be trusted.

"I did, but they're no longer working there," said Cindy. "Why are you asking?"

"Detman gave me the name of one of the detectives that was investigating the Stein case. He also mentioned that this detective was getting real friendly with Madeline Stein. I want to find out how close he was, without drawing any attention."

"Who are we talking about here?" asked Cindy.

"A detective named Robert Shane. Does that ring a bell?" asked Racer.

"Never heard of him," replied Cindy. "But I can contact my friend and see if he knows anything about Shane."

When they got back to the station, Cindy went right to the phone. Talking to a guy by the name of Jim, Racer could hear Cindy ask for a big favor. Hanging up, she told Racer, "The Clubhouse Bar in Springdale in an hour."

On the way to Springdale, Racer asked Cindy where she knew Jim from. Cindy explained that the Fairfield and Springdale police departments had worked a large sting operation together a little over a year ago and that Jim was the contact in Springdale. She had worked with him for about three months before the case was closed. She was sure that he could be trusted. Racer explained that this was a little different. They were talking about another cop here. Cindy commented that if he didn't do anything wrong, he shouldn't have anything to worry about.

"Where is this Clubhouse Bar?" asked Racer.

Once they reached Springdale, Cindy gave Racer directions. They finally pulled up outside of a small neighborhood bar with a neon sign that displayed a racehorse and jockey. There were about a dozen cars parked outside. Racer knew that if the bar was full of locals, they would stand out like a sore thumb, so he decided to enter the bar first and take a look around before Cindy entered. He asked Cindy what Jim looked like.

"You can't miss him. He looks just like Mister Clean from the television commercials. He even has the gold earring in his right ear."

Racer slipped out of the car and headed for the entrance to the bar.

Racer stood in the doorway as the door closed behind him. He could feel everyone checking him over. He ignored them and headed for a couple of empty stools on the right side of the bar. When he got to one of the stools, he gave a quick look around and sat down. There were about 25 people in the place and it was loud and smoky.

Racer ordered a draft, and as he sipped it, he tried to see if Mr. Clean was there. He didn't see anyone fitting that description. So he just waited.

He saw the front door open and Cindy enter. Everyone's head in the place turned to see who it was. Cindy walked across the bar and took a stool two down from Racer. She ordered a Tom Collins from the bartender and looked around. Then all of a sudden, a large muscular guy was standing next to her. Racer had no idea where he came from. The man whispered something into Cindy's ear and she followed him to a table.

Racer could see the table right from where he was seated. A woman was already seated at the table. Cindy and Jim were in a heavy discussion. Racer would bet that this Jim character would be a little reluctant to roll over on a fellow officer. They were there for about half an hour when Cindy got up and made her way to the door. Racer watched as Jim drained his beer and headed for the bar. Racer waited a couple of minutes and followed Cindy out.

On the way back to Fairfield, Racer asked Cindy how her conversation with Mr. Clean went. She told Racer that he was a little reluctant to say anything about Shane until she told him that his information was important to a case she was working. He finally gave in. "He told me that Shane was a good cop as far as he knew. He also told me that Shane headed the investigation of the Stein porn ring and that he was the one that nailed Mr. Stein." Cindy said she asked how close he was to Madeline Stein. "He told me that word around the station was that Madeline and Shane were playing house for certain favors. I asked Jim directly if the favors had anything to do with keeping her name out of her husband's case. He told me that was the word. I then told him I wanted to know if Madeline Stein had appeared in any of the videos that her husband shot. He said that he didn't know for sure but Shane had mentioned it."

"What about Shane?" asked Racer.

"Jim told me that he was a lieutenant now, which might make it tough on doing a check on him," said Cindy. "You know, rank has its privilege. That's about it. So where do we go from here?"

"The big thing right now is to wait for that envelope to arrive at Amanda English's place. If it has what I think it has inside, we can lower the boom on Danny boy until it hurts. And I still want to find out about those videos that Madeline Stein appeared in. I would love to play them for her," said Racer with a big smile.

When they got back to station, Racer walked Cindy to her car. A light rain was now falling. They stood there standing toe to toe, and Racer all of a sudden had the urge to kiss her. It was definitely an awkward moment. Instead, he told her that they had a very productive day. Cindy nodded and got in her car. They said their goodnights and Racer watched as she pulled out of the police parking lot. Walking to his car, he thought about Cindy. He had to keep his distance. He didn't want things to become complicated between them. They were starting to work well together and he didn't want to ruin that.

CHAPTER SIXTEEN

Racer woke up at around five in the morning. He had a strange feeling that something was wrong. Sitting down at the kitchen table with a cup of coffee, he started to fit the pieces of the puzzle together. If he could only figure out who the killer was, he could wrap up this case, except he felt as if he were missing something. He ran through the cast of characters. It had to be someone in the ring. Very possibly Madeline Stein or someone working for her. Would Danny have enough guts to do it, or was Susan the one? It sure wouldn't surprise him if it was an individual or the whole group. It was fortunate that no one had turned up dead lately. But he didn't want to press his luck.

Taking his coffee into the living room, Racer sat down in a chair by the patio doors. Cindy had gotten one of those brown envelopes with photos taken of her, but no one had contacted her yet. And now Danny had mailed an envelope to Amanda English. Things were starting to heat up, he thought, and then the phone rang.

"Detective Racer, this is patrolman Lewis. I got a call to a fire and I think you should get over here."

"Hey, I'm in homicide, Lewis, not arson," said Racer.

"I know, that's why I called you," said Lewis.

"Then tell me what's going on," said Racer.

"We got called to a fire scene but when my partner and I got here, I realized that it wasn't a fire at all. Smoke was coming out from under the garage door. It was exhaust from a car. When we broke into the garage, we found a car running with a young man in the front seat. He was pronounced dead at the scene," said Lewis.

"What's your location?" asked Racer.

"We're at an apartment on Herbert Street," said Lewis. "We

found an envelope on the front seat next to the body and it's addressed to you."

"Don't let anyone touch that envelope. I'll be there in about 10 minutes," said Racer, knowing what the uneasy feeling was when he woke up.

"I'm sorry, but there are detectives on the scene and they already took control of the envelope," replied Lewis.

"Do you happen to know their names?" asked Racer.

"It's a Detective Harlin that has the envelope," said Lewis.

"Lewis, I want you to go to Detective Harlin and tell him not to open that envelope. It is evidence in a murder investigation," said Racer.

"I'll do my best but I can't guarantee anything," said Lewis, hanging up.

Racer called Cindy immediately. "Get dressed. I'll be there in five minutes to pick you up."

"What's going on?" asked Cindy in a sluggish voice.

"I'll fill you in when I get there," replied Racer.

Getting dressed, all Racer could think about was Harlin with that envelope in his hands and it ticked him off.

Racer was outside of Cindy's apartment in four minutes. She wasn't outside yet. He was ready to start blowing the horn when she appeared in the doorway. Racer reached across the front seat and pushed the passenger door open. Cindy jumped in and fastened her seatbelt.

"What's the big hurry?" she asked.

"It's Danny Tonelli," said Racer. "A patrolman by the name of Lewis just called me. They found Danny dead in a closed garage with his car running. He left an envelope addressed to me next to him on the front seat of his car."

"Then why the hurry?" asked Cindy.

"Guess who's on the scene? Harlin, and he has the envelope," replied Racer.

"Then we better step it up," said Cindy.

Racer punched the accelerator and the speedometer started climbing. At this time of the morning there wasn't much traffic to contend with. When they pulled up in front of Danny's apartment, the fire engines were just leaving. The only vehicles left were two patrol cars and an unmarked detective's car. Climbing out of the car, Racer jogged up the driveway to the garage. Cindy was right behind him. A black patrolman stopped Racer before he got hallway up the drive.

"Are you Detective Racer?" asked the patrolman.

"Yeah, and this is my partner Detective Darling."

The patrolman nodded toward Cindy and then turned his attention back to Racer. "I'm Lewis, the one who called you. I gave your message to Detective Harlin and he just chuckled but he did give me the envelope," said the patrolman, handing Racer the envelope.

"Did the lab boys have a chance to go over it?" asked Cindy.

"I'm not sure," said Lewis.

"Is Detective Harlin still here?" asked Racer.

"Yes, sir, he and his partner are in the garage, still going over the car."

"Did the M.E. take the body yet?" asked Cindy.

"Yes, Detective Harlin released it to the coroner's men," replied Lewis.

"Do you know who called it in?" asked Cindy.

"The owner of the house," replied Lewis. "She called 911 and reported it as a fire, so they dispatched the fire department and a patrol car."

"Think she's still up?" asked Cindy.

"I'm sure of it. She's been watching us through the window shades ever since we got here," replied Lewis.

"Cindy, go and see what you can find out from her," said Racer, pointing toward the house.

"Detective Harlin has already talked with her," said Lewis.

Racer motioned for Cindy to keep right on going. She headed for the house and Racer headed for the garage. Harlin and Piakowski were going over the car when Racer walked up on them. Piakowski noticed Racer first and nudged Harlin. Harlin leaned away from the car and turned to face Racer.

"Well, well, look who's here. If it isn't Super Detective Racer. Are you here to take this crime scene over, too?" asked Harlin.

"I came to pick up an envelope that I believe is addressed to me," replied Racer.

"The patrolman has it. Go see him," replied Piakowski.

"One of these days you're going to stick your nose where it doesn't belong and someone is going to chop it off," said Racer.

"Are you always this crabby in the morning or is it your time of the month?" asked Harlin.

Racer glared at him and then turned away. He headed back to the house to see if Cindy had anything. When he got there, Cindy was still inside. Racer took this chance to open the envelope and see what was inside. It was a letter. He sat down on the porch step and read it.

To Detective Racer,

I wanted you to know that I didn't kill anybody. I swear I didn't. As a matter of fact, I really liked the women that I took pictures of at the store. My job was to pick up the girls and slip them a sedative so they would do whatever we wanted. But I never hurt them in any way. I just couldn't stand being suspected of murder. I would tell you who was doing the killing but I honestly don't know. Please forgive me for what I am about to do.

I decided to work for Madeline Stein because it sounded good, but once I got started she wouldn't let me out. I must go now. I'm sorry for everything that I did.

The letter was signed, Danny.

Racer read it over one more time while he waited for Cindy. *Damn*, Racer thought, *why didn't Danny come to me for help? I gave him every chance to confide in me.* Just then the door opened behind him and Cindy came out of the house.

"Do you want to see Danny's apartment?" asked Cindy, with the elderly woman who owned the apartment standing next to her.

"Sure, let's take a look before Harlin goes through it," said Racer, pulling himself up.

Racer and Cindy followed the woman up to Danny's apartment. When they got to the door, the woman opened it with her key and told Racer and Cindy to take their time; if they needed anything, she would be downstairs having tea. Racer waited until the woman departed and then they entered the apartment. The place looked the same as it had the day before. The only thing that made it look like someone lived there was an empty soda can sitting on the end table next to the sofa. Racer and Cindy started going through each of the small rooms carefully. They didn't want to miss anything. They hadn't found anything until they opened Danny's closet and saw a metal box on one of the shelves. Racer took it down and put it on Danny's dresser. It was locked. They looked for a key but couldn't find one.

"I'll bet it's on Danny's key ring and Harlin probably has it by now," said Racer.

"So how do we get it opened?" asked Cindy.

"We don't. Not here anyway," replied Racer.

They made sure that everything looked just the way it was when they came in. Racer knew that Harlin and Piakowski would be searching the place when they got done in the garage, but he sure wasn't going to leave the box behind.

Racer tucked the box under his arm and they headed for the door. Cindy pulled it closed behind them. They stopped to see the woman downstairs to thank her and tell her they were done. As they left, Racer noticed Harlin and Piakowski heading for the house.

It was a couple of minutes before eight when they arrived at the station. Racer put the metal box in his filing drawer and locked it. He then made a copy of Danny's letter and went to the lab. Racer moved through the lab, looking for Sidney. He found him sitting at his desk with a cup of coffee and a Danish in front of him. When he saw Racer and Cindy, he got up and greeted them.

"I thought that you forgot about me. I hadn't heard from you in a while," said Sidney.

"Well, I have something for you," said Racer.

He handed Sidney the envelope with the letter from Danny inside. Racer explained to Sidney the circumstances behind the letter. Sidney shook his head and told Racer that he would get right on it.

"Thanks," said Racer. "I'll be waiting for your call."

When Cindy and Racer got back upstairs, they noticed that the light in Detman's office was on. Racer headed in that direction. Stepping into the office, Racer asked, "Did you hear about Danny Tonelli?"

"Yeah, I heard. Is his death going to hinder the investigation?" asked Detman.

"No, it shouldn't. As a matter of fact, it might help me when I have a chat with Susan Thompson."

"Remember, the captain wants his update tomorrow," said Detman.

Racer nodded and told Detman that he would catch him later. Heading back to his desk, Racer noticed Cindy talking with a couple of the other detectives by the coffee machine. Sitting down at his desk, he picked up the phone and dialed. It took a couple of minutes before Marge Smyth answered.

"Marge, this is Racer. Where can I meet you? Someplace private."

"It sounds important. How about two o'clock at the lake?" asked Marge.

"See you there," said Racer, hanging up.

Cindy returned just as Racer retrieved the metal box from the filing cabinet and placed it on the desk. Reaching into his pants pocket, Racer removed a penknife. Slipping the blade of the knife into the keyhole, he turned it forcibly back and forth until the lid popped open. Racer flipped the top open and looked inside. There were a number of envelopes with the initials of the dead women on them. He removed the first envelope with Elizabeth Farley's initials on it and opened it carefully. Inside he found several strips of negatives. He held them up to the light and saw that they were nothing you would write home to mother about. He passed them to Cindy and then took the next envelope. This one was for Barbara Molino. The contents were the same for each envelope that he opened.

"I'm sure that someone would be upset if they knew that we had this box," said Racer.

"And who do you think that person would be?" asked Cindy.

"It seems like the name Madeline Stein just keeps popping into my head," said Racer.

Before Racer closed the box there was one more envelope with the initials C.D. inside. It was the negatives that Danny had taken of Cindy in the dressing room at the Designer Dress Shop. As Racer started to hold them up to the light, Cindy grabbed them out of his hand.

"Whoa, wait a minute! They're evidence in a murder case," said Racer.

"Bull! I'm going to burn these," she replied.

Racer put all the envelopes back in the box and snapped the lid closed. There was nothing in there that could link Danny with anybody else. All it proved was he was a peeping tom.

"Do you think that Danny really killed himself?" asked Cindy.

"Yeah, I'm afraid so. Otherwise, he wouldn't have left the letter. Take the box with all the negatives down to Sidney and have them developed. Tell him to get anything else he can off the box and envelopes and make sure he keeps this quiet. Maybe those pictures can tell us something," said Racer.

"Do I have to give him all the negatives?" asked Cindy.

"You can keep yours out for now," replied Racer, "but we can't destroy them. At least, not yet. Sorry!"

Watching Cindy leave, Racer grabbed the phone and made another call. Twenty minutes later Cindy returned with the report from Sidney. She slid it across the desk. Cindy told him that there was nothing on the envelope but Danny's prints with the exception of Harlin's, the patrolman's and Racer's.

"I figured that. I was pretty sure that Danny committed suicide. Did you give him the negatives?"

"I sure did, and I told him to keep it under his hat," said Cindy.

"Good," said Racer, as the phone rang.

Racer grabbed the phone and listened for several seconds, nodding his head.

"Thanks Steve. I owe you one," said Racer, returning the phone to its cradle.

"Did Steve come up with something?" asked Cindy.

"Steve said he couldn't find any of the videos floating around, but he did find a couple of the photos that were used for advertising the films. He's going to drop them off at my apartment tonight, but that isn't the best part. Guess who bought up all the videos just after Mister Stein kicked the bucket?"

"Let me guess, Shane," said Cindy.

"Bingo! You have just won yourself a cigar," said Racer.

"Why would Shane buy up all the videos of Madeline Stein?" asked Cindy.

"Apparently, he was closer to Madeline then anyone thought, so close that he wanted to protect her or even one better: blackmail her later when he needed a little money."

"Do you really think that he was blackmailing her?" asked Cindy.

"No, more like her partner. You might have to get together with your buddy Mr. Clean one more time. I think there are a few questions I would like to get answered about Detective Shane. We have to be real careful that he doesn't get wind of it," said Racer.

"I don't know how willing Jim is going to be to talk to me again about Shane. I got the feeling that he wasn't going to say anymore on that subject," Cindy replied.

"Who else do you know in the Springdale department that could help us get a look at those files without anyone else knowing?" asked Racer.

"Jim was the only one that I knew and could trust," said Cindy.

"Damn! Who else could we trust?"

They both looked at each other and said, "Sidney."

"The departments share evidence at times and Sidney must have a contact there. Someone that could be trusted," said Racer.

Racer and Cindy pushed through the doors to the lab so loudly that all the technicians turned in their direction. Racer asked if Sidney was around and a tech pointed toward the photo lab. Racer left a message with the tech to have Sidney call him as soon as he was done. They headed back upstairs.

"I'm going to drop in on Susan Thompson. I want you to stay

here and wait for Sidney. Explain what we need and see if he can help us. I should be back in an hour or two," said Racer.

Racer pulled into the mall outside of the Designer Dress Shop and parked. He noticed Susan Thompson's dark Buick in one of the spaces reserved for the employees. He had an eerie feeling that someone was watching him. Slipping out of the ZX, Racer casually looked around but didn't see anyone. After entering the shop, he looked for Susan Thompson but didn't see her. There were two salesclerks in the store and both were busy with customers. He stood by the counter and waited. One of the clerks kept looking over his way and smiling.

At the first chance Racer had, he slipped behind the curtain into the back room. He peeked into the small office, which was empty. Making his way along the aisle, he came to the area that was directly behind the dressing room wall. Racer started going over the wall carefully. A lot of boxes were piled against it so he had to move them out of his way. There was a small sliding door hidden behind the boxes. He guessed that it probably looked directly into the dressing rooms. He put the boxes back and had just finished when a voice came from behind him.

"May I ask what you are doing back here?" asked the voice.

Racer turned and saw the salesclerk who had been smiling at him. He identified himself and asked if Susan Thompson was around. The salesclerk told him that Susan had taken a break in the coffee shop at the mall and would be back soon.

"I'll wait then."

The salesclerk looked at him for a moment and then explained that he shouldn't be in the back. It was strictly for employees. Racer apologized and followed the salesclerk back to the front of the shop. As they were walking, he asked her if she knew Danny Tonelli.

"Not really. I usually work nights and he worked days. I would only see him when we changed shifts," replied the clerk.

Just then the chimes on the front door sounded and Susan Thompson entered. When she saw Racer, her face turned ashen.

He moved along side of her and took her arm. "I think we need to talk in private. I have a couple of questions to ask you," he said.

Susan led Racer to the small office in the back and closed the door.

"When was the last time that you saw Danny alive?" asked Racer.

"Yesterday, just before he left the shop," replied Susan.

"Did anything seemed to be bothering him?"

"No, not at all. As a matter of fact, he seemed in an especially good mood."

"Do you have any idea what Danny did in his spare time?" asked Racer.

"How would I know that?" replied Susan.

"I thought maybe the two of you might have some of the same interests, say maybe photography," said Racer.

Her face went pale when Racer said that. She caught her breath before she told Racer that she and Danny didn't hang around together. Therefore, she had no idea if they had anything in common or not. They were just employees at the dress shop and they both worked for Madeline Stein. That was it.

"How far did the employee-employer relationship go?" asked Racer.

"I don't understand what you're asking," said Susan, puzzled.

"I think you do. I just want you to know that when Danny died, he left me a letter. He said that the only thing that he was guilty of was coercing young women into having their pictures taken."

"Look, Detective Racer, I don't know what Danny did on his own time and I don't much care, but if you have any accusations to make, then make them. Otherwise you can leave," said Susan.

"That's funny. That is just what Danny told me just before he turned up dead."

Susan got up and moved to the door. She opened it and stood there.

"Thanks, Susan, I'm sure we will be talking again soon. And next time it will be at the station," said Racer, getting up out of his chair.

Racer was thinking of his meeting with Marge Smyth on the way to the station. If he played his cards right, he could use the press to his advantage. He had to be real careful on what kind of information he gave her. If he leaked the right kind of story, it most assuredly would send some people scrambling. Susan Thompson had to be worried. Danny had taken the easy way out…if committing suicide was easy. It did prove one thing, that Danny Tonelli wasn't the killer.

Racer pulled his cell phone out and called Cindy to see if she had a chance to talk with Sidney. When he finally got her on the line, she told him that she was still waiting. Cindy also informed Racer that Amanda English had called and said that she had received a large brown envelope and would wait to hear from him before opening it. Racer told her to wait for Sidney and he would pick her up in an hour. Cindy acknowledged this and hung up. Racer made a U-turn and headed for Amanda English's place.

Parking in front of Amanda English's place, Racer got out of the car and headed for the front door. After knocking, he could hear someone approaching the door from the inside. It opened and Amanda was standing there.

"Detective Racer, I'm glad you got my message. Come on in."

Racer walked past her into a small hallway. To the left was the kitchen and small dining room, and to the right was the living room. Racer followed Amanda into the living room and took a seat on the sofa. Amanda picked up the brown envelope from the coffee table and sat down next to Racer.

"Is this the envelope you mentioned the other day?" asked Amanda.

"I'm pretty sure it is," replied Racer.

"Well, can I open it now?" asked Amanda.

"Amanda, the material that is in this envelope might not be something you would want anyone to see," cautioned Racer.

"You already have a good idea of what is in here, don't you?" she asked.

Racer nodded.

Amanda opened the envelope and removed its contents. There were several eight by ten photos. As Amanda looked at them, her hand went to her mouth and she gasped in shock. Racer slowly reached for the pictures. Amanda pulled them away. "I can't show these to you," said Amanda, embarrassed.

"Look, Amanda, I have a good idea what those pictures show. I do need to see them. It is real important to my case."

Amanda reluctantly handed the photos to Racer. Then she turned away from him. The photos were almost identical to the ones that Cindy received. One of the photos showed Amanda naked from the waist up. Racer took the pictures and put them back into the envelope. He explained that she would probably receive a phone call in a couple of days from someone trying to set up a meeting to talk about the pictures. The people who sent the photos were going to try and blackmail her.

"Amanda, if that call comes, agree to a meeting and then call me right away, even if they tell you not to contact the police," said Racer.

"You want me to meet these people? I can't do that," said Amanda, noticeably shaken.

"You aren't the first woman that this has happened to, but I want to make sure that you will be the last," said Racer. "Your safety is my main priority, and I won't let anything happen to you."

"All right, I'll do it," Amanda agreed reluctantly.

Racer told Amanda how much he appreciated her help. As he got up to leave, Racer could see Amanda's eyes riveted on the brown envelope in his hand. He did his best to assure her that he would take good care of the pictures in the brown envelope.

When Racer got back to the station it was deserted. He was steaming about those pictures of Amanda and thought about the women that were being taken advantage of. He knew that it was time to start squeezing some people. He was tired of playing games. He knew that Cindy and Amanda had received pictures but he didn't know how many others there were out there. When Sidney got those negatives developed, maybe he could get something off of them.

Racer went to his desk and found a note from Cindy. It told

him that Sidney had called and she was down in the lab. Racer looked at his watch: quarter to twelve. He didn't want to miss his appointment with Marge Smyth. Right now it might be the best weapon that he had available. He headed for the steps, and when he reached the lab, he saw Cindy and Sidney seated in his office. Racer headed right for it.

"Well, I got your pictures developed," said Sidney. "He had quite a collection of females there. There were a couple of pictures that had several people in them. I think you might be interested in them first. I was telling Cindy that I know a lab tech that works in the Springdale police department. We went to school together. We are pretty good friends. I think he can be trusted."

"Good," said Racer. "When can I meet him?"

"That's already taken care of. We will get together after work tonight at Barney's. Believe it or not, he never misses ladies' night," answered Cindy.

"Now can I get a look at those pictures?" asked Racer.

"Sure, they should be dried by now. You wait here and I'll go get them for you."

After Sidney was gone, Racer handed Cindy the brown envelope. She looked at the photos one at a time.

"These are almost identical to mine," said Cindy. "How did Amanda English take it?"

"She was embarrassed, but she did agree to help us. As soon as they make contact with her, she'll call me," said Racer.

"I'm still waiting for my call," said Cindy.

"We don't know how long it is from the time the victims receive the photos until they contact them," said Racer, just as Sidney returned to his office.

He had a packet of photos with him. Racer took them and started flipping through them one at a time. As he finished with one, he passed it to Cindy. There were photos of all the victims: Elizabeth Farley, Barbara Molino, Mary Wagner and Cheryl Portsmouth. There were also photos of three other women, including Cindy, but there was none of Amanda English. As Racer looked through them, he saw other people in the photos as Sidney had said. One was Danny, one was a young woman with blond hair and the last one was definitely Susan Thompson. Racer could see that Danny and the young woman were posing for the pictures, but Susan Thompson looked like she was arranging the people for the shots. That could mean Susan Thompson might be the photographer.

Racer started talking out loud. "Danny Tonelli was the catcher and also posed with the women. Susan Thompson was the photographer and Madeline Stein was the leader of the pack. She used her studio to develop the pictures and took care of marketing the finished product. She probably learned how to do that from her husband. But who the hell is the killer?" asked Racer.

"Good question. If we knew that we'd have the case solved," said Cindy.

Racer realized that he had been talking out loud.

"It has to be someone close to the operation. Someone who knows how the process works. Right now we know of two people who have access to a car like that. Susan Thompson owns one, and Robert Shane has one assigned to him through the Springdale police department. The statements from the security guard and Mrs. Caldwell indicate that it was a man that visited the victims just before they were killed."

"So you think it could be Shane?" asked Cindy.

"I don't know, but we have to see those files from the Stein pornography case."

Racer shoved the photos into the same envelope that contained Amanda English's pictures. Leaving the lab, Sidney said that they would all meet at Barney's around seven. After Sidney was out of sight, Racer took Cindy's arm and asked her what Sidney meant by "We'll all meet at Barney's." Cindy explained that she promised Sidney he could attend because it was his friend and he set up the meeting. She added that she didn't see any harm in it, and it might make his friend feel a little more relaxed.

"Okay, but you better keep an eye on Sidney. Remember, we have to keep this under our hat. Peterson can't catch wind of what's going on," said Racer.

When they left the station, Racer began to drive out of town. "I thought we were going to lunch," said Cindy.

"We are. We're going on a picnic lunch out at Miller lake."

On the way, Racer stopped at a sub shop and picked up a couple of sandwiches and some drinks. He figured they could get to the lake and have their lunch before Marge Smyth showed up.

The lake was completely deserted when they got there. Cindy was still leery of what was going on. Racer parked the car and they both headed over to a picnic table about 50 feet from the water. It was a beautiful day. The sky was partly cloudy and the temperature was in the eighties though Cindy could feel coolness coming off the water.

After they sat down, Racer pulled the sandwiches and sodas from the bag and placed them on the table.

"Are you going to tell me what we are doing here?" asked Cindy.

"What do you mean? We're here to have lunch," he replied.

Cindy glared at him and bit down on her sub.

After they were finished, Racer collected the garbage and dumped it into one of the barrels. Then he strolled down to the water's edge. Cindy watched and wondered how everybody saw Racer as such a hard guy. She enjoyed working with him. She knew that he was tough and could bend the rules to suit him, but he also had his good side. She would never hesitate, knowing that Racer had her back. As she was staring at the water, she could feel someone standing behind her. Cindy jumped up and turned to see Marge Smyth standing nearby. Now she knew why they were there. Racer had set up a meet.

"Where's your partner?" asked Marge.

"He's down by the water. I'll get him," said Cindy.

Cindy walked down to get Racer. He was standing by the water's edge throwing stones into the lake like a little kid.

"Marge Smyth is here looking for you. Why didn't you tell me that was why we were here?" asked Cindy.

"Cindy, you have to understand that this has to be kept extremely quiet," said Racer. "No exceptions. Not even Detman can find out. The less everyone knows the better off we'll be. If you have any reservations about what I'm doing, then you better go sit in the car. I don't want to drag you into anything that you're not comfortable with."

"I understand what's going on and you don't have to worry about me. But you could have trusted me," said Cindy.

"I did," said Racer. "You're here."

"What's up?" asked Marge lighting a French cigarette.

"If I give you a story that is newsworthy, how soon would it appear in the paper?" asked Racer, sitting down across from her.

"Hey, if it is something real good, I still have time to catch the morning edition," said Marge, leaning on the picnic table with both elbows.

"Look, I want to make a deal with you, but you have to keep it confidential."

"I'm listening," said Marge, completely focused on Racer.

"I'm going to tell you a story that I want you to print, but you can't ask any questions right now. If everything comes out the way I plan, I'll give you the exclusive rights to the entire story. How does that sound?" said Racer, cocking his head toward Marge.

"Pretty damn vague. It's hard to say yes when I don't even know what the hell you are talking about," she replied, blowing smoke out the side of her mouth.

"Remember, you came to me asking questions concerning the recent murders," said Racer.

"Yeah, I remember, and you basically told me to go to hell. But now I guess you can use old Marge."

"I think that it will be advantageous to both of us. But you have to promise to print only what I tell you," said Racer seriously.

"And if I do this, you will give me the exclusive rights to the entire story?"

"That's the deal," said Racer.

After his meeting with Marge Smyth, Racer told Cindy this was the leverage that he needed to create a crack between Susan Thompson and Madeline Stein. As they drove back toward town, Cindy asked, "When did you decide to call Smith?"

"I came up with the idea yesterday and phoned her," replied Racer. "You have to realize that what I just did could get me kicked off the force. So it was real important not to have anybody eavesdrop on us. That way, I knew no one would find out."

"I understand. You're secret is safe with me," said Cindy.

Racer said that he had to make a quick stop by his apartment to see if Steve had dropped off those pictures that he had come up with.

When Racer got to his apartment, he parked the ZX out in front and asked Cindy if she would like to come in for a few minutes. She accompanied Racer inside.

Unlocking the door to his apartment, he held it open so Cindy could enter. There was an envelope lying on the floor. It must have been slid under the door. Racer picked it up and moved toward the kitchen while Cindy slowly took in the apartment.

"You might as well sit down for a few minutes while we take a look at what Steve came up with," said Racer, ripping open the envelope. Inside were two black and white pictures. It appeared as if a professional took them. The first one showed a young girl standing next to a large dog. She wore a fluffy bath robe open at the top to reveal an ample amount of the girl's cleavage. One of her legs was visible under the robe. The girl looked like she had blond hair. The second photo was of the same girl, and this one was taken from behind. The robe had slipped to the floor and she was standing there naked. Her back was to the camera but she was half twisted around so you could see a partial shot of her face. Racer was sure that they had been taken for promotional purposes.

"Well, what do you think? Is it Madeline Stein or not?" asked Racer.

"It's not real easy to tell. Not only are they in black and white but they're so grainy."

"I know, but they might be good enough to shake Miss Stein up."

"But what if it isn't her?" asked Cindy.

"Then we'll all be shocked," replied Racer.

Cindy put the two pictures side by side and studied them.

Racer glanced at his wall clock and saw it was getting close to five. He asked if she was getting hungry. Cindy held her hand up and then turned the photos toward Racer.

"Look at the bottom right hand corner of each photo and tell me what you see."

Racer studied the pictures one at a time. After a few seconds he said, "What am I suppose to be looking for?"

"There appears to be some kind of writing here," said Cindy. "Like it might have been erased."

"So?" asked Racer.

"What if the person in the picture had autographed those photos and then later it was removed for some reason?"

"Then we'll see how good Sidney really is. Maybe he can raise that writing for us," said Racer, placing the photos back into the envelope. "We better get going."

It was five-thirty when they arrived at Barney's. The crowd was still sparse and there was plenty of places to sit. Racer wanted to make sure that they had a table with a little privacy, so he picked a table on the opposite side of the room. Racer left Cindy sitting at the table and went to the bar. Barney was sitting at one end, watching some court show on television. "Hey, can I get some service here?" asked Racer.

"Just keep your pants on. I'm the only one here right now," said Barney.

Barney's bartenders didn't come on until seven. When he finally broke away, Barney poured Racer a beer and mixed a Tom Collins for Cindy. Barney put the drinks in front of Racer as he tossed a twenty on the bar. Racer picked up the drinks and headed back to the table.

It was around six when Sidney showed up with his friend in tow. Racer waved to them as they came in. When they got to the table, Racer asked what everyone was drinking and headed back to the bar. Barney took his order and started getting the drinks. As Racer waited, he looked around: The place was starting to fill up. Everyone wanted to get a good seat for the show, which Racer found out was a bikini contest. Returning to the table, Racer found Cindy, Sidney and his friend were all involved in conversation.

Racer passed the drinks out and sat down. He listened to Sidney tell everyone how much he liked working in the lab and how seriously he took his job. And then he realized that he forgot to introduce his friend.

"Everyone, this is my friend David Hughes. He is a lab tech with the Springdale police department," said Sidney. "I'm sure he will be able to help us."

"You can call me Dave. All my friends do."

"Well, let's get started," said Racer. "What I really need is a look at the file from the Stein pornography case that detective Robert Shane worked on. I want to know if you can help us with that."

"That could be a big problem," said Dave, his smile fading immediately. "The file has been sealed under court order and it can't be opened for another two years."

"Who sealed it?" asked Racer.

"Detective Shane had one of the county judges do it because of its sensitive material, since it concerns some of the local citizens," answered Dave. "The judge agreed."

"So you're telling me there is no way to get a look at that file for another two years?" said Racer.

"Not exactly. There is a way, but it will be risky, and if we get caught it could cost us our jobs for ignoring a court order," replied Dave.

"This is only between me and you. There is no reason for anyone else to take a chance. Everyone knows that I'm the black sheep in the department. That's why I got demoted to Traffic," said Racer, sternly. "So David, what's your plan?"

As Racer drove Cindy home, he could tell that she was still disappointed. She hadn't said a word since they left Barney's. He pulled the ZX to the curb in front of her apartment and, before he could say good night, she was half way to the front entrance. Racer waited until he could see the lights in her apartment go on. He felt bad about cutting her out but it was the only way. If Peterson found out about him getting into a closed file, it would be adios. And he didn't want to catch her up in that.

On the ride home, his mind became a total blank. It was the first time since he started this case that it wasn't working overtime. Raindrops started hitting his windshield, and he watched them as they became streams flowing down into the cavern where the wipers hid. He felt totally relaxed. As a matter of fact, he was so relaxed that he almost ran off the road.

Racer wasn't home 10 minutes when the phone rang. He was almost tempted to let it ring but instead he picked it up. It was Cindy on the other end.

"Racer, I have something you might want to listen to." It was Cindy.

"When I got home I turned on my answering machine and there was a message for me. It isn't your everyday message."

Telling Cindy that he was on his way, Racer hung up the phone and rushed back out to his car. As he raced to Cindy's apartment, unpleasant thoughts were running through his head. He flew into the driveway, hit the brakes, jumped out, and jogged all the way to the entrance. When he got to Cindy's apartment, he only had to knock once and the door opened. Cindy was wearing a cream-colored robe closed tightly around her body. Racer went directly to the couch and sat down. Cindy went to the answering machine and hit the play button. In a split second, a voice came on.

"Cindy my darling, I know you're a cop. You better keep your nose out of my business or that pretty face of yours won't be so pretty. Pleasant dreams." Then the phone went dead.

Racer looked at Cindy, and he could tell that she was a little shaken by this.

"Do you recognize the voice?" he asked.

Cindy shook her head.

"One thing we know for sure: Its a man's voice," said Racer.

"Do you think that's our killer?" asked Cindy.

"I would say that it's a pretty good chance," said Racer.

"But why did he risk calling me?"

"Look at it this way. Danny Tonelli took some illicit pictures of you in the changing room with the possibility of coercing you into a photo session. But someone else also saw those pictures and checked them out. Someone with connections. Someone who knows you're a cop."

"But why would they threaten a cop?" asked Cindy.

"You aren't only a cop, but you're also a woman with a pretty face," said Racer. "They probably think they can intimidate you. They also know that you have seen the bodies they've left behind. So they plant a seed and wait to see how it grows."

"Do you think that it's Shane that's doing the killing?" asked Cindy.

"He's the only one I can think of that had the inside dope on this porn ring. Then he builds a close relation with Madeline Stein to maneuver his way in. He could easily find out who the women were and use his badge to get into their homes. He knows how the system works, so it's easy for him to cover his tracks."

"And that is why you need to get into that file," said Cindy.

"That's why. I'm sorry if you're disappointed. I'm not cutting you out of the case. I just don't want you to lose a promising career for a stunt that I pull. I'll keep you filled in on everything I find out," said Racer, with his hands folded in front of him.

"Just be careful," said Cindy, with a forced smile.

Racer nodded as he said, "I better get going. We have a meeting with Peterson in the morning and after he reads his morning paper, he might not be in such a good mood."

"You think this article will work?" asked Cindy.

"I don't know, but I sure hope it will. Maybe the killer will think twice before he commits another murder," said Racer.

He got up and walked toward the door with Cindy beside him. When they got there, he turned to face her. She leaned over and kissed him on the cheek.

"What's that for?" he asked in surprise.

"That's for trying to protect me," replied Cindy.

Racer looked deep into her eyes and was hypnotized for a second. He finally broke the trance and left before he did something stupid.

CHAPTER SEVENTEEN

On the way to the station the next morning, Racer stopped off at a convenience store to pick up the morning paper. When he got back into his car, he opened the paper to find the article written by Marge Smyth, which was right on the front page in the lower right hand corner.

DOES CRIME PAY

The latest murders that have plagued Fairfield since June may be linked to a pornography ring that is taking advantage of young women in this town to satisfy their lust for sex. According to reliable sources, the women are most likely being drugged and used by the leaders of the ring to fill their fantasies. Once they have been used, they are discarded and left for dead.

The local police won't comment on this case, but sources have suggested that some very prominent local people might be involved.

This ring might be linked to the pornographic activities that took place in Springdale several years ago. Some of the original members of the Stein pornography case might have resurrected their business, thinking that there is still money to be made. If you have been caught up in this illegal business and found yourself lucky to escape any injury, please contact the Fairfield Police Department. All contacts will be kept in strict confidence.

Racer read the article and thought that Marge did a pretty good job with the little bit of information that he gave her. Now, maybe this would rattle a few cages and at least keep anyone else from getting hurt. *This should really spice up the meeting with Peterson this morning*, Racer thought as he started up the car.

Detman was sitting on Racer's desk waiting for him when he got to the squad room.

"You know the captain is going to go through the roof when he reads this story," said Detman, tossing a paper on the desk. "Do you know anything about it?"

"Hey look, this reporter has been following me around ever since I got this case," said Racer. "She apparently has finally put two and two together and is coming up with four."

"How close is she?" asked Detman.

Racer just shook his head. With that, Detman slid off Racer's desk and headed back to his office. As Cindy walked up she caught the end of the conversation.

"Apparently, people have been reading the paper already," said Cindy.

"Yeah, when I got here Detman was waiting for me."

"Did you tell him where the story came from?" asked Cindy in a hushed voice.

"Heck no," said Racer. "But I'm sure he has a pretty good idea."

Cindy asked, "Do you think it will show dividends?"

"I sure hope so. After our meeting with Peterson, we are going to pay Susan Thompson another visit and see if she has a change of heart about talking to us."

"What about Madeline Stein?" asked Cindy.

"We'll get to her later. I want as much ammunition as I can get before I speak to her again," said Racer.

Just then the phone rang. They both looked at it and Racer picked it up. He was sure that it was Peterson. Instead, it was Sidney. He informed Racer that the pictures of Misty Blue were done. Racer said that Cindy would be right down to get them.

When she was gone, he called Susan Thompson's home. He let the phone ring about 20 times before he hung up. As he placed the receiver in the cradle, the phone rang immediately. It was Peterson's secretary. The captain wanted to see him in five minutes. Racer told her that he'd be there. Racer checked his watch and waited for Cindy. When he saw her starting to enter the squad room, he got up to meet her.

"We have an appointment with the captain," said Racer.

When they got upstairs, Peterson's secretary told them to have a seat. While they were waiting, Racer wanted to know what Sidney found out. Cindy pulled the pictures from the envelope and handed them to Racer. On the bottom corner of each picture there was a signature. Racer had to look closely to make it out. He read it in a whisper, "With love, Misty Blue. Now we have to see if we can match this to Madeline Stein's handwriting."

Before Cindy could answer, the secretary told them the captain would see them now.

They both went to his office door and gave a brief knock.

"Come in," Peterson's voice boomed.

They pushed the large oak door open and entered. Peterson wasn't sitting behind his desk. Instead he was over on the leather couch, sitting next to Detman. They were discussing something quietly. Peterson looked up and motioned for Racer and Cindy to have a seat. He finished what he was saying to Detman and moved back behind his desk. Peterson seemed unusually calm at the moment.

"Well, what do the two of you have for me this morning?" asked Peterson.

"Captain, we have a pretty good idea that the four victims were unwilling members of a pornography ring being run between here and Springdale. We suspect that the victims were being blackmailed, drugged and then taken advantage of," said Racer.

"I already know that much. What I'm trying to figure out is why I had to read it in the *Fairfield Press* instead of hearing it from my own detectives. I already placed a call to Marge Smyth and asked her who her source was but, as you can guess, she told me that information was confidential. You don't have any idea who leaked this information?" Peterson yelled, his face turning red.

"I don't have any idea. It could have come from anybody associated with the case," said Racer.

"Tell me, detective, is there anything else I should know about this case? Or should I wait to get my information from the newspaper?" said Peterson.

"Only one thing," said Racer. "We know that Danny Tonelli was right in the middle of this whole mess."

"Do you think that he was the killer?" asked Peterson.

"No, sir, just one of the drones."

"Who else do you think is involved?" asked Peterson.

"Right now, we're not quite sure. We are presently questioning some of his known associates," answered Racer.

"You better not be holding anything back on me," shouted Peterson. "The chief has already been on the phone and he isn't happy about this leak. The press has been bugging the hell out of him and he keeps telling them that there is nothing to report, and then this story surfaces. It makes him look like an idiot. From now on, I want you two clowns to keep Detman posted on every move you make. Do I make myself understood?"

Racer and Cindy both nodded.

"Good, then get your butts out of here," said Peterson, shooing them away.

Heading for the stairs, they heard Detman calling them. They ignored him.

They slid into Racer's ZX and pulled out of the lot, headed for the Designer Dress Shop. They had to get a sample of Madeline Stein's handwriting for comparison. Cindy mentioned that if they went to the dress shop, they might spook her. So she told Racer she had a better idea. "Her bank must have a signature card or canceled check on file."

"Good thinking. Now where does she do her banking?" asked Racer.

"First National on Cherry Street," said Cindy. "I remember from the background check I did on her."

When they arrived at the bank, Racer showed his badge and told the guard they needed to speak with the bank manager. The guard escorted them through a group of cubicles and stopped in front of a glass door. The black lettering on the door read, Oliver Henderson, Bank Manager. The guard tapped on the door, and led them in. After introducing Racer and Cindy, the guard excused himself.

"Good morning, I'm Oliver Henderson, the bank manager," said the elderly gentleman in a three-piece suit. "What can I do for you this morning?"

"Well, sir, we are here on official police business. We understand that Madeline Stein has her accounts here. We need to get a copy of her signature card," said Racer.

"Is Miss Stein in some kind of trouble?" asked Mr. Henderson, a little concerned.

"No, sir," replied Racer. "We need the signature so we can verify some documents presented to us. But this has to be kept confidential. Not even Miss Stein can know."

"Detective Racer, you understand that bank records are confidential documents. I'm afraid without Miss Stein's permission I can't give you anything," said Mr. Henderson.

"I'm not asking for you to divulge any information about her accounts. All I'm asking for is a copy of her signature. I'm sure that it wouldn't hurt anyone."

"No one will know where you got the signature?" asked Mr. Henderson.

"Correct, sir," said Racer.

"Wait here and I'll see what I can do for you," said Mr. Henderson as he got up from his desk and left the office.

"Think he will give it to us?" asked Cindy.

"I don't know why not. All those cards are used for is to verify the signature of the person wanting access to their safety deposit box. Those cards are kept in a metal file box sitting on the desk of the bank receptionist, where anyone can view them."

Mr. Henderson was gone only a short time. When he returned, he had a manila folder with him. Opening the file, Mr. Henderson slid a photocopy of the signature card across the desk to Racer.

"I really appreciate this," said Racer. "You have no idea how this will help us."

"I hope this helps you verify those documents for Miss Stein," said Henderson, as he shook hands with Racer and Cindy.

When they got outside, Racer told Cindy that he had a person in mind that would be able to match those signatures. She nodded, and they both got into the car.

"Who is this person we are going to see?" asked Cindy.

"Someone that I met a few years ago. He's real good at what he does," said Racer.

Racer pulled up in front of an old dilapidated building on Fellows Street. The building looked like it should have been condemned years ago.

When they got inside, there was some semblance of a front desk, but Racer never stopped. Up the steps he went. When they reached the second floor, Racer turned right and stopped at apartment 209. He put his ear to the door first and then knocked loudly. Cindy stood back by the stairs, her hand on the butt end of her Sig Sauer. She could see the door open a crack. Racer put his hand on the door, gave it a push and disappeared inside. Cindy ran to the door, not knowing what to think. Racer was standing next to a man in his fifties in pajamas and a bathrobe. She gazed past them and saw that the apartment looked like a bomb had just been dropped on it.

"What the hell are you doing here?" said the man to Racer.

"I need a favor," said Racer, seriously.

"That's all you ever want. When will my debt be paid?" asked the man.

"Look, all I want is you to match up a couple of signatures for me," said Racer, showing the man a twenty.

The man snatched the twenty and said, "Give me the damn signatures and let me take a look at them. Remember, this is the last time. No more favors."

Racer handed the man the signature card and the two photos of Misty Blue. He took them and disappeared into another room.

"Who is that man?" asked Cindy.

"He was my first partner on the force," said Racer.

"What happened to him?" asked Cindy.

"We made a raid on a warehouse one night. There was a ring of kids stealing electronics from local stores. He went in the front and I took the back. All I heard was a gunshot. I ran in and found him lying on the floor with a young kid standing over him with a gun. The kid was in shock. I walked up and took the gun away from the kid and knelt over Arnie. All he could say was, they're only kids, only kids. I found out that the bullet hit his kidney and caused considerable damage. The doctor told him that he wouldn't be able to return to the streets, so the department gave him a desk job. He couldn't handle it and went out on a disability retirement a year later."

"And that is why he is so angry at you?" said Cindy.

"You see, Arnie didn't want me to press charges against the kid holding the gun. He wanted me to go easy on him. He said the kid had his whole life in front of him and he didn't want me to ruin it. Arnie tried to convince me that the shooting was an accident."

"And you wouldn't do it," said Cindy.

"He was pissed off at me for a long time," said Racer. "I guess you could say he still is. But at least we have an understanding now."

Cindy's eyes went pass Racer and focused on the man who had just entered the room. He confirmed that the signatures matched. There was no doubt. Racer thanked him. On the way out, they could still hear Arnie grumbling.

It was now time to pay a visit to Susan Thompson and see if she had a change of heart.

First, Racer checked the Designer Dress Shop only to find it was Susan Thompson's day off. Sliding in next to Cindy, Racer checked his notebook to see where Susan lived. Pulling back out on the street, Racer headed south on Callie Drive.

Turning onto Hunington Lane, Racer approached Susan's house. He noticed that a dark colored Buick was parked in the driveway. Parking across the street, they walked over to the house. The house appeared quiet. The shades were pulled tight and the outside lights were still on. Racer knocked on the front door and they waited. No answer. He motioned for Cindy to take a look around back. She disappeared around the corner of the garage. Racer knocked again, with a little more authority. He was just about to give up when he heard the lock draw back and the door open.

Expecting Susan Thompson, instead Racer found himself staring at a well-built guy standing in the doorway. Racer guessed that he was probably six-foot-four and in the neighborhood of two hundred and twenty pounds. He had a mustache and light beard and looked to be in his mid-thirties. Racer could see that he must have woken him up.

"Yeah, what do you want?" asked the guy.

"I'm looking for Susan Thompson," said Racer, as he flashed his shield.

"What is this all about?" asked the guy.

"I have some questions to ask her. May I ask who you are?" asked Racer.

"I'm Brian," said the guy. "Susan's my mother."

"Well Brian, can I talk with your mother?" asked Racer.

"She's not here. When she has the weekend off, she goes up to Harper's lake. We have a cabin up there," answered Brian.

"When do you expect her back?"

"Not until late Sunday night," said Brian. "Now can I go back to sleep?"

"Sure," said Racer. "Oh, by the way, do you mind if we take a look at the Buick?"

"Why?" asked Brian.

"We've received a report of a stolen car similar to your mother's. We just want to make sure that everything is okay," said Racer.

"I don't see any harm in that," said Brian. "Wait, I'll get the keys."

While Brian went back inside, Racer walked over to Cindy.

"I didn't know she had a son," said Cindy.

"Me either. Susan isn't home. Apparently she goes away for the weekends. She has a cabin at Harper's Lake," said Racer.

"That's a good two hours drive from here," said Cindy. "And as I remember, it's pretty secluded up there."

Brian Thompson returned to the front door with a set of car keys in his hand.

"Isn't this your mother's car?" asked Racer.

"It is," said Brian.

"Then how did she get to the lake?" asked Racer.

"Oh, I have a Trans Am and mom loves to drive it, so we switch cars sometimes."

Brian walked over to the Buick and unlocked the driver's side door. As he did, the phone inside the house started ringing. Brian excused himself and left them alone with the car. Racer unlocked the back door and crawled inside. Cindy was already in the front seat. They went over the car the best they could in the short amount of time they had. Cindy was ready to pull the trunk release when Brian returned.

"I really have to go," said Brian. "I got called into work early."

"Sure, thanks for your help," said Racer, as Brian ran back into the house.

As they walked back to Racer's car, Cindy said, "We might have another suspect. Brian Thompson had access to the Buick and could have known what his mom was involved in."

"I agree that he had access to the car. I wish we could have gotten a peek in the trunk but I'm not so sure that he is aware of what his mother is doing," said Racer. "Besides, would you tell your son that good old mom is involved in a porno ring?"

"Maybe you're right, said Cindy. "I'll run him through the system anyway."

CHAPTER EIGHTEEN

Racer's cell phone rang. He recognized the number right away. Answering the call, it was Marge Smyth on the line.

"Yeah, what's up?" asked Racer.

"I received a strange phone call about an hour ago. It was a male voice warning me that if I want to stay healthy I had to drop the story on the pornography ring," said Marge.

"Did you recognize the voice?" asked Racer.

"No, but it was real convincing," replied Marge.

"If you need protection, I'll arrange it for you," said Racer.

"Thanks but no thanks," said Marge. "I've had phone calls like this before. It usually is nothing but noise."

"Okay, but be careful. If anything else happens, call me right away."

After hanging up, Racer thought, *That article is already showing results. If the killer's making threatening phone calls, it wouldn't be long before he'll make a mistake.* Racer looked up as Cindy returned from running Brian Thompson's name through the system.

"Nothing," said Cindy. "He has no record on file here or in Springdale, so I'm running him through the FBI's computers. We should hear something before the end of the day."

"No use waiting around here. Want to take a ride?" asked Racer.

"Sure, where to?" asked Cindy.

"Let's see if we can find the Thompson place at Harper's Lake," replied Racer.

Race pulled off the highway into a dirt parking lot. There were two gas pumps positioned in front of a small grocery store. The place looked like something out of the fifties. The pumps had lighted globes on top, with the flying horse emblem stenciled on them. The store reminded him of the Beverly Hillbillies. It was made out of weathered wood with scrubbing boards and wash tubs hanging from the walls. He could imagine what the inside looked like.

Entering the store, Racer headed for the counter and Cindy headed for the cooler. Racer could see an old woman, probably in her seventies, manning the cash register. Racer wanted to know if she could point out the directions to the Thompson cabin.

The woman studied him before she answered, "When you leave here you take a left. Go up the hill until you get right on top. There is a road to the right. Go down that road until you come to the lake. Turn left and it's the fourth cabin."

"Thanks a lot. I really appreciate it," said Racer as he paid for the sodas.

Racer followed the old woman's directions. When they got to the road by the lake, Racer made the left and started counting off cabins until he came to the fourth one. A sign hanging from one of the trees alongside of the driveway read, *Jim Thompson's Place—No Trespassing*. Racer pulled into the stone-covered driveway and followed it up to a cedar log cabin with a large screened-in porch. He brought the ZX to a stop and mentioned to Cindy that the place looked deserted. He didn't see any car parked outside.

Racer and Cindy got out and looked around. The cabin was surrounded with pine trees and it faced the lake. The air was cooler there than in the city. It was quiet except for the birds chirping. Racer asked Cindy to see if anyone was home. While he took a look around back.

There was a good size building right behind the cabin. Walking up to it, he tried to see inside, but there were drawn curtains on all the windows. Trying the front and side doors, he found them both locked. Then he noticed that there was a window up by the peak of the roof that had no curtains on it. As he stood staring up at the window, Cindy came up behind him. "It appears no one is home," she said.

"Let's see if we can find a ladder around here," said Racer.

They found an old wooden ladder by a woodpile. They carried the ladder over to the building and stood it up so it came to rest right under the window. He made sure that the ladder was steady and told Cindy to hold on to it. He climbed the rungs one at a time until he came to the window. It was dirty but he cleaned it off with the side of his hand. The only thing that he could see was a loft filled with cardboard boxes. He noticed a hole in the floor that must have led to the floor below. Racer tried the window, which was unlocked. Looking around, Racer slid the window up. In a second, he was inside.

Once inside, he immediately went to the hole in the floor. There was a fold-up ladder that had been left in the down position. Racer slowly descended the ladder, careful to make sure that no one was there. Seeing that he was alone, he went right to the front door and slipped the bolt back. "Look what I found," he said. "It's a photo studio." Racer helped Cindy return the ladder back to where they found it. Then they entered the building together.

The first room was set up like a miniature photo studio. There were a couple of hi-tech cameras mounted on tripods, lighting, and several different background scenes. One was a bedroom scene and the other was a scene that could be converted from a living room to a den to a fun room, set up with toys that were definitely not for children.

"I think we just found where the photo sessions took place," replied Racer. "It's nice and secluded. Out of the way. Not easy for anybody to see what is going on."

Racer asked Cindy to keep an eye out for anybody while he looked around. Cindy went outside and leaned against the car as Racer started to go through the place. He made sure that he put everything back exactly where he found it. Looking around, he found 35mm film, stacks of negatives of the local landscape and several photos of Susan's son. All of a sudden he heard the car horn blow. Racer moved to the door and watched as a car turned into the driveway. Racer slipped the latch and closed the door behind him. He walked over to where Cindy was standing and waited.

It was a Trans Am, the car Brian Thompson had described.

Susan Thompson got out of the car and was totally surprised to see Racer and Cindy standing in her driveway.

"How did you know where I was?" asked Susan, surprised.

"We stopped by your house and Brian told us where we could find you," said Racer.

"I see. I like to come up here on the weekends to get away from the city. My husband inherited this place before we were married and when he died, I just couldn't give it up."

"I can't blame you," said Cindy. "It's gorgeous up here."

"Why don't you come in and I'll get you something cool to drink," said Susan, leading them to the cabin.

When they were inside, she motioned for Cindy and Racer to have a seat around a solid wood table on the screened porch. Leaving them for a couple of minutes, she returned with a tray holding a pitcher of lemonade with three glasses full of ice. Placing it on the table, she took the pitcher and poured each one of them a glass of lemonade. After everyone was settled, Susan finally asked what they were doing there.

"I think you have a good idea. Our investigation has uncovered your operation," said Racer.

"What operation are we talking about?" asked Susan, acting surprised.

"The operation of taking pictures of unsuspecting victims at the dress shop and coercing these women into posing for you," said Racer.

"I don't have any idea what you are talking about," said Susan Thompson sternly.

"Well, let me enlighten you. There's a secret panel behind the dressing rooms where Danny Tonelli would take photos of unsuspecting women trying on sexy garments. The film is given to Madeline Stein, who uses her studio in Springdale to develop it. A set of proofs are given back to Danny for delivery to the victims, with a note inside blackmailing them. The victims then get a phone call setting up a meeting. At the meeting in some nice restaurant, the victims are drugged, I'm guessing with one of those date rape drugs. This way they would do whatever you wanted."

"All I'm hearing is Danny took the pictures, Madeline Stein

developed them and Danny drugged the women. Why are you coming to me?" asked Susan, nervously.

"Once the victims were drugged, they were driven up here and the photo sessions began. When it was over, they were returned to their home and that was that. One big problem came up, though. The women started turning up dead. What happened? Did they threaten to go to the cops so they had to be eliminated?" asked Racer.

"That is quite a story, detective, but I don't know anything about it," replied Susan.

"This could be a big problem for you, Susan. We can prove everything. You see, that's what happened to Danny. He realized that we were getting close, so he took the easy way out. He'd still be alive if he would have worked with us," said Racer.

"Supposing you're right, what do I get?" asked Susan.

"I'll do everything I possibly can to get you immunity from prosecution, but I can't promise you anything until you tell me what you know," said Racer.

"Let me think about this," said Susan with a worried look in her eyes.

"I'll give you 20 minutes and that's it. Then I'll have to get a warrant for your arrest."

"I will tell you one thing and that's the fact that Madeline Stein is not behind this so-called operation," said Susan.

"Think about what I said. You have 20 minutes."

Cindy and Racer got up and headed outside. Walking down to the lake Racer checked his watch. Lingering by the lake, they never let the cabin out of their sight. They were there about 30 minutes when Racer motioned for them to head back to the cabin.

When they got to the front door, Racer knocked but on one answered. He tried the door and it was open. They both stepped into the cabin with their weapons drawn. They checked each room but no Susan Thompson. When they got to the back door, Racer could see someone moving in the building behind the cabin. Racer called to Cindy and they both rushed toward the building. Racer signaled for Cindy to watch the front while he headed around to the side door. He squeezed in and closed the door behind him. Susan was in the front room where all the equipment was set up. Racer made it to the doorway and stopped. Susan was by a small desk, going through a box of papers. He stood there watching her. He wanted to see what she was up to before approaching her.

After shuffling through the papers, Susan stopped and began to read a sheet of paper with a picture stapled to it. Then, all of a sudden, she ripped up the paper and picture. After tossing it into a trash can, she went back to the box of papers.

"Time's up," said Racer as he holstered his weapon and stepped into the room.

Susan must have jumped a foot off the floor. She was noticeably startled. "I was going through some of my old papers and cleaning house," said Susan.

"How convenient. Then you don't mind if I have a look."

"I believe the law says something about having a warrant before you can go through people's things," said Susan.

"Not if that person gives you permission. Look, Susan, believe it or not, I'm trying to help you. You know that four women are dead. Four women you photographed. Don't you think that's strange? And if you continue to withhold information, I won't be able to help you anymore. That means you could wind up going to prison not only for pornography but as accessory to murder."

As Racer talked, he moved over to the front door and let Cindy in.

Susan finally gave in. "Okay, what do you want to know?"

"The best thing to do is start at the beginning," said Racer pulling a notebook and pen from his jacket pocket.

Susan took a deep breath, and explained to Racer and Cindy that after Madeline Stein found out about her being an amateur photographer, with her own studio, she was approached about using her studio for photo sessions. "She wanted a chance to see my studio, and she told me that if it met with her approval she would pay me $500 a session, plus expenses. Since it was a time in my life when I was in a financial bind, I jumped at the chance."

"Madeline Stein never said what kind of pictures she was talking about?" asked Cindy.

"No, I didn't find out until later," said Susan. "Madeline told me that she would take the film and develop it at her studio in Springdale."

"What happened after that?" asked Racer.

"One day Madeline took a ride up here and looked the place over and was impressed, especially by how secluded it was. She felt that it would be perfect for what she wanted to do. A few weeks later she came up to me with an address and told me to be there at nine o'clock that night."

"Didn't you ask any questions?" asked Racer.

"I started to but she just walked away," said Susan.

"Do you remember the date for that first session?" asked Racer.

"All I can remember is it was three days before that first girl was killed," said Susan. "I packed up my equipment and headed for the address that Madeline had given me. When I got their, I found Madeline, Danny Tonelli, and some girl that I never saw before. This is when Madeline explained that I was going to shoot some photos of this girl in a variety of poses and backgrounds. The photos would then be presented to a leading men's magazine," said Susan.

"How did you feel about that?" asked Racer.

"I didn't ask a whole lot of questions. The woman seemed loose and enjoying herself. She did everything that was asked without any complaints. She even threw in a few poses herself. When we finished the session, Madeline took the film and the girl got to keep the clothes. I never saw the finished photos. Madeline kept them," said Susan.

"Did anyone stayed behind? Or went back for anything?" asked Racer.

"No, we all left together," replied Susan.

"Why did you say that you thought that Madeline wasn't the leader?" asked Racer.

"Just a couple of things that happened during the last few months. Madeline was chewing Danny out for something and she mentioned that the boss would not like it if he found out," said Susan, staring up at both of them.

"Those were the words that she used?" asked Racer.

"Yes, the exact words. Another time, when we came out of one of the shoots, there was a car parked across the street. Madeline walked over to it and talked to someone inside. I'm pretty sure that it was a man, though I never really got a good look."

"What kind of car was this person driving?" asked Racer.

"It was similar to mine, a dark blue or black Buick," replied Susan.

"Have you been told of any more photo sessions that will be coming up?" asked Racer.

"Yes, that is why I'm up here this weekend. I'm getting the studio ready for a session that is supposed to take place either Wednesday or Thursday."

"How is this next session supposed to be set up?" asked Racer.

"I don't know. I asked who was going to take Danny's place and she told me that wasn't my business."

"So you really don't know who the subject is then?" asked Racer.

"I have no idea," replied Susan.

"I want you to go along with the plan," said Racer. "I'll get in touch with you on Tuesday and tell you exactly what I want you to do."

"I'll do whatever you want," said Susan, her eyes filling with tears.

Racer decided that it was time to head back. He reminded Susan not to mention a word to anybody about their conversation.

Racer and Cindy got back to the station around six. Walking to his desk, Racer found several messages waiting for him. "Let me take a look at these and then we can get out of here," he said.

After reading one of the messages, Racer picked up the phone and dialed.

"Hi, this is Detective Racer, I got your message. No, that's okay, I'll be right over," said Racer and then he hung up the phone.

"Who was that?" asked Cindy.

Racer held his hand up and dialed Marge Smyth's number. She had left a message on her answering machine to meet her at Barney's at nine that night. Then he answered Cindy.

"Amanda English received a phone call late last night. It was from an unidentified male. He wants to meet her concerning the pictures," said Racer.

Crossing the squad room, Sidney intercepted Racer and Cindy. He told Racer that the meet with David Hughes was set for Sunday morning at seven, at the old gas station on route 409 just on the outskirts of Springdale. Racer nodded as they headed for the stairs.

Racer drove to 9027 Cumberland Circle and parked in front. When they got to the front, Racer knocked softly. A short but handsome man answered the door.

"I'm Detective Racer and this is my partner Detective Darling."

"Nice to meet you. I'm Amanda's husband, Tim. Come on in, Amanda's in the living room."

Mr. English led them into the living room and motioned them to have a seat. He took a spot beside his wife. He mentioned he just got home from a business trip, and Amanda told him everything. He was concerned about his wife's safety.

"Amanda, can you tell us about the call?" asked Racer.

"At around eleven last night I got this strange phone call. It was a man's voice asking me if I had gotten the photos. I asked him who he was but he just ignored me. I told him that I had received an envelope with several pictures in it and that I didn't appreciate someone intruding on my privacy. Then he got nasty. He told me to shut up and listen. He said that if I didn't want my husband to see these pictures that I should meet him on Wednesday and that they could talk about it," said Amanda, noticeably upset. "I told him that I didn't care if they did tell my husband about those pictures. I would explain what had happened." She reached for a tissue and then continued. "He asked, how would I explain to my husband the other people in the photos? When I asked what people, he assured me that he could do wonders with a photo. I'd be surprised what situations he could put me in. He said I would receive a phone call at five o'clock sharp Wednesday and I should follow the instructions exactly. And before he hung up, he made sure that I understood that if I told anybody about the call something serious could happen to me."

"I'm really concerned about my wife's safety here, detectives," said Mr. English.

"Mr. English, it is really important that your wife keeps that meeting. I need her to play along with these people so we can set a trap and bust their pornography ring. In doing that, hopefully we'll catch a killer."

"Where are these photos? The ones that were originally taken," asked Mr. English.

"I'm sorry, but they're evidence," said Racer.

"You feel confident that you can guarantee Amanda's safety?" asked Mr. English.

"There will be someone with Amanda all the time. She will never be alone," said Racer. "Look, this is probably the best opportunity that we'll have to catch these people. I'm sure that you don't want this to happen to anyone else."

"I'd need to talk this over with Amanda, if you don't mind. If you could call us tomorrow we'll let you know our decision," said Mr. English.

"I understand. I'll give you a call tomorrow around noon, and please keep this between us," said Racer."

"We understand," replied Mr. English.

When Racer and Cindy got outside, Cindy asked what he thought their chances were of having Amanda's cooperation.

"I don't think that Amanda will be the problem. It's going to be her husband."

"I probably can't blame him," replied Cindy.

CHAPTER NINETEEN

When they arrived at Barney's, Racer pointed out a table to Cindy by the jukebox and headed for the bar. On the way, he scanned the place to see if Marge Smyth had arrived, but he couldn't find her. He grabbed a couple of beers, threw a ten on the bar and headed back to his table. On the way, Racer heard his name being called from the hallway that led to the restrooms. He turned and saw Marge Smyth leaning against the wall. "Come on over and join us," said Racer, nodding toward the table.

Instead, Marge waved for him to come over. As Racer approached her, he could tell that she was noticeably shaken. "Are you all right?" he asked looking around.

"I have a big problem. I got another phone call. I'm sure it was from the same guy that called before. He threatened me again. He wants me to drop the story, but that's not the worst. On the way here, someone tried to run me off the road," said Marge.

"Look, you're safe with me," said Racer.

"But what if he's here, watching me to check out who I'm talking to?" said Marge.

"I don't think he would risk being identified," said Racer.

"You have an idea who he is, don't you?" asked Marge. "You're setting me up."

"Look, I told you this story could flush some scum to the top. This guy is just trying to intimidate you," said Racer. "Come on, let's go over and sit down."

"I wondered what happened to you," said Cindy as her eyes went to Marge Smyth.

Racer sat down and explained the situation to Cindy. Leaving the two girls alone, he went back to the restroom area and called Detman on his cell phone.

"Harry, this is Racer. I need to arrange protection for Marge

Smyth, and I need it done quietly."

"It has something to do with that article she wrote, doesn't it?" asked Detman.

"I can't get into that now. You'll just have to trust me on this," said Racer.

"Okay, I'll see what I can do. Where are you?"

"We're at Barney's. I can keep an eye on her until you arrange something. Just let me know when I can turn her loose."

"Stay there for at least another half-hour and I'll call you back," said Detman.

When Racer got back to the table, Marge and Cindy were in conversation. Racer sat down across from them.

"I really need to get going," said Marge.

Racer leaned across the table and said, "Look, I'm arranging for some protection for you. When you leave the bar you won't have to worry about someone attacking you."

Marge laughed loudly, then quickly looked around to see if anyone was looking at her. "Just think, a investigating reporter that needs protection. There goes my reputation of being a toughie."

"Better your reputation then your life," said Racer, as his cell phone rang.

"Yeah," he said into the phone putting his free hand over his ear. Listening for a couple of minutes, Racer finally hung up. He explained to Marge that everything was taken care of. She wouldn't even know she was being watched. Marge thanked Racer for his help. Just then Barney approached the table with another round. Placing the drinks in front of everyone, Barney asked if anyone wanted to dance. Marge said that she had rough day and really needed to get home, but Cindy took him up on his offer.

Racer didn't remember too much about the night before. But he did remember getting in about three in this morning. He squinted at his watch and saw that it was one in the afternoon. Rain was striking gently against his bedroom window. He was still fully dressed except for his shoes. As he tried to get up, it felt as if his head were split right down the middle. Putting a hand on each side, he tried to push it together with no luck.

Finally gathering enough strength, Racer pulled himself from bed and struggled into the kitchen. He headed right for the coffee maker and turned it on. Grabbing a cup out of the cupboard, he sat down at the table. He was sitting there with his head in his hands when the phone rang. The ringing almost knocked him off his chair. The crack in his head just got a little wider. He stumbled over to the phone and yanked it off the hook, more to stop the ringing than to answer it. It was Mrs. English on the phone. Her and her husband wanted to meet with him at four that afternoon. Racer said that was okay.

Hanging up the phone, he went to the coffee maker and poured a cup of coffee. As he carried it back to the bedroom with him, he started to slowly undress. Nothing like a hot shower to clear the head of all those cobwebs.

Racer and Cindy pulled up outside of Amanda English's place at three forty-five. The rain had stopped and the late afternoon sun was straining to break through the clouds. They got out of Cindy's car and headed to the house.

Racer knocked on the screen door and waited. It took only a few seconds for Amanda English to answer. After opening the door, she invited them in.

Racer and Cindy moved past her and waited. Her husband was already sitting in the living room. "Have a seat," said Tim.

"Detective, we have decided to go along with your plan," said Amanda. "We want to help stop this horrible thing from happening to anyone else."

"I think you made the right decision," said Racer.

Racer explained the plan to Amanda and Tim. He stressed the fact that Cindy and he would be nearby every step of the way. And once these people were behind bars, everyone would be able to sleep a little easier at night. Racer thanked them both and told Amanda that he would call her Tuesday night to set up the time. When Cindy and Racer got up and moved toward the door. Tim followed them out.

"Detectives, I am going to hold you solely responsible for my wife's safety. Do you understand?" said Tim, staring at Racer.

"Yes sir, I understand perfectly. Don't worry, everything will be all right," replied Racer.

They shook hands and left.

It had turned into a beautiful afternoon, and Racer decided that they should take a ride out to Madeline Stein's place. Cindy pulled away from the curb and headed for the highway.

When they got to the Stein place, Cindy parked on a back street where the back of the house was visible. Madeline Stein was sitting outside in a lounge chair by the pool, watching a blond man play tennis with an automatic ball server. Madeline was wearing a bright pink bikini with a beach wrap over her shoulders. Then one of her goons appeared, whispered something into Madeline's ear and left. A minute later he was back with a gentleman in sports clothes and dark sunglasses. Madeline offered him a chaise right next to her and they soon got into a conversation. It seemed to get quite heavy at times. All of a sudden, the man reached into his pocket and pulled out a roll of bills with a rubber band around it. The goon returned and handed a package, wrapped in brown paper, to Madeline. Madeline took the money and handed the package to the gentleman.

"What do you think is in the package?" asked Cindy.

"How about videos?" said Racer.

The guy got up and gave Madeline a kiss on the cheek, and the goon escorted him out.

Racer said, "Probably one of the distributors she uses for her merchandise."

"Check this out," said Cindy. "Here comes our tennis player."

The blond athlete took her hand and helped her up. After giving her a firm kiss, he led her into the house.

"A little afternoon delight," said Racer. "Let's get around to the front of the house and wait for this guy to come out."

Cindy pulled the car around to the front of the house and found a spot that gave them cover. They sat there for a good hour before the blond man came out and walked across the driveway to a white BMW. Racer noted that he had changed into a gray pin-stripe suit. Madeline followed him, wearing a white fluffy bathrobe. Pausing before he got into his car, the blond man gave her a long, passionate kiss.

The white BMW pulled out of the driveway and headed for the highway, where it made a right hand turn toward Springdale.

"Did you check the license plate?"

"Yeah, it read F U Z Z 1," replied Cindy.

"How unique," said Racer.

They followed the BMW until, a mile from Springdale, it turned off onto a dirt road marked with a sign that read "Harley's Place." They knew that it would be hard to follow the BMW down a dirt road, so Racer told Cindy to pull over. The hot afternoon sun caused the dust to fly off the tires. They both watched as the car traveled about a mile down the road and stopped.

Racer waited several minutes and then told Cindy to continue slowly, keeping one eye open for the white car. All of a sudden, Racer spotted it, parked in front of a large brick house. A young boy was playing basketball in the driveway. As they passed the mailbox, Racer took notice of the name on the mailbox: Mr. and Mrs. R. Shane. He then told Cindy that they could head back to town.

On the way back to Fairfield, Cindy said, "Remember Susan telling us that Madeline Stein wasn't the boss?"

"Yeah, I remember," replied Racer.

"Then it has to be Shane. He learned the operation during his original investigation of old man Stein. He must have waited until things cooled down and then got Madeline to start everything back up again," said Cindy.

"I'm sure he realized how profitable it was. The temptation must have been too hard to resist."

"Don't you think that he'd be afraid that Madeline would turn him in?" asked Cindy.

"Oh, I'm sure he has some very damaging information on Madeline to protect himself from that," said Racer.

"Kind of a romance made in hell," said Cindy. "What do you think you will find in that sealed file tomorrow?"

"Something that will substantiate everything that we just said, I hope," said Racer. *We better have all our ducks in a row if we intend to link a cop to a porn ring. Especially when there is a killer involved*, he added silently to himself.

Cindy dropped Racer off at home and made him promise one more time that he would see her after his meeting with David Hughes. He promised and got out of the car. After watching Cindy pull away, he entered apartment and went right to the answering machine. The only message on it was from Steve Howard, who wanted Racer to call him. Racer thought that maybe a visit to the club would be more appropriate.

Racer got to the club around eight-thirty. It cost him five bucks just to get in. Racer headed for the bar where he ordered a beer and asked the bartender if Steve was around. The bartender placed a frosted Bud in front of him and left for a minute. After taking a sip of his beer, Racer noticed Steve moving in his direction.

"Hey, I got your message," said Racer as Steve reached him. "What do you have for me?"

"I ran across a guy that you might be interested in meeting," said Steve. "He works at a place called the Palace Massage Parlor over on Market. I told him that you might be interested in buying some vintage skin flicks with Misty Blue in them."

"Does this guy have a name?" asked Racer.

"Just ask for Bull," said Steve.

Racer pulled up outside of the Palace Massage Parlor. Palace wasn't quite the word that Racer would have used to describe the place. It was an old, rundown motel with a pink neon sign. Inside it was dark and musty. The only lighting was a pair of lamps with pink lampshades. There was a counter located next to a long hallway, and behind it was a middle-aged woman with a low cut dress. He could see another room off to the right with several couches and about half a dozen women sitting around. The woman behind the counter asked Racer what he was looking for.

"I'm looking for a guy by the name of Bull," said Racer.

"What do you want with him?" she asked.

"I understand that he has some videos for sale," replied Racer.

"Are you a cop?" she asked sarcastically.

"Look, Steve over at The Jungle told me that Bull had some videos for sale. If he's not interested, that's fine with me," said

Racer, as he pulled away from the counter.

"Wait. Let me get him," said the woman as she disappeared behind a curtain.

Racer walked over to the doorway and started looking the girls over. They were all dressed in some form of lingerie. When he started to exchange smiles with the girls, a squirrely-looking guy came through the curtain and motioned him into a small room about the size of a closet.

"What can I get you?" he asked.

"I'm looking for a couple of videos starring a girl by the name of Misty Blue. Steve said you can help me."

"I didn't know these movies were so popular," said Bull.

"Why do you say that?" asked Racer.

"Several months ago, another guy was in here. Bought up all the movies I had on this Misty Blue broad," said Bull.

"If he bought up all the copies, then why am I here?" asked Racer.

"I recently came across three more videos. One is called the Call of the Wolf Girl and the other is Blue Angel," said Bull. "Are you interested?"

"I thought you said there were three," asked Racer.

"Yeah, there's three. The third one doesn't have a name," replied Bull, shrugging his shoulders.

"The guy that bought up the other videos, what did he look like?" asked Racer.

"Didn't pay that much attention," said Bull. "Do you want the movies or not?"

"Yeah, how much for all three?" asked Racer.

"A hundred," said Bull.

Racer reached into his back pocket and pulled his wallet out. He barely had enough to cover the hundred. The guy reached up onto a shelf lined with videos and pulled out three cassettes. Racer handed him the money; Bull handed Racer the videos.

Pushing the curtain aside, Racer stepped out into the entrance-way. He gave the girls one more smile and left.

Arriving home, Racer grabbed a beer from the fridge and sat down in front of the television. He slipped the first tape, into the

VCR and waited for the screen to come to life. Racer watched about half of it before he turned it off. Then he began to watch Call of the Wolf Girl, which was worse then the first one.

As he watched the videos, Racer hit the pause button frequently, trying to identify Misty Blue. It wasn't easy. The tapes were old, worn and grainy. In one of the close-ups, he was almost positive it was Madeline. Then he put in the last video. It was a complete orgy from the start. The girl's faces were hard to see because they were always turned away from the camera. Finally, hitting the stop button, he fell back in his chair. He had to get some sleep. His meeting with David Hughes was set for seven. Pushing himself out of the chair, he finished his beer and shuffled off to bed.

CHAPTER TWENTY

The next morning, Racer was up early and on the road by 6:00, bound for the old gas station. The highway was empty all the way to Springdale; It was Sunday and everyone was still in bed. When he arrived, he drove up along side one of the pumps and waited. The old Texaco building was all boarded up except for a side door. He could see where the boards had been pulled away. It was probably a nesting place for the homeless. From where he sat, he could see up and down the highway for about a mile. The morning sky was starting to turn a brilliant red. He would bet that they were in for a storm later on. Slipping out of his car, he walked around to make sure the place was deserted. He didn't find any signs of life. He leaned against the side of the car and continued to wait.

After five more minutes passed, a Honda approached from the east. Racer watched as the car slowed, pulled into the gas station and stopped alongside of the ZX. David Hughes was sitting behind the steering wheel. He was alone.

David climbed out and walked around to meet Racer. Both men were standing between the two cars when the first shot rang out. Racer heard the pop and turned to face the grove of trees across the highway. His hand was already going for the .357 under his coat. David didn't know what was going on. Before Racer's gun was clear of his holster, the second shot rang out. This time David ducked. Racer felt a sting in his left arm but never took his attention away from the line of trees across the highway. Then he saw the glint of sunlight hitting bare metal. He ran around his car and crouched behind one of the abandoned gas pumps. The third shot took out the glass globe on top of the pump. Shattered glass rained down on top of him. He looked back at David to see if he had taken cover and saw that he was between the two cars. Racer realized that he had to separate himself from David, so he followed the line of pumps to the last one. He hoped that a car would come along, giving him cover.

Racer made a mad dash across the highway just as a truck went by. When he got to the other side, he threw himself on the ground and listened. He could hear someone running through the brush and followed the sound. By the time he got to a clearing, an old pickup truck was pulling away. Looking for a plate number, Racer fired several shots, hoping to hit one of the truck's tires. There was no plate on the truck. After the truck disappeared, he noticed that his left arm was bleeding and blood was running down into his hand. Removing a handkerchief from his pocket, he covered the wound and ran back across the highway to the gas station.

David Hughes's car was gone. Racer checked the highway and it was empty. Getting back to his car, Racer noticed a large white envelope lying on the front seat with a note attached to it. He also noticed that one of the bullets had grazed the top of his car, leaving a long, narrow scratch. His pride and joy had been violated.

Getting in the car, he read the note attached to the envelope. It said, "Sorry I couldn't stay. I hope that this information can help you. I took a big chance getting this. Use it wisely." And it was signed by Dave.

Racer opened the white envelope and looked inside. There were a dozen reports from the Stein pornography case. Racer shoved them back into the envelope and sped out of the gas station, onto the highway. He hit eighty and kept it there all the way back to Fairfield. He could feel the warmth of his blood as it ran down his arm. He knew that he had to get it cleaned out and bandaged, but there was no way he was going to a hospital. Gunshot wounds had to be reported. The first place that came to mind was Cindy's.

Racer drove to Cindy's building and parked close to the entrance. Checking his watch, it was eight-fifteen. That whole episode hadn't taken more than 30 minutes. Knocking on Cindy's door, he could hear some rustling coming from inside.

Cindy pulled the door open and Racer stumbled inside.

"What the hell is wrong with you this morning?" asked Cindy.

Then she saw the blood on the doorframe and the blood-soaked handkerchief around his arm. "My God! What happened?"

"Nothing, just your normal Sunday morning drive," replied Racer, holding his arm.

"You dummy!" cried Cindy. "I told you I should have gone along."

"Yes, Mother," said Racer just before he passed out.

When Racer came to, he was lying in bed with a blanket pulled up around his neck and a bandage on his left upper arm. He could hear Cindy in the next room, talking with a man. He knew the voice but couldn't place it. His head was kind of foggy. He looked under the covers and saw that all he had on was his shorts. He thought back to the shots that were fired at him and David Hughes. David left him a white envelope with the documents in it. But what did he do with it? He threw the covers back and swung his feet over the edge of the bed. His clothes were folded over a chair in the corner of the room. He was about to put his pants on when the door opened and Cindy came in with Detman right behind her.

"I should have known," said Racer, looking at Detman.

"I needed help with you. Harry was the only one that I could trust," said Cindy. "Besides, he is your best friend."

"How much did you tell him?" asked Racer.

"I told him that you had a meeting this morning and that's it," replied Cindy.

"Well, how about if you let me put my pants on and then we can talk?"

Once they were gone, Racer slipped his pants on. He picked up his shirt and saw that the left sleeve was blood-stained, and there was a tear where the bullet had passed through. He slipped his feet into his shoes and started for the living room. That was when he noticed the envelope on the dresser. Racer picked it up, folded it in half, and slipped it into his jacket pocket.

His left arm was throbbing like a toothache, and the bandage was already spotted with blood. When he got to the living room,

Racer sat down on the couch, next to Detman.

"Do you think that it was a set-up?" asked Detman.

"No, because David had left an envelope and message behind," answered Racer.

Racer also mentioned that he wasn't quite sure who the gunman was shooting at. When the first shot rang out, he and David were standing together, so either one of them could have been the target.

"Maybe he was trying to get rid of the two of you," said Detman.

"Possibly, but I think it was David he was aiming for. He probably was followed," replied Racer.

"Did you have a chance to read the documents that David left behind?" asked Detman.

Racer said that he was too busy ducking bullets. He pulled the envelope from his jacket pocket, and pulled the papers out. Racer divided the sheets up between the three of them. They spread the papers out on the table and spent the next several minutes looking them over.

"The only one that was arrested was Mr. Stein," said Racer. "They caught two of the models, but they were given immunity for their testimony. Madeline's name isn't even mentioned anywhere."

"Shane and his partner, a Tom Decker, handled the whole case," said Cindy.

"There really isn't much in here except for Mr. Stein and the models' names. Isn't it strange that his main model was a girl called Misty Blue and she isn't even mentioned in here once. I'm starting to believe that Shane had this case file sealed so no one would start suggesting that there was a cover-up," said Racer. "There isn't even any mention of the contacts that Stein had for distributing his skin flicks."

"They didn't even interview Madeline Stein," said Cindy.

"Shane was probably overjoyed that Stein died, so he didn't have to bring any of this out in court. He just kept it all for his own personal use," said Detman.

"Maybe we should have a talk with Tom Decker and see what he has to say about all this," said Cindy.

"Sounds good to me," said Racer. "The first thing tomorrow morning."

"Let me see if I can track down those two models," said Detman. "Maybe they can add something to this."

Racer took the next hour explaining to Detman the trap they were setting, with the help of Amanda English, and how they were going to spring it. Detman wasn't too happy about using a civilian as bait without the captain's okay, but reluctantly agreed.

"You aren't real happy about investigating Shane, are you, Harry?" asked Racer.

"If you feel he might be dirty, then he needs to be taken off the street," said Detman. "Do you think that it might have been Shane who took those shots at you?"

"It sure is a possibility," said Racer. "Or he could have hired someone. I'm sure he has plenty of connections."

Racer was up early the next morning. He could still feel the throbbing left arm. In the bathroom he removed the bandage that Cindy put in place the day before. His arm had a nice deep indentation. The bleeding had stopped but the healing process was just getting underway. Racer opened the medicine cabinet, took out some antiseptic and clean bandages and placed them on the counter top. Then he took a much-needed shower.

Afterwards, he dried off his arm carefully and applied the liquid from the brown bottle. The sting from the antiseptic caused Racer to grit his teeth. Then he applied the clean dressing with two strips of adhesive tape. Then he went into the bedroom to get dressed. Cindy had driven him home so he would have to stop at her place and pick his car up. Then he would head out to the gas station and see if he could come up with any clues on who might have fired those shots. On the way to the kitchen, Racer retrieved the morning paper. He was stunned to read that David Hughes was involved in a serious traffic accident. Witnesses stated that his vehicle collided with an old Ford pickup truck on Highway 6. It went on to say that Mr. Hughes had sustained multiple chest injuries and a broken leg. The driver of the pickup truck fled the scene before police arrived. The highway patrol was investigating the accident. This time Racer was sure who the target was: David Hughes. He would have to call Detman and see if protection could be arranged for David. Whoever was behind this might not stop until he was dead.

At 20 minutes after seven, he put on his sports jacket carefully and went outside. Cindy was already waiting for him in the ZX. Racer slid in and handed Cindy the article on David Hughes.

"Then the gunman was after David," said Cindy.

Racer nodded.

"How's the arm?"

"Sore," replied Racer. He told her to head for Highway 6. He mentioned that they were going to make two stops: one at the gas station where the meet took place, and the second would be to the hospital where David Hughes was.

When they saw the Texaco sign, Racer told her to pull in and park next to the first pump. "This is were I parked, and Hughes pulled his car up right beside me. We were both facing in the same direction. Now, let's see if we can find anything that might lead us to the shooter," said Racer.

They got out of the car and started looking around. Racer checked the gas pumps and Cindy walked over to the old building. They spent about 30 minutes looking with no luck. Racer finally walked over to the ZX and followed the scratch that ran across his roof, lining it up with a boarded-up window. He directed Cindy toward the window and joined her there. They moved their hands across the boards, and Racer was sure it was there. Cindy looked but couldn't find anything, so she moved inside. A couple of minutes later, Cindy hollered, "Is this what you're looking for."

Racer went inside and found Cindy standing by the back wall behind the old wood counter. There in the wall was what appeared to be a bullet hole. Racer pulled out his pocketknife and craved the wood away from the bullet. He didn't want to mar it any more then he had to. "We'll get this to Sidney when we get back," he said as he held up the bullet. "It's a guess, but I would say that it came from a 30.06. Now let's take a look across the street and see if we can find anything."

Crossing the street, they came to a small clearing. Racer pointed out the area where the shooter must have been standing. The grass was still bent down and a couple of tree branches were broken. They scanned the area for a while but all they could find was the tire marks that the truck had left.

"We might as well head for the hospital. Maybe we'll have better luck with David."

Twenty minutes later they were pulling into the hospital parking lot. Stopping by the front desk, Racer asked what room David Hughes was in. The receptionist informed them he was in the Intensive Care Unit. Reaching the third floor, Racer stopped one of the nurses and asked for David Hughes' room. She wanted to know if they were immediate family. Racer showed the nurse his shield. She asked them to wait a minute.

The nurse walked over to a house phone and dialed. Speaking into it, she kept shaking her head and looking at Racer and Cindy. Finally she hung up and returned to them.

"Dr. Hutchinson will be with you in a minute," she said. "He's the doctor in charge."

A few seconds later, Racer watched as a tall gray hair man approached them. He wore a long white hospital coat and carried a clipboard. "Hi, I'm Dr. Hutchinson. I understand you want to see Mr. Hughes."

"That's right," said Racer, identifying themselves.

"I'm sorry to tell you this but Mr. Hughes passed away around five this morning. We did everything that we could but the internal injuries were too serious," said the doctor.

"Do you intend to perform an autopsy on the body?" asked Racer.

"Not on a traffic accident, though we will run a tox screen," replied the doctor. "If you need any more information you'll have to contact the Springdale police or the county highway patrol. I'm sorry."

"Thanks, doc," said Racer.

When they reached the lobby, Racer called the Springdale Police Department and identified himself as an insurance agent. He explained that he was trying to find out where the pickup truck had been taken so he could get pictures for the file. He was told that it had been towed to the county impound until the investigation was closed. Racer decided to go there immediately.

When they arrived at the impound lot, Racer asked Cindy to go inside and see what she could find out. He was going to look around and see if he could spot the truck. He didn't have to go too far before a large German shepherd stopped him, so he peered through the chain link fence and waited for Cindy. It only took a couple of minutes before Cindy and a county officer came out. Stepping down into the yard, the officer unlocked the gate and put the dog on a chain. The officer's name was Griffin.

"Officer Griffin was the first one on the scene," said Cindy, as they walked over to a partially destroyed Ford pickup. Racer recognized the truck right away.

"Officer, what exactly have you found out so far?" asked Racer.

"It was apparent that the pickup truck had pulled out of a dirt road right into the path of Mr. Hughes' vehicle. The pickup truck was empty. It was amazing the driver could walk away from the accident," said Officer Griffin. "I found Mr. Hughes crushed between the steering column and the front seat. His legs had been jammed up under the dashboard. I knew that he was in serious condition. I radioed for the paramedics and med-vac. After I helped Mr. Hughes, I searched the area with several other officers but we couldn't find anything. Then we started thinking that maybe the truck had been parked and the brakes failed and it rolled out onto the highway."

"If that was the case, the driver would have come looking for the truck," said Racer.

"That's true," said Griffin. "That's why we discounted that idea. Besides, the truck doesn't have any plates on it and there isn't a house in the area for miles."

"Did you find anything in the truck?" asked Racer.

"Nothing," replied Griffin. "Since Mr. Hughes passed away this morning and the driver fled the scene, I requested that the crime lab go over it."

"If you find anything else, give me a call," said Racer as he handed Griffin his card.

Back in the car, Racer said, "Let's get back to the station and give the slug we found to Sidney. Maybe he can come up with something."

Back at the station, Racer headed for the lab to drop the bullet off with Sidney. Racer found out that Sidney had taken the day off to comfort Daniel Hughes's family. They had been real good friends for quite some time. Looking around in Sidney's office, he found an evidence envelope. Slipping the slug in, he sealed the envelope and filled the information out on the outside. Getting back upstairs, he noticed that Cindy was in Detman's Office. Detman saw him and motioned for Racer to join them. When Racer entered the office, Cindy picked up a slim sheaf of papers and handed it to him.

"Take a look at this. It's the report back on Brian Thompson."

Racer took the report and sat down. He read it to himself. Brian Thompson had enlisted in the Navy out of high school. His first brush with the law was right out of boot camp. He was accused of assaulting a female officer and was thrown in the brig. Instead of a court martial, the Navy decided to give him a General Discharge for dishonorable reasons. Six months later, he was arrested on suspicion of rape and aggravated assault. He beat the rape charge but got 12 months for the assault. A year later, his girlfriend signed a complaint that he'd beaten her into submission and taken liberties with her. When it came to trial, she dropped the charges. And then came the last entry on the report. Brian Thompson had been paroled from a three to five year prison sentence for attempted murder of a woman companion that he had picked up in a nightclub. He had threatened her with a switchblade and cut her face.

"Now I know why Susan Thompson never mentioned that she had a son," said Racer, finishing the report.

"I just got off the phone with Brian's parole officer before you came in," said Detman. "He's been keeping a close eye on Brian since he got out and so far he's has been a good boy. He has a steady job and reports in when he has to."

"Where does he work?" asked Racer.

Detman checked his notes, "He works at some warehouse over on Belmont for a retail chain. Always on time and never misses a day."

"I think we need to pay Brian a visit," said Racer.

"Should we call the photo session off?" asked Detman.

"Definitely not. It goes on as planned. At first we didn't have any suspects, and now we have a barrel full. We have to find out which one is rotten."

CHAPTER TWENTY-ONE

Monday after lunch, Cindy and Racer paid a visit to Norman's Department Store warehouse on Belmont Avenue. After identifying themselves, they asked for the manager, and a well-dressed man introduced himself as Joe Peoples. Racer asked Mr. Peoples if there some place they could talk in private.

Mr. Peoples led them to an office away from the main warehouse. Once inside, he closed the door behind them. Cindy and Racer took chairs in front of an old mahogany desk. When they were seated, Racer told Mr. Peoples they were there to find out some information concerning a worker by the name of Brian Thompson. Mr. Peoples wasn't surprised since Brian was an ex-con. Racer stressed that it was just a routine visit and wanted it kept confidential. Mr. Peoples nodded.

Racer then started to ask Mr. Peoples a variety of questions concerning Brian's work record. Mr. Peoples answered every one of them without hesitation until it came to the one concerning Brian's friends. Mr. Peoples apologized, but he couldn't think of anyone that Brian was friends with. Racer stood up and thanked him for his help. He gave Mr. Peoples one of his cards and asked that if anything else came to mind to give him a call.

Leaving the warehouse, Racer mentioned that it was time to give Shane's old partner a visit. On the way, Racer told Cindy about the videotapes he found concerning Madeline Stein, alias Misty Blue.

"Is she in the videos?" asked Cindy.

"It wasn't easy to make her out, but in some of the close ups you can recognize her," said Racer.

Racer motioned for Cindy to pull over at one of the gas stations coming up. Racer removed his cell phone, and Cindy headed for the store. Racer placed a call to the Springdale Police Department. When the desk sergeant answered, Racer asked for Detective Decker.

"Sorry, but Detective Decker retired about six months ago," said the sergeant.

"Do you know where to?" asked Racer.

"He packed up and moved to sunny Florida," replied the sergeant.

"Thanks," said Racer and hung up.

When he turned back toward the car, Cindy was leaning against the passenger door, holding two Cokes.

"Well, we can scratch that one off our list," said Racer.

"Dead?" asked Cindy.

"Might as well be. He retired to Florida."

When they finally returned to the station, the report on the bullet was sitting on Racer's desk. Picking up the report, Racer read it. The bullet was fired from a 30.06 rifle. The lab ran it through the system with no match. So all he had to do was find the rifle. When he looked up from the report, Detman was standing right in front of him. Racer handed the report to Cindy to read.

"How many people do you think we will need Wednesday?" asked Detman.

"I think that we can handle it," said Racer, "though we might need a sentry. And I think Sidney can handle that."

"The lab tech," said Detman and then he realized he was shouting.

"We need someone that we can trust and that can keep his or her mouth shut. I already know that Sidney can do that. And on the other side, I'm sure that he would like nothing better than to catch David Hughes' killer."

"You ask him. That way he is your responsibility. If anything goes wrong, it will be your butt on the line," said Detman.

"Okay, let's meet tomorrow morning to talk over what we're going to do. We'll meet at the Golden Kettle on Stevens around eight, and I'll buy breakfast," said Racer.

When Detman was gone, Racer suggested to Cindy that they stop by the Designer Dress Shop and see how Susan Thompson was holding up.

When they reached the dress shop, Racer decided to send Cindy in to talk with Susan Thompson, figuring a female wouldn't raise too much suspicion. Racer watched Cindy cross the parking lot and enter the shop, his attention focused on the entrance. After about 10 minutes, Cindy came out of the shop and headed in his direction. When she got close to Racer's ZX, she changed direction, and Racer realized that something was wrong. He started the car and pulled out of the space heading for the main drive.

Checking his rearview mirror, he saw a blue Grand Am parked behind him, a big guy at wheel. Racer decided to circle the mall before picking Cindy up. He spotted her down by the bus stop, sitting on the wood bench. He picked her up, turned back into the lot and parked.

"What did you find out inside?" asked Racer, keeping a close eye on the Grand Am.

"I talked with Susan and she told me that everything was still a go."

"How is she holding up?" asked Racer.

"She's a little scared. She feels that she's being watched, and I think she's right. I saw the Grand Am parked behind you," said Cindy.

"They must be tailing her," said Racer.

"She talked with Madeline Stein and was told that this might be the last session for a while." She thinks the guy running this whole thing is getting jumpy," said Cindy.

"The heat must be getting to them. That means we're getting close," said Racer.

"Apparently, the only reason they're doing this one is they have obligations to take care of," said Cindy.

"That means they have a paying customer who wants his merchandise," said Racer.

"She's afraid she might be in danger," said Cindy.

"Has she been threatened?" asked Racer.

"No, she just has that feeling," said Cindy.

Racer knew what she meant as he glanced over at the blue Grand Am. It was the same car that kept popping up. "Even though the car is registered to Madeline Stein, the two thugs must work for Shane. They're watching everyone to make sure they stay in line," said Racer.

"You don't think that they would hurt Susan, do you?" asked Cindy.

"No," replied Racer, "At least not until after their last photo shoot. They need her right now and don't want to draw any more attention to themselves. What did you say to Susan about Wednesday?"

"I told her that everything was set and we would be in touch," replied Cindy.

Racer put the car in reverse, backed out of the parking space and headed for the exit.

Racer and Cindy stopped by the lab when they got back to the station. They found Sidney sitting at his desk, sipping a cup of coffee and filling out reports. He motioned for them to come in. Sidney looked haggard. It had to be a tough time for him.

"I'm sorry I got your friend involved in this," said Racer.

"Hey, it isn't your fault. It's the bastard that rammed his truck into Dave's car. Have you found anything out about it?"

Racer explained their conversation with the county patrol officer. He didn't want Sidney to know that Robert Shane was their prime suspect in David Hughes' death. Then Racer got down to why they were there. "Sidney, I have a proposition for you. I want you to join us Wednesday night when we break this case wide open. I know I can trust you to keep this under your hat. No one outside of Detman and us is aware of this."

"You can count on me," said Sidney excitedly. "Do I get to carry a gun? I can hit a fly at a hundred paces and I have the trophies to prove it."

"I know but those targets don't shoot back," said Racer.

"I understand," said Sidney, with a little disappointment in his voice.

Racer explained that everyone involved was going to meet at the Golden Kettle tomorrow morning at eight. Sidney assured Racer that wouldn't be a problem.

Getting back to their desks, Racer and Cindy started to go over everything they had so far. They wanted to make sure they didn't miss anything. Cindy asked, "What if this porn ring isn't tied into the murders? What if our killer is someone outside of the circle? We could be wasting our time here."

"I know that's a possibility, but we have to trust our instincts," said Racer. "Everything points to someone who knows the operation."

Racer started to go down the list of evidence they had collected. The notes concerning the clothing they found at each scene and how it led them to the Designer Dress Shop. The empty film canister. Evidence that Danny Tonelli was drugging the victims and assisting in the picture taking. Everything pointed to the adult film business. Then there was the connection between Robert Shane and Madeline Stein. "There are two main things missing," said Racer. "The murder weapon and the dark colored Buick."

"But that is what Susan Thompson drives," replied Cindy.

"I know, but Shane has one assigned to him by the Springdale Police Department. So right now, we don't know for sure which one it is."

"Why not a warrant?" asked Cindy.

"It will alert everyone to what we are doing, especially Shane, and I don't want that to happen," said Racer. "Besides, after Wednesday night, I'm sure that Susan Thompson will give us anything we want."

Racer continued going down the list of evidence. The women all had sex before they were killed, so either they knew the killer or he gained entry under some kind of false pretense. They also had a statement from Susan Thompson concerning the adult film business. Everything seemed to be in place to set the trap. All Racer could hope for was that Shane would be nearby.

Racer and Cindy realized the danger that the two women would be in: Amanda English as the victim and Susan Thompson as the informer. You never knew what a killer would do when his back was against the wall, since he had nothing to lose. The trap would have to be set carefully. Every angle would have to be covered. Racer couldn't take the chance that anyone would get away.

"Let's call it a day," said Racer. "We'll need to get all the sleep we can tonight. We are going to have a couple of busy days ahead of us."

Cindy agreed. No Barney's tonight.

It was around six when Racer got home. He fell backward into his recliner in front of the television. He pushed the button on the remote control and the TV came to life. The evening news was just coming on. All Racer could think about was how tough this case had been so far. It was a shame that some innocent people had to pay the ultimate price, like David Hughes, not to mention the four victims. Racer really wasn't paying much attention to the news. The last thing that he remembered was the weatherman saying something about tomorrow being partly cloudy.

It was eight-forty when Racer arrived at the restaurant, and everyone gave him a hard time for being late.

"Sorry," said Racer. "I'm usually always on time. I don't know what happened." Racer paid the price for his tardiness. When the waitress came to take orders, his colleagues made sure that Racer picked up the check for everyone. While they were waiting for their breakfast, they started to lay out their plan for Wednesday night. Everyone was given an assignment. Before Racer could ask if there were any questions, the waitress was back with a tray full of dishes.

When she left, Racer asked the others to recite their assignment.

"Sidney, you can go first."

"I'm the sentry," said Sidney. "I'll be sitting by the T in the road and take notice of every car that enters or exits the road. I'll write down the plate number and the type of car they're driving."

Racer then looked at Detman, who spoke around a mouthful of eggs. "I'll be at the end of the driveway, out of sight. I'm to make sure that no one approaches the cabin that shouldn't be there."

That left Cindy.

"My part is easy," she said. "I'll take my place by the front door to the studio and I'll keep an eye on everyone who enters. Susan

Thompson will leave one of the curtains open a crack so I can watch everything that is taking place inside. When I see Racer enter the cabin from the side door, I enter from the front."

Everyone stopped eating and looked at Racer.

"I'm the one who will give the signal to start everything in motion," he said. "Shane sometimes sits outside the residence to make sure everything is going all right. If this happens, we can't afford to let him get away. Sidney, if that happens, you have to block off the road and not let him out. The lieutenant will give you that signal. Make sure you do not stay in the car. Once you pull it across the road, get out. Remember, at this point we don't know exactly who is going to be there or how dangerous they might be. It is possible that our killer will be one of those people."

"Remember people, we must protect the safety of Amanda English at all cost," said Detman. "We can't allow anything to happen to her."

"Cindy and I have a meeting set up with Susan Thompson Wednesday morning to go over everything one last time," said Racer. "Once that has happened, we can all head for the lake."

They chatted for about another hour before they broke up. It was already ten-fifteen when they finally left the restaurant. As Cindy and Racer headed for their cars, he reminded Cindy that he wanted her to stay with Amanda English every step of the way.

Cindy said, "I understand. She'll never be out of my sight."

Racer pulled his cell phone out and made a call, while Cindy slid into the driver's seat. When Racer got off the phone, he opened the door and climbed in beside her.

"We have an appointment with Amanda and her husband at four-thirty this evening. She wants to make sure her husband is home when we come over. And for lunch we are meeting with Marge Smyth."

"Why did you call her?" asked Cindy.

"Remember, she did us a big favor, and I promised her that I would give her the first shot at this story when it broke. I'm not going to go back on my word."

"Okay," said Cindy as she put the car in gear and pulled out of the driveway.

Racer directed Cindy to drive to a place called the Red Baron Steakhouse, located outside of town on Drecker Road. When they got there, the parking lot had only a spattering of cars. It was 10 minutes to one. They pulled into the far corner of the lot and waited. Marge was suppose to arrive at one o'clock.

At about one-twenty, she finally pulled into the lot. Cindy watched her park next to the side entrance of the restaurant. After she was out of her car, Racer and Cindy walked over to greet her.

"You're late," said Racer. "Run into any problems?"

"Traffic was heavier than I thought," said Marge as they walked toward the entrance.

When they got inside, they had to wait before being seated. Racer didn't know why; there were very few people in the place. "Why'd you pick this place?" he asked "It seems dead."

"I always come here when I want to keep my meetings private," said Marge.

Finally, the maitre d' showed them to a table near the front window, which gave them a perfect view of the parking lot. After they ordered drinks, Racer informed Marge of what was going to happen tomorrow. He made sure that he left out some of the important parts, thinking that she didn't need to know everything. Racer told her that a bust was going to take place and that it had to do with the adult film ring that she had written the article about. Now he was going to pay her back the favor by giving her the first crack at the story. Racer told her to be at the little grocery store at Miller's Lake at ten o'clock. Racer had her promise that she wouldn't say a word to anyone.

On their way back to Fairfield, Racer looked at his watch and realized that they had about two hours to kill before their meeting with Amanda English. He knew exactly where he wanted to go. Cindy pulled the car to the curb in front of Arnie's place.

"Don't tell me that we have to go through this again," she said.

"Don't worry," said Racer. "His bark is worse then his bite."

Racer rang the doorbell and saw Arnie peek out through the curtains. He opened the door and told Racer to go away.

"Peace," said Racer.

"What do you want now?" asked Arnie

"Hey, I'll buy you a couple of beers at Barney's if you can give me any information you have on a detective by the name of Robert Shane," said Racer.

"I knew you wanted something," said Arnie.

"Look, this case we're working on, his name keeps popping up," said Racer.

"On what side does it keep coming up?" asked Arnie with a serious look on his face.

"Why would you ask that?" said Racer.

"Look, why the hell don't you come right out and ask me what you really want," said Arnie. "Stop beating around the bush."

"Okay, I will. What connections does Shane have with Madeline Stein?" asked Racer.

"Shane had a good thing going for him. He was bedding Madeline. Can't blame him. He was investigating Stein's adult film business and Stein's wife was suspected of being one of the stars. The way I heard it, Shane made a deal with her husband to keep her name out of the reports in return for some sexual favors. That's the way the story goes."

"You mean he made the deal with the husband and not Madeline?" asked Cindy.

"That's right. The deal was that old man Stein would plead guilty to the porn charge and Shane would leave his wife out of it."

"How long did this thing go on?" asked Cindy.

"It could still be going on for all I know. The hell of it is, Shane has a beautiful wife. You know what's funny about the whole thing?" said Arnie. "No one gave a damn."

"Have you heard of anything else that he might have been mixed up in?" asked Racer.

"There were some stories going around after that about Shane shooting his own movies. I guess everyone thought since he was sleeping with Madeline, he'd taken over the movie business. Nothing like making some spare change on the side," said Arnie.

"Was there any truth to those stories?" asked Racer.

"None that could be proven," said Arnie. "And if he is, who gives a damn?"

Racer and Cindy dropped Arnie off at Barney's and stuffed a twenty in his pocket. After watching him go inside, they headed over to the English's.

When they arrived, Tim wasn't home yet. Amanda invited them in and offered them something to drink. Racer had a cup of coffee and Cindy had her usual Diet Coke. They sat around making small talk waiting for Tim to arrive. He arrived about five minutes later and excused himself almost immediately. After he left the room, Amanda questioned Racer.

"Do you think that everything is going to be all right?" asked Amanda.

But before Racer could answer, Tim returned. He had shed his sports coat and tie, then rolled up his sleeves to the elbows. He looked ready for business. Racer waited until Tim took a seat next to Amanda before speaking.

"I'll explain to you everything that is going to take place tomorrow. If you have any questions, please save them until I'm done," said Racer.

After Amanda and Tim agreed, Racer explained that Amanda would be directed to a nice restaurant for conversation and a meal. This is where she would be blackmailed, using the pictures they sent her in the mail. "Sometime during the meal, they will slip something into your drink," said Racer. "It's nothing that will harm you but it will make you feel uninhibited. Kind of like having a few too many. Once the drug takes effect, they will drive you off to a secluded area and hold the photo session. Don't worry, we know exactly where they are going to take you." He assured them that Cindy would be with Amanda every step of the way. Once they reached the location of the shoot, Racer and his team would be waiting. "First thing in the morning, I'll put a tap on your phone. That way, Cindy and I can listen to everything that the contact person would say."

"How far will you allow this to go before you stop it?" asked Tim with concern.

"You have to understand that we have to catch them in the act.

So we will have to allow them to take some pictures before we can make any arrests," answered Racer.

"So that means Amanda will actually have to pose for them?" asked Tim.

"I'm afraid so. But I give you my word that those pictures will never leave our hands."

"That's what you tell us now, but how about that drug Amanda has to take? What kind of effect will it have on her later?" asked Tim.

"We know for a fact that the drug isn't harmful and it doesn't have any side effects," said Racer. "By morning, she won't even know what happened. That's what they count on."

All the time they were talking, Amanda wrung her hands. She was noticeably nervous.

"Can you guarantee Amanda's safety?" asked Tim sternly.

"Yes sir, I can," said Racer.

"I want to be here tomorrow but I have to go out of town," said Tim. "Something came up and my boss needs me to visit one of our biggest accounts. I couldn't tell him what's going on, so I have to do this. Detective Racer and Detective Darling, I'm putting all my trust in the two of you. If anything goes wrong, I will hold you personally responsible. I'll be calling you throughout the day to see how things are going."

"Don't worry," said Cindy to Amanda. "Nothing is going to happen to you. I will be with you all the time. You might not be able to see me but I'll be there."

Racer and Cindy got up and excused themselves. When they got to the front door, Racer paused and turned toward the young couple. "Try to get some sleep tonight. We have a big day ahead of us."

CHAPTER TWENTY-TWO

Racer watched as the telephone truck pulled up outside the English house at eight sharp. George Spanos stepped from his truck with a clipboard under his arm and knocked on the door. George worked for the department. Amanda English answered and let him in. Racer and Cindy were sitting down the street, watching the house. Racer would leave when the phone truck did, but Cindy would remain with Amanda the rest of the day. Racer knew that Detman was sitting around the corner in a panel truck, waiting for the tap to be completed. They would wait until Amanda received the call setting up the meet; then they would leave and carry out their respective assignments.

Racer also had to touch base with Susan Thompson to make sure she understood exactly what she was supposed to do. Racer did not want any screw-ups. He reminded Cindy the only way they would communicate was by cellphone. The police radio would be off limits. He got out of Cindy's car and joined Detman in the panel truck.

The temperature was only 70 but it was supposed to reach 90 before the day was out. Hopefully, the call to Amanda would come early in the day. They had been in the van about two hours before the phone finally rang. Everyone fell silent. They listened as Amanda answered, but it was only her husband. He was just checking to see how she was holding up. They only talked for about 30 seconds and then said their good-byes. Racer could hear the tension in their voices. It was ten-thirty before the phone rang again. Amanda picked it up on the fourth ring.

"Hello," said Amanda but there was no reply. "Hello," said Amanda one more time but again no answer. Then there was a dial tone.

"What do you think?" asked Detman.

"Could be our man," said Racer. "He's just checking things out."

Twenty minutes later the phone rang again. Amanda picked it up on the fifth ring this time. "Hello," she said in a shaky voice.

"Amanda, are you alone?" asked the man's voice in a whisper.

"Yes, who is this?" she asked.

"Don't ask any questions. Just follow my instructions," said the man's voice.

"What do you want me to do?" asked Amanda, getting more nervous by the second.

"I want you to take a cab to the Club Paris. There will be a table reserved for you. Just sit there and your escort will meet you. Don't mention this conversation to anyone or bring anyone with you. You will be followed. It you don't do as I say, those nice glossy pictures of you will find their way into the wrong hands. Understand?"

"Yes, I'll be alone," said Amanda.

"Okay, be there by six and don't be late. And remember, don't breathe a word of this to anyone," said the voice.

Before Amanda could say anything else, the phone went dead. Detman put a trace on the call. It came from a phone booth at a convenience store outside of the city. They recorded the conversation so they could get a voice match later. Now, it was time for them to disperse. Racer and Detman left, but it was the responsibility of George Spanos to continue the tap on Amanda's line, just in case the guy called back and changed the instructions. Racer walked back to his car and picked Detman up. Heading back to the station, Racer got on his cellphone and filled Cindy in on the phone conversation. He also made sure that she was aware that someone could be watching Amanda. She acknowledged this and hung up.

When they get back to the station, Detman called the local sub shop for sandwiches. While they were waiting, Detman's phone rang. As he listened, his eyes went to the ceiling, Racer knew it had to be Peterson. After he hung up, he told Racer that Peterson wanted to see them in his office early Friday morning for an update. Racer smiled and told Detman they might be able to give Peterson an early Christmas present.

Detman just nodded.

After they finished their lunch, Racer called the Designer Dress Shop and ask if Susan Thompson was there. He was told she was at lunch and wouldn't be back for another half-hour. Racer ask where she was having lunch and explained that it was very important that he get hold of her. He told them that it had something to do with a natural gas leak. He listened and then hung up the phone. Stopping by the lab to get Sidney, they headed for the Mesa Café in the Mall.

Racer confirmed with Detman that they would meet at the little grocery store at seven sharp.

It took them about ten minutes to get to the mall. Racer ran six red lights and a few stop signs. He circled the mall until he found the Mesa Café, and then he parked so that the car was hidden from the cafe.

"Sidney, go in and see if you can spot Susan Thompson," said Racer, giving him a picture of the woman. "Tell her that I want her to stop in the ice cream shop on the way back to the store. I'll meet her there."

Racer watched Sidney cross the parking lot and enter the cafe. Then he took time to survey the lot. He wanted to make sure that no one else was watching. When he was sure, he got out of the car and walked over to the ice cream shop. When he saw Susan come out of the café, he entered the shop and ordered a chocolate chip cone. He took a seat and waited for her. In a few seconds, Susan entered the store and sat at a table next to Racer. Racer made casual conversation while he looked around to make sure they weren't being watched. When he was sure they were alone, he went on to tell Susan what was going to happen that night. He purposely left out the part about the phone tap and the tail on Amanda English.

"I will be at the cabin around seven-thirty tonight," said Racer. "It will give me time to set up."

"My stomach is all in knots over this," said Susan.

"Just relax. Everything will be all right. Has anyone tried to contact you about tonight?"

"Madeline called me first thing this morning. She wanted to make sure that the studio will be ready," said Susan.

"Did she mention who was going to be there?" asked Racer.

"No. She just said they will be there at around nine," replied Susan.

"Just go on about your day as you usually do," said Racer as he finished his cone.

Before they all headed up to Miller's Lake, Racer drove past the English house to make sure everything was on schedule. He drove straight through the first time. Cindy saw him but didn't make any effort to make contact. Racer circled the block and parked about a block away. He called Cindy on his cellphone. "How is everything going?" he asked.

"Fine except for my bladder. I think it is about ready to burst," answered Cindy.

"Go ahead and take a break. I'll watch the place until you get back," said Racer.

Racer watched as she pulled away. Then he turned to Sidney and told him to keep an eye on the house. He got out of the car and strolled over to where the van was still parked. Racer tapped on the rear door and it opened a crack. Racer showed himself and George let him in. "How is the phone tap going?" asked Racer.

"Slow," replied George. "The husband has called two more times but that's it."

Looking at his watch, Racer left the van and headed back to his car.

After sliding in beside Sidney, Racer asked, "anything going on?"

"No, just a kid delivering the paper," answered Sidney.

About 45 minutes later Cindy pulled back into her space. Racer got back on his cell and asked if everything was all right.

"Yeah, it probably will be for a few more hours," replied Cindy.

"We'll see you later," said Racer. He had one more stop in

mind before they started their trip.

"Are you ready for dinner?" asked Racer.

"Sure, I could eat something," said Sidney.

"I know just the right place," said Racer, heading for the Club Paris.

Racer pulled into the parking lot at the Club Paris. Sidney looked a little surprised. "I don't think we are quite dressed for this," he said.

"Don't worry, you're with me," said Racer with a sly smile.

Sliding out of the car, they both walked across the parking lot and headed for the restaurant's entrance.

They both walked inside and stopped by the maitre d'. They were both a little under dressed with sport jackets and slacks.

"Gentlemen, I'm sorry, but the Club Paris requires that all gentlemen have a coat and tie in the dining room," said the maitre d'

Racer pulled the maitre d' aside and whispered into his ear. Finally, the maitre d' motioned for them to follow him. Sidney and Racer were seated at a table that gave them a complete view of the dining room. Racer gave the man a tip and thanked him for his help. When the waiter arrived, Racer ordered his usual and Sidney had coffee. Racer then got up and told Sidney that he would be right back.

"What's up?" asked Sidney, when Racer returned.

"I wanted to see if I could find out what table was going to be used for the meet tonight," said Racer.

"Did you?" asked Sidney.

"The only table that it could be is the one back in that little room. It's reserved for a woman by the name of Helen Wallace. Recognize the name? I don't."

"Me either," replied Sidney. "Do you have any idea who the contact will be?"

"I don't know, but I would love to stick around and find out. But we won't have the time. Besides, Cindy will take care of that part," said Racer.

The waiter returned with their drinks and asked if they were ready to order.

After dinner, they returned to the car and headed for the highway. Racer mentioned that they should be there by six-thirty. He watched as Sidney settled in, placing his head against the headrest. In a few minutes, Sidney was sound asleep. Racer thought that Sidney might as well get some sleep because it was going to be a long night. At six-twenty-three Racer pulled into the grocery store lot. As he maneuvered his car around the side, he noticed Detman's car already there and parked out of sight. He pulled up alongside of Detman and parked.

Racer gave Sidney a little shake to wake him up.

"Are we here all ready?" asked Sidney.

"Yeah, you were zonked out," replied Racer.

Racer climbed out of the car and started walking toward the store. Sidney was about three steps behind him. When Racer got inside, Detman was sitting on a bench, sipping at a soda. Racer walked over to the cooler and grabbed two sodas, giving one to Sidney. He paid the old woman behind the counter and sat down next to Detman.

"What time do you think everyone will get here?" asked Detman.

"Susan was told to have everything ready for nine. Cindy will give us a call as soon as she gets in range of the cabin," replied Racer. "That should give us plenty of time to get into position."

It was seven-thirty when Cindy contacted them. She phoned that they were about an hour away. Racer looked at his watch and mentioned that they were a little early.

"Call us every 15 minutes to give us your position," Racer said into his cell.

"Right," said Cindy as she hung up.

"This way we will know exactly were they are all the time," said Racer to Detman and Sidney.

Racer decided to go to the cabin, so he and Sidney drove off, with Detman right behind him. When they got to the final turn before Thompson's cabin, Racer stopped. Detman pulled right in behind him. They all got out and huddled on the side of the road.

"Sidney, this is where you are going to keep watch," said Racer. "The lieutenant is going to let you use his car, and he'll ride with me."

"You better not let anything happen to it," said Detman, giving Sidney the keys.

Before they left Sidney, Racer reminded him to keep out of sight until it was time; they would contact him just before Cindy arrived. Racer and Detman jumped into the ZX and headed for the cabin. When they got to the cabin, Racer backed his car into a small opening in the trees. Walking toward the cabin, Racer checked to make sure his car couldn't be seen from the road. That's when the second call came in from Cindy. They were about 45 miles from the lake. Racer acknowledged the call and passed the information on to Sidney. Racer noticed that all the blinds and curtains were drawn tight, with the exception of the ones he had designated, which were left open just a crack. Racer tapped on the door, and Susan Thompson answered immediately. Holding the door open, Detman and Racer entered. Racer introduced Detman to Susan.

"The lieutenant will be stationed at the bottom of the driveway to make sure that no one gets through our net. Do you have everything ready?" asked Racer.

"About half of the shooting will take place in the front room here and the rest will be shot in the back room, which is set up as a bedroom," said Susan.

Racer walked into the back room to check it out. Detman was right behind him. He looked around and saw only one window and the door that he just came through. "We will make the arrest as soon as we have enough evidence to get a conviction," said Racer. "Now, you'll be arrested with everyone else. Don't worry, we'll take care of you later. But we have to make it look like you're being treated the same as everyone else."

"I understand," said Susan.

It was eight-fifteen when the next call came in from Cindy. She said that they were stopped at a gas station on the highway and everyone was sitting around. Racer assured her that they might be doing this to make sure they weren't followed. They were just 15 minutes away. Racer instructed her to make one more call, and that one would come when they made the turn off the highway. The call came 10 minutes later.

"How many people are we dealing with?" asked Racer.

"Four," answered Cindy.

Racer mentioned that Detman would point out where to park her car, before taking up her position. Racer signed off for the last time. He then turned to Detman and told him it was time to head down to the end of the driveway. Racer reminded Detman to call when they made the turn for the cabin. Racer called Sidney to warn him that they were headed in his direction. A few minutes later, Detman's call came. Racer slipped out the side door and took his position by the side window. Though his view was limited, it would be enough to see what he needed.

Racer could see the glow of the headlights as the car pulled into the driveway. The gravel crackled under its weight as the car inched up to the cabin. It was a red Cadillac. He watched the car doors open. Madeline Stein and Amanda got out of the back seat. Madeline had her arm around Amanda's waist, as if trying to steady her. A guy and girl got out of the front seat and they all headed for the cabin. Racer recognized the girl as one of the sales-clerks from the Designer Dress Shop but he didn't recognize the guy. At first he was hoping that it was Robert Shane, but no such luck. Madeline tapped on the door and waited for it to open.

When the light hit Amanda, she seemed to come to life, though her eyes were a little glassy. In a second, they were all in the cabin and the door shut behind them. Racer moved to the window. When he got there, he saw the guy move Amanda to the loveseat and helped her sit down. The guy, whose name was Georgie, wasn't very big. He was almost a carbon copy of Danny Tonelli. He appeared to be about five-ten, 180 pounds with real dark hair. The girl was a redhead, about the same size as Amanda but a little more top heavy. Racer watched as Madeline talked with Susan; Then Madeline turned to the redhead, named Carol. Racer heard something about taking Amanda into the bedroom and get-ting her ready. Then she told everyone that they would start shoot-ing when Amanda and Carol returned. After that, they would move into the bedroom where Georgie would be Amanda's part-ner. Carol went to Amanda and helped her out off the loveseat. She picked up a duffel bag from the floor, and both women went off to the bedroom. All everyone could do now was wait.

While everyone was getting ready in the cabin, a dark Buick LeSabre approached from the highway and headed toward the cabin. The rear lights were out so there was no way to see the license plate number. Both Sidney and Detman watched it move slowly past the cabin. A couple of seconds later, it made a U-turn and headed back. When it got near the cabin, it pulled off the road and the headlights went out. Whoever it was didn't leave the car.

Racer watched as Carol re-entered the room with Amanda in tow. Amanda was wearing a short green robe, and Carol had changed into a low-cut red dress. The girl positioned Amanda back on the loveseat and moved away from her. Across the room, Susan Thompson was adjusting the camera and lights while Madeline Stein took a chair behind the camera. After a couple of minutes, Susan looked through the viewfinder and told everyone she was ready. Madeline then told Amanda to remove her robe and place it on the floor in front of her. Amanda did as she was told. Amanda was wearing a black lace teddy under the robe. It was low cut in the front and back.

Madeline now became the director. She moved Amanda through a series of poses both on the loveseat and floor. All the time Susan was clicking the camera. Though the poses were provocative, Amanda never removed the teddy. After a series of photos were taken, Amanda was told to sit back on the loveseat and relax. Georgie was there with a drink, which he gave to Amanda. Racer was sure that it was probably laced with a drug to keep her loose and cooperative.

Madeline put Amanda and Carol though a series of poses together. Racer noticed a red light go on; it was from a video camera that Georgie was holding. Susan was snapping pictures as fast as she could, and Georgie was moving in closer and closer. Madeline continued to move the women through their poses. When the last picture was snapped, she hollered for everyone to take a break. Racer took this as his cue.

Racer talked into his cellphone and gave the signal to go. He removed his .357 from his shoulder holster and started counting to five. When he hit five, he burst through the side door. He did exactly what he wanted to do, catch everyone by surprise. Racer shouted for everyone to stay exactly were they were and not to move. He knew that Cindy was outside the front door and if anyone made a move, she would stop them. Georgie put the camcorder down and then made a move toward Racer. Racer stuck the barrel of the magnum in his face. Racer then told Carol to unlock the front door. She did as she was told. Cindy came through the front door and went right to Amanda. She grabbed the robe up off the floor and threw it around Amanda's shoulders. Racer told everyone to put their hands against the wall. Carol asked if she could get dressed. Racer motioned toward her clothes. As he went down the line, he read them their rights and put the cuffs on. He got on his cell, telling Detman that everything was secure and to come on up.

As Detman entered the cabin, Racer could hear a car engine rev and tires spinning on gravel. Two seconds later, everyone heard the crunch of metal as two cars collided.

"What was that?" asked Racer, looking at Detman.

"There was a car parked out on the road, watching the cabin. When I started heading up the driveway, it sped off. Apparently the roadblock stopped him," replied Detman.

"Let's go see," said Racer. He told Cindy to keep an eye on their prisoners and he and Detman headed out to see if Sidney was okay.

When they got to the roadblock, Racer could see that the dark Buick hit Detman's car broadside. The impact was so great that both cars traveled a good thirty yards down the road. Seeing the damage, Detman let out a string of curses. The whole side of his car had been smashed. Racer checked to see if Sidney was all right and then ran to the Buick. The driver was slumped over, his face buried in the deflated airbag. Racer yanked the door open and pulled the man back against the seat. It was Robert Shane, no doubt about that. He had been knocked unconscious.

"As soon as your prisoner wakes up, read him his rights," Racer told Sidney. "And don't forget to cuff him."

Detman got on his cell and called for a couple of wreckers.

"Bring Shane up to the cabin as soon as he can move," said Racer.

Racer pulled Detman away from his car and they both headed back to the cabin. On the way, Racer gave Tim English a call to tell him that the bust went just as planned. He said how relieved he was and thanked Racer for taking care of his wife. When they got close to the cabin, they could hear the redhead blaming Madeline Stein for getting her into this mess. Once they were inside, Racer directed Cindy to take Amanda into the bedroom and get her dressed. He then collected all the film and videotapes that were used for the shoot. After stuffing them into his pockets, he asked Detman who he wanted to question first.

"I'll take the kid first," said Detman.

Detman grabbed Georgie by the collar and told him they were going to have a nice chat. The guy looked at him and then at Madeline, but Racer blocked his view. Detman led him into one of the back rooms. Cindy returned to the room with Amanda. Helping her back down on the loveseat, Cindy sat down next to her. Racer told Cindy that Detman had Georgie and that he was going to try his luck with Madeline Stein. Racer grabbed Madeline by the arm and took her into one of the bedrooms.

"Would you like to make a statement first?" Racer asked.

"As far as I'm concerned, you can go to hell," said Madeline. "And if you have anything else to say to me, you can address it with my lawyer."

"You know, you're in a lot more trouble then you think," said Racer.

Madeline sat there and glared at him. Racer then went through the whole scenario for her. He stressed the point that, right now, they were all suspects in a murder investigation. That seemed to loosen Madeline's tongue a little.

"You can't pin those murders on me. I had absolutely nothing to do with them," said Madeline.

"Well, let's put it this way: I can tie you to all the women and I have a motive, blackmail," replied Racer, staring right into her eyes.

"You don't have anything," said Madeline. "As you can see, the women did it of their own free will."

"Oh, free will. Does that include putting drugs into their drinks?" asked Racer.

Madeline swung her head away from his glance.

"One of you or all of you are going to be put away for a long time," said Racer.

"You're crazy," said Madeline.

"You know, there is a funny thing about the law. If just one of you did the deed, the rest of you are culpable," said Racer. "So since you like taking pictures of women, you'll probably find some willing candidates in prison. Though you might be the subject of their affection."

Madeline slammed her mouth shut and wouldn't say another word. Racer grabbed her by the arm and led her back into the studio. When they got there, Detman had already returned Georgie and taken the redhead, Carol. Racer was about ready to interview Susan when the door flew open. Sidney pushed Shane into the room. Racer quickly looked around the room to catch everyone's reaction. Madeline's face went from a rosy color to an ashen white. No one else had much of an expression, which gave Racer the impression they didn't recognized him. Racer told Sidney to take Shane into the back bedroom and stay with him. He checked on Amanda; she had snuggled up to Cindy and fallen sound asleep. *Hopefully, she won't remember too much about tonight*, thought Racer. He glanced at his watch. It was nine forty-five. He told Cindy that he was going outside to make a call, and that he'd be right back.

Stepping outside, Racer removed his cell phone and dialed Marge Smyth.

"Yes, ma'am. Could you check to see if a Marge Smyth is there? asked Racer. "It's important. I'll wait."

As he waited, he thought about how well everything went. They had put a big dent into the adult film business and taken a giant step in catching their killer.

"Racer, is that you?" asked Marge Smyth. "Where are you?"

Racer filled her in on what happened and told her to be at the station in an hour. She started to ask a question but Racer hung up.

Returning to the studio, Racer found Detman finishing up with the redhead. Everyone was back in the front room. Racer motioned for Detman to join him in the alcove.

"What did you come up with?" asked Racer.

"Georgie's real name is George Visser. He has been working for Madeline Stein, doing odd jobs. She offered him a chance to make some extra money and he took it. He claims that Madeline told him that everything was on the up and up, which we all know is a crock. He also told me that he delivers packages for her out of the studio in Springdale. Next was the redhead. Her name is Carol Harding. She works for Madeline at the Designer Dress Shop. Her story is a carbon copy of Georgie's except she doesn't do any delivering. She claims that this is only her second photo shoot."

"Well, you got more than me. Madeline clammed up on me, said I have to go through her lawyer. But I think that might change now that she knows we have Shane."

"I guess it's time for us to have a little chat with Detective Shane," said Detman.

"Can't wait," replied Racer.

When they entered the bedroom, Shane was lying on the bed with his head propped up with a pillow. Sidney was sitting on a small dresser with his eyes fixed on his prisoner.

"Did he have anything to say?" asked Racer.

"All he said was, he wanted to know what was going on," said Sidney.

"That's what we are going to find out," replied Racer.

Walking over to the bed, Racer grabbed Shane by his shirt and pulled him up into a sitting position. He could see blood on Shane's head where there was a good-sized bump.

"Well, Detective Shane, what brings you all the way out here tonight?" asked Racer.

"I've been investigating the Stein photo shop for months now, on suspicion of pornography. I was afraid that the ring Mr. Stein started had been started back up by his wife. So I started checking it out by following Madeline Stein here tonight," said Shane.

"Why did you run then instead of joining in on the bust?" asked Detman.

"I thought that you all were part of the ring and I didn't want to try and do anything myself. So I decided to go and get help," said Shane.

"Sounds like a good story to me, lieutenant," said Racer, looking at Detman.

"Yeah, a well rehearsed one," said Detman.

"Well, I hate to ruin your night any further, detective, but we have evidence that not only are you a part of this ring, you're probably the leader," said Racer.

"You're crazy," said Shane rubbing his head.

"Let's put two and two together for you. You started up a relationship with Madeline Stein. Her name never appears on any of the police reports and her movies start to disappear. You found a good money-making operation and moved right in."

Shane stared at Racer for a second and then turned to Detman. "You better call the guys in the white jackets. I think your buddy here has gone off the deep end," said Shane.

"If anyone has gone off the deep end, it's you," said Detman. "And you don't have a life jacket either."

Now came the nutcracker.

"Over the last three months, four women have turned up dead. Your people photographed all four of them. After these sessions, they all had their throats sliced. The car that was seen at all the murder scenes is exactly like yours and not only that, the description that we got from an eye witness matches you to a tee. So, not only do we have you for pornography but we also have you for suspicion of murder."

"I don't have a thing to say to you," said Shane. "You're loony."

"But that's not all," said Racer. "We have the little matter of David Hughes and how that truck so conveniently rolled out in front of him. And then there are the shots that were fired at me. So you see, Detective Shane, you have a lot more questions to answer."

"You talk a good story but we both know it takes proof to convict," said Shane. "And besides, I'm a cop."

"That's the whole problem. There's a cancer in the department and we have to cut it out," said Detman.

"If you have anything else to say, you can say it to my legal representative," said Shane.

Racer and Detman helped Shane off the bed and led him back into the front room. It was time to load everyone up and get them to the station.

They loaded Madeline, Carol and Georgie into the Cadillac with Detman as the driver. He thought this was great. A trade off, his smashed car for a new Cadillac. Detman backed the Caddie out of the driveway while Cindy went to get her car. They loaded Robert Shane and Susan Thompson into the back seat and Racer watched as Cindy left right behind Detman. Back in the cabin, Racer shook Amanda gently. Her eyes opened but she had a hard time focusing. Racer and Sidney helped her to her feet and escorted her outside. Racer thought that the cool night air would do her good. As Sidney held on to Amanda, Racer closed all the doors and windows and made sure they were locked. They then walked Amanda around to the front of the cabin and eased her into a chair on the front porch. Sidney stayed with her while Racer went for his car. He wanted to make sure that he got Amanda home safe and sound. And he was going to do it personally. They positioned Amanda in the front seat of the ZX and put her seat belt around her. Sidney squeezed in and Racer got behind the wheel. Before they turned onto the highway, Amanda was sound asleep again.

Racer pulled the ZX into Amanda's driveway. The lights were all on. He had barely brought the car to a stop when Tim appeared at the front door. Amanda was still asleep in the front seat. Tim approached the car, and Racer motioned for him to be quiet. He opened the passenger door carefully, released the seat belt and picked up his wife from the front seat. He carried her into the house and went directly to their bedroom. Racer held the door opened and then took a seat in the living room. Sidney was still trying to pry himself out of the car. When Tim returned to the living room, he took a seat opposite Racer. "Can you fill me in on what happened tonight?" asked Tim.

Racer took the best part of an hour explaining what took place. He made sure that he left out a lot of the graphic stuff.

"Is it over now?" asked Tim.

"Yes, it's over," said Racer confidently.

"I'm glad. I really appreciate everything that you've done for Amanda."

"This is what I get paid for," said Racer. "I'm glad that everything turned out okay."

As Racer stood to leave, he reminded Tim that Amanda should sleep right through till morning. They shook hands and Racer left.

Driving Sidney back to the station, Racer felt good. He was so sure that he could sweat Madeline Stein and Robert Shane until they admitted everything. He would use them against each other. Out of that should come the killer.

CHAPTER TWENTY-THREE

It was after midnight when Racer and Sidney entered the station. It was already like a circus. Everyone was there: the Chief, Captain Peterson, an assistant District Attorney and a half dozen lawyers. As he scanned the room, he saw Cindy talking with Marge Smyth. He started walking toward them when Detman intercepted him.

"I see the press is already here. You wouldn't know how they found out about this so fast?" asked Detman.

"Hey, what do I know?" replied Racer, continuing across the room toward Marge Smyth. When Racer reached Marge, he asked, "Do you have enough for your story?"

"I think so," she replied. "I might even get a raise out of this."

Racer, Cindy, the captain, the assistant district attorney, and the lieutenant met in Detman's office. Racer explained everything that took place, including the evidence they had on the suspects. Then he let the bombshell drop. He suspected that Robert Shane was the killer. Peterson hit the ceiling. "Are you going to stand there and tell me that a detective like Robert Shane is not only involved in this adult film ring but was also killing these women?" he asked loudly.

"Yes sir, that is exactly what I am telling you," said Racer. "That is why I need two search warrants tonight."

"Who do you need them for?" asked the assistant District Attorney.

"I need one for Madeline Stein and the other for Robert Shane," said Racer calmly. "They have to cover everything they own houses, cars, businesses, and anything that they can use to store personal property."

"What exactly are you looking for?" asked the assistant District Attorney.

"Mainly, I'm looking for the murder weapon and the rifle that fired those shots at me," said Racer. "I'm looking for anything that ties Shane to David Hughes' death."

"And Madeline Stein?" asked the assistant District Attorney.

"With Madeline, I'm looking for information, such as names, addresses, records of sales anything that will blow this thing sky high," said Racer.

"Do you believe you'll really find these things?" asked the assistant District Attorney.

"Yes," said Racer without any hesitation.

The assistant District Attorney then turned to Detman.

"And what do you think?" he asked.

"I'm behind Racer one hundred percent," said Detman.

Then it was Peterson's turn. He went on to tell everyone that he wasn't comfortable with accusing a cop of murder. It was enough to have him on pornography charge. But if everyone were in agreement, he would consent to the warrants.

"I'll have the warrants for you by three," said the assistant DA.

"How long can we hold them?" asked Cindy.

"Until their hearing, which will be tomorrow afternoon. Then the judge will determine what happens after that," said the assistant DA.

"You better get started on those warrants," said Peterson.

The assistant DA nodded his head and left the office.

"All I can say is, you better be right," said Peterson when he left the office.

"How are we going to do this?" asked Detman.

"What I thought is, Cindy and myself would take Shane, you and Sidney would take Madeline and, as much as I hate to say it, Harlin and Piakowski could take the dress shop and photo studio," said Racer. "We have to be quick about it."

"Sounds like a plan to me," said Detman.

"Did you get the glass from the restaurant?" Racer asked Cindy.

"I got it and Sidney is already downstairs working on it," she replied.

Racer then turned to Detman. "Do you have one of those large brown envelopes I can borrow?" asked Racer.

Detman opened his top desk drawer and pulled one out. Racer took it and placed the five rolls of film and the videotape in it. He sealed the envelope and handed it back to Detman. "Here, lock this away somewhere and guard it with your life," said Racer.

Detman took the envelope and placed it in one of the filing drawers, which he closed and locked. Just then one of the duty officers stuck his head into the office. "Racer, Shane wants to talk with you," said the officer. Racer looked at Detman and they both headed for the door.

"Alone," said the officer. "He made that very clear. Sorry, lieutenant."

Racer walked over to the desk, where Shane was sitting all alone. "I hear you want to speak with me," he said.

"Is there someplace we can talk in private?" asked Shane.

Racer motioned for Shane to followed him into one of the interrogating rooms. Racer closed the door and told Shane to have a seat. Shane sat down at the small table in the center of the room. Racer stayed standing waiting to hear what Shane had to say.

"Look, just between you and me, I swear that I didn't have anything to do with those killings," said Shane. "I know that you are going to search my place but you won't find anything. I didn't kill anybody."

"Does that include David Hughes and the bullet that was put in my arm?" asked Racer.

"Daniel Hughes was a friend," said Shane. "I would never do anything to harm him and I definitely did not fire a rifle at you. I don't even own one."

"We'll see, won't we?" replied Racer.

"What kind of deal do you think I could get if I tell you everything?" asked Shane, changing the subject.

"Everything?" asked Racer.

"Yeah," said Shane. "The names and phone numbers of all the people involved. And I'm sure you would be surprised who some of those people are."

"You know as well as I do that I can't make any promises, but

I can talk to the district attorney and see what can be done," said Racer.

"Then see what you can do," said Shane.

Racer escorted Shane back to the desk. After sitting him down, he turned back toward Detman's office. He could see that the assistant DA had returned. He told Racer that a courier should arrive within the hour with the warrants. Detman then informed Racer that he had called Harlin and Piakowski and they should be there any time. Then he asked Racer what Shane wanted.

"Nothing," said Racer. "Nothing at all."

Twenty minutes later, the courier arrived with the warrants and right behind him was Harlin and Piakowski. Racer spent the next 15 minutes explaining to the detectives what was going down. The assistant DA then distributed the warrants. Harlin and Piakowski were anxious to get started. Racer told everyone they would start at the first sign of daylight. Which wasn't far away. That would also give Sidney time to finish up in the lab. So all they could do now was wait.

One by one, they all headed for the coffee maker. Racer wished he were at Barney's downing one of his cold drafts. Going to the window, he could see the raindrops starting to hit against the glass. Racer was thinking how much it had been raining lately, when Sidney entered the office.

"No doubt, it was a sedative," said Sidney holding the lab report.

Racer took the report from him and read it. He then turned to Cindy and asked who had put the drug into Amanda's drink.

"It was Georgie," replied Cindy, "but it came out of Madeline's purse."

"Have you matched prints yet?" asked Racer.

"A perfect match with Georgie's," replied Sidney.

"Good. Now we have a little leverage," replied Racer.

Finally five o'clock came. It was time for everyone to get started. They had to get a head start because once the arraignments started, bail would be set and Madeline Stein and Robert Shane would be the first ones out for sure. That meant that there was a good chance that evidence would disappear. The three teams made

their way to the door. When they got outside, they had to make a
mad dash across the parking lot. The rain was coming down in
sheets now and it was almost impossible not to get wet.

Racer was the lead car on the way to Springdale. Every time
he checked in the rearview mirror, Harlin and Piakowski were
right behind him. Racer got to his turnoff, made the right and
watched as Harlin's car continues on to Springdale. When he
pulled up outside of Shane's house, there was only a single light
burning. Before he got out, Racer told Cindy that she might as well
wait. Then Racer slipped out of the car and ran to the house. The
rain was coming down just as hard as it was an hour ago. He
hugged the house tight to shield himself from the rain. He rang the
bell and waited. After a few seconds, he tried again. A few more
seconds passed before the door opened a crack.

"Who is it?" asked the woman standing behind the door.

"It's the police, ma'am," said Racer as he removed his shield
from his pocket.

"I'm sorry but Bob isn't home right now," said the woman.

"We're not here to see him," said Racer. "I have a search warrant to search the premises."

Mrs. Shane seemed a little confused looking out on the group
of detectives standing out in the rain.

"Mrs. Shane, can we please come in?" asked Racer. "It is quite
wet out here."

"I'm sorry, sure," said Mrs. Shane, motioning for them to
come inside.

Once inside the house, Racer identified himself and Cindy as
detectives with the Fairfield Police Department. Racer could see
the confusion on Mrs. Shane's face.

"Why do you have a warrant to search my house?" she asked.

Racer explained to her what had happened the night before.

Apparently, Robert Shane didn't even have the courtesy to call
his wife and tell her what had happened. Racer felt sorry for the
woman.

"What do you think you'll find?" asked Mrs. Shane, sitting
with her hands in her lap.

"The warrant gives up the right to search for anything that is associated with this case," said Racer. "And that includes any type of weapon."

"I know Bob has several handguns locked in a cabinet along with a couple of shotguns," said Mrs. Shane. "I can show them to you, if you wish."

"Yes ma'am," said Racer. "Can you tell me if you husband owns or has owned an old pickup truck?"

"No," replied Mrs. Shane. "One thing Bob doesn't like is old vehicles. He's not very handy around cars, so as soon as they start to give him trouble, he trades them in. I don't think we ever had a car more than three or four years."

"Ma'am, if you don't mind, we would like to get started with our search," said Racer.

Mrs. Shane told them that they were free to go wherever they wished, but she did ask if they could leave the back bedroom until last. Her two boys were sleeping in there.

"Yes ma'am, we can do that," said Racer.

Racer and Cindy searched the house and garage for about two and half-hours and all they came up with where the weapons that Mrs. Shane had told them about. They did find a couple of hunting knives that they collected for analysis. Next, they went through the cars parked in the garage and come up empty. As they went through the house, Cindy noticed a fold-down stairway that led to a storage space above the house. Racer climbed up while Cindy continued her search.

Racer found four locked check boxes pushed off to the side. He hollered down to Cindy and then passed them to her. Then went to Mrs. Shane and asked if she had a key for them. Mrs. Shane informed Racer that she never saw them before.

"Do you have any idea where your husband might keep the key to them?" asked Racer.

"Let me look in his desk. It's in the den," said Mrs. Shane. "He keeps all his spare keys there."

Several minutes later, Mrs. Shane returned with a key ring and handed it to Racer. He took the keys one at a time and tried them. The first box finally opened. There was a ledger, canceled checks and a small phone book. Racer kept trying until he had all the boxes open. The other boxes contained pictures and negatives of various women in different types of poses with or without clothes on. Some of the women were by themselves and some were with partners. He shielded them from Mrs. Shane. When he was done, he put everything back into the boxes and closed them.

"Have you found what you were looking for?" asked Mrs. Shane.

"We'll be taking these with us," replied Racer.

It took them another 20 minutes to finish up. When they were done, all they had to show for their efforts were the hunting knives and the check boxes. Racer signed a receipt for what they were removing from the premises and handed it to Mrs. Shane.

"Detective, does this have something to do with Madeline Stein?" she asked. "I'm not dumb. I know that my husband was seeing her. He kept telling me that it was only business but if I asked any questions he'd shut me off."

"Yes ma'am, it was a business," said Racer. "A business that has gotten your husband in a lot of trouble."

"Will I be able to see him?" asked Mrs. Shane.

"Check with your husband's attorney," said Racer. "He will be able to help you."

As Cindy and Racer left the house, the rain had stopped for the moment. The sky was still cloudy, and it was evident that the rain wasn't completely over.

"It is such a shame," said Cindy as they got into the car.

"Yeah, a beautiful wife and a couple of lovely kids and he's out screwing around."

Racer and Cindy approached the desk sergeant at the Springdale Police Department and asked for Shane's captain. All they got was a cold stare. Finally, Racer leaned over the desk and told the sergeant either he could pick up the phone and call him, or Racer would go upstairs and find him himself. The sergeant reached over, picked up the phone and dialed.

"Second floor, take the hall to the end and ask for Lieutenant Baldwin," said the sergeant.

"Thanks," said Racer flatly.

Climbing the stairs to the second floor, they took the hallway all the way to the end as the sergeant told them. The door was marked Vice in large black letters. Racer pushed it open. Several detectives where sitting around their desks, going through paperwork. Racer approached the first one and asked for Baldwin. The detective looked them over, then pointed to an office in the back corner. Racer and Cindy headed in that direction. As they approached, a young-looking man emerged from the office and greeted them.

"I'm Captain Baldwin," he said.

"This is detective Darling and I'm Racer."

"Come on in and have a seat," said Baldwin as he closed the door behind them.

"I understand that you arrested one of my detectives last night," said Baldwin. "That really concerns me. Lieutenant Shane is a real credit to the department and has received many commendations. I sure hope that you haven't made a big mistake. I'm sure after all is said and done, Lieutenant Shane will be exonerated of all charges. Now detectives, what can I do for you?"

"We have a warrant to go through Shane's things," said Racer flatly.

The smug smile disappeared from Baldwin's face. "Is that really necessary?" he asked.

"Yes, captain, it is," said Racer firmly.

"Then follow me," said Baldwin.

Racer and Cindy followed him out of the office. He led them to a desk in the middle of the room. Racer asked Cindy to go through Shane's desk as he followed the captain. Baldwin led Racer to the locker room and pointed out Shane's locker. There was a lock on the handle.

"You won't have a key to this, would you?" asked Racer.

"I'm afraid not," replied Baldwin.

Racer removed his gun from his holster and hit the lock several times with the butt of the gun. The lock finally fell open. Racer removed it and tossed it on the wood bench between the lockers. As he went through Shane's locker, Baldwin never left his side. Racer went through a change of clothes, a shaving kit, but didn't come up with anything out of the norm. Reaching the back of the top shelf, he found a leather case. Inside was a 9mm Beretta. That was it. Racer closed the locker and hung the lock back in handle.

When they rejoined Cindy, Racer asked if she had found anything.

"Nothing, it's clean," said Cindy.

"Thanks for your cooperation, captain," said Racer sarcastically.

Baldwin never said another word. He just watched as they left.

Outside the rain had started again. It would be a long ride back to Fairfield. When they arrived at the station, the rain had come to a stop. The thick clouds were starting to break up and the sun was trying to poke through. It was a little after noon when they entered the squad room. It was full of activity. Detman noticed them right away and was out of his office waving to them. Racer and Cindy moved in that direction. They could see Harlin and Piakowski were already there. They entered the office and collapsed into chairs.

"The two of you look like crap," said Detman with a smile on his face.

"Thanks lieutenant, we love you, too," said Cindy.

"I just wanted everyone to know that Peterson has scheduled a meeting for one-thirty this afternoon," said Detman. "The Chief and District Attorney will be there with him. So he wants everyone involved with the case to be present. So I wanted to make sure everyone is on the same wavelength. Also, I got a call from Vice raising holy hell about why they weren't involved in this thing. So there will be some wounds to heal. Now, I called out for sandwiches and soft drinks. They should be here any minute."

"While we are waiting, we might as well go over what we found," suggested Harlin.

"Good thought," said Racer.

"Let me go first," said Detman. "We searched Stein's house,

cars, guest house and grounds. We came up with a stack of negatives and several videotapes. Sidney has them, down in the lab right now. But that was it."

Harlin went next.

"The photo studio was a bonanza," said Harlin. "We found a filing cabinet full of eight by tens. There also was a separate file on a lot of the girls they must have used. Apparently, the women in Fairfield weren't the only victims."

"We'll have to check to see if any of those women have turned up dead," said Detman.

"Will do," said Piakowski.

Harlin then mentioned that the files of the four dead women had red dots on them. They were the only files marked that way.

"That might be a good sign," said Detman.

Racer told them about the four metal check boxes that they had found at Shane's house. They were filled with pictures as well as negatives. "The one thing that might prove to be the big find is a ledger with names and phone numbers. With a little luck that could be their distribution network," said Racer.

"What about Shane?" asked Detman.

"All we found were several hunting knives," said Racer. "We dropped them off by Sidney on the way up."

The disappointment could be read in everyone's face. They had enough evidence to put Shane, Madeline Stein and the rest away on pornography charges, but there was nothing pointing them to who had committed the murders.

"What if, and I'm saying if, Shane didn't commit these murders? Where do we go from here?" asked Detman.

Racer just stared at him with a blank look. Then the door swung open; the sandwiches had arrived. After they finished eating, Detman motioned for Racer to join him outside the office.

"You know we have enough evidence to convict on the charges centering around the adult films," said Detman, "but that wasn't the reason for this whole damn investigation.

"Well, we know that Shane drives a car similar to the one that has been identified at the murder scenes," said Racer. "He also knew the women, where they lived and could have used his badge to gain entrance. That would explain no forced entry marks. He also could have used blackmail to force them to have sex with him. Therefore, no evidence of rape."

"You built a good circumstantial case against him, but I don't know if it's enough to convict," said Detman. "The big question is, why kill these four and not all of them?"

"Physical attraction," said Racer.

Detman just shook his head.

Something in the back of Racer's brain was throbbing. The idea of a guy like Shane, with a beautiful wife, small kids at home, running around with Madeline Stein, committing murder and rape just to satisfy his lust was hard to stomach. Racer looked over Detman's shoulder and saw Sidney approaching with a hand full of envelopes. When he reached them, they all went back into the office.

Sidney handed Detman one envelope at a time and explained the contents. Most of the reports centered on the negatives, photos, videotapes and the ledger. Then they came to the report on the hunting knives. It read that the knives had traces of blood on them. But the blood belonged to animals, probably deer. Detman tossed the report over to Racer.

"Well, it's time," said Detman. "Our presence is required on the fourth floor."

As soon as they entered the conference room on the fourth floor, Peterson pulled Detman aside. The Chief of Detective and the District Attorney was already there. Racer avoided all the brass. He wasn't much for rubbing elbows with the upper crust of the department. Detman finally broke away from the captain and returned to the group. His eyes went directly to Racer.

"The Captain wants you to review the case," said Detman. "And unless any questions are asked of a particular individual, Racer is the only one who will speak. Is that clear?"

Everyone muttered his or her acknowledgment.

"Is that all he said to you?" asked Racer.

But before Detman could answer, Peterson called the meeting to order. He took the first five minutes giving an introduction into the case. He stressed the heat that the department had been under to solve this case. Although he didn't mention a name, everyone understood whom he was referring to. Peterson talked about how the murders had terrorized the city and women everywhere felt unsafe. But now, due to the recent bust, everyone could sleep safe at night again. Then he introduced Racer and gave him the floor.

It only took Racer about 10 minutes to discuss the case from beginning to present. He made sure that some of the more sensitive information was not mentioned. At the end of his talk, he presented some of the evidence they had against the suspects. He stressed the point that Susan Thompson had been a great help to them in breaking the ring. Then Peterson interrupted.

"I would like to mention that the District Attorney, myself, Lieutenant Shane and his lawyer had a very productive meeting this morning, before he went to his hearing," said Peterson. "Shane is willing to turn state's evidence for a deal. But I must add that one thing he is very adamant about is his lack of involvement in the murders. And after listening to the circumstantial evidence we have, I might tend to agree. What other avenues do you have to follow?" asked Peterson, looking directly at Racer.

"All I can say right now is there are a lot of people sitting in prison convicted on circumstantial evidence," said Racer. "They all claim to be innocent."

"I understand that, detective, but we are talking about convicting a cop of murder," said Peterson.

"We are still exploring all avenues open to us," said Racer. "The murder investigation is still open."

Racer could see the look of concern on the faces of the Chief and the District Attorney. He knew that Peterson had ambushed him. After the meeting, he cornered the DA. "What are the chances of getting an indictment against Shane with what we have?" asked Racer.

"As far as the pornography charges, not a problems, but with the murder charge, it would depend on the grand jury," said the DA. "I will admit, I have seen people sent to prison on less evidence, but I would feel a whole lot better if we had a stronger case. Shane is a detective who has been decorated for his service to the department, and you better make sure that you have the right man before we proceed on the murder charges."

After the District Attorney and Racer split up, Cindy caught up with him.

"What's our next step?" asked Cindy. "It doesn't sound like everyone is convinced Shane is the killer."

"You got that feeling too," said Racer.

"Well, I guess we have to come up with some evidence that positively links Shane to the women," said Cindy.

"I want you to go back downstairs and call the county sheriff's department and see if they have come up with anything on that truck," said Racer.

Cindy nodded.

When Cindy and Racer reached the first floor, he told her to go ahead and make her phone call, he was going down to the lab and see Sidney. They both were dragging but they wanted to cover all the loose ends before they called it a day. As Racer headed for the lab, he kept running Shane through his mind. Was Shane innocent or trying to build doubt in everyone's mind about the murders? Pushing through the lab doors, Racer asked a tech in a white lab coat if Sidney was around. She said he was in the viewing room. Racer knew that she meant the morgue. As he approached the steel doors, Racer could see a light flickering from a small room off to the left. He opened the door and peeked in. Sidney was sitting there watching porno flicks.

"What the heck are you doing?" asked Racer with a big smile on his face. "These videos are for private viewing only."

"Just sit down and take a look at this," said Sidney. "Pay particular attention to the woman with the long blond hair."

Racer stared at the screen and his eyes lit up. "I'll be damned," said Racer. "It's Shane's wife, or someone who looks an awful lot like her."

"That was the same thing that I was thinking," said Sidney. "Maybe that is how they met."

"Possible, very possible," said Racer. "And that could be why he is so quick to make a deal with us. He probably doesn't want this to get out. Can't say I blame him."

Sidney finally turned the projector off and looked at Racer. "That's all I can find," said Sidney. "If you only could get me that rifle, we might have something positive."

Racer was having a heck of a time making it back up the stairs. Not only was he tired but he was starving. That sandwich at lunch wasn't enough to fill his big toe. Everything had quieted down in the squad room. Cindy was sitting at her desk, sipping a diet soda.

"Well, did you find anything out?" asked Racer.

"No," said Cindy. "The guy who has been investigating the accident isn't there right now but they are going to have him call me as soon as he gets back, and that is not until around eight tonight."

"I don't know about you but there is no way I will make it till eight without something to eat and a little nap," said Racer. "So how about some dinner?"

"I'm with you," said Cindy. "My stomach is starting to growl. How about a steak place?"

They strolled across the parking lot heading for Racer's car. The sky was starting to cloud up again. A short time later, Racer pulled up in front of the Steak Joynt Restaurant. Cindy told Racer that it was her turn to treat. He just shook his head. "Look now, you have been buying all my meals lately," said Cindy. "I'm starting to feel like a kept woman."

"Don't worry about it," said Racer. "Us homicide cops make big money."

They were ushered to a nice quiet table. When the waiter approached to take their drink order, Racer ordered a bottle of white wine with two glasses.

"What's the occasion?" asked Cindy.

"We have to celebrate our bust," said Racer. "No one else is going to congratulate us."

CHAPTER TWENTY-FOUR

Detman was just leaving when they returned to the station.

"The two of you better go home and get some sleep," said Detman. "I don't want two fried cops working for me."

"We're just gluttons for punishment," said Racer.

"I don't want to see you two before noon," said Detman as he walked away.

When they reached the squad room, Cindy's phone stopped ringing. The squad room was completely empty. Everyone was signed out on the board. Getting to their desks, they collapsed into the chairs. Racer put his head in his hands and closed his eyes.

"Can I interest you in a cup of coffee?" asked Cindy.

"Sure," replied Racer.

As she stood by the coffee maker, pouring two cups of coffee, her phone started ringing again. Racer got up and grabbed the phone on the third ring. "Racer here." He held the phone away from his ear and said, "It's for you."

Cindy walked back to her desk with two cups of coffee. She put them down and took the phone from Racer. "This is detective Darling," said Cindy. "I called to see if anything turned up in the David Hughes case."

After listening for several minutes, Cindy thanked the person on the other end and hung up.

"They found a fingerprint on the driver's door. It appears the truck was stolen from a farmer over in Coatesville. He's going to fax it over," said Cindy.

"That's great. Now we can wrap this thing up as soon as we tie it to Shane," said Racer. "Well, let's go and see if it's on the way."

Cindy grabbed her cup of coffee and followed Racer into the outer hall. Racer was four steps ahead of Cindy as he headed for the fax room. The fax was already coming across the wire. While they were waiting, Racer grabbed the phone and dialed Sidney. The girl who answered said Sidney had gone home. She gave Racer his home number. Racer dialed again. When a woman answered, Racer asked for Sidney. He was told that Sidney had just stepped into the shower. Racer asked if she would give him a message to call Racer when he got out. He thanked her and hung up.

"I have the fax," said Cindy.

"Let's head to the lab and wait for Sidney to call," said Racer.

When Sidney called, Racer told him that they had a fingerprint taken from the driver's door on the pickup truck that David hit. All they needed was to match it to Shane. Sidney explained that he had promised his wife that they would go out for a nice dinner tonight. He had made reservations at the Park Place Restaurant.

"I'll tell you what, if you can match this print to Shane, I'll buy you and your wife dinner," said Racer.

Sidney reluctantly agreed.

"He's on his way," said Racer as he placed the phone back on the cradle.

It was nine o'clock when Sidney pushed his way through the swinging doors. He explained to Racer that he only had 30 minutes to match that print and get to the restaurant. The Park Place did not hold a reservation past the allotted time.

As Sidney passed Cindy, she handed him the fax of the print the county sheriff's department took from the door of the pickup truck. Sidney went to a computer and brought up Shane's file. Then he placed the print onto the glass of a scanner and closed the cover. Hitting a button, the scanner went into motion. It took about 30 seconds when the screen flashed red and the message "no match" came up.

"It doesn't match," replied Sidney.

"Damn," said Cindy.

"I don't believe it," said Racer.

"Fingerprints don't lie," said Sidney. "I'll send it off to the feds tomorrow and see if they can come up with anything."

"The county cops have already done that," said Cindy. "They're still waiting for an answer."

Then suddenly Racer said, "Pull Brian Thompson's file."

"Can't this wait until tomorrow?" said Sidney as he looked at his watch.

"Sidney, just pull the file," said Racer.

Sidney punched Brian Thompson's name into the computer and his file came up. He pushed the button for the scanner and again it went into motion.

"You don't think that he is involved in this, do you?" asked Cindy.

"I don't know, but we should find out in a few seconds," said Racer.

"Why him?" asked Cindy.

"Look at it this way," said Racer. "His mother drives the same kind of car as Shane and, as we know, has access to it. Susan is the photographer that has been taking the pictures. And I would be surprised if Brian doesn't know about that. Besides, his record isn't exactly clean."

This time it took him a little longer but when Sidney raised his head, he was smiling.

"Son-of-a-bitch," said Racer. "I screwed up."

Racer pulled his cell phone and dialed Detman. He stood there, drumming his fingers on the table waiting for Detman to answer. It took about twenty rings before someone came on the line.

"Harry, I know who the killer is and I need a search warrant right now," said Racer.

"Hold on," said Detman. "This morning you were telling everyone that Shane was our killer."

"I screwed up," said Racer.

"So you want me to believe you now," said Detman.

"Damn it, Harry," shouted Racer into the phone. "We have proof. Sidney just matched a fingerprint that was taken off the pickup truck that killed David Hughes. It belongs to Brian Thompson."

The line went silent for a minute.

"Okay," said Detman. "I'll get the warrant and meet you in front of the Thompson's place in half an hour."

"We'll be there," said Racer as he hung up.

Sidney was patiently standing there looking at his watch. Racer reached into his pocket and pulled out four twenties and told Sidney to have a good bottle of wine.

"Thanks," Racer said. "You just broke the case."

Racer didn't spare any rubber getting to the Thompson place. They were sitting outside the house in fifteen minutes. It was now misting. They would sit and wait for Detman to get there. Both cars were sitting in the driveway. Susan's dark Buick LeSabre and Brian's car. As they sat there the dampness was creeping into the car. The mist was now turning into a light rain. It was really putting a chill into the air.

Racer kept the car running so he could keep the windows clear. Just then, he saw a figure come from the back of the house. It was hard to tell who it was. The figure was dressed in a bulky raincoat and was carrying an umbrella. The person got into the Buick and started the engine. The lights went on and the car started backing out of the driveway. When the car got into the street, it headed in the opposite direction that Racer and Cindy were parked.

"Do you think that was Brian?" asked Cindy.

"I don't know but I sure wish that Harry would hurry with that warrant," said Racer.

Racer glanced into the rearview mirror and saw a pair of headlights approaching from a distance. The car slowed up and pulled in behind them. Detman got out of the car and walked up to Racer's window.

"Let's go, it's party time," said Detman with the warrant in his hand.

Cindy and Racer got out of the car and joined Detman. They all walked up to the Thompson's house and rang the bell. Racer motioned for Cindy to take the back. No one answered. Detman rang the bell again. The rain was starting to fall harder and the longer they waited, the wetter they got. Finally, on the third ring Susan Thompson answered the door in her housecoat. She was definitely surprised to see them.

"Are you going to arrest me again?" asked Susan.

"Can we please come in?" asked Detman.

Susan stepped aside and allowed them to enter.

"We are really here to talk to your son," said Racer. "Is he home?"

"You just missed him," said Susan. "He is meeting some friends at the bowling alley."

"Mrs. Thompson, we have a search warrant here that gives us the right to search everything on the premises," said Detman.

"What are you looking for?" asked Susan. "I've cooperated with you fully."

"I know you have," said Racer. "This has nothing to do with you."

"Then why are you here to see my son?" asked Susan.

"We have some questions we'd like to ask him on a different matter," said Detman.

"Look, just because he was in jail doesn't mean the police have a right to harass him every time something happens," said Susan a little upset.

"I understand," said Detman.

"He hasn't done anything," said Susan. "He works hard and stays home most of the time. He goes out a couple of nights a month to meet his friends and that's it."

"Mrs. Thompson, can we search the house?" asked Detman politely. "And we would like to start with your son's room."

Racer went to the back door and stuck his head out. Cindy was hunched under the overhang to keep from getting to wet. "Go ahead and get the car," said Racer.

Cindy nodded and headed back to the driveway.

When Racer rejoined Detman, they headed for Brian's bedroom. Susan Thompson showed them into a medium-size room toward the back of the house. She stood guard in the doorway as Detman and Racer searched the room. They went through all the drawers in the dresser and nightstand and found nothing. But when they got to the closet they found a shoebox with several pairs of surgical gloves. They also found a wallet with a false police identification card and a detective's gold shield. Racer turned to Mrs. Thompson. "Have you ever seen these before?" asked Racer.

"No," replied Susan shaking her head.

"Did you ever mentioned to your son about the photo sessions?" asked Racer.

"I don't know," said Susan. "I might have. But I didn't mention anything about what we were doing at the photo shoots."

As they continued their search, Cindy entered the house carrying a rifle with a scope and a box of 30.06 shells. "Look what I found in the trunk of the car," she said.

"I guess you never saw them before either," said Racer.

"No," replied Susan. "I mean, yes, I saw them. He goes hunting with his friends. He asked me not to say anything because he isn't allowed to have weapons. What exactly is going on here?"

Ignoring the question, Detman asked, "Where specifically did your son go tonight?"

"To the bowling alley over on Rolling Hills Boulevard," said Susan.

Racer then turned to Cindy.

"We need to match the rifle with the bullet we found," said Racer.

"What bullet?" asked Detman with concern on his face.

"The one I found," said Racer. "Don't ask so many questions. I'll explain it to you later."

"Sorry I asked," said Detman. "I'm only the lieutenant here."

Detman took the rifle from Cindy and told them that he would take it to the lab. He'd have a ballistics check done on it to see if he could get a match. If it matched, he'd call the DA for a warrant to arrest Brian Thompson. Racer informed him that Sidney had the slug. He went on to tell Detman that Sidney was having dinner with his wife at the Park Place Restaurant.

"Don't worry, I'll find him," said Detman.

Susan, who had been listening to their conversation, all of a sudden burst into tears.

"My son hasn't done anything," she said. "You can't send him back to jail. He has been trying so hard to stay out of trouble."

Cindy put her arm around Susan and tried to console her.

"We really have to go," said Racer. "This is really turning into an awful long night."

When they got outside, the rain was coming down in sheets. Thunder was rolling and lightning was cracking. They made a mad dash for Racer's car. Detman went back to the station, and Racer and Cindy headed for the bowling alley on Rolling Hills Boulevard. It took Racer about 10 minutes to make the 30 minute trip. He dropped Cindy off at the side entrance and told her to be careful. Then he drove his car to the main entrance and parked it right by the front door.

When he got inside, he saw Cindy standing by the side door. The place was packed. It must have been the weather that brought everyone indoors. Racer walked down to the opposite end of the building and then slowly made his way back toward Cindy. When he finally reached her, he told her that he didn't see Brian. Racer then went to the counter. "Could you please page a Brian Thompson?" Racer asked the cashier. "Just tell him to come to the counter."

Then Racer stepped out of sight and waited. He listened to the page but didn't see anyone make a move toward the counter. He asked the cashier to give it one more shot. This time he saw a guy from alley 24 walk toward the counter, but it wasn't Brian Thompson. Racer watched as Cindy followed right behind him. When the guy got to the counter, Racer could hear him tell the cashier that Brian wasn't there.

"Excuse me," said Racer. "Did you say that Brian wasn't here?"

"Yeah," said the guy. "He was supposed to be here at nine but didn't show up."

"You won't have any idea where he might be, would you?" asked Racer.

"Who the hell are you?" asked the guy.

"Just a friend," said Racer. "I wanted to surprise him, and his mother told me that he would be here."

"Well, he isn't and I don't know where he is," said the kid.

"Come on, Cindy. I think I know where Brian Thompson might be," said Racer, running out to the ZX with Cindy right behind him.

Racer started the car and pushed the accelerator to the floor.

It fishtailed out of the parking lot and into the street. Once he straightened the car out, Cindy asked him where he thought Brian was.

"I'm afraid to say," said Racer, "but I think he's headed for Amanda English's house."

"How would he get in?" asked Cindy. "He doesn't have his fake identification."

"What if he has more than one?" said Racer. "I can't take that chance. The last four women who had photo sessions with Susan Thompson are now dead, and I don't want that to increase to five."

Racer thought to himself that he wouldn't be able to live with himself if anything happened to Amanda. He had given his word to Tim and Amanda that nothing would happen, but now he wasn't so sure.

CHAPTER TWENTY-FIVE

Carefully approaching Amanda English's house, Racer noticed a dark Buick parked about a half block away. He parked right in front of it. The rain was still falling heavily to the ground. He noticed several lights on in the house.

"I'll take the back," said Cindy as she slid her .38 out of her purse.

"I'll give you two minutes to get in position," said Racer.

Racer watched as she crossed the street in the rain, then disappeared around the corner of the house. He counted off two minutes and stepped out into the rain. As he approached the house, he noticed how quiet it was. He felt good about the Buick still being there. It probably meant that Amanda was still alive. When he got to the front of the house, he tried to see in the windows. They were covered with curtains and he couldn't see anything. Next, he went to the front door and tried the knob. It was locked. He carefully put his shoulder against it and gave it a push. It didn't budge. Moving to one of the windows, he applied a little muscle and it slid open. He squeezed through the opening and tumbled into the front room. Drawing his .357, he slowly made his way through the downstairs. Pausing, he hear noises coming from one of the back rooms. When he got to the door where the noise was coming from, he gave it a short power kick. The door blew open in a shower of splinters.

Brian Thompson and Amanda English were in bed. Brian was on top of her, ripping at her clothes. There was tape on Amanda's mouth and her hands were tied to the bed. When Brian saw Racer, he jumped off Amanda and leaped through the window. Shattered glass flew everywhere. Racer ran to the window but couldn't see anything in the rain and darkness. All he could do was holler to Cindy that Brian was coming her way. He went back to the bed, untied Amanda's hands and removed the tape from her mouth. She burst into tears. He asked if she was all right and Amanda nodded. Racer ran to the back door and threw it open. He slowly moved into the darkness, not knowing what to expect. A car was starting in the distance. Racer slid along the house until he came to the corner. Cindy was sitting on the ground holding her head.

"Are you all right?" asked Racer.

"Yeah, I'm fine. I feel like a damn fool. He blew through that window and knocked me right over."

Racer ran to the front of the house as the Buick was pulling away from the curb.

"Put out an APB on the Buick, then take care of Amanda," hollered Racer. "I'm going after him."

Racer ran to the ZX and jumped in. He started the car and hit the accelerator. It only took him several seconds and he was right behind the Buick. He chased Brian Thompson through town and out onto the highway. Racer called in the chase and told the dispatcher to get hold of Lieutenant Detman. Brian made a couple of sharp turns trying to lose him, but Racer stayed right on his tail.

"Harry, Cindy is with Amanda English. You better get some medical help and a policewoman over there," said Racer.

A few seconds later, Detman came on the radio. "I was with Sidney. He matched the bullet to the rifle. Brian Thompson's our man," said Detman. "I'm waiting on the arrest warrant."

"Good. Pick Cindy up and I'll get back to you," replied Racer and signed off.

The roads were slick from the rain, but the ZX handled them without any trouble. Every time the Buick spun out, Racer was right behind it. Brian was heading back toward town when he made a sharp left at the city limits and almost hit a van head on. Racer hit his brakes and started to fishtail but pulled out of it as he downshifted and hit the accelerator again.

Detman came back on the radio and asked what Racer's position was. Racer informed him that they were headed west on Sandpiper Road. Racer pushed the accelerator down harder and the ZX lurched forward. He didn't want to lose Brian. The rain was hitting the windshield so hard that the wipers had a hard time keeping up. He saw the taillights of the Buick disappear up ahead. When he got to that spot in the road, he saw the entrance to the new shopping mall that was under construction. It was probably about half completed. Racer hit his brakes and slowed down. He downshifted the ZX and pulled into the entrance. The driveway and the entire parking lot were all stone. They hadn't laid the concrete yet. As Racer slowly approached the building, he called Detman back on the radio.

"Harry, I'm at the entrance to the new shopping mall," said Racer.

"Okay," said Detman. "I have Cindy with me. We should be there in ten minutes."

Racer acknowledged that and signed off. He turned around the corner of the building and saw the Buick sitting up ahead. He approached it cautiously. Pulling up alongside of it, he saw that it was stuck in the mud. The car had gone off the stone area and got mired down. There was an opening into the mall about fifty yards ahead. Racer aimed his car into the opening so his lights would shine into it. He stepped out into the rain, made his way to the opening and stopped. There were some night-lights on but they didn't give off enough light to see into all the corners. Racer had to decide if he was going to wait for Cindy and Detman or enter the mall now. He didn't want to lose Brian, so he decided to go in.

Racer hugged the wall as he slowly made his way, passing one store at a time. Each one had only one light shining from the ceiling, which created a lot of shadows. As he moved on, Racer noticed that the corridors had a single sting of lights hanging from the ceiling. Only one out of every six lights was lit. There had to be a switch or something to turn the rest on, he thought, but where? He heard another car pull up outside on the stones. That had to be Detman and Cindy. He retraced his steps back to the entrance. Cindy and Detman had pulled up alongside his car.

"What's the situation?" asked Detman.

"I followed Brian in here. When I got to his car, it was empty and stuck in the mud. It looks like he's taken refuge in the mall," said Racer.

"Can we get him out of there?" asked Detman.

"The big problem is lighting. There is some but not enough," said Racer. "Too many dark corners."

"What do you suggest?" asked Detman.

"There is a string of lights going down the center of the corridor but I don't have the slightest idea of how to turn them on," replied Racer.

"If I'm not mistaken, construction usually runs them off of a generator. All we have to do is find it," said Detman.

"It's probably not in the open. They usually try to hide them so no one steals them," replied Cindy.

"Don't worry, I'll find it," said Racer.

They decided that Detman would watch the front, Cindy would watch the back and Racer would search for the generator. They split up and went about their assignments. Racer walked around the outside of the building until he came to a hole in the wall. It was so dark in there he couldn't make out anything. He ran back to his car and aimed his lights in that direction. Bingo, there it was. The only problem was that it was chained to a cement pillar with a padlock on the engine. Racer drew his .357 and hit the lock with the butt of his gun. After several blows it wouldn't budge. Finally, he took aim and fired. The lock flew open. He removed the lock from the hasp and hit the start button. The motor groaned but wouldn't start. Racer pushed the start button again and held it. This time the motor came to life. Now he looked for a switch that turned the lights on. There was an electrical box mounted to a two-by-four stuck in the ground. It also had a lock on it. He didn't want to take a chance of firing at it and destroying the whole box. He tried his gun butt on the lock and it gave way after a couple of hits. Racer removed the lock, threw the box opened and hit every switch. The lights came on one string at a time. In a few seconds, the whole building was lit like a Christmas tree.

Racer ran to the opening and slipped back into the building. He made Detman and Cindy aware of his moves. Staying close to the wall, he started checking each store one by one. When he came to the first doorway leading in from the outside, Cindy joined him. Racer stayed about 10 feet in front of Cindy as she covered him. When they got to the center of the mall, Detman joined them. Detman went down one side of the aisle and Racer down the other. They got two-thirds down the aisle when the lights started to dim.

"I hate to ask, but did you check the gas before you started the generator?" asked Detman.

"Damn!" said Racer. "You should have told me that before I started the generator."

Moving through two more stores, the lights went out. All they had were the night-lights.

"Why are these lights still on?" asked Cindy.

"They must be hooked into the power lines," replied Detman.

Racer heard a noise up ahead. He held his hand up and they all stopped dead in their tracks and listened. He heard it again. It sounded like someone was moving away from them. Racer picked up the pace. When he got near the end of the corridor, he could see a figure moving in the shadows. Racer hollered for Brian to stop and give himself up. Just then a shot rang out. The bullet hit the concrete wall right in front of Racer and sent powder and stone flying into the air. Everyone hit the floor in a hurry.

"Well, at least we know he has a gun," said Racer.

They could hear Brian moving again. This time he seemed to be in a hurry. As Racer moved down the corridor a little further, he could see a stream of light that must have been coming from outside.

"There has to be an opening up there," said Racer as he moved in that direction.

Racer started running toward the light. He hollered back to Detman to circle around outside and try to cut him off. Cindy stayed right behind Racer. When Racer got to the last store opening, on the left, he peered in. A large opening in the wall led to the outside. A second shot rang out, but this one was not aimed at him. Racer ran to the opening and could see Brian Thompson sprinting through the rain toward the road. Racer climbed through the opening with Cindy right behind him. Racer told Cindy to get the car and head for the road. Racer started after Brian on foot.

It was raining so hard now that it stung his eyes as he ran. He was slowly gaining on Brian as they both trudged through the water and mud. Racer felt like he had weights on his feet. There must have been an inch of mud on each shoe. Racer saw Brian stop and turn toward him. His right arm went up and Racer went down as two more shots ripped through the night. Racer went headfirst into a large puddle. Not only was he soaked but he was completely caked in mud.

At this point, Racer felt confident that he could have gotten off a good shot, but he wanted Brian alive and in one piece, so he continued to run after him. Racer could see Brian dart up onto the road and look both ways. *Must be looking for a vehicle to jump into*, he thought. As Brian stood there, Racer was closing the gap between them. He lungs were starting to sting as he drew in the damp night air. Cindy was coming up behind him with the car now. Racer could hear the engine getting closer. Finally, Racer reached the road.

Brian Thompson had paused long enough for Racer to catch up to him. As Brian turned to face Racer and get off another shot, Racer sailed through the air and hit him with both feet square in the chest. This sent Brian backward and the gun flying off into the mud. Racer knew that Brian was a big guy. His arms were the size of most people's thighs. He probably worked out in prison a lot. Racer went to throw another punch but Brian blocked it and grabbed Racer around the chest. He was squeezing so hard that Racer was having a hard time breathing. Finally, Racer cupped both hands and popped Brian's ears with his palms. Brian dropped Racer onto the asphalt.

As Brian staggered backwards shaking his head, Racer brought the heel of his right foot up and caught Brian in the solar plexus. Brian bent over and grabbed his stomach. This gave Racer a chance to bring up his left knee and catch Brian right under the chin. Racer could hear his mouth slam shut and bone crack. Brian fell over backwards and hit the road hard. Racer started to relax. Brian lay in the rain for a few seconds and then slowly got back to his feet. Blood was running out of his mouth and nose. Racer saw something shiny in his suspect's right hand. It was a switchblade.

"Are you going to use the same knife on me as you used on those defenseless women?" shouted Racer, taking a defensive stance.

Brian started moving toward him, swinging the knife back and forth. When he was two steps away, Brian made a lunge at Racer. Racer sidestepped him and grabbed his arm as he went by. He yanked it up behind Brian until he dropped the knife and then gave it one more push. There was a loud pop and Brian fell to his knees, howling. Racer figured he owed Brian one more for the scratch he put in the ZX. He walked around to face Brian, who was kneeling in the pouring rain. His eyes were fixed on the ground.

"Brian, you have the right to remain silent," started Racer. As Brian looked up to meet Racer's eyes, Racer caught him with the heel of his right hand square on the nose. Blood flew everywhere and Brian hit the ground hard for the second time. This time, he stayed there.

"You have a right to an attorney and to have him present during questioning," said Racer, exhausted.

He heard the car pull up behind him.

Cindy jumped out and ran over to him. "Are you all right?" she asked.

"I think you should ask Brian that question," said Racer as he pointed to the figure lying on the road.

"Is he dead?" asked Cindy.

"No, but I think he might be in need of some medical help."

"I already radioed for back up and an ambulance, said Cindy. Detman's been hurt."

"Go ahead and cuff him," said Racer as he ran back to the car and drove away.

When Racer got to Detman, he was sitting on the front seat of his car, holding his arm.

"Are you okay?" asked Racer.

"I think I broke my arm again," replied Detman with a grimace. "When Thompson turned to fire at me, I jumped out of the way. I slipped on a pile of bricks and fell."

"Are you okay to drive?" asked Racer.

"I think so," said Detman. "Did you get him?"

"Damn right I did. I'll meet you up on the road," said Racer, getting back in his car.

Racer headed up to the road where Cindy was guarding the suspect.

When the ambulance arrived, Racer pointed to Detman first. They checked his arm and put an air splint on it. Then they went to Brian Thompson who was sitting, cuffed, in the back seat of one of the police cars that were now on the scene. They eased him out of the patrol car, placed him on a gurney, loaded Brian and Detman into the back and closed the doors. Racer told one of the patrol officers to follow the ambulance to the hospital. Cindy and Racer both stood in the rain and watched as the ambulance, with its red and white lights flashing, sped out of sight.

Racer tossed his keys to Cindy. "You drive my car back and I'll take Detman's."

"Harry might not appreciate you driving his car with all that mud on you," said Cindy.

"Don't worry, it's only a rental," said Racer. "I'll meet you at the hospital."

Racer stood there for a minute and watched as Cindy drove off into the night. Then he walked back to Detman's car and collapsed into the front seat. He was tired, wet and muddy. All he really wanted was a hot shower and a nice warm bed, but he knew that he wasn't going to get either for several hours yet. He swung his legs into the car and started it up. The rain was a drizzle now. The forecast for tomorrow was sunny, with a high in the eighties. He sure hoped that the weatherman was right this time. He was sure as hell getting sick of this rain. Leaving the patrolman to do their jobs, he headed back to town.

When Racer reached the hospital, Detman was sitting with Cindy in the waiting room with a brand new cast on his arm.

"How is Thompson doing?" asked Racer.

"You did a pretty good number on him," said Detman. "He's going to need a little more medical attention than I did. They're going to keep him in the hospital overnight for observation. I have two officers guarding his room."

"All I want right now is a hot shower," said Racer.

"Cindy, take this man home, and that's an order," said Detman.

Cindy nodded and took Racer by the arm. She led him out of the hospital and helped him into his car. Detman followed them outside. "Take it easy now and get some sleep," said Detman. "We'll get everything straightened out tomorrow."

It was one in the afternoon when Racer finally came to. The sunlight steamed through his window. Lying there, he vaguely remembered getting home. He was so tired he couldn't remember taking a shower and falling into bed. He threw the covers back and grabbed a pair of shorts, put them on, and headed for the kitchen to make some coffee. While it was heating up, he shaved and got dressed. Returning to the kitchen, Racer poured himself a cup of coffee just as the phone began to ring.

"I just got a call from Detman. He wants us in his office by three," said Cindy.

CHAPTER TWENTY-SIX

When Cindy and Racer got to the station, everyone started to congratulate them on a job well done. Detman came out of his office as soon as he saw them.

"Well, word's out," said Detman. "The two of you are heroes. Marge Smyth was here an hour ago and the Chief gave her the whole story."

"Good. That will make us even," said Racer looking around.

"The Captain has scheduled a news conference for three-thirty and he wants everyone associated with the case there, especially the two of you. So we might as well head up to the conference room. The brass is probably already there," said Detman.

"Great," replied Racer. "By the way, how's the arm?"

"Fine," said Detman, carrying it in a sling.

As they made their way upstairs, Detman told them that they had questioned Brian Thompson that morning. Harlin and Piakowski had taken care of it.

"Great, the blind leading the blind," replied Racer.

"Never mind that," said Detman. "He didn't want to talk at first, but when the prosecutor started to shove all the evidence in his face, he finally decided to make a statement. And even with his lawyer there, he admitted to the murders."

"They'll probably cop an insanity plea," said Racer.

"I don't know about that. He told us that he learned about the adult film business from his mother. He started to follow her to the sessions and would search her stuff," said Detman.

"How about the phony badge and identification?" asked Cindy.

"Apparently one of the guys he was in prison with got them for him. He told Harlin that all he wanted was to have sex with them, but things got out of hand. Once he killed the first girl, it became easier each time," said Detman.

"What a sicko," said Cindy.

"How did he find out about the meeting with David Hughes?" asked Racer.

"He didn't. He was really following you. The day that you visited the Thompson place, he knew that something was up, so he decided to start following you," replied Detman.

"Why the hell didn't I pick that up?" asked Racer.

"Probably because you never expected something like that. He said that when he followed you to that gas station, he was aiming at you."

"But why David Hughes?" asked Cindy.

"He pushed that truck out in front of Hughes' car because he thought that Hughes was helping Racer," said Detman.

When they got to the conference room all the television cameras were set up. There was a podium at the opposite end of the room with several chairs lined up along side of it. The Chief, Peterson and the District Attorney were all sitting there, chatting. As Detman, Cindy and Racer approached, everyone got up and started clapping their hands and patting them on the back. *What a circus!* thought Racer.

The news conference, like most, featured a lot of rhetoric. The Chief read off a chronological list of the events that led up to the breaking of the pornography ring and the arrest of Brian Thompson as the Fairfield Murderer. He then gave praise to Lieutenant Detman for running such a thorough investigation and to the detectives that finally broke the case, Racer and Darling.

After it was all over and the cameras were turned off, the DA came up and told Racer that with the evidence they had collected, he'd have no trouble prosecuting the suspects. Racer nodded and saw Peterson approaching. He told Racer that he wanted to see him in his office first thing Monday morning.

"I'll be there," said Racer.

Sitting in Detman's office, Harry and Cindy were kidding Racer about the big promotion that Peterson was probably going to give him. Racer just smiled and thought about the meeting and the deal that they had made when Racer took the case over. That was probably why Peterson wanted to see him, he thought.

Racer looked at Detman and said, "You know, Harry, it sure feels nice to be back in homicide."

"We were damn lucky to get you back," said Detman. "And let's not forget this young lady here. She did one heck of a job as your partner."

"You don't have to tell me that," said Racer. "She can be my partner any time."

"You two better stop before I start to blush," said Cindy.

As the reporters filtered out, they offered their final congratulations. Even Harlin and Piakowski came over to shake hands with Racer and Cindy after they returned from their interrogation with Brian Thompson. Even though Racer had to swallow hard, he thanked Jim and Bob for their help on the case. Detman then mentioned that it was time to celebrate. Everyone grabbed their coats and headed for the stairs.

Racer was in the District Attorney's office the next day at ten o'clock. He wasn't feeling the best because of one too many drinks the night before. The DA told Racer that Cindy called and would be about 10 minutes late. When she arrived, they went over the reports, made a couple of changes and signed off on them. The DA then went over the two cases with them. The pornography case was first. He explained the charges against Robert Shane and Madeline Stein. He also told them that Susan Thompson was holding to her promise of testifying against them. In the second case, Brian Thompson would be facing four counts of first degree murder, a second degree murder charge and several minor charges, including his assault on Racer. Everything was in order. Before they left, the DA told them he would be in touch on trial dates. Racer and Cindy shook his hand and departed.

After they were outside, Racer told Cindy that he was going to take it easy the rest of the day. All he had planned was the Monday morning meeting with Peterson. Cindy mentioned that she had promised to spend the weekend with her parents. After they said their good-byes, Racer watched her walk away from him. She stopped and waved as she got into her car and drove away.

Racer awoke to a partially cloudy sky on Monday. He quickly showered, shaved and dressed before heading out. He stopped at a local coffee shop, grabbed a large coffee and drove to the station. He was feeling great.

When Racer got to his desk, he found a note confirming his meeting with Peterson this morning taped to his phone. The captain wanted him in his office at nine sharp. Looking up, Racer saw Cindy enter the squad room. She looked beat.

"Well, how was your weekend?" asked Racer.

"Not so good. All I did was act as a referee between my mother and my kid brother. It seems like he has a drinking problem, and all they do lately is fight."

"Sorry about that. Maybe you should have stayed in town with me," he replied.

Cindy smiled and said, "Maybe I should have."

"Well, I'll see you later. I have to head upstairs for my big meeting with Peterson. Maybe we can talk about this at lunch, my treat," said Racer.

He smiled down at her, patted her on the shoulder and then headed for the stairs.

Peterson's secretary ushered Racer right into the Captain's office and informed him that the Captain would be right with him. She then excused herself and closed the door. Racer took a seat in one of the black leather chairs and started drumming his fingers on the arm. In a few minutes Peterson entered.

Captain Peterson walked around his desk and sat down. He pulled out one of his foot long cigars and lit it up. He sat there for a moment, blowing blue rings into the air. Finally, he gave his attention to Racer.

"Well Racer, let's get right to the point. Remember that deal we made when you were reassigned to homicide?" asked Peterson. "Well, the whole thing is off. Starting next week, you'll report back to the Traffic Division."

Racer just about jumped out of his chair.

"What the hell are you trying to pull? I solved this damn case for you just as I said I would. Those two flunkies Detman had on the case couldn't find their butt with both hands. I got you good press and saved the department from embarrassment. I did everything that I said I would, and now it's your turn to hold up your end of the deal," shouted Racer.

Peterson laughed. "You're lucky that you have a job right now. You removed departmental files without permission. You endangered a civilian by using Amanda English as bait; you were wounded in the line of duty and never reported it, and you used unnecessary force on Brian Thompson at the time of his arrest. We'll be lucky if he doesn't sue us."

"That's a bunch of bull," yelled Racer. "What unnecessary force are you talking about? The guy had a gun, and when I disarmed him, he pulled a switchblade on me, which turned out to be the murder weapon."

"You didn't have to lay him up in the hospital with two broken ribs, a fractured jaw, broken nose and several broken teeth," said Peterson. "And I can bet that I know where those leaks to the press were coming from."

"You rotten son-of-a-bitch! You used me like an old whore. You're no better then some of the scum I deal with on the street," said Racer in a threatening voice.

"Too bad. You can take it to the Chief, but he backs me up. He is scared that someone might sue us."

"What about Cindy?" asked Racer, trying to restrain himself. "What little treat do you have for her?"

"She is only on loan from the Vice squad. So the same day that you return to Traffic, she will be returning to Vice. She really doesn't have a say in the matter," said Peterson, with a smirk.

"What will the press think when they find out that their heroes have been demoted after solving the most celebrated case in Fairfields' history?" asked Racer.

"I'll tell them that the two of you are going back to your assigned departments. Of course, I will tell everyone how the department appreciates your work and dedication. But if the two celebrated cops want to argue the matter, then the truth might come out about the mishandling of the case, and how maybe we could have saved some of those women if it had been handled correctly," said Peterson. He was obviously enjoying this.

"Well, if you think that you are going to use me every time you can't solve a case, you're very mistaken," said Racer. He reached into his pocket and pulled out his wallet, which contained his gold shield and police identification. Racer opened it up, stared at the badge for a few seconds and then tossed it on Peterson's desk. His .357 was next.

"Captain, you can take those and stick them were the sun doesn't shine. I guess in the long run this is what you wanted all the time," said Racer calmly.

Peterson glared at him.

"I quit," said Racer, and left the office.

Racer entered the squad room and walked right up to Cindy. But before he could say a word, Detman opened his office door and hollered for them to get in there. Racer could tell from Detman's tone that he was serious. Cindy frowned and she seem to know that something was wrong.

"What is going on here?" she asked.

"I have a feeling you are about to find out. And you're not going to like it," said Racer, feeling sorry for Cindy.

Detman slammed the office door behind them.

"Sit your butts down," said Detman. Then turning his attention to Racer, he said, "What in the hell happened in Peterson's office?"

"All you need to know, lieutenant, is that I no longer work here," said Racer.

"Is someone here going to tell me what is going on?" asked Cindy.

"Go on, lieutenant, tell her where she will be reporting Monday. Tell her what her reward is for helping to solve this case. Apparently the Captain has already informed you."

"Cindy, starting next Monday you are going back to Vice," Detman said quietly.

"Yeah, that's your reward for doing such a good job. Isn't that a kick in the pants? But more likely, it's because you worked with me. This was all set up since the beginning. Isn't that right, lieutenant?" said Racer.

"Look Cindy, you were on loan to homicide, and we agreed once the case was closed you would return," said Detman. "There isn't anything that I can do. Your lieutenant asked for you back and the captain agreed. I tried to get the loan made permanent but I was over-ruled. When I pressed the matter, I was told to mind my own business."

Racer got up and headed for the door.

Cindy looked at Detman and said, "You have to be kidding about Racer. He's the best homicide detective we have."

"Peterson seems to have his mind made up and there's nothing I can do about it," replied Detman, looking at Racer.

Racer got up and headed for the door. Pausing in the doorway, he turned and said, "I guess this is it. It was only a matter of time until Peterson found a way to get me out. First I was angry, then disappointed, but now I feel relieved. I just want you to know I really enjoyed working with everyone. Well, I'll see you around." Then he left.

After work that Monday, Cindy stopped in at Barney's, hoping that Racer might be there. She walked up to the bar and asked if Racer had been in.

"Yeah, he was here. Left about an hour ago. It's a shame what they did to him. He's a damn good cop. All he ever tried to do was protect the citizens of this city from the bad guys," said Barney.

"Did he say where he was going?" asked Cindy.

"No, he just grabbed a six pack and left. He looked pretty low."

"Thanks," said Cindy as she left. She drove over to Racer's apartment but didn't see his car anywhere. Going up to his apartment, she knocked several times. There was no answer. Then a light went on in her head. She ran outside, jumped into her car and sped away.

An hour later, Cindy pulled into the gravel parking lot at the lake. She found Racer's car parked under one of the large shade trees. He was sitting on the ground, leaning against the car. Cindy got out of her car and walked over to him. Two of the cans in the six pack were already empty and Racer was sipping on the third.

"Nice out here, isn't it? So peaceful and quite. No one to bother you or fight with."

"Are you all right?" asked Cindy.

"Never better," said Racer.

"What are your plans now?" asked Cindy.

"I'm going to take that trip that I never had time to take. Now I have all the time in the world. Maybe Peterson did me a favor."

"You don't believe that. You are one of the best detectives on the force and you belong there. Tomorrow I'm going to see the Chief and have a talk with him," said Cindy. "And then...."

Racer stopped her. "Cindy, don't worry about me. Take care of yourself. You have a promising career ahead of you. Don't mess it up trying to defend me. Besides, I'm sure that Detman won't allow you to waste away in Vice. He'll keep trying to get you back in Homicide. Sooner or later they'll give in. Who knows? Maybe you'll get a chance to be Harlin's partner," said Racer somberly. Then he threw his head back and laughed loudly.

"I don't want to be Harlin's partner or anyone else's," said Cindy. "You're my partner and that is how I want it to stay."

"Look, keep plugging away. Don't let things like this bother you. This has been coming for a long time. Why do you think I was transferred to Traffic? Peterson has been trying to get rid of me for years. I just gave him the opportunity, that's all."

"You aren't going to fight it, are you? You're giving up," said Cindy.

"If that is what you call it, then yes," replied Racer. "Now have a beer and shut up."

Racer handed her a beer and they sat together staring out over the endless waters of the lake.

THE END